LONG WAY OUT

A Novel

by Rand Bishop

Long Way Out
© 2024, Norman Randolph Bishop
DBA Weightless Cargo Press
ISBN: 978-1-7330299-3-3
Email: nrandbishop@gmail.com
Editor: Patrick Merlihan
Cover Art and Design: Kristi Ryder

Dedicated to my brothers in HOW (Husbands Out to Wives), in gratitude for providing me a lifeline and a loving, accepting community; and to Sebra, who continues to teach me the meaning of unconditional love, the value of happiness, and the art of having fun.

Introductory Note From the Author...

While *Long Way Out* is a work of fiction, it is not simply a fabricated story, nor is its narrative unique to a single character in a book. The novel's protagonist, Russell Deacon, represents countless men snared in similar real-life quandaries. After dutifully following the normative script, by marrying women and fathering children, such men find themselves unable to deny or quell same-sex attraction. Thus, many resort to seeking furtive, anonymous sex with other men. And, although they may long to live openly and honestly as their whole, complete selves, they see no other choice but to do whatever they believe is necessary to keep their queer identities hidden.

This all-too-common cycle of deception not only bears the constant risk posed by sexually transmitted infections. Such duplicity is also a recipe for shame, guilt, clinical depression, anxiety, and even suicide ideation. This author hopes that *Long Way Out* provides a compelling and entertaining reading experience. But, more importantly, it is my fervent hope that some will see themselves in this story, understand they're not alone, and find evidence in Russell's eventual emergence from deceit and isolation that the journey to honesty is worth it, and that light, love, and a measure of personal peace awaits outside the closet.

Rand Bishop
Newport, Oregon

ONE

Russell was terrified, panicked. In one potentially fatal moment of weakness, he had risked exposing himself to the killer virus. He grasped for an excuse, a scapegoat: *Blame it on the alcohol.* "Too much to drink," after all, had been the explanation the last time he'd been fellated by an older man — a quarter-century ago. That event, however, although momentous and unforgettable, hadn't been further complicated by the fear of falling victim to a deadly plague. Back then, "I was drunk" was merely a self-deceptive copout uttered by an insecure, conflicted kid, tightrope walking the precarious cusp between adolescence and manhood. It was also a feeble attempt at denying how absolutely incredible, how transcendent it had felt to be pleasured orally by a superbly skilled gay lover.

At 18, Russell simply wasn't ready to admit the inconvenient truth. "It's just not my thing," he told David. "I just let you do it because I knew how much you wanted to." In the moment, Russell was clueless as to how wounded David had been by this flippant review. "I was shit-faced and horny," he further rationalized. "It was no big deal."

Russell never had any serious moral hang-ups about homosexuality or gay sex. And, even then, he was genuinely pleased, even proud — privately, of course — to have had the experience. It meant he could check "sex with another man" off his curiosity

3

list. But, it wasn't something he'd ever want to do again. To etch his denial in stone, Russell proceeded to persuade himself that one single, enormous, earth-shaking ejaculation had purged every last micro-droplet of queerness from his system. Blowjob #1, he convinced himself, had cleared the pathway ahead for a smooth, productive life journey, uncomplicated by ambivalent sexuality and all the untidy, bothersome drama that comes with it. But, surprise, surprise! That sense of certitude didn't last. The truth won't slumber forever, no matter how many times you bludgeon it on its ornery, impenetrable skull. And, when that nagging inner voice awakens, a fella's left with two choices: pay attention and accept it, or keep covering your ears, declaring, "I can't hear you!" Choosing option two, Russell would go on to learn, eventually backfires on men like him.

For decades, Russell subjected himself to extended, self-imposed periods of quasi-straightness. Still, he couldn't help but notice stuff, even when he wanted more than anything to look away. Sooner or later, a guy's gonna bump into this and that. Blind pig. Acorn. Turns out, lust-obsessed gay and bi men are everywhere. And, when one has his antennae up, another is not difficult to locate — and not necessarily evidenced by limp-wristed flamboyance. After all, anyone can spot the Nancy boy. But, he doesn't have to be a flaming queen, trumpeting his queerness unabashedly with stereotypical lisps, gestures, and attire. He might be the square-jawed, broad-shouldered dude pushing a grocery cart down the supermarket aisle, the burly truck driver taking a coffee break at a highway rest stop, or the stylish metrosexual grinning coyly from behind the wheel of his vintage Porsche, as he waits for the light to change.

Initially, Russell answered his same-sex impulses by masturbating to gay Internet porn. Then, his curiosity began steering him to places where men meet for casual, anonymous sex — park paths, public restrooms, adult book stores — but only to observe other men coupling, while servicing himself. So, Russell had managed to reach his 40s without engaging in any actual, direct physical contact with other men, with the sole exception of David's magical sword-swallowing performance, decades earlier.

It was 1994. AIDS was still rampant. Russell and Tess had been hitched for 13 years. Their marriage had produced two sons. Russell reveled in the role of faithful husband, father, and provider. Risking catching any STI was unthinkable. And, under no circumstance would he ever roll the dice on that murderous monster, HIV. Then, one night, Russell entered the Madame X Adult Emporium, purchased five bucks worth of tokens and slinked back into the video booth area. What set this particular evening apart from previous visits is that Russell wasn't stopping by on his way home from work to gift himself a quickie happy ending.

Shortly after five p.m., Russell was headed for the elevator, when a shiny, hairless head poked out through an open office door.

"Rusty Boy," the man called out.

"Yeah, Ed," Russell responded. "What's up?" *As if he didn't know.*

"Yeah. Hey, Dude. Tonight's the night, right? You gonna get off your high horse and join me and Mike at McCormick's for some beers?" Rumor had it that Ed was circulating an office pool to guess the date when highfalutin' Russell Deacon would finally condescend to go out and toss a few back with the testosterone twins. On a normal evening, Russell would have been armed with a legitimate excuse. One of the boys needed to be picked up after karate; there was a PTO meeting; he had to mow the lawn before the thunderstorm hit. On this particular night, however, Russell was at a complete loss for a reason to turn down Ed's invitation. Tess had picked up the boys early from school. And, by now, they were well on their way to Knoxville to celebrate her mother's birthday. So there he was, caught like a bass on a hook. And, Ed was reeling him in. *Why*, Russell chastised himself, *did I ever tell Ed about how much I was looking forward to a four-day bachelor weekend?*

Ed attempted to sweeten the deal: "Mike promised to tell us all about that chick with the..." The lasered glare from Mary Ann from the marketing department halted Ed midsentence. Seeing the blush flow into Ed's cheeks and forehead amused Russell. Every male employee in the office had learned to cut a wide swath to avoid Mary Ann's scorn. The woman made Betty Friedan and Doris Lessing sound like Mormon sister wives.

"Anyway," Ed continued, picking his language more carefully under the intense glower of the company feminist. "You know Mike's gonna have some good stories. And, the Rockets are playing the Pacers. So..." The expression on the man's pink, pie-shaped mug begged an answer.

Russell murmured an obligatory *"Fuck!"* under his breath and repeated it several more times, for good measure. Then, this is what he couldn't believe he heard himself say out loud: "Cool. McCormick's. Guess I'll see you guys there, then."

Ed's jaw dropped open, as his eyes widened. He shook his hairless head in shock and surprise. "Anybody got Thursday, April thirteenth?" he bellowed. "If you do, congratulations! You're the WINNERRRRR!"

Russell didn't typically do shots. On this occasion, the extra alcohol was an effort to mute the misery of having to endure Mike's overbearing barrage of self-aggrandizing, misogynistic bullshit. And, as the evening wore on, Ed's high-decibel verbal explosions — "OH! Did you fuckin' see that shit?" — and violent high-fives after every Sam Cassell three-pointer and Clyde Drexler dunk left Russell loopy as a punch-drunk boxer... on top of having tipped across the line into inebriation somewhere around 9:15. As he wobbled out of the pub onto the sidewalk, Russell gazed up to see purple neon search lights sweeping across the southern sky. "Hmmm," he murmured to himself. Taking a little stroll in the brisk Spring air seemed like a prudent idea. It would be smart to do some sobering up before climbing behind the wheel.

The closer Russell got to the amethyst glow, the quicker and harder his heart pounded against his ribcage. Although he could feel his face flushing hot, a chill seeped down his neck to his shoulders. By the time he rounded the corner on Demonbreun, his teeth were chattering. Despite a temperature of 68 degrees Fahrenheit, Russell was freezing from the inside out. By the time he reached for the handle on Madame X's purple door, his entire arm was twitching uncontrollably, from shoulder to fingertips.

Every triple-X adult business greets a customer with a similar smell: bleach being the predominate tone, blended with a trace of human perspiration, and finished with a subtle note of spent spermatozoa. This certain, familiar olfactory stimulus always triggered the same physical response. Russell's chubbing organ was like a trained circus cat eager to jump through hoops of fire for the reward to come. By the time he parted the beaded curtain, the shivering in Russell's shoulders had calmed. He paused inside the entrance, giving his eyes a chance to adjust to the darkness. After a minute or so, he could make out several men, each striking his own variation on a pose, leaning back casually against the video booths, smoking cigarettes. As if their moves had been choreographed and rehearsed, heads swiveled, one, then the next, placing Russell under squint-eyed scrutiny, each man sizing up the newcomer, to determine if he matched their preferred profile for a casual, spontaneous sex partner. One slender fellow smiled. Automatically, and purely out of politeness, Russell smiled back. Then, he quickly averted his eyes, hoping he hadn't sent out the wrong signal. Even in circumstances where names are rarely exchanged, the last thing Russell wanted was to mislead someone.

Russell spied a closed booth door with its red light lit. The adjacent booth was empty. So, he slipped inside, making sure to turn the lock behind him. He stacked his tokens neatly on top of the video monitor. Before he could insert the first token, the door handle jiggled, then jiggled again, followed by three hurried knocks. "Shit," Russell muttered. He was relatively sure who it was. Opening the door a crack confirmed his suspicion. There stood the slender fellow with whom he had just traded smiles.

"Want some company?" Slender Fellow asked, with a suggestive Cheshire-Cat grin.

"No thanks," Russell lied. Immediately, a pang of guilt struck his heart for any feeling of rejection Slender Fellow might have been feeling. In fact, there was nothing Russell wanted more than to invite him in. An electric thrill wave rippled through his body as he pictured the two of them in this confined space, lit only by the flickering video monitor, exploring each other's naked skin. It took every morsel of self-control Russell could muster to pull the door shut again, leaving the possibility for that imagined scenario outside.

Slender Fellow, however, was not to be denied so offhandedly. After another rapid knock, Russell heard his voice through the door. "Are you sure?"

"Yes, I'm fucking sure," Russell spat back. "Jesus! FUCK *OFF*!"

"Okay, okay! You don't have to be an asshole!" Russell hated the thought of hurting anyone's feelings. He hadn't actually been angry with the guy. He knew what that initial exchange of smiles had implied. Slender Fellow had been following the unwritten rules to the letter, adhering strictly to anonymous-hook-up protocol. Russell had sent out mixed signals, by returning a coded smile, then ducking into a booth. Slender Fellow had every right to presume he would be welcomed inside.

Stewing in alcohol-marinated self-recrimination, Russell pushed a few tokens into the slot. In a second, the screen lit up with hard-core porn. A pair of hermaphrodites performing fake sex for the camera was not Russell's cup-a tea. He changed the channel again... and again. Finally, Russell's channel surf landed on a visual he found considerably more enticing: a swarthy, well-endowed, 30-something fellow lying on a bed masturbating. Russell removed his shirt. With his eyes fixed on the screen, he pinched a nipple with one hand, while unzipping his fly with the other.

When Russell's lucky stars were aligned, the video screen was not nearly as arousing as what was happening on the other side of the plywood wall. Best case scenario, two guys would be getting it on in the next booth — preferably, engaged in oral. Such a serendipitous occurrence allowed Russell to watch the live action through the glory hole while he self-pleasured at a safe distance. This time, however, there was only one person in the next booth. And, he was peering at Russell through the circular opening. Russell found it equally titillating to have another guy watch him masturbate. So, upon the realization that he was being spied on, Russell's erection inflated to maximum arousal. He lowered his pants and undershorts to reveal the star of the show, now standing bold and tall. He spit into his palm and began caressing the shaft, all the while maintaining eye contact with his audience of one, who was peeking through the circular cutaway like a Bowery Boy stealing a gander at the game through the outfield fence. Russell took a break from stroking himself to avoid an early climax. In response, his neighbor licked his lips, as if slavering for a lick of a rapidly melting ice cream cone. Then, the man further demonstrated his intention by opening his mouth wide enough to nearly fill the hole, thus making his eyes disappear. Russell was surprised to observe that the exposed orifice was devoid of teeth.

As the ravenous voyeur closed his mouth and resumed licking his lips in a silent plea, Russell could make out the deep wrinkles of advanced age. The melancholy in the man's eyes was like an unspoken confession. "I'm old and lonely," they conveyed, "desperate for human contact." Russell had already rejected someone in a way that might have caused emotional distress. He could hardly bear to do the same to the desperate, elderly gent in the next booth. *After all*, he assured himself. *I'm a kind, loving person. There's not a mean bone in my body.*

For years, Russell had answered his same-sex attraction from afar. So, why now, why here, like this, with some wrinkled, toothless octogenarian? Russell had been tempted by numerous, far more attractive guys in much more alluring situations and still managed to remain at arm's length. Was this sudden lack of resolve simply due to brain cells addled by alcohol? Could that really be an adequate excuse? Then, Russell began to see this fraught playlet from an angle that made him the hero. If he had to guess, this sad, old gent, had likely been imprisoned in a dark, isolated closet for three-quarters of a century. Russell was congratulating himself in advance for his magnanimity. But he knew the real reason he was about to break his long-standing, no-contact policy: he was a horny, drunk, closeted, bisexual man with a hard-on staring into a willing, eager, open mouth.

When his soldier's helmet first touched the old man's tongue, a fierce tremor pulsed through Russell's entire body. Still, it wasn't too late to correct course and make the safer, more sensible decision. But, no. Russell had abandoned common sense on a barstool at McCormick's Pub. A second later, the man was inhaling Russell's member like a starving refugee. The inside of the fellator's mouth was leathery, as if his salivary glands had run dry. Still, he sucked greedily, like a baby goat on its mama's teat. This was nothing like how Russell had remembered glorious Blowjob #1. On that long-ago night, he'd been lying naked on his back on soft sheets, as David took every inch of his eager, rookie erection lovingly and tenderly into his soft, wet, veteran mouth and throat. Blowjob #2 had Russell on tip toe, pressing his chest, palms, and the side of his face flat onto a hard, cold wall, while pushing his loins flush against the unforgiving surface around a hole cut by a skill saw. Feeling more and more physically uncomfortable, Russell feared that, if he didn't finish soon, he would lose his erection. To hasten his climax, he began undulating, bumping his thighs against the partition.

Even after Russell blew his load, the old gent's mouth felt dry. Russell withdrew. The man whispered, "Thank you." Russell coughed, then mumbled a thank you in return.

In his mind, Russell was already asking... *Oh, my Lord in Heaven! What have I done*?

TWO

"So, what makes you think you might have been exposed?" The direct but casual nature of the nurse's voice suggested that she had posed this identical query to myriad other patients — mostly, Russell presumed, men. He wondered how many of them had been as terrified as he was at that moment. Russell felt oddly comforted by the supposition that he wasn't the only idiot on the planet to impulsively play Russian roulette with his health. Still, he'd never pictured himself taking a cruise on that ship of fools.

Despite her matter-of-fact demeanor, the nurse seemed earnest, genuinely concerned, and interested. Russell gave her the 30-second elevator-pitch version of the previous night's blunder. "So, did you *give* oral sex?" she inquired. "Or, were you on the receiving end?" Russell's answer provoked a grin, followed by a little chuckle. The nurse's amusement didn't seem the least bit mocking, but rather sweet, caring, and sympathetic. Here he was, a 44-year-old man in an examination room, feeling like a kindergartner who'd just charged through the screen door and into his mother's arms, sobbing about some mean thing a neighbor kid had said. Mom was about to repeat that old saw about sticks and stones. The nurse's grin widened into a soft, full-fledged smile. "Russell," she began, seeking eye contact. For the last 14 hours, Russell's mind had been entertaining every worst-case scenario imaginable. Why in heaven's name was this woman taking so long to finish her statement? "Receiving oral," she conveyed, "is probably the safest kind of sex you can have."

A sheepish grin creased Russell's lips, as a reservoir of renewed hope flooded into his heavy heart. Suddenly, he felt like another kind of fool altogether: naïve, alarmist, overwrought. He blushed to think that he'd blown up a nonthreatening, late-night misstep into such a huge, urgent, life-and-death drama. He'd even petitioned a God he was not sure he believed in for mercy and pledged to mend his ways, should he be spared from this dreaded malady. Certainly, if God exists and actually listens to our prayers, He, She, or It would have frisbeed Russell's plea onto the "when and if time allows" pile. *Nevertheless,* Russell reasoned, *I can't be faulted for saying a little just-in-case prayer, can I?* At that moment, whatever embarrassment he felt was totally eclipsed by another dominant emotion: profound relief. "So," Russell stammered through an involuntary grin, "is that it? Am I free to go?"

"No, no," she replied, good naturedly, "you're here. We might as well test you." Clearly, Russell's respite from anxiety had been premature and unwarranted. The nurse then pivoted on the heels of her sneakers, scooted over to the counter, slipped on a pair of disposable vinyl gloves, and began making preparations for the testing process.

"So, there's still a chance..." Russell wondered aloud.

"There's *always* a chance," she answered. "Please lower your trousers and your undies. This won't take long. You'll be out of here in two shakes of a lamb's tail." Russell was thinking to himself... *A single shake would be preferable.* Tentatively, with renewed trepidation, Russell followed the nurse's instructions, scooching his pants and shorts down around his knees. He then leaned his bare buttocks back against the stiff, chilly paper sheet covering the examination table. When the nurse turned around again, her expression had transformed from amused friendliness to one-hundred-percent-business. She approached Russell with intention, holding a small, clear plastic jar in her left hand, and a small obelisk-shaped instrument in her right. As she drew near, Russell could see that the instrument appeared to be made of greenish-tinted glass, perhaps hexagonal, approximately two inches long and a sixteenth of an inch in diameter. The nurse placed the jar down on a nearby tray and reached out to take Russell's limp noodle into her gloved left hand. Oddly, the mischievous organ that had gotten him into this mess no longer seemed to be attached to his body. He felt like a medical student auditing the procedure from an overhead observation platform. "This might be a little uncomfortable," she warned, "But, please, stay as still as possible. Ready?"

"No," Russell muttered through gritted teeth, nervously making light of a circumstance the word awkward didn't come close to describing.

"Sorry," she said, before proceeding to insert the glass shaft into the tiny opening of Russell's urethra. Russell was no longer a detached observer. The pain of the initial centimeter of penetration informed him that the penis in her hand was most definitely directly connected to his central nervous system. It took everything he had to quell the impulse to jerk away. When the nurse began slowly pushing the tiny, glass hexagon inside him to its full length, Russell immediately got a clear hint of what torture must feel like. Had he been a captured combatant at that moment, he would have been wishing he had bitten down on the cyanide pill, while willingly blathering confessions to the most heinous crimes imaginable.

Emerging from the office elevator, Russell's stinging urethra had teamed up with a throbbing headache — two nagging reminders of the previous night's inebriation and the impulsive activities that followed. While he liked the nurse's hopeful prognosis, he was not looking forward to a fretful weekend, sitting by the phone in an empty house, awaiting test results. Having beelined directly to the breakroom to pour a cup of coffee, he was not particularly thrilled to find Mike Terzian there, hunched over the counter, perusing the sports section of *The Tennessean.*

"Rusty Boy!" As usual, Mike's voice was boisterous enough to peel paint off the walls. "You must-a been pretty damn thirsty last night!" The vigorous, heavy-handed back slap that followed resulted in hot java sloshing onto Russell's hand. Wincing from the burning sensation and reaching for a paper towel, the only response he could manage was a forced, squint-eyed grin. "Boy, Howdy!" Mike joked. "You sure made up for all those nights when you pussied out."

"Sometimes ya just gotta let it all hang out. Go with the flow," Russell replied, making an effort to appease the office chauvinist with generic vagueness.

"I hear ya, Bucko. But, I hope you weren't dumb enough to drive home in that condition."

"No, I took a walk first... you know, to sober up."

"Good, 'cause a D.U.I. ain't worth it. If ya know what I mean." If Mike possessed any special expertise, it was a penchant for articulating the obvious.

"I do," Russell agreed, shuffling to make his exit.

"Wait a minute," Mike bellowed. His expression indicated that two and two were adding up. "I *thought* that was you." Mike smiled knowingly, as if he and Russell now shared a secret.

These words halted Russell in his tracks. "I'm sorry?" He was asking for clarification, while still hoping Mike wasn't saying what he worried he was saying.

"I was truckin' back to the ol' homestead, toolin' down eighth, past that porn place. You know the one with the purple neon search lights. What's it called?"

"Madame X," Russell stated. It would have been futile to feign ignorance. From the very moment this business began adding heliotrope into the color palate of the Nashville skyline, the

Southern Baptists had been trying to shutter the place. Every other week, a news blurb appeared in the paper about this never-ending controversy.

"What's that place like?" Mike asked.

"What do you mean?" Russell queried, feigning innocence. "Why would you ask me that?"

"Oh..." Mike deliberately cranked up the gotcha tone. "So, that *wasn't* you."

"Look, man," Russell said, staring directly into his macho workmate's beady, brown eyes, "I don't have a single clue what you're talking about."

"Okay, okay. Jesus, Dude!" Mike chuckled. "Don't get your panties in a wad."

"And, what is *that* remark supposed to mean?" Russell knew better than to poke the bear. But, he was having a crap day. It couldn't get much worse.

"Well, I heard..."

"I don't give a rat's ass what you heard, Mike!" By now, Russell's face was flushing beet red, his throat was as dry as roofing shingles on an August afternoon, and the throbbing in his head was rendering him nearly blind.

"Just sayin'," Mike continued. "Next time your ol' lady's outta town, you should check out one of those oriental massage parlors just a few more blocks south on eighth. Those little slant chicks know what they're doin'. And," at this point, he modulated his voice into a hissing whisper, "... you'd be less likely to catch the gay there."

By now, Russell was choking on a bitter recipe of emotions: equal parts fury over a bigoted asshole's brazen disrespect mixed with abject humiliation over the prick's slightly veiled insinuations. "I'll be sure to keep that in mind," Russell muttered, jaw clenched and rigid, before wheeling around to march out of the breakroom.

As usual, Mike's had to have the last word. "I mean, there's nothin' like a happy ending..."

"Can you just shut the fuck up, Mike?" Russell barked, plenty loud enough for the entire floor to hear.

Reverberations of Mike's guffaw accompanied Russell's perp walk down the long corridor. Right on schedule, Ed's shiny bean poked out from his office door. "Everything okay, Buddy?" he asked.

"A-okay," Russell lied, as the first teardrop trickled its way down his cheek. "Everything is hunky-fucking dory."

"Okay, team," Russell barked. "Time for ground-ball drills." The response, several boyish, high-pitched groans, indicated that this was one of the Pirates' least popular practice routines. "Come on, you guys," Russell said, with three quick hand claps. "The quicker we get started, the quicker the drill will be over." A gaggle of 10-, 11-, and 12-year-olds snatched their mitts, loped lethargically onto the field, and lined up single file behind the shortstop position. It felt odd to be coaching a Saturday morning practice in the absence of his sons. Just then, out of the corner of his eye, Russell noticed a shaggy-haired boy on the sidelines, displaying his bright-blue, popsicle-stained tongue to a child in the bleachers. "Hey, Carter!" Russell asked. "You gonna join us?"

"Yeah, Coach," Carter responded, jump-shooting his popsicle stick off the rim of the trash bin before shuffling across the third-base line toward his teammates.

"Aren't you forgetting something?" Russell inquired. The youngster looked back through creased, questioning eyes. "Or," Russell continued, "are you planning to field grounders with your bare hands?" Carter pursed his lips, silently confessing his momentary space out by shooting a pointer finger at his coach and returning to the dugout to fetch his glove.

"That kid would leave his dick in his shorts if it wasn't attached." Carter's father, Bryan, wasn't an official Little League coach. Still, he was always willing to help out. Russell and the rest of the coaching staff valued Bryan's participation, even though his cocky swagger and darkish sense of humor occasionally rubbed some parents the wrong way.

Russell proceeded to swat balls across the infield dirt... to one boy, then the next in line, and so on. Some were fearless, fully capable of fielding a briskly punched grounder. Others, at least, made a decent attempt at swatting down the ball. Several turned their heads at the last second, letting the orb skitter through their legs or bounce past them into left field. Only a few were capable of making an accurate throw to first. Some got it there on a bounce. Others chucked it over the assistant coach's head into the dugout or against the chain link fence. One particularly large, clumsy lad succeeded in blocking the ball, before making several attempts at picking it up, only to drop it, then kick it. After chasing the elusive thing past second base, he finally got a grip, and hurled his toss over the bleachers into the parking lot, where it bounced three times, narrowly missing a young mother pushing a stroller, before thudding against the door panel of a stationary Pathfinder.

"Don't worry about it," Russell advised, in a vain attempt at encouragement, while trying to muffle a laugh. "You've got one heck of an arm, Tyler. Keep working on your accuracy."

"Hopeless," Bryan observed. His eyes, however, were not looking at the chubby boy with the erratic arm, but somewhere else altogether. Russell had become familiar with the walking trail that circled the grove of trees beyond the outfield fence. On occasion, he had prowled the several tributary pathways that veered off the main trail into the woods. And that was where Bryan's attention appeared to be focused, observing as one man in a tank top and jogging shorts approached another fellow sitting on a trailside bench. After a conversation lasting no longer than five seconds, the jogger trotted away from the bench and, about 10 yards down the trail, took an abrupt left, vanishing into the stand of trees. After the jogger was out of sight, the other fellow rose from the bench to follow him into the woods.

"Bryan..." Russell said. Bryan snapped out of his reverie and turned his head, realizing Russell was extending his hand.

"Oh, sorry, Coach," he muttered, offering the scuffed, grass-stained baseball. It was at that moment that Russell took notice of Bryan's eyelashes, which were unusually long and quite beautiful. He'd already been taken by Bryan's eye color, a cool, Paul-Newman-like shade of blue, made even more striking in contrast to a thick head of tousled coal-black hair, wafting in the spring breeze. Russell's eyes traveled down to Bryan's taught forearm, forested in ebony hair. Meanwhile, it wasn't escaping Bryan how intensely Russell was studying him, like an artist poised to lay brush to canvas. Ridiculously handsome men like Bryan catch people staring at them on a regular basis, without remark. Russell's gaze, however, contained something beyond simple admiration or manly envy. "What?" Bryan asked, suggestively.

Now, Russell realized, he was the one lost in reverie. "Nothing." As Russell took hold of the baseball, one of his fingers grazed against one of Bryan's. The electricity was supercharged. Bryan grinned. No words were necessary. The two men's understanding required no verbal confirmation. And, still, the communication was complete. In that one, instantaneous moment of contact, the doors to their most-personal selves blew open. They both suspected something about the other, something essential and private, something only comprehensible to men like them.

THREE

"The boys are having such a great time with their cousins, I hate to yank them away." The pause that followed led Russell to suspect there might be more to the story. "And, actually," Tess finally continued, "Dad is not doing so great."

Normally, calling Russell so early on a Sunday risked rousing a slumbering Godzilla. This morning, however, the unexpected wake-up call was merciful, having liberated him from a disturbing nightmare. In his dream state, Russell had rolled over to reach out across the bed. Instead of finding the familiar smoothness of his wife's toned arm, his fingers came in contact with some loose, crepey skin. He quickly recognized the face looking at him from Tess's side of the bed as that of the toothless fellator from Madame X. Responding to Russell's touch, the aged fellow exhibited a broad smile, revealing gums that glowed neon pink. Eagerly, he skooched closer, showing every intention of kissing Russell on the lips. If this wasn't sufficiently frightening, several bloody lesions became visible on the man's wrinkled neck. At this terrifying sight, Russell's attempt at a scream failed to produce an audible sound. "So," Russell muttered drowsily into the telephone, "you're saying there's good news and bad news."

"Sort of," Tess responded. "Hank and Rory are having the time of their lives with Eric and Josh. On the other hand, my dad's Parkinson's is..." A particular waver in her voice indicated she was barely holding it together.

Perhaps, Russell thought, steering the conversation in a more pragmatic direction might skootch his wife away from the emotional cliff. "How much school do you think the boys can afford to miss?"

Knowing this was a totally speculative question, he didn't wait for an answer. "You know, Hank already had to skip one Little League practice."

"I know, Babe," she said. "But..." Russell heard the unmistakable carping of his mother-in-law in the background, to which Tess responded, "I'll be there in just a minute, Mom."

"Look," Russell began. "I get it... I totally..."

"I have to go, Babe," Tess interrupted. "Mom needs me. Can we talk later?"

"Okay," Russell said, making his best effort at sounding patient and understanding. "I love you. Hug the boys for me. Give my love to your folks, too."

"I will. I love you, too."

"I miss you, Tess." There was no response. She had already disconnected the call.

Weighted down by that satisfying kind of exhaustion that only comes from putting in consecutive hours of physical labor, Russell pushed his mower into the tool shed. After locking up his tools, he surveyed the yard, taking stock of how much tidier it appeared: a major improvement from when he'd initiated his landscaping chores earlier that morning. A firefly rose up out of the fresh-cut lawn, twinkling in the twilight. Then a second, and a third. A minute later, Russell's little hunk of terra firma was sparkling like a magical, miniature Milky Way. He felt the itch of a no-see-em bite on his ankle. A soft evening breeze lifted a rank odor from his armpit to his nose. He was definitely overdue due for a hot shower.

It felt luxurious to be standing naked under a steamy, cleansing cascade, listening to the random, chaotic percussion of water splashing against tile. Vigorously, Russell lathered a bar of Irish Spring, and ran his soapy hands over his arms, shoulders, and neck, as a swirling, grime-tinted cyclone of suds and water vanished down the drain. As the short hairs around his man breasts bristled against his palm, his nipples began to harden. Of late, Russell had found himself drifting into enticing fantasies of running his hands over another man's furry pectorals, pinching and sucking an imaginary lover's nipples. To this thought, his always on-call soldier responded posthaste, inflating like one of those balloons birthday-party clowns twist into bunnies and poodles. Running the sudsy bar down his belly and over his thighs, Russell dispatched his fingertips to explore the tender flesh between his upper legs. Feeling a slight wobble in his knees, Russell carefully widened his stance to stabilize his footing. No reason to take unnecessary chances. It's difficult to imagine a demise more mortifying than cracking one's skull while copping a wank in the shower.

Russell had no reason to feel guilty or ashamed. These compulsions were normal and natural. He was a mortal man, after all, with an active, insistent libido. His behavior wasn't covert, risky, or self-destructive. Rather, this was a harmless, healthy outlet for his same-sex impulses. Of course, he'd been telling himself a similar story for years. Experience had made him an expert at compartmentalization, rationalizing his clandestine, voyeuristic adventures, while sneaking stealthily along a park trail, or leering through a glory hole, heart pounding in his throat, spying on other men doing the thing he so desired, but never dared to do. Only three nights ago, he'd exploded that imaginary shield of protection into a million shards. In doing so, he had put his own physical well-being and, by extension, his wife's in jeopardy. This was the fact he couldn't purge from his mind. Even in the throes of self-pleasure, the wrongness of his transgression and the risk that misstep represented plagued his thoughts. And, being a superb mind reader, Russell's erection began to soften. He lathered up again and resumed stroking, gripping harder, and picking up the pace, only to feel his uncharacteristically recalcitrant member shrinking in his hand. "Come on, Buddy," he coaxed, assuming the role of player-coach, "You can do this!" If he'd ever had trouble bringing a stiffy to climax, he couldn't remember when. "It's okay," Russell reassured his wilting partner in crime, "stress will do that to ya."

Despite missing his family, Russell found some consolation in the knowledge that the wife and kids wouldn't be walking through the door at any moment. What if Tess came home hot-to-trot, as she sometimes did after they'd slept separately for any length of time? Without the assurance of negative test results, acquiescing to her desires would be ill-advised. A horny wife would place Russell in an impossible predicament, struggling to explain his lack of interest. What words in the English language wouldn't have resulted in Tess feeling undesirable? And, worse yet, what excuse wouldn't risk raising a red flag of suspicion? Then, it suddenly occurred to Russell that he and Tess hadn't made love in months, maybe not this entire year — and, it was mid-April! *Why was that*, he wondered? Why hadn't the idea of initiating marital sex even crossed his mind? And, more curiously, why hadn't Tess brought it up or complained about the scarcity of their sexual activity? When she was feeling frisky, Tess was never shy about sending up a flare. "Maybe we should do it," she'd say, with no more passion than if she was suggesting making popcorn. And, 20 minutes later, after they'd finished going through those well-practiced motions, she'd invariably sigh and remark, "That was a good idea."

After turning off the shower, Russell looked down at his flaccid friend dangling between his legs. "You're an asshole," he said, with a woeful chuckle. "You know that?"

Russell was in the home stretch of his sales pitch when the cell phone in his pocket startled him with an abrupt vibration. He had only owned the device for a month. And, every time it pulsated to signify an incoming call, he nearly jumped out of his skin.

"You okay?" inquired the prospect, a jowly, mustachioed fellow in his early fifties.

"Oh, yeah," Russell reassured him. "I'm just not used to... I just got this damn thing," he confessed, pulling the phone from his pocket and trying to figure out how to send the call to voicemail. With a quick glance at the caller ID — Davidson County Health Services — Russell's heart jumped. Within a few seconds, his entire face was burning hot. And, as perverse as it may seem, his penis misread an incoming phone call that had something to do with sex as a signal to chub up.

"Do you need to take that?" the prospect asked. "I mean, I can only give you a few more minutes. But, if you need..."

"No, no, no," Russell insisted, faking a laugh. "It's not important." By that point, the device had mercifully ceased vibrating on its own. Unfortunately, Russell's concern over his health status did not abate. Knowing that his STI test results were available served to rocket his anxiety to another level.

It had taken weeks of unrelenting persistence to get this meeting with the owner of a modest-sized home-stairlift business. Distracted as he was, Russell hadn't brought his "A" game. But, until the phone began vibrating, his confidence had been on the high side. He was a seasoned veteran of the sales game. And, reading the room led him to believe that a few more strategically chosen questions would give him a better than 50-50 chance of closing the deal.

The previous night, Russell had crawled into the sack, bone weary from laboring all day in the yard. Adding to his physical exhaustion, he'd attempted to mute the mind babble with three, tall vodka/sodas, heavy on the vodka. Still, the nagging self-speak would not be silenced. Four onerous words, articulated by a caring, friendly nurse, as she prepared to shove a glass obelisk up into his urethra, ping-ponged between the walls of Russell's fevered cranium: "There's always a chance. There's always a chance." As long as that dreadful outcome still remained a longshot possibility, Russell's overactive mind was pulled toward the worst of all possible worst-case scenarios like a needle to a magnet. Minute after tedious minute ticked slowly by, as he lay there stewing: *Is there any gentle way of informing my wife that I succumbed to compulsive same-sex desires by sticking my junk through a hole in the wall and letting someone I'd never met before and will likely never encounter again gobble up the very part of my body I pledged exclusively to her 13 years ago like a banana popsicle?* The scariest unknown of all: *How would Tess respond to such unwelcome news?* This was something Russell hoped he would never have to find out.

As Russell tossed and turned, he was less concerned about how miserable it might be to suffer a slow, withering death and far more fixated on the fact that a positive HIV test would force him to unveil the truth about his same-sex urges and pursuits. In his twisted, egocentric mind, Russell wasn't remotely ready to take responsibility for his careless actions. He was far more content singing "Poor, Poor, Pitiful Me," while picturing himself as a victim of circumstance, a guiltless pawn affected by powerful factors beyond his control. Wallowing in gloom led Russell's insomnia-plagued brain to entertain dark, tragic thoughts: Tess and the boys motoring westward on Interstate 40; a drunk driver careening across the highway divider at high speed, wiping out his entire family in a random, fiery, head-on collision. In that imagined plotline, in spite of his transgressions and fatal diagnosis, unanimous sympathy would be directed toward the suddenly childless, grieving widower, not the innocent, collateral victims of his weakness and poor judgment.

Russell walked out of the sales meeting with yet another, "Give me a week to think about it," a clichéd professional pleasantry that frequently led to a pass. But Russell was far less concerned about a phone call he'd be making in a week than the one he was about to return. Russell sat in his car staring at his cell phone. He was tempted to throw the cursed thing onto the pavement and stomp it into pile of useless chips and wires. But doing that would only postpone the inevitable. Finally, he gritted his teeth, pushed the requisite buttons, placed the device to his ear, closed his eyes, and held his breath. "Hi, Russell," the recorded message began, "This is Nancy, from the lab at Davidson County Health Services. I'm calling to let you know that your test results are in. In the interest of your privacy, I'll need to relay this information to you personally. Please call me at..." The remainder of the voicemail provided him with office hours, plus return phone and extension numbers.

"*Fuck!*" Russell shrieked. In the adjacent parking space, a young mother swiveled around from buckling a wiggly toddler into a car seat to launch a disapproving glower in his direction. A pre-teen boy peaked over her shoulder in Russell's direction, tittering gleefully over this spontaneous, profane exclamation.

"What are you laughing at?" the mother admonished the youngster. "There's nothing funny about that kind of language!" The poor kid couldn't help himself. At that age, hearing a grown man holler the O.G. of four-letter words invariably rises to the peak of hilarity. "You want a whipping?" his mother threatened. "Cause I'll beat your sorry, little ass!" The collateral damage from Russell's potentially fatal mistake was already being felt outside the boundaries of his immediate family.

Russell's hands were trembling so severely, he misdialed several times, inspiring several more expletive outbursts. As the woman in the adjacent vehicle backed out of her space, she lasered a parting sneer in Russell's direction. Anxiety spiking, he couldn't have cared less about what some tight-assed, abusive mother thought about him. By the time he heard ringing on the other end of the line, tears were clouding his vision. Somehow, he managed to push the correct digits to reach the proper extension. The call went to voicemail.

The playful phrase "playing phone tag" was invented shortly after the advent of the answering machine. On this particular day, for Russell, playing phone tag was less a game and more akin to psychological torture. He was just north of Briley Parkway on I-24 when the phone buzzing resumed. The suspense was too much to bear. Heart pounding and hands shaking, Russell signaled and jerked his vehicle into the right lane, provoking a startling, sustained honk. A speeding box truck promptly pulled up to the Celica's rear bumper, as if the driver was threatening to ram it from behind. Then, the driver amplified his rage by laying on his horn again for an additional three seconds. With the phone still buzzing like a hive of bees, Russell managed to maneuver onto the shoulder. Perspiration on his fingers led to a phone fumble. Fortunately, he was able to re-snag it before it tumbled between the seats. "Yes, hello. This is Russell."

"Oh, good," the woman's voice said. "Hi. I'm glad we finally connected. This is Nancy from the Davidson County Health Department."

"Okay," Russell said, clenching his jaw and squeezing his eyes shut to arm himself for the anticipated report.

"I have the results of your lab test from... let's see, last Friday, the 14th, I think it was."

"That's right," Russell agreed.

"Okay. Good. So, just to ensure that I'm talking to the correct person," she said, "could you tell me your birthdate, please?" As Russell answered that and a pair of additional queries for the purpose of confirming his identity, he tried his best not to reveal how increasingly nervous and impatient he was becoming with the passing of every exasperating second. "Well, Russell," she said. "From what I'm seeing here, it looks like you have nothing to worry about."

Even though this was the likeliest outcome, it had yet to fully register. "So," he asked, "what does that mean... exactly?"

"Well," she elaborated, "you tested negative... for all STIs."

"Including HIV." Russell was making a conscious choice to articulate this as a statement, not as a question.

"Correct," she stated. Russell finally allowed himself to exhale. "So," she continued, "you're good to go."

"Well, that's really super news," Russell exuded, "super, super news!" The positive nature of this cross-the-board negative report was beginning to penetrate the emotional wall he'd been constructing for days. Meanwhile, he was suddenly self-conscious about having just uttered the word "super" three times in a single sentence, like a 90-year-old fuddy-duddy describing a corn dog at the county fair.

"But, Russell..." The woman's voice lowered audibly in pitch to emphasize the seriousness of what she was about to ask. "Do you use condoms?"

"Of course," Russell fibbed. He likened sex with a condom to taking a shower in a wetsuit. "Most of the time, I mean. This one time, I didn't."

"Well then," she interrupted, "this time, you got lucky. Next time, your luck might not hold out."

"But, the testing nurse told me that receiving oral sex is relatively safe. Is that true?"

"Look," Nancy responded, "when you exchange any bodily fluids at all with someone whose health status and sexual history you don't know, nothing is a hundred-percent safe. Even sex with a condom. Just be smart. Reduce the risk as much as you can, and you should be fine." Russell, however, was already incapable of absorbing or comprehending the professional advice he himself had requested. These words of caution were being drowned out by the devil on Russell's shoulder rasping, *Hey, Dude, just keep being lucky*!

For the next five minutes, Russell sat in his car on the shoulder of the Interstate weeping like a baby. "Thank you, God," he murmured, casting his tearful gaze heavenward. After drying his eyes and blowing his nose, he turned the key and revved his engine. A glance in the rearview mirror to double-check for oncoming vehicles revealed a pair of happy, but extremely bloodshot eyes. His gratitude to some omnipotent, paternalistic deity was already ringing hollow. Surely, a higher power had little or nothing to do with those test results. Russell only cared about one fact: *I'm off the hook*. For three days, he had been totally immersed in a percolating vat of fragility and uncertainty. Now, one clear health report had rendered him bulletproof. In his mind's eye, he immediately began envisioning innumerable elicit pleasures to come. As Russell traced the return route to the office, the strict, self-imposed guidelines he'd long imposed upon himself were seeming overly cautious. The next time there was a knock on a peep-booth door, he would no longer arbitrarily rule out physical contact, especially if that knock offered the possibility of being on the receiving end of an expert blowjob.

FOUR

"You're certainly in a chipper mood today." Chatty observations of this nature were rarely articulated by the office's most uncompromising feminist. Russell had been making a particularly pitiful attempt at whistling the refrain from Bobby McFerrin's "Don't Worry, Be Happy," as he and Mary Ann waited for the elevator.

Russell stopped mid-whistle. "Well, Mary Ann, life is short. It really doesn't make sense to waste precious time wallowing in negativity."

"What exactly are you saying?"

Russell quickly realized that if he failed to respond with pitch-perfection, he might very well find himself in hot water. It was clear what Mary Ann was really asking: *Are you suggesting that I'm a Debbie Downer or,* in plainer, cruder terms, *a bitch*? Luckily, the opening elevator doors gave him a momentary reprieve to consider a passable reply. Russell took a half-step back, offering a nod to suggest that the lady enter the car first. Mary Ann offered him a pithy sneer for his chivalry, but took him up on it anyway, while assuming the haughty carriage of royal entitlement.

"Wait, wait! Hold that elevator!" Russell pushed the "open-door" button to give Ed time to scoot inside. The presence of a third person, Russell assumed, would insure a change of subject during the ride down to the garage. "Mercy bo-kups," Ed exclaimed, in deliberately botched French. As the car commenced its descent, Ed took notice of the mindless grin creasing Russell's mug. "Look's like somebody's been enjoyin' bein' off the leash!" he teased.

30

"Not really," Russell answered, crisply.

"Well, then," Ed pried, "Pray tell... what's with the good mood?"

"That's what Mary Ann was just asking about," Russell said, unable to hold back a grin. "Right, Mary Ann?" She, however, was pretending to be listening to voicemails on her new, company-issued Nokia phone. The two men traded smirks. It was common knowledge that there was no cell signal in the elevator. "Anyway," Russell continued. "At the risk of tallying up unhatched chickadees, I'm feelin' pretty darn good about the stair-lift company." To the frequent frustration of Ed and others on the sales team, Russell tended to keep the status of pending accounts hush-hush until they were signed, sealed, and filed away. This time, however, he was dangling a carrot purely for the purpose of distracting a chronically indiscreet coworker from whatever other suspicions he might be entertaining.

"Way to kick ass, Bro!" Ed exclaimed, raising his right hand for an expected high five. Purposefully, Russell ignored this juvenile gesture. Still, he took note that Ed did have at least one admirable quality, being as he was, capable of delighting in a teammate feathering his pockets with a big commission.

"Thanks, Bro," Russell said, putting sarcastic emphasis on the word "Bro" as he shot a sidelong glance toward Mary Ann. She continued fake-listening to her phone, while savoring a private chuckle over Ed's clownishness.

"You-da-man!" Ed exuded, before finally lowering his still un-slapped palm. Russell's optimism about this particular sale aside, his grin was really about having received the best possible news about his health status. And, the parts of his male anatomy dangling under that soon-to-be feathered pocket were also living in a kind of gleeful anticipation that Ed couldn't possibly comprehend. The elevator doors opened at the garage level. "Après vous, Mademoiselle," Ed said to Mary Ann, sweeping his hand, palm up, toward the exit with exaggerated gallantry.

Mary Ann looked up from her phone, locked eyes with Ed, and muttered a flippant, "Fuck you."

"That'll be the day, M'Lady," Ed joshed, before following her out into the clangy, cavernous, underground garage. As they'd done dozens of times, Ed and Russell proceeded to trudge in the direction of their assigned parking spaces. "That woman hates my fuckin' guts," Ed stewed. It baffled Russell how this guy could remain so clueless. Sure, Mary Ann was a tough nut to crack. But at least 90-percent of the blame for this chronic disharmony fell on Ed's shoulders. After all, you don't win the hearts and minds of women like Mary Ann by acting as poster boy for every unappealing masculine trait imaginable.

"Yep," Russell agreed. He was about to change the subject when any chance of verbal communication was drowned out by the rumble of a revving engine reverberating off the cinder block walls, immediately followed by a deafening screech of tires. As Russell suspected, the source of the racket was Mike, at the wheel of his immaculately restored, early-70s-era Dodge Charger. The muscle car pulled up alongside Ed and Russell, matching their pace as the passenger-side window rolled down. Identifying a more sympathetic audience, Ed repeated his complaint to Mike about Mary Ann, who was legging it 10 yards behind, now engaged in actual conversation on her phone.

"I wouldn't fuck that bitch with your dick!" declared Mike. This jingoistic wisecrack made "Bro" Ed's day, sending him roiling in peels of belly laughter. Meanwhile, Russell didn't break stride, nor did he relinquish his grin. He pointed his key remote at his Celica, which responded with a pair of high-pitched Toyota beeps. Nothing could have better signified the stark difference in the world views of two men than the ground-shaking roar of Mike's Detroit-built V8 next to the timid hum of Russell's fuel-efficient, four-cylinder Japanese import. "Hey!" Mike addressed Ed. "The bee-otch may think you're an asshole. But, at least she knows you're not queer bate like Rusty Boy." Mike proceeded to underline his offensive punchline by pumping his accelerator like a lion claiming supremacy on the Serengeti. Refusing to give a bully like Mike the pleasure of ruining his good mood, Russell pretended he hadn't heard the insult. Not getting his desired response, Mike peeled out like a spoiled, zit-cheeked punk on senior skip day.

By now, Mary Ann had caught up. Unlike Russell, she wasn't feigning deafness. "Oh, God!" she teased, through a sly, off-kilter smile, "tell me it's not true, Russ!" She added perfect punctuation to this wisecrack by tossing her Prada valise into the boot of her BMW E36. Russell had to squelch the urge to ask Mary Ann the same question she'd posed to him five minutes earlier, as they awaited the elevator... *What exactly are you saying*? He cringed at the possibility that Mary Ann might possess a super-acute sense of gaydar. Maybe, she'd always harbored suspicions that he was queer and closeted. On the other hand, it seemed altogether uncharacteristic for this woman to care even the tiniest whit about Russell's sexual orientation, or to waste mental energy pondering the secret sexual preferences of any man, for that matter.

No one would have considered Mary Ann a natural beauty. But she devoted considerable effort and invested substantial resources into optimizing what native appeal she possessed. And she was not above using her sexual allure to gain advantage. Russell chuckled at an ironic realization: Mary Ann's sardonic quip conjured up memories of schoolyard flirtations, when a girl being mean to a boy (or vice versa) was actually the first sign of a crush. And, although it seemed silly, he would have liked to think that this female juggernaut found him somewhat attractive. The slamming of Mary Ann's trunk echoed off the concrete walls like a bomb, portending more explosions to come. Because, for better or for worse, Russell Deacon drove out and away from that parking garage and immediately set upon blowing up everything in his life — bit by bit.

For some inexplicable reason, the crunching noise of each individual step seemed louder than normal. Except for some bird chirps and a distant airplane, Russell's leather dress shoes treading the woodland path, stealthily, intentionally, provided the only sound.

Twenty minutes earlier, he'd been motoring along his usual route, harboring every intention of heading directly home. Then, it crossed his mind, with Tess and boys out of town, no one was expecting him. He considered swinging by Boston Market. But dinner could wait. And, in truth, the hunger gurgling in his gut was for something other than roasted chicken. As had occurred countless times before, craving drowned out rationality and impulse seized the wheel. There was little he could do to deny it. The Celica drove itself into the left turn lane, as the clicking of the turn signal sent a suggestive Morse Code message directly to Russell's groin. Swinging through the intersection, he sensed his tingling genitals siphoning blood away from his other extremities, arming up to answer the call of duty. His heartbeat quickened. His face flushed. And, his bowels stirred.

When Russell's thoughts began entertaining certain possibilities and there stood a chance those possibilities might soon be manifested, his sphincter muscles would immediately loosen their grip. As the Celica's tires ground noisily across the gravel parking lot, the necessity of locating a toilet was becoming urgent. An Andy Gump stood a stone's throw from the jogging trail. Finding the fiberglass out-building occupied was disconcerting. Luckily, the door swung open and out bounded a thin, spikey haired, bleach-blonde fellow, clad in a multicolored tank top and a pair of skimpy, canary-yellow running shorts. "It's all yours," he lisped, with a wily grin. Yellow Shorts lingered for a few seconds to check Russell out from head to toe. Although Russell was still dressed in his work clothes, his square attire didn't inhibit a positive review. "Nice," Yellow Shorts assessed, before pirouetting to bound, deer-like, in the direction of the trail. The man's brazenness made Russell blush. Still, he felt flattered that someone found him desirable.

Ten minutes later, there he was, newly purged bowels and all, taking loud, crunchy steps deeper into the woods. The evidence of prior clandestine couplings — cigarette butts, condom wrappers, and wads of tissue — lay strewn here and there, under the larger trees, behind thickets, and between boulders. It always disturbed Russell to witness how thoughtless some men were to leave such detritus on the forest floor. Still, he knew that this particular kind of litter invariably meant that he stood a good chance of coming across guys in the act. Deep-throated laughter wafted through the trees. The source of the merriment was not far away. Russell stopped, like a kid playing statue tag on the grammar-school playground and waited, hoping to get a bead on where the noise was coming from. In the absence of leaf-and-twig-crushing footsteps, he was able to pick out the low, indistinct hum of sporadic chatter. Cautiously, he began guerilla-ninja-ing toward the sound.

He found them on a slope at the edge of the creek. One of the men was standing, head tilted back, eyes closed. The second fellow had his back to Russell, crouched down on his haunches, with his face next to the standing man's crotch. It didn't take Sherlock Holmes to discern what was going on. And, if there had been any question about it, confirmation came when the standing man spoke. "Oh, yeah," he urged, "suck it. Take it all." Russell had ferreted out his ideal voyeuristic scenario: A clear view of two guys getting it on, both oblivious to his presence. With his eyes fixed on the action, Russell loosened his belt, unzipped his fly and lowered his trousers and undershorts down past his buttocks. He had always found it unsatisfactory to simply pull out his willy and have at it. Achieving optimum gratification required feeling the outside air on his ass and thighs. He worked up a mouthful of saliva, spit a wad into his palm, and began lubricating his throbbing hard on. Each consecutive stroke assured him that he would soon be contributing a dollop of milky protein nutrient to the forest floor.

Russell's self-pleasuring was picking up momentum, when a twig under his right foot snapped, prompting the standing man to open his eyes. Immediately recognizing those pale-blue orbs, under that thick mop of ebony hair, Russell's jaw dropped open. Bryan identified Russell as well. Not appearing to be the slightest bit self-conscious about what, to Russell, seemed a particularly awkward happenstance, Bryan exhibited a broad smile. In contrast, Russell simply stood there, cock in hand, gawking in disbelief. Countless men perused places like this for the purpose of hooking up. Certainly, there had always been a remote chance that a coincidental meeting might take place. But, it had always seemed the longest of longshots that Russell would ever run into someone he knew at the very minute that person was getting his knob gobbled.

Bryan waved a friendly "come on over" gesture, a clear, unambiguous invitation to join in the fun. Russell's automatic reaction was a subtle shake of his head. Bryan's return shoulder shrug said, "Whatever, Buddy. Suit yourself." Then, he closed his blue eyes again and resumed encouraging his partner. "Oh, yeah," he said, "you love it, don't you!"

While the serendipity of this situation was unnerving, it was also enormously exhilarating. Russell couldn't simply retreat, not while sporting a yet-to-be-satisfied, rock-hard erection. He needed to finish before making his escape. Turning to the side to avoid further eye contact with Bryan, Russell was startled to discover someone lurking behind him. As his aroused package came into view, Yellow

Shorts cast a lustful gander down at the thing in Russell's hand and reiterated his earlier assessment: "Nice." Eyes fixed on the prize, Yellow Shorts reached out, with the clear intention of stroking it. By now, overwhelm had rendered Russell a tad woozy. Only a couple of minutes ago, he'd been on a glide path toward safe, blissful, solo sex. In the interim, he'd been invited into a three-way by his volunteer-assistant Little League coach and a man in the loudest, least-modest jogging shorts on the planet was attempting to grab his junk.

Russell's reaction was totally instinctual. He slapped the man's hand away. "Don't you dare touch it!" he hissed.

"Okay! Okay!" Yellow Shorts blurted. "You don't have to be a bitch about it."

Hastily, Russell pulled up his undershorts and pants. Without zipping up or buckling his belt, he set off stomping through the brush toward the path, grasping his trousers to keep them from falling down. Wrinkled shirt tails wafting like ballpark pennants, dress shoes indiscriminately shattering twigs and pulverizing fallen leaves, he charged hurriedly away from the creek-side orgy. Despite his frenzied state, Russell was still very much aroused. He had failed to achieve relief in the shower the night before. This circumstance risked a painful case of blue balls. So, after putting what seemed a safe distance between himself and the others, he ducked behind a large boulder to finish the deed.

Russell's ejaculation arrived with a moan of such ultimate pleasure, it might well have been audible in the next county. However, he had no more than three seconds to savor the sensation before he detected footsteps approaching on the path. Feeling the presence of another person on the other side of the boulder, Russell held his breath. Panic pressure welled up in his temples and forehead. The wooziness returned. He leaned his shoulder blades against the stone to prevent from toppling over. "Way to get 'er done, Coach!"

Recognizing Bryan's voice provided momentary relief. Still, standing there in the woods with his private parts still exposed, Russell wasn't about to trade witticisms. With his entire body still quivering from orgasmic release, the scene seemed so absurd that he had to muffle a chortle.

After what seemed an interminable few seconds, the footsteps resumed and faded into the distance. Russell finally felt free to exhale. That Bryan had demonstrated sufficient discretion to refrain from further invasion into his private self-pleasuring was to be appreciated. Still, with that one dubious compliment — "Way to get 'er done, Coach!" — Bryan had reminded Russell that, after years of secrecy, someone finally had his number. Then again, Russell had Bryan's number, too. These two men had just shared a secret so personal, so confidential, and so potentially volatile that it could never be revealed — to anyone else, ever. What they would do about it — or what they chose *not* to do about it, for that matter — was a question for another day.

FIVE

One common assumption about queer boys and men is that they have zero interest in or talent for sports. This notion isn't exclusive to the straight world. It also pervades amongst gay men — totally understandable, because so many suffered harassment and ostracization on the school playground for not displaying the same "masculine" traits and athletic inclinations as their male peers. A second conventional supposition presumes that every gay and bi person becomes painfully aware of their "difference" from early childhood. While these generalizations often ring true, in both cases, Russell Deacon was the exception.

Baseball had been a Deacon family tradition for generations. Russell's paternal grandfather spent his early adulthood barnstorming across the country with a semi-pro team before going on to coach in the minor leagues. Being "Deke" Deacon's firstborn grandson, it was taken for granted that Russell would not only pursue the national pastime with vigor, but would excel on the diamond. On the day Russell was born, Deke was beaming proudly at the pudgy, pink-cheeked babe when a vision came to him: of Russell, grown up, taking the field in uniform, as a scrappy, switch-hitting, base-stealing, all-star shortstop.

Russell did indeed grow up to swing from both sides of the plate. He also developed a particular passion for and, ultimately, a distinct alacrity for playing ballgames. The balls he played with, however, were of a considerably softer texture. Russell also discovered a shared interest with an untold number of other men in pursuing an alternative national pastime. However, unlike the sport Russell's father's father pictured him playing, these activities are seldom scheduled and never played under the lights in front of a cheering crowd. Instead, such games break out spontaneously, in shadowy spaces known only to those with the curiosity and compulsion to take part. Not only do teammates usually prefer to remain nameless, they rarely take the field with the same players. Still, they play nonetheless, and not to outscore an opponent, but to assume their positions for the purpose of achieving a win-win. Russell shuddered to think how profoundly disappointed Deke, who passed away when Russell was three, would have been to learn what kind of switch hitter that cherubic, swaddled infant grew up to be.

While Russell showed athletic promise as a youngster, certain factors dissuaded him from sustaining his sporting aspirations into his teens. First, he stopped growing in ninth grade. Thus, while his teammates continued to get taller and stronger, Russell had already peaked out at five-foot seven. As the pitches started coming in faster, his bat simply couldn't catch up. Too, he lacked a cutthroat competitive spirit. He'd always loved donning the uniform, taking the field, and playing the game. But, he never considered winning the most important thing. Finally, pubescence arrived later for Russell than it did for most of his peers, made more conspicuous by his late-September birthday, which made him one of the youngest boys in his grade level. By seventh grade, wisps of hair were showing up in the armpits and crotches of the other boys. Meanwhile, the lunar landscape of Rusty Deacon's scrotum remained conspicuously pink and fallow. Thus, dressing and showering in the junior-high locker room left him feeling painfully self-conscious about his under-developed body.

Long after he was finally visited by puberty, he would experience discomfort in any situation where his private parts might be exposed to other guys. A big part of this chronic anxiety came from an ever present fear that he might get an erection. And, the more he pondered the embarrassment of this possibility, the more likely it became. In retrospect, this involuntary tendency might have provided him some evidence of same-sex attraction. Instead, for more than a decade to come, there was a short circuit in the connection between what his heart wanted, what his body lusted after, and what his mind was willing to believe. In truth, Russell always felt a strong attraction to girls. As early as fifth and sixth grades, he would initiate spin-the-bottle games. But, kissing a girl then was less about sex and more about some childish ideal of paperback-novel romance. Enthralled by Mike Hammer mysteries and film-noir detective movies, his masculine role model was the private eye in a fedora, who drank straight whiskey from a chimney glass, smoked Lucky Strikes and, at some point in the story, took the blonde in his arms and planted a wet one on her voluptuous, painted lips. That was the scene he pictured himself playing out whenever the bottle's neck came to rest pointed in his direction.

By eighth grade, however, sexual conquest had leapt to the forefront of his every conscious thought. Russell lived in constant obsession about if and when he might make his way to first base, second base, and beyond. Had he known what the future had in store, he would have found it particularly ironic that baseball vernacular was so commonly used to score sexual achievement.

Russell and Tess's firstborn son, Henry (named after his maternal grandfather and affectionately known as Hank) had inherited some of his bloodline's native athleticism. However, the boy's legs were heavy and he showed little real passion for the game. Their younger boy turned out to be an entirely different creature altogether. Rory was a natural athlete. As soon as his hand was big enough to hold a baseball, he was all in. Too, he was born with the quality Russell lacked: a fiercely competitive nature. When Hank turned nine, his father wasn't the one to suggest that he sign up for Little League. Pressure came in the form of a dare from little brother Rory. Being as naturally gifted as he was, Rory's impatience over having to wait two long seasons before officially joining the team was understandable.

Russell harbored no designs on coaching or managing a youth squad. But, while he hadn't been on a ball field in decades, he couldn't help but feel that his background — and his heritage — made him more qualified than the three fathers charged with captaining the Pirate crew. Observing the team getting pummeled, game after game — the kids hadn't even been schooled in the sport's most rudimentary aspects — made it increasingly difficult for Russell to hold his tongue. He consciously attempted to frame his coaching feedback in the form of "helpful suggestions." The last time he took the team manager aside to share some tips, the response was swift and candid. "Look, Russ," Bob Christy responded, "if you think you can do a better job, you're welcome to it."

To Russell's pleasant surprise, helping the boys improve their skills, build self-esteem, and discover team comradery proved enormously gratifying. With Coach Deacon at the helm, the Pirates showed measurable improvement from one contest to the next. Eventually, they developed a confident swagger. And, having ended the previous summer's campaign — Russell's first full season as manager — by reaching the second round of the regional playoffs, a nibble of victory had made them hungry for more. Thus, the 1994 season began on a positive, optimistic note.

For any coach, in any sport, the first game of the year can be a source of nervous anticipation. Coach Deacon was no exception. He couldn't help but fret about how his players would respond when faced with real-time, three-dimensional competition. To be certain, Russell was pleased to have his sons back at home and on the ballfield. Still, the specter of opening day held additional anxiety. The trepidation Coach was feeling on the cusp of this summer's first contest was less about the game and more about coming face-to-face with a certain volunteer assistant. Russell walked onto the field with his gut churning like a cement mixer. His sweat glands were working overtime, to the extent that he could hardly grip the bat to hit ground balls to the infielders. Tension had been building throughout the week. That Bryan had skipped the Tuesday and Thursday practice without explanation led Russell to surmise that his hunky helper must be avoiding him. Then, to Russell's surprise, Bryan showed up on Saturday morning, all smiles, cocky as ever, as if Monday's chance encounter in the woods was either too meaningless to acknowledge or had been selectively plucked from his memory. By all outward appearances, for Bryan, today was like any other Little League Saturday. He sauntered onto the field as that same blue-eyed, overly confident, ready-to-be-of-service, volunteer coach. It quickly became apparent that what happened in the grove beyond the outfield fence would have no bearing on today's game.

Pre-season Pirate practices had been going relatively smoothly. The squad had several solid returning players. Bryan's son Carter, now 12, had experienced a growth spurt and was demonstrating real progress swinging the bat. Over the winter, Carter had also developed a fairly reliable slider, which he was able to throw for strikes. Hank and Rory, 11 and 9 respectively, had been working with Russell to improve their skill sets. And Rory, now entering his first campaign in uniform — after champing at the bit over the course of two, excruciatingly tedious summers — was eager to make an on-field contribution and prove himself.

In the fourth inning, with two outs and a runner on third, Rory got his shot. It was a critical moment, with the score knotted, six to six. Russell's younger son stepped into the batter's box and proceeded to very strategically use his diminutive stature and limited vertical strike zone to his advantage. The high, hard fast ball that had resulted in big brother Hank striking out twice provided the shorter Rory with four consecutive balls and a free pass. But, Rory wasn't content with simply drawing a walk. Much to the surprise of the Pirates' first base coach, he seized his very first opportunity to take off in a dead sprint for second base. The catcher was so taken off guard that he rushed his throw, which sailed over the shortstop's head into center field, enabling the Pirate runner on third to waltz in and score standing up. From that juncture on, it was no contest. Their rattled opponents, the Angels, pretty much fell apart, handing the Pirates an easy 12-6 victory... thanks in large part to Rory's heroics.

After the game, as Bryan finished collecting the bats and the rest of the equipment, he asked, "Anything else I can do for you, Coach?"

"I don't think so," Russell responded. "Thanks, Buddy, as always, for your help. See you at practice on Tuesday?"

"Tomorrow," Bryan corrected him. Seeing the clueless expression on Russell's face, Bryan offered what he assumed was a reminder: "We'll be seeing each other tomorrow evening." Not having a clue what Bryan was talking about, Russell stood there for a moment, his brain shuffling through a deck of possibilities. Certainly, Bryan couldn't be suggesting that they might run into each other in the woods again. "Dinner," Bryan said, "...tomorrow night, at your house. Diana said Tess invited us over."

"Oh, right," Russell stammered, blushing beet red, and forcing a chuckle to pretend he'd forgotten. If Tess had informed him about this, he had no memory of it. And, considering to whom the invitation had been extended, this is not something that would easily have slipped his mind. "Great!" Russell said, trying to dredge up a drop of enthusiasm. "Tomorrow it is. See ya'all then."

"I don't know why you're being so weird about this." Tess was clearly exasperated. She and her hubby had been volleying this issue back and forth for an insufferable 20 minutes.

"Well," Russell responded. "I don't think there's anything wrong with the man of the house wanting to be consulted. I mean, you know... I'd, I'd..." He was flailing to find words that wouldn't be interpreted as sexist. "A guy kinda likes to have some say about what happens in his own home once in a while."

"Do you not like Bryan? I mean, Hank and Carter have been getting pretty tight. I think it would be good for Hank. I mean, Diane's a little too cozy with Jesus, but..."

"I don't know, Babe," Russell interrupted. "I saw you two in the bleachers, cluckin' away like a pair of hens in the barnyard." So much for his desire to avoid misogyny.

"Oh, man!" Tess exclaimed. "How could I have forgotten?"

"Forgotten what?"

"That I'd married a male chauvinist pig!" At that point, Russell's usually ultra-classy spouse started snorting like a hungry sow and tickling his rib cage, as if he were four years old.

"Stop it!" Russell demanded.

"Sorry, Babe," Tess said, retracting her fingers from his ribs. "I forgot. Opening day always throws a wet blanket over your funny bone. Grumpy ol' coach. I get it."

Russell wanted to tell his wife how uncomfortable he felt with the idea of socializing with Bryan. But, he couldn't think of a reason that would have made a lick of sense — no reason outside the truth, anyway. "I just don't like getting blindsided," he complained, "hearing about my own social plans that way. You know, from somebody else."

"You always seemed fine with spontaneous arrangements like this before."

"What if I'd made other plans? That would be like super awkward."

"What other plans?"

"I don't know..." She had him cornered. He was at a loss for a comeback.

"See?" she said, soothingly, placing the palm of her hand on his chest, as if to calm his racing heart. "You're getting all worked up about nothing."

Yes, Russell was worked up. Not, however, about nothing. He had a totally legitimate reason for feeling unsettled about the social plans his wife had made without his consultation. That reason, however, couldn't possibly be shared with her.

SIX

"**F**uck you, lard ass!" Rory lambasted Hank. "You couldn't steal a base if it was like six inches away!" The bickering was well into its second day. Russell had worried that a more athletically gifted, more-assertive little brother joining his average-skilled, less-motivated big brother's Little League team might become the source of fraternal friction. Since yesterday's game, Hank had ragged Rory relentlessly about his choice to steal second base without receiving a cue from the coach. What made Rory's act of self-determination particularly irksome to the elder boy was that it had made his upstart pipsqueak brother the game's MVP.

Russell was about to chastise Rory for this profane taunting of his pear-shaped older sibling when the doorbell rang. To evade discipline, Rory streaked to the foyer to welcome the evening's guests. Seeing Rory at the door, Carter exuded, "Whoa, Dude! You're a badass!" The two boys engaged in double high-, then double low-fives, while Hank looked on from the stairs, wearing a hangdog expression. Diane remained outside on the porch, smiling like a prom queen, a Bing Cherry pie cradled in her arms in a perfect portrayal of the docile southern homemaker. No one else noticed Bryan and Russell locking eyes. Bryan shot Russell that amazing smile. Russell wanted to send one back in return. His expression, however, remained blank and unchanged.

"Come on in, you guys!" Tess called out from the kitchen. "Make yourselves at home." Carter followed Hank to do battle with monsters in the virtual world. Diane glided to the kitchen to deliver her pie. Bryan put his arm around Rory's shoulders, and proceeded to extol the kid's tenacity as they strolled toward the back patio. Russell was left standing alone in the foyer, feeling like an invisible guest in his own home.

"My Lord, Tess!" Bryan exclaimed, wiping his perpetually smiling lips with a red-and-white-checkered cloth napkin. "This chicken is to die for!"

"Well, there's plenty left, if you want more," Tess announced, tongs in one hand and a tray of legs and thighs in the other. Unlike most typical patriarchal American households, the king of the Deacon family barbecue was the queen of the house. Tess was the grill master. Russell was the clean-up crew.

"You know I'd love to," Bryan responded. "But I'm stuffed. I guess my eyes are bigger than my stomach." Bryan's big eyes may have been looking up at Tess as he turned down another thigh. His fingers, however, had found Russell's thigh under the patio table and were inching slowly but surely toward more private parts. Like Rory's choice yesterday to steal second base, Bryan's brazen move came without permission from the coach. There could hardly have been a more inappropriate setting for such an advance. And that, for Russell, is precisely what made it even more exciting. As Bryan slid his palm under the leg of Russell's cargo shorts, the edge of his pinky brushed against the tip of a rapidly inflating erection. Only the cotton fabric of Russell's tighty-whities prohibited direct, finger-to-glans contact.

"Who wants dessert?" Tess asked. "Diane brought a beautiful pie. Homemade, right?"

"Baked from scratch, of course," Diane drawled, as if any other answer would do.

"We've got Dryer's French Vanilla, if anyone wants theirs á la mode," Tess announced. "Russ..."

"Yes, My Love," Russell dreamily responded, as Bryan's smallest digit surreptitiously massaged the tip of his raging boner.

"Maybe you could get off your lazy rump," Tess half-joked, "and fetch the pie and ice cream."

"Oh, I don't know," Russell said, tossing a subtle side glance at Bryan. "Doncha think we could wait a few minutes? You know, to give this scrumptious meal a chance to settle down."

"Okay, then," Tess countered, "maybe you could make yourself useful by brewing up some of your world-renown free-trade java."

"Oh, my!" Diane cooed, a la Scarlet O'Hara. "Coffee sounds absolutely divine."

"Alrighty," Russell responded, with a note of surrender, "I guess I can fulfill that wish. And, on my way to the kitchen, maybe I can make myself even more useful, by bussing a few items."

"At last," Tess said, exhaling a mock sigh. "The man of the house justifies his existence." At this, Diane tittered like blushing nun, to think that any wife could express such overt disrespect for her hubby, especially in the presence of company. While scanning the table for an adequate crotch shield, Russell removed Bryan's meandering mitt from his leg, giving it an affectionate little squeeze in the process. The salad bowl seemed best for screening the tenting in his groin area. He was sidling around the table, holding the bowl strategically, like a vaudeville fan dancer, when Diane reached for the salad tongs.

"I just love fresh fruit in a summer salad, don't you?" she said. "Wouldn't want any of these yummy goodies to go to waste." She then proceeded to pick out the remaining half-dozen green grapes, placing them, one by one, on her empty plate. Aware of what Russell was hiding under the bowl, while witnessing his wife pluck out select testicular shaped pieces of fruit proved enormously amusing to Bryan. Russell, on the other hand, couldn't wait to commence bow-legging his way across the patio and into the house.

"Your back bothering you, Babe?" Tess called out.

"Little bit, yeah," he fibbed.

"You know that can't happen again," Russell informed Bryan. The sun was sinking into the western horizon as the two men stood on the furthest edge of the backyard, beyond earshot of their spouses. Bryan's choice earlier in the evening to play under-the-table pocket pool had been nonconsensual, poorly timed, and came with a risk Russell found unacceptable.

"Oh, come on, Coach," Bryan teased, tilting his head slyly to one side and assuming an ultra-lascivious leer. "You know you loved it. Your dick was standing up like a flagpole."

"Look," Russell insisted, "I'm dead serious. What happened earlier can never happen again."

"You mean," Bryan presumed aloud, "that it can never happen *here*... at your house, on the patio, in the presence of the ladies. Right?" Russell attempted to utter an unambiguous "No!" They could never engage in such shenanigans, not here, not anywhere, not ever! His recalcitrant tongue, however, refused to formulate the word. A sexy, irresistible man was offering an open invitation to be his fuck buddy. At least, that's what Russell was reading in the not-so-subtle subtext. It was something he'd only fantasized about, while placing such an appealing arrangement light years beyond the realm of possibility. Seeing the silent longing in Russell's befuddled eyes, Bryan stated, matter-of-factly, "Look, I like you. I'm attracted to you. You have needs. I have needs. Where's the problem?" Never before had Russell experienced such a strong desire to kiss another man. Never had he felt such a powerful urge to rip the buttons off the front of a guy's shirt, to run his palms over forested pectorals, to lick an armpit, and bite a nipple. Once again, Russell tried to speak. But words were still caught in his constricted throat. It was as though a flutter of sparrows had invaded his chest. "I don't know, Russ," Bryan said. "Maybe I'm wrong."

This was the very first time Bryan had called Russell by his name. Russell's knees buckled. He nearly swooned. Finally, he was able to mutter something audible. "Say it again," he demanded quietly.

"Say what?"

"My name," Russell insisted. "Say my name."

"Okay," Bryan responded, obviously perplexed by this peculiar plea. "Russ." The thrill tremor traveling down Russell's spine sent his feet into a wiggly, cartoonish dance step. Observing the weirdness of this herky-jerky movement made Bryan titter. Russell looked at Bryan. Bryan looked back at Russell, then broke into a full-fledged guffaw. Russell, in turn, couldn't hold back his laughter at the absurdity of it all. So, the two men stood there on the lawn, under the twilight sky, for several consecutive minutes, belly laughing uncontrollably. By the time this prolonged spate of levity began losing steam, Russell's abdomen was aching and tears were streaming down his cheeks.

"I'd better go in now," said Russell.

"You okay, Buddy?" Bryan inquired.

"Yeah," Russell managed. "I'm good. I just have to..." His voice trailed off as he set out tottering, weak-kneed across the lawn toward the house.

"So," Tess offered, "that wasn't so bad, was it? I mean, correct me if I'm wrong. But it looked to me like you and Bryan were really enjoying each other's company."

Bryan, Diane, and Carter were gone. Russell was on kitchen-scouring detail, wiping up the last bit of cleaning solution from the granite counter top. "Yeah," he agreed, keeping his head down, concentrating on the job at hand. "He's okay I guess."

"What were you guys laughing about?"

"When?"

"When? I thought you were going to wet your shorts."

"Oh, it was a joke," Russell claimed. "Stupid actually."

"Care to share? I could use a good laugh."

"You wouldn't get it," responded Russell. "It's..." He needed to avoid this line of questioning. "Besides, I can't really remember the whole thing."

"I see," Tess quipped. "I'm just a mere female. I could never..."

"That's not what I meant," he declared. "And, you know it."

Tess grabbed a large, stainless steel pot from the dish rack and began drying it with a dish towel. "Such a good-looking man," she remarked, as she hung the newly dried pot from its hook above the range top.

"Really?" Russell replied, as if he'd never noticed.

"Oh, come on, Russ! Don't tell me you wouldn't die to have those blue eyes."

"Next time I see him," he promised, "I'll take a closer look." Imagining when his next encounter with his hunky, potential fuck buddy might be and under what circumstances sent blood rushing back into Russell's genitals.

Meanwhile, Tess had bellied up from behind, slipped her hands under her hubby's biceps, around his torso, and over his chest. As she laid her head tenderly against his back, she said, "I love you."

"Love you, too, Babe," was the automatic reply.

Tess's hands wandered down under Russell's apron to discover his soldier, now standing at the ready. "Well, well, well," she purred. "Looks like someone has been feeling neglected." Russell swiveled around, looked his wife in the eyes, took her cheeks in his hands, pulled her lips to his and kissed her with a passion he hadn't shown her in years. Not wanting to squander the moment, she took him by the hand. Leaving his apron on the kitchen floor, Russell obediently followed her upstairs to their bed.

It had been at least seven months since they'd made love. In the aftermath, the couple lay there for a while under the sheet, like they often did before the kids came along, bare skin pressed against bare skin. Finally, Tess broke the silence. "Why do you suppose you didn't cum?" It was a reasonable question. In her mind, Russell must have been as dammed up with love juice as she'd been.

"Oh, I don't know. I'm really tired," he theorized. "There's a lot of stress at work. And I'm a little worried about Hank. He's having a hard time with his little brother outperforming him on the ball field."

"I get that," she said, before giving him an affectionate little neck smooch just below the earlobe. "Well, you just let me know when you're in the mood again... and we'll give it another shot."

SEVEN

Ironically, a closeted bisexual man's compulsion to seek out casual, anonymous sexual encounters with other men often has a lot to do with the very same factors that should logically warn him against engaging in such behavior. So it was with Russell Deacon. The cloak-and-dagger secrecy, the solitary sleuthing into forbidden territory added an extra degree of excitement unmatched by any other sexual exchange. Russell had come to crave the rumbling in his belly, the chill in his shoulders, the hot flush in his cheeks, the array of adrenalized sensations that invariably preceded a plunge into unpredictable currents. And, by simply observing and noticing things that happen every single day in every single town, thrill seekers like Russell eventually stumble into places where such clandestine couplings are likely to take place.

Russell first became cognizant of the existence of such secret rendezvous spots while taking his young sons, then seven and five, for a nature hike through a county park. Russell, Hank, and Rory were only a few minutes into their Saturday excursion, traversing a trail through the forested area leading to a natural granite edifice known as Rooster Rock. They had just rounded a switchback when Russell spied the illicit goings on. No more than a dozen strides into the shade, under a large Douglas Fir, one man was going down on another man. Russell stopped dead in his tracks, splaying his arms out like a lieutenant silently ordering his platoon to refrain from advancement. "What's wrong, Dad?" Hank queried.

"I think I forgot something in the car," Russell improvised, simultaneously ripping his gaze away from the pairing in progress and sensing an unforeseen, involuntary, electrified tingle in his man parts.

"What?" Hank asked. "What did you forget?"

"We have to go back," Russell insisted, swiveling a quick about face. Suddenly, it was of the utmost importance to put maximum distance between his two young sons and what was happening in the dappled shadows beneath the evergreen canopy.

Ninety minutes later, the intrepid father-son trio sat atop Rooster Rock, wolfing down PB and J sandwiches, when Rory asked, "What were those men doing, Daddy?"

"Which men?" Russell responded, all too aware which men his youngest son was curious about. Picturing the scene in the woods, Russell's soldier perked up once again.

"You saw them," Rory contended. "I know you did." Even as a kindergartener, Rory refused to let anyone get away with even the tiniest hint of obfuscation.

"Oh, right. Now, I remember," Russell confessed. "Well..." he said, pretending to be hazarding a guess, "maybe one of them broke a shoelace and his friend was fixing it for him."

"Okay. Makes sense, I guess." Rory accepted this bogus theory with a head nod, while slurping the last noisy drops from his juice box.

"Whoa!" Hank exclaimed, pointing to the sky. "Is that an eagle, Dad?"

Happy to have the subject changed, Russell located the raptor sailing across the blue sky with grandeur and grace. "I think that's a red-tail hawk," he guessed. "We'll have to look it up in the *World Book* when we get home."

"Cool!" said Hank. This wholesome tableau had every potential of being a significant, bonding father-son moment. As the feathered predator tucked its wings and swooped down below the level of the tree tops, Russell hoped his boys would remember it that way. His mind, however, was busy speculating when he might be able to steal away solo to pay the Rooster Rock trail a reprise visit. And, when that opportunity presented itself, he wondered if he would come across yet another covert, male-on-male hook-up under the fir trees.

Over the three years to follow, Russell became extremely adept at keeping his "real life" — as a sales rep, husband, and father — separate from his same-sex interests and pursuits. Even though, over time, he devoted an increased amount of time to his voyeuristic compulsions, he was still maintaining what, to him, felt like a healthy and functional balance between his dual personas. Inside the house and at the office, Russell played the straight-man role convincingly. Outside those conscientiously controlled environments, he was constantly cruising for his next opportunity to seek out and observe men having sex. Russell's perfect track record at negotiating these two disconnected lives eventually gave him a distorted level of self-assurance. Overconfidence, however, can lead to sloppy behavior which, in turn, risks disappointing a spouse or, worse yet, rousing suspicion. This was a lesson Russell would learn the hard way.

It happened the night Russell's traveling college roommate was expected for dinner. Russell was motoring home from the office with more than adequate time to accomplish a short list of honey-do's before his ex-roomie's ETA. As his preferred homeward route took him directly past Centennial Park, he figured he might as well take a quick look-see. For someone like Russell, who had developed a finely honed radar for hook-ups in progress, an early-evening swing past and around The Parthenon told myriad stories. Two cars parked snugly parallel to one another; the driver of one car leaning against the open driver-side window of the other. Flirtatious conversation between the two men, followed by one of them sauntering around the other's vehicle, opening the passenger door, and sliding in. Russell had even memorized vehicles driven by regulars who frequented the men's bathrooms. Experience had taught him who the aggressive, grabby ones were, and to avoid entering the small, cinder block structure by the duck pond when a certain Jeep was parked in a nearby space.

On this particular evening, however, such activity in the park was scarce. After two complete laps, Russell pulled over into the shade. He was paging through the *Nashville Scene* when an SUV pulled up and into the adjacent spot. The driver motioned for Russell to roll down his window. Russell complied. And, without so much as a perfunctory, "Hi. How're ya doin'?" the guy leapfrogged over any and all small talk. "What do you like?" he inquired.

Russell knew exactly what his query meant. Still, he played naive. "What do I like?" he asked in return.

"Well," the man responded, with a wry smile, "do you like getting sucked?"

The fellow's brazen question took Russell totally by surprise. After all, a more typical park meet-up would go something like this...

Guy One: "Hey."

Guy Two: "Hey."

Guy One: "Nice evening."

Guy Two: "Yeah, perfect."

These introductory murmurings might be followed by a pause, during which the two men would check each other out with closer scrutiny, while trading a couple of shy smiles.

Guy One: "Any special plans for tonight?"

Guy Two: "No. Not really. I'm just on my way home from work. Thought I'd stop for a few minutes and get some fresh air."

Guy One: "Yeah. Me, too." At this point, one of them might dare to cup his own crotch, to make his intentions and interests absolutely clear. From there, only after it was firmly established that both men were (a) there to hook up and (b) interested in doing so with each other, would they turn to the "what are you into" page in the script.

On this particular evening, however, all of that usual verbal foreplay had been edited from the conversation in advance. *Did Russell like to get sucked? Was this guy kidding? Is the Pope Catholic?* "Yeah, of course," said Russell.

"Okay, then," the fellow answered, re-starting his engine. "Follow me." Before Russell had a chance to respond, the SUV was backing out. Then, the vehicle sat there, idling, with its driver's intense eyes looking at Russell in his side mirror, as if daring him to turn down this audacious proposition.

A dozen red flags were waving. The fellow could have been a vice officer. Still, in spite of the obvious danger signs, Russell's internal daredevil grabbed the steering wheel. As he followed the stranger home, Russell chastised himself repeatedly for being stupid and weak enough to even consider accepting this invitation, especially when he was resolved to prevent this man from carrying out the act he'd so audaciously offered to perform. Still, Russell stuck to the fellow's bumper. After no more than a half mile, the SUV slid into the driveway of a tiny, yellow-brick box of a house. Russell pulled in next to the curb and watched, as the man sashayed to his mailbox to fetch an armful of mail. A faint voice was shouting, almost indiscernible, as if reason was crying out from the bottom of a well. "Don't turn off that engine!" the distant warning demanded. "Put the car in drive and beat it!" But, by now, Russell was under the sway of two bosses... the fellow waving come hither from his porch and the stiff shaft in his trousers. Russell killed the motor, climbed out, and pocketed his keys.

The dwelling was not significantly larger than a typical two-bedroom apartment. The living room had been converted into a beauty salon, with an old-school, swiveling barber chair dominating the space. Folding tables were strewn with hair products, alongside the various tools of the hairdressing trade. "Come over here," the host commanded. As if he had no will of his own, Russell obeyed. Spying the obvious bulge in Russell's crotch, the hairdresser licked his lips, and muttered, "Ooo, la, la! Whatever do we have here?" As he reached for Russell's belt buckle, Russell took a stride back. "Just relax, Honey," the man said, "this won't hurt one little bit." By now, he'd snatched Russell's belt and unhooked the buckle.

"Look," Russell managed to utter. "Please. Stop. For just a minute."

"Okay," said the hairdresser, withdrawing his hands from Russell's by-now, half-unzipped pants. He struck a Baryshnikov pose and looked down his narrow, pointed nose, directly into Russell's eyes. "Is there a problem?"

"Not exactly." Russell spoke haltingly. "I said I liked, you know... blowjobs. I mean, what guy doesn't? Right?"

"Right." Once again, the eager hairdresser grasped for Russell's zipper. "Wish granted."

"No! Hold on!" Russell protested loudly. He felt like a frightened, lost, little boy. "Look," Russell continued, deliberately dialing back his vocal level by several decibels, "I really appreciate you wanting to do this. I really do."

"You appreciate it? What the fuck does that mean? Believe me, you'll appreciate it a lot more when I'm deep throating your Johnson."

"I'm sure I would," Russell admitted. "But..."

"But what?"

"Well..." Russell took a deep breath to summon up his resolve. Meanwhile, his host put a hand on a hip, cocked his head to one side, and widened his eyes, silently indicating that, while he was all ears for the moment, he wasn't about to wait all night. "It's... it's just not gonna happen."

"Okay, then, why are you here?" the flummoxed fellow snapped. "What do you think *is* gonna happen?" While he appeared to be genuinely peeved, he was also indicating that he might be flexible enough to consider accommodating an alternative scenario.

Okay, Russell thought to himself. *Maybe this wasn't such a horrible idea after all.* "Well," he proposed. "I'd like to... you know, do it myself. And, I'd like it... if... if you watched."

"Okay. If you wanna pass on the best blowjob in Tennessee," the hairdresser quipped, forcing a pinched smile, "ain't no skin off my back." He nodded in the direction of Russell's bulging crotch. "Show me what you got." Tentatively, Russell unveiled his package and, as had always been his habit, he proceeded to pull his boxer briefs and pants down below the cheeks of his buttocks. "Oh, my," the hairdresser remarked, with a note of remorse, "such a lovely one, too."

While masturbating in front of another man was usually a turn-on for Russell, he felt like he was on display, as if his engorged penis had been transformed into a performing sea lion. "Go ahead," the hairdresser commanded, assuming the voice of a bitchy schoolmarm. "Do your thing, Honey. Get your rocks off." At the moment, Russell was hard-pressed to determine if he was being mocked or if his host was actually offering encouragement. Of course, Russell's most insecure self-speak decided that this guy was determined to humiliate him out of spite. And, for the first time ever, in a circumstance when such an opportunity presented itself, Russell's erection began to soften and droop.

Witnessing this sad unfurling, the hairdresser remarked, "You've got a lovely cock, Honey. Now you know where I live. So, don't be a stranger. You just drop on by any ol' time. But, next time, be prepared to shove that pretty thing down my throat." There would be no next time.

Russell had left his pager in his car. The screen display showed three missed notifications... all from Tess. His head still dizzy, as if he'd just endured a brain-bruising rollercoaster ride, he sped to the closest 7-Eleven and grabbed a payphone.

"Didn't you get my pages?" Tess queried.

"What pages?" Sensing a crisis brewing, Russell quickly realized that more concern was called for. "I'm sorry. What's going on?"

"Well, James has been here for a half hour."

"Fuck!" Russell exclaimed. "What time is it?"

"Almost six-thirty."

"Oh, Jesus. I'm really running late."

"Ya think?" she spat back, sardonically. "Where the hell have you been? Did you pick up the sweet peppers and the olive oil?"

"Of course I did." This statement was a fabrication. But he dared not provoke additional indignation from his already fuming spouse. One lie, however, naturally leads to the next, and the next, and so on. And now, he had to come up with another excuse for why he wouldn't be home for at least another half hour. Russell began spinning a veritable litany of falsehoods. He'd had a last-minute, late-afternoon sales appointment in Goodlettsville; a fender bender on the Interstate had tied up traffic; his pager was acting up.

"Well, just get here as soon as you can," Tess said.

"You know I will, Babe. Still love me?" The lack of response meant one of two things: either his furious wife had already hung up, or she was intentionally leaving him dangling in the frosty breeze, without an iota of reassurance.

For a time in his teens, Russell harbored aspirations of becoming a stage actor. With that goal in mind, he auditioned for and won roles in several high school theatrical productions. Twenty years after abandoning those ambitions in favor of an elusive concept called "security," his thespian background was coming in handy. It took an Oscar-level performance for Russell to walk into his own home with a smile on his face. Tess, too, pulled off a masterful charade of pleasantry for the benefit of their guest. Russell was about to inquire why places hadn't been set at the table for Hank and Rory. But the pizza box protruding from the trash can answered his question before he had a chance to ask.

Tension between Russell and his fed-up wife wasn't a side dish, but sauce for the main course. Tess was finding it difficult to chew with a rigid jaw and clenched teeth. And, her being forced to endure unrelatable reminiscences between two erstwhile college mates made suffering through the evening that much more challenging. James, either oblivious to the bad vibrations or pretending to be so, paid high compliments to the chef. Russell took his own praise to absurd extremes, exuding exemplary reviews for each and every item on the menu. He knew his five-star ravings were ringing hollow. And, with his gut tied in knots, he, too, could hardly eat. Still, while poking at and pushing his food around on his plate, he did manage to swill close to a liter of wine.

Inebriated and fatigued, Russell stood at the sink, scrubbing pots and pans. He began envisioning his house of cards teetering and fluttering to the ground in disarray. For the first time since Blowjob #1, internalized confusion about his sexual identity was making the road ahead appear iffy and precarious. And, there was no one he could talk to about it.

EIGHT

Russell wasn't in denial. He'd even spoken the word bisexual out loud — and more than once — just never within earshot of loved ones or workmates. He justified this choice under the pretext of protecting everyone else from unwelcome, potentially messy information. Russell had yet to grasp the reality that his sexual orientation was as vital to the entirety of who he was as any one of his limbs, as crucial to his health and longevity as were any of his major organs. In a matter of speaking, he had tap danced through more than two decades of adulthood on one leg. Still, self-delusion told him his life wasn't broken. So, it didn't need fixing.

The innate irony in maintaining this kind of dual persona seems obvious. Untold numbers of men — many of them, like Russell, married to women — go to great lengths and considerable risk to satisfy their closeted desires. And, even though names are rarely exchanged, a single, fleeting, chance encounter instantly makes these men aware of one of the most intimate, essential, and personal details about each other. Russell was concealing a fundamental part of himself from friends and family members who, for good reason, presumed they knew the real Russell. Meanwhile, the real Russell was exposing that same fundamental part of himself to strangers who didn't know him at all. What Russell kept from the closest and dearest people in his life, he willingly put on display for folks he cared nothing for and who, in all likelihood, he would never encounter again. In fact, Russell's sexual attraction to other men was the sum total of what those other men knew about him and all Russell knew about them as well.

Sustaining this pretense came with periods of high anxiety. In their original incarnations, these frets mostly centered around the health risk, the possibility of endangering his wife's wellbeing or, absolute worst-case-scenario, getting found out. But one thing Russell had never lost a wink of sleep over was the possibility of falling in love with another man. Then, along came Bryan to throw a monkey wrench into Russell's not-broke-why-fix-it, one-legged pogo dance. Bryan had left no ambiguity regarding his interest in taking the next step with Russell. All Russell had to do was give the go sign and the two men could begin exploring the kind of adventure Russell had never before considered feasible. As assertive as Bryan tended to be, it seemed out of character for him to sit back and let Russell make the next move. So, as Russell prolonged his fence straddling, he began to wonder how long Bryan would be willing to wait for a wishy-washy potential fuck buddy to give him the thumbs up.

For nearly three weeks, Russell was caught, helplessly riding a pendulum of emotions, swinging first to one extreme, then pulled by gravity to sweep back to the opposite oscillation. Some mornings, he arose convinced that he needed to cut off what seemed a certain catastrophe at its roots. By that same afternoon, he'd be drifting off into lusty reveries, with his niggling inner voice saying *you'd be a fool to pass up such a dream setup*. But, before he could take that step, his feet would get cold again, his cranium echoing with what ifs: *If I did give the high sign, what if I couldn't go through with it? What would that make me in Bryan's eyes? What if we gave it a shot, and it didn't feel right? Where would that leave us?* And, oh dear! *What if one of us got his heart broken?*

By stark contrast, Russell never battled timidity in professional settings. On the job, he was armed with a smile, a business card, and a well-rehearsed script. He was there in an official capacity, representing a reputable corporate institution and a quality product. Knowing that a salesman's first job is to sell himself, he wore affability like a finely tailored suit, one he could slip into and out of at will, without so much as snagging a toenail. Every sales vet also knows that an unreceptive response must never be taken personally... *Ya win some, ya lose some. Every "no" just gets you closer to the next "yes." Rejection comes with the territory.* Russell could recite Zig Ziglar in his sleep. With Bryan, however, Russell *was* the product; and, not just a part of him, the whole kit and caboodle, soup to nuts, inside and out. Thus, even though his customer was itching to take a test drive, Russell found himself paralyzed with doubt, afraid of getting in over his head, incapable of closing the deal.

On the con side of the ledger, everything about accepting Bryan's proposition stood in contradiction to Russell's most basic policies of self-protection: Avoid physical contact; never share personal information; and don't be with the same person more than once. Adhering strictly to this playbook functioned double duty, by preventing exposure to STIs and scotching any possibility of emotional entanglements. Now, Russell was contemplating tearing up the very rulebook he had authored for himself just to see what might happen with this impossibly handsome, undeniably sexy, but also promiscuous guy. Russell knew that sexual contact with Bryan presented another, very real potential peril, by exposing him to whatever germ Bryan might have picked up out there in the woods.

Still, even *those* blaring alarms failed to quash Russell's Bryan fixation. He daydreamed about running his hands through the dark fur forest on Bryan's chest. In vivid, sensual detail, Russell imagined rubbing his nose and cheek against the soft skin between Bryan's upper legs. He envisioned nibbling Bryan's scrotum, fondling his stiff soldier, licking its helmet like a lollipop, clutching the cheeks of Bryan's muscular buttocks and plunging the entire shaft down his throat. Of course, Russell had never actually indulged in any of the pleasures playing out so luridly on his mental porn screen. The fact that Russell had zero hands-on experience and, therefore, could claim zero expertise when it came to the things he so longed to do added yet another reason for prolonging the stall.

Russell was finding it nearly impossible to stop such mind meanderings from affecting his concentration at the office. But these focus issues became far more irksome on the Little League diamond, with the object of his obsession standing nearby, always poised and ready to be of service. *Oh*, Russell mused to himself, *Bryan could service me anytime. Just say when and where, Big Guy, I'll be there.* Russell's self-discipline was growing weaker with every passing week. If Bryan had dropped trou on the pitcher's mound in full view of the packed bleachers, Russell would have fallen to his knees and gobbled him whole.

Then, upon the midway point of the Pirates' season, Bryan's wife brought Russell's *Catch 22* a chapter closer to its conclusion by tendering a return dinner invitation. "What do you say, Babe?" Tess asked. "I told Diane I needed to ask you."

"I bet Lady Antebellum loved hearing that," Russell joked.

"Shut up," Tess shot back, playfully. "You are *so bad* sometimes!" Russell's better half had no idea how true this statement was. "Anyway," Tess continued, "she said Bryan was totally into it. Actually, I think she told me it was his suggestion." Russell's heart skipped a beat. He felt faint. Hearing that this dinner invite had been Bryan's idea made it an unambiguous signal. This was the impetus he needed to finally make his move, one way or the other. Knowing that he was approaching a critical fork in the road ahead made Russell's knees wobble. He clutched the bar stool to prevent from folding onto the kitchen floor like a marionette with broken strings.

"You okay, Babe?" Tess inquired. "You look sort of..."

"Shaky, yeah," Russell muttered, taking a seat. "I'm okay now."

"Are you sure?" She was sincerely concerned. "Maybe we should call the doctor."

"No, no, no!" he insisted. "I'm fine. Just a little dizzy spell. Happens now and then. Only lasts a second."

"Russ! If you've been having dizzy spells, you should..."

"*I'm fine!*" Russell snapped, with far more intensity than he'd intended. The expression on Tess's face was one of shock, with a dollop of fear. Her husband lashing out this way was out of character.

"I was just..." Tess began. She couldn't seem to find the words.

"I know, Babe," Russell said. "I'm sorry. But, I *am* fine. And," — he summoned up his inner salesman, deliberately modulating his voice to convey cheerful enthusiasm — "And, I'm also totally fine with having dinner at the Bailey's!"

"Okay." A note of skepticism still lingered in her voice. "I'll confirm it with Diane."

"*Book it!*" Russell exclaimed, exhibiting a grotesque smile and slapping his hand on the granite counter top. Tess looked at her husband as though she suspected an alien creature had slithered in and seized control of his body. More often than not, Tess's intuition could intercept and decode another person's thoughts before that person even had a chance to unscramble them. Now, it was Russell trying to get a glimpse into his wife's head. And, if she was thinking what Russell suspected she was thinking, her hunch was correct. Russell's body — and his soul! — *had* been invaded. What she couldn't have suspected was that the invasive creature hadn't come from outer space. His name was Bryan. He had electric-blue eyes, thick, black hair, and a wicked smile to die for.

Upon a Sunday evening in early July at six-thirty p.m., Russell, Tess, Hank, and Rory stood on the porch of a red-brick lot hog, nearly identical to every other domicile in an upscale, Disneyesque housing development. As the front door opened, Russell's heart leaped in anticipation. Acting in the butler role, Carter extended a greeting. "Hi, Coach." With his attention fixed over Carter's shoulder, scanning for the boy's father, Russell missed this salutation.

"Don't mind him," Tess said. "He's rude. His mother didn't raise him right."

Peals of laughter from the three boys caught Russell's attention. "What?" he queried. "Did I miss something? What's so funny?"

Just then, the object of Russell's obsession materialized, costumed for the occasion in barbecue apron and chef's hat. Russell found Bryan's guise so adorable, it was all he could do to restrain myself from scooting over and giving his host an affectionate smooch on the lips. "Come on in, you guys!" Bryan was offering a wave with his oven-mitted hand when he caught something alarming in the corner of his eye. "Shit!" he exclaimed, before vanishing as quickly as he'd appeared. A patio door was heard sliding shut. The next noise was Bryan's distant voice shouting, "Get the fuck out of here! Damn it! God-damn, fucking pest!"

The neighbor's cat yanking an eight-pound salmon off the marinating tray and onto the grass was merely the first debacle in what was to become an evening rife with mishaps. Diane scalded the rice, which was very garlicky as it turned out, making it impossible for Tess to eat, even if it had been properly prepared. The wine Russell brought had gone bad. The pie was undercooked, and the ice cream had melted into something resembling cold clam chowder. Under other circumstances, such a comedy of errors might have resulted in laughter over the absolute absurdity of it all. However, a final event — this one totally non-accidental — served to bring the occasion to its unceremonious conclusion. And, in a matter of a quick, inexplicable two minutes, a burgeoning friendship between two families found itself standing at a premature dead end.

Diane was already mortified by how poorly the evening had gone. But, her embarrassment couldn't possibly provide adequate justification for the words that spewed so callously from her mouth. And, to further aggravate this offense, the context of those words revealed her blackest heart. Russell had never cared for women like Diane. Although he wasn't one to toss individuals into generalized buckets, he couldn't help but see Diane as a stereotype, one from which, in his eyes, she never deviated. Russell had met a thousand Dianes — prissy, entitled, white, southern Christian girls, mired in a starched, outdated tradition of presumed moral superiority, quiet judgment, and disingenuous gentility. Learning that Diane had attended Clear Creek Baptist Bible College only reconfirmed Russell's initial impression. That she applied her undergrad degree to the sole purpose of snagging a handsome, successful husband also fell in perfect box step with generations of debutante culture.

Co-eds of such conservative Christian institutions wear promise rings to flaunt their pledge to remain virgins until their wedding nights. At the same time, they spend weekday evenings in their dorm rooms deep-throating bananas, preparing to dole out blowjobs to their Friday- and Saturday-night dates. She who waits not for marriage to do the deed God created for the exclusive purpose of making more little Christian babies is most definitely flirting with eternal damnation. Meanwhile, here in the mortal world, the randy little slut runs the risk of being shamed and shunned by her snotty, holier-than-thou sorority sisters. Imprint that inexplicable moral code on a girl whose rite of passage spawned from cotillion classes — learning the exact firmness of a just-firm-enough handshake and how to avoid stepping on a waltz partner's freshly buffed Florsheims — and, whose debut into "respectful society" involved being put on display like a prize calf adorned in a dozen petticoats, and you get Diane. Too, you get suburban neighborhoods populated by phony, shallow, vindictive women from the same mold, whose lives revolve around unquestioned obedience to their husbands, maintaining a fixed smile no matter what, and popping out perfect replications of Great, Great Grandmother Beauregard's pecan pie.

"I can't eat this," Hank blurted. "The crust is like... all gooey." The boy's unsolicited culinary review was indisputable. Diane should have left the pie in the oven longer. Speechless discomfort descended upon the dinner table like autumnal drizzle. Everyone felt the chill. For the first time since the meeting of these two families, Diane relinquished her Miss America smile to expose the wrinkles around her collagen-injected lips. She just sat there, making no pretense at refinement, jaw clenched, her squinted eyes shooting lasers across the table at poor, painfully candid Hank. Certainly, a proper gentleman from Diane's crinoline-lined ecosphere would have kept such commentary to himself. A true son of the Confederacy would have gobbled up every crumb of his hostess's under-baked pie, and asked for seconds. Still, not a single soul spoke up on behalf of the half-baked pastry.

To Russell's surprise, even Tess couldn't muster up sufficient motivation to offer Diane reassurance. Nor did she insist that Hank offer an apology for his rudeness. "Would you like to be excused from the table, Hank?" Tess asked.

"Mmm, hmmm," her son mumbled, guiltily.

"I'm sorry," she replied. "Let's try that again. Hank, would you like to be excused?"

"Yes, Ma'am."

"Yes, Ma'am, what?"

Providing defense counsel, Carter whispered a prompt into Hank's ear. "May I please be excused?" Hank asked.

"Now you're talkin'!" Tess hinted a smile. "Was that so difficult?" A bit of a smirk crossed the boy's face, as he awaited permission to leave the table. "Yes, Hank, you may be excused."

Russell had brought a bubble-making kit, thinking it might keep the boys outdoors for a little longer. Fresh air would be much better for their youthful lungs than the stale, stifling atmosphere in front of the Nintendo screen. Hank, Rory, and Carter commenced floating large, glistening orbs over the grass. While Rory and Carter attacked the wobbly soap balloons like Wallace's warriors on the *Braveheart* battlefield, Hank invented a less violent, clownish approach, twirling across the lawn like a wood nymph, leaping into the air, contorting his portly frame in slapstick attempts to burst the bubbles with his nose and forehead. Tess and Russell found genuine amusement in their older son's silly, improvised, backyard ballet. Seeing him playing with such uninhibited, joyful exuberance was a rare treat. Diane, however, still smarting from an honest statement made by an 11-year-old child, was entertaining other thoughts. "You guys better watch out with that one," she warned, her eyes leering at Hank's Isadora Duncan parody in progress. "If you don't cut this behavior off right away, you might just have a fairy on your hands."

This tactless, wholly uncalled-for judgment of the boy — and of Tess and Russell as parents — plunged the ambient temperature to unprecedented depths of discomfort. Russell might have spoken up, and not the least bit civilly, had his wife not cut him off before he could make matters even worse. "Oh, dear!" Tess exclaimed. "Look at the time!"

"Oh, dang!" Russell was catching her drift. "What time *is* it, Babe?"

"Well, let's see..." Tess checking her watch was a dead giveaway, revealing her sudden "concern" about the lateness of the evening for what it was: a deliberate tactic to prevent an unpleasant confrontation and make way for a quick exit.

"It's only eight-fifteen," interjected Bryan. "I thought we were gonna play Balderdash."

"Pictionary," Diane corrected him, with the absolute certitude of someone who desperately needed to be right about something. "We were going to play Pictionary."

"But you know I hate Pictionary," Bryan argued. "I suck at that game."

"Everybody sucks at something," quipped Russell. *Perhaps*, he was thinking, *a little levity might ease the tension.* Bryan and Russell exchanged knowing glances, both acknowledging the subtext of a certain verb.

"So true. So true," Bryan agreed, faking pensive seriousness. "So, what do you suck at, Coach?"

"Well, Sir. In my lifetime, I've sucked at lots of things." Despite the fraught nature of the moment, Russell allowed a wry grin. "But, not Pictionary."

"Look out!" declared Bryan. "The gauntlet has been thrown down! Does that mean the game is on?" The wives had no clue their hubbies were speaking in coded language.

"Absolutely," Russell responded, locking eyes with the man he'd been fantasizing about for weeks. "But not tonight."

"Criminy!" exclaimed Bryan. "I was dying to find out who sucks more."

"Well, Darlin'..." By now, Diane had repositioned her debutante smile mask across her taught, rigid face. "I guess we're just going to have to wait for next time to find out." Then, in blue-blooded southern-plantation speak, she drawled, "Apparently, our guests have grown weary of our company."

In her world of artifice, Diane had just issued a cue, to which a true friend would respond with something like, "Oh, don't be silly, Diane! We treasure every single moment with you and your lovely family." However, the re-assurance she anticipated didn't materialize. And, in the ensuing silence, that well-practiced smile once again became too heavy a lift.

NINE

Russell sat perched on a kitchen stool, nursing a second cup of morning coffee. Hovering over a sheet of note paper, he made his dozenth attempt at composing a missive to Bryan. Some opening lines had been scuttled before he'd managed to pen a second word. Other drafts survived a complete sentence, even a sentence and a half, before being hastily crossed out. For Russell, one single, mean-spirited remark from Diane, directed at his older son, had triggered a temblor of emotion. Thus, the playful flirtation between Russell and the offensive woman's husband had taken a tectonic shift onto extremely unstable terrain.

Tess had her own way of dealing with the issue: avoidance. After the previous Saturday's Pirates game, Bryan was helping load equipment bags into the trunk of Russell's Celica, when Diane pulled up to collect him. "Where the heck is Tess?" she queried Russell. "Is everything okay?"

What Russell wanted to say was, "What do you think, Diane? Do you think everything is okay?" Instead, he punted. "Yup, Diane. Everything is hunky-dory. She's just... you know, really busy."

"Well," Diane replied, "surely, she can't be too busy to come out here and help me cheer the Pirates. Tell her we miss her sweet face, okay?"

"Will do," Russell said, with minimal effort at making a terse, manufactured smile look sincere. "You can bet on it."

Bryan brushed off his hands and flashed his pearly-white signature smile. Then, he paused for a moment to place a hand on Russell's forearm, sending an electric charge shooting through Russell's body. "Good game, Coach," he said, before about-facing to slide into the shotgun seat.

Through the closed passenger door, Russell heard Diane inquire, "Are they mad at us for some reason?" Russell was confused. Why, he wondered, hadn't Bryan reached out to reassure him, in no uncertain terms, that he didn't share his wife's homophobic mindset. Surely, Bryan couldn't possibly condone those thoughtless, hurtful words. Russell looked at the page, now covered with scribbled-out scrawls. In abject frustration, he crumpled it into a ball.

He had managed to enter *Dear Bryan* on a fresh sheet when Hank's voice startled him. "Hey, Dad." Nervously, Russell covered the salutation with his forearm. Observing his father's peculiar behavior, Hank wrinkled his eyes and scrunched his mouth. The boy's curious expression prompted Russell to concoct an unrequested explanation. "Carter's dad and me... we've kinda been wondering if we should invest in a couple of those new composite bats. They're not cheap. But, you guys are having such a great season, we were thinking, you know... it might be... like extra incentive, or whatever."

"Cool," Hank mumbled. The lackadaisical nature of the boy's reply indicated that he was far less interested in the content of his father's communiqué in progress or what bats his Little League squad might use in their season-long quest for a playoff spot, than he was in perusing the pantry shelf. Having found the box he was looking for (Apple Jacks), Hank snatched a bowl from the cupboard and plodded to the fridge for milk. As he reached for the two-percent, he announced, "Carter thinks his dad might be gay." Hearing this statement, uttered so off-the-cuff and matter-of-factly, Russell's heart leapt into his throat and commenced pounding like a house-beat kick drum. "Pretty weird," Hank opined, as he dumped cereal into the bowl, followed by a sloppy pour of milk, much of which splashed onto the countertop. "I mean, pretty freakin' weird, right?"

"Are you going to clean that up?" Russell asked — a deliberate attempt at diverting the course of conversation.

"What?" As usual, Hank was either oblivious to his slobbery, or simply didn't care about what untidiness he might leave behind for his parents to mop up. Following his father's eyes, he had to acknowledge the white puddle and the rivulet of milk snaking its way toward the edge of the countertop. "I'll get to it," he promised, toting his bowl toward the table.

"No," Russell retorted. "You'll do it now."

"I don't want my cereal to get soggy," whined the boy.

"Tough life, Kiddo," Russell scolded. "You waltz in here. You open the pantry. There's food. Billions of kids don't have it so good. How would you like it if..."

"Okay, okay!" the boy interjected. "I hear ya. Cool it with the lecture, Pops." While Hank occasionally revealed a snarky side, he was beginning to exert a new level of assertiveness, even defiance. Russell felt reluctant to read the boy the riot act in fear that it might deflate his newfound confidence. Lord knows, the chubby, pre-pubescent lad could use a supplementary cache of that all-too-illusive character trait. Still, Russell's paternal authority was being disrespected. So, he wasn't about to remain mute. Meanwhile, as the father mulled over what to say, the son proceeded to unroll a half-dozen paper towels and wad them up for the purpose of thwarting the spill.

"You should use that rag and sponge by the sink," Russell stated. "You're wasting paper."

"Maybe you're the one who's gay, Dad," Hank quipped, attacking the countertop with half-assed haste, doing more spreading of his spill than cleaning it up. By this point, white liquid was dribbling down onto the drawers and drawer pulls.

"For Chrissake!" Russell erupted, marching around the kitchen island to grab the aforementioned rag and sponge. He pushed his son aside with evident impatience and started doing damage control.

"I didn't mean it, Dad," Hank repented. "I know you're not gay. And, I wouldn't care if... you know."

"What's this talk?" Tess asked, as she shuffled into the room.

"Apparently," Russell retorted, "Jolly Prince Henry is incapable of pouring milk on his cereal without creating a sticky lake in the kitchen."

"Well," Tess remarked, "If Hank made the mess, he should clean it up. If you keep coddling the boy, Russ..." The glower Russell shot in his wife's direction stopped her mid-sentence. "Well," she demurred, "Obviously, you know what I'm talking about." That's when the page on the kitchen island caught her eye. "What's this," she inquired, wryly, "a love letter?" Russell was at a complete loss for words. It was barely seven a.m., and his day had already turned into a steaming, stinking pile of manure. And, hearing that Bryan's son had been having misgivings about his father's sexuality only multiplied this mounting angst. What, he couldn't help but wonder, might have triggered Carter's suspicions? And now, serious or not, Tess was expressing suspicions of her own.

"Hank," Tess addressed her son. As the boy looked up at his mother from his Apple Jacks, Russell sneaked the note pad off of the countertop. "Your father and I won't always be here to clean up your messes. The faster you learn that, the sooner you'll start taking full responsibility for your actions, the happier you'll be, and the more successful you'll be. Are you hearing what I'm saying here?"

"Yes, Ma'am," Hank burbled, through a mouthful of partially masticated cereal.

"One more thing," Tess stated. "And, this is important. No matter how your friends use it, the word gay is not to be used as an insult or a way of saying something's not cool. Is that clear?"

"Yeah, but," Hank began, "I wasn't..."

"I mean," Tess interrupted, with a chuckle, "you might think your dad is uncool. But, I can assure you, he is *not* gay." She placed her hand tenderly on Russell's shoulder. "Are you, Babe?" For Russell, this seemed like the perfect cue to drown out any further conversation by grinding some more free-trade coffee beans.

"You are literally the most depressed person I've ever met." This unabashed remark from Mary Ann came out of the blue.

After a particularly dismal start, Russell's day had done an abrupt and welcome shift toward the sunnier side. Arriving at the office, he was immediately bolstered by the sight of the contract for the stair-lift company policy lying on his desk, fully executed and notarized. He had worked diligently to court this account. It wasn't the biggest sale ever. But, having been in a bit of slump of late, finally landing this fish provided a long overdue measure of self-satisfaction. Too, closing the deal would surely put some handsome plumage in his cap and boost his profile around the office. These factors made Mary Ann's unsolicited observation about Russell's emotional state all that much more unexpected.

To Russell, his job seemed to be the sole aspect of his life in which he felt completely comfortable and settled. His marriage, though by all appearances stable, even ideal, was not what it appeared to be. Tess, after all, believed herself to be married to a straight, devoted husband. And, while Russell actively disproved that notion on a regular basis, she had no reason to suspect otherwise. The Pirates were midway through the best season of Russell's coaching tenure, as yet undefeated, and winning their games by substantial margins. Still, Russell had been unable to take sustained joy in coaching Little League, due to the constant presence of a certain someone with whom he constantly imagined getting naked — a circumstance he yearned for, but had yet to write himself a hall pass to allow.

In the interim between dinner party #1, when Bryan first put certain tempting ideas out there on the table, and the more recent reprise disaster, during which Bryan's spouse trumpeted her bigotry, Russell's dilemma had been a simpler, more binary internal deliberation — not exactly simple to resolve, just more cut and dry. It was basically *should I or shouldn't I*, presaging the ultimate resolution of *will I or won't I?* The devil on one shoulder represented the pro side of the debate: *Go ahead, jump in! You know you want to. You'll always regret it if you don't.* The angel on the side of caution made a sober and convincing counter case based upon risks and possible consequences: *Don't be impulsive and foolish. Think about everything you stand to lose. If you succumb to your weakness, you may very well regret it for the rest of your life.* Post backyard barbecue #2, another voice began chiming in, revealing a third angle Russell hadn't anticipated being part of the debate. We might call this one the voice of moral principle. Diane's attitudes regarding homosexuality didn't directly pertain to Russell's yet-to-be-made, final decision about whether to get down and dirty with her willing husband. Still, it did seem important to know whether Bryan shared her bias. Perhaps, Russell worried, Bryan was one of those self-loathing, closeted men who behaved one way, while simultaneously holding disdain for others with similar needs and desires.

Up until now, Tess and Russell had never felt compelled to discuss the possibility of having a gay son. But, to one degree or another, every parent ponders the prospect and considers how they might feel and/or respond under such perplexing circumstances. If Carter were to express ambivalence about his sexual orientation or gender identity, it seems improbable that his mother would show much compassion. Diane, Russell guessed, would be far more likely to insist on sending a sexually confused offspring to conversion therapy for the cure. The question remained: would Bryan exhibit more understanding and support? Would he be willing to stand up for the boy, in spite of his wife's myopic intransigence?

Prior to Diane broadcasting her intolerance, Russell had been on the verge of making a decision. But the woman's bigotry, along with her husband's lack of response, had called a timeout on Russell moving forward. And, before he could give Bryan the high sign, Russell needed to know where his potential fuck buddy stood. Russell kept running this conundrum through his puzzled brain. Still, he had yet to find an acceptable way to broach this thorny issue. After all, even a husband who is painfully aware of his wife's character flaws often feels obliged to leap to her defense, should she come under criticism from a third party. Russell definitely wanted to avoid being confrontational, as in, "So, Bry, how do you really feel about your spouse's homophobia?" Perhaps he should simply be frank about how disturbed he and Tess had been by Diane's insensitive remark and the implication her words made about their parenting. A strategically asked question might get the dialogue started, something like, "How did Diane's statement strike you?" after which, Russell might offer Bryan an easy escape... "Surely, you can't be on board with that kind of attitude."

But the longer an issue like this languishes in awkward silence, the tougher bringing it up becomes. Thus, due to Russell's continual, ever-increasing discomfort, when he was in Bryan's company, he conscientiously cut a wide swath around any subject that didn't pertain to the basic pragmatics of coaching Little League. Too, Russell very deliberately steered clear of those woods, for fear of once again catching Bryan in the act.

"I'm not depressed," Russell contended.

"Right. Whatever." Mary Ann's response dripped with disbelief.

"No, seriously," Russell insisted. "I'm not a depressed person. I have no idea why you'd say such a thing."

"Get help, Russell," she advised. Aghast at the woman's brazenness, Russell watched, tongue-tied, as Mary Ann exited the breakroom.

TEN

"No way!" Russell exclaimed. "You've gotta be kidding me!" David had aged very little over the 20 years since Russell had last seen him.

"Hello, my old friend," gushed David, opening his arms and grinning like a jack o' lantern. Russell, gob-smacked, and buzzing with a swarm of chaotic emotions, strode directly into the hug.

"How *are* you?" Russell asked, as if anyone could possibly answer such a loaded question in a single sentence.

"Good, good," David answered, tears welling up in his eyes, as he released an audible sigh of relief and resignation. Certainly, Russell assumed, additional details would be forthcoming. For now, other curiosities begged for attention.

"Well, come on, you guys," Russell demanded. "I'm dying to know! How did this happen? I'm... Well, I don't know what to say!"

Tess had been observing this reunion from behind the kitchen counter, beaming proudly for having so successfully pulled off the surprise. "Well, David..."

"I..." David butted in, then immediately realized his rudeness. "Go ahead, Tess. Sorry."

"No, no, no," she insisted. "By all means, you go ahead." Butterflies fluttered in Russell's belly. He was on pins and needles, preparing to hear some explanation as to how and why the man responsible for glorious Blowjob #1 two decades ago was now standing in his home, apparently at the behest of his wife.

Originally, David recounted, he and Tess had met four years earlier at the Georgia Bridal Show in Atlanta. She was there to introduce her line of artificial-silk boutonnieres and corsages. David — this came as no surprise to Russell — was running the event. Tess, being a newbie within the insular world of wedding planners, dress

81

designers, and cake makers, was frustrated and flailing. Sensing her consternation, David offered her a sympathetic ear and some helpful tips. If not for David's encouragement and sage advice, Tess might not have returned to the event that, four years hence, had become her most essential lifeline to the lucrative wedding industry. Tess's annual interaction with David had remained cordial, but businesslike, until this past Spring, when David invited her out for drinks with a group of the most prestigious vendors from the bridal world. Chitchat over cocktails revealed that Tess was married to someone named Russell Deacon. As serendipity would have it — or, perhaps, David suspected, Karma at work — this turned out to be the same Russell Deacon who, back in the summer of 1976, had interned for a company where David was a co-founding partner. Tess, who took over the story from here, was pleased to hear David speak about seeing real potential in the younger Russell. Then again, an open, supportive spirit seemed entirely consistent with David's character, as she had come to know him.

When David emailed Tess, indicating that he was scheduled to be in Nashville to attend a July trade show, she insisted that he come over for dinner. While accepting the invite, David suggested that Tess keep his pending visit a secret. Imagining how much more fun a surprise reunion would be, Tess agreed enthusiastically. (In fact, David was harboring serious trepidation about seeing Russell again and feared that, should Russell catch wind of their plans, he might put the kibosh on the idea altogether.)

Blowjob #1 took place during the summer between Russell's freshman and sophomore years of college. Russell was thrilled about being accepted for a summer internship at GRMN8, Atlanta's most cutting-edge advertising agency. Effete, ruddy-cheeked David Martin Mangold represented the "M" in the company moniker. At

24, he was the youngest partner in what was becoming a buzzworthy success story.

Russell, just shy of 19, green as a leprechaun's cap, and eager as a three-month-old beagle, was one of a handful of summer gofers. David, being closer to Russell's age than the rest of the execs, seemed cool as a banana popsicle, and exhibited a thousand-percent more pizzazz than anyone else for whom the interns becked and called. Young Russell, in particular, felt immediately drawn to David and inspired by his young boss's energy and sardonic sense of humor. Too, he had never met someone who inhabited homosexuality without the slightest hint of shame. David also wore southern-ness like a finely tailored seersucker suit. In his throaty rasp and lilting drawl, he somehow managed to stretch a single vowel into three separate vowel sounds. For Russell, David was like a surrogate Tennessee Williams.

Within days of Russell's arrival, David began showing special interest in the pretty, blond lad, inviting him into his office, prying into details about his life. "Do you have a girlfriend?" David asked, an innocuous query on its surface, but one that, considering the characters involved, carried its own pointed subtext. It just so happened that Russell was enmeshed in the kind of emotional crisis that, for an 18-year-old, feels like the end of the world. A month earlier, his longtime girlfriend's mother had inadvertently discovered birth-control pills stashed in the back of her daughter's dresser drawer. This revelation resulted in a threat from the girl's parents: should she insist on seeing Russell again, they would no longer pay her college tuition. Eliza was Russell's first real love. Now, their relationship, already strained by the distance between two university campuses, had been put into limbo.

David began inviting Russell over to his tony Buckhead apartment in the evening to hang out. There, David would uncork a bottle of wine and spin a record album — his favorite of that long-ago summer being Barry Manilow II, featuring the passionate breakthrough hit, "Mandy." The pair passed the time gabbing about movies, music, books, current events, and simply enjoying each other's company. Although he made no secret about his sexual orientation and candidly admitted being attracted to Russell, David was never aggressive or pushy. Eventually, he informed his youthful protégé that, should Russell ever be curious about having sex with someone of his own gender, he (David) would be available for a freebie trial run, no strings attached. It was an offer that remained on the table, but one Russell didn't seriously consider — for most of the remainder of the summer, that is.

David shared anecdotes about growing up in Fort Worth and honing his ever-sharp wit for his own self-preservation. On occasion, he'd also pursued relationships with girls to beard his real inclinations. Russell was pining away for Eliza, suffering an unremitting heartache over their forced estrangement. After listening to Russell's sad nightly update, David would offer to massage the tension out of the younger man's shoulders (whatever tension remained after several chilled glasses of Liebfraumilch). Gradually, as the weeks rolled on, Russell's inhibitions melted away. He was becoming more comfortable in physically proximity to David and with having a gay man's gentle hands touching his body. He was, after all, starving for physical human contact. The conversation gradually turned away from old wounds to the here and now, and finally to the near future. Russell harbored no strict moral hang-ups that might have prevented him from accepting David's open invite to try a gratis, no-obligation, same-sex sampler platter. He'd come to know David as someone he could trust. So, at long last, Russell admitted that he was indeed curious.

And so it came to pass, one fateful night, after indulging in at least double their usual volume of vino, David walked Russell back to the no-frills living quarters the company provided for its summer interns. Inside a tiny bedroom, they undressed silently, as to not draw undue attention from slumbering roommates. As he slipped under the sheets of his single bed, Russell's heart was pounding in his ears and his hard-on was pulsating in anticipation. David followed. Although that first whisker-stubbled kiss felt strange and altogether new, Russell was surprised not to be revolted as another man's tongue mingled with his. The foreign flavor of David's kiss served as a delicious appetizer, priming Russell's palate for the main course to come. And what David did next with his well-practiced tongue switched on the flashing neon lights and set off the earthquake sirens.

It soon became evident that, while David was an ascending star in the advertising world, he'd already achieved hall-of-fame status in the bedroom. David ducked down to treat Russell's nipples with some playful biting and ran his tongue around his armpits and back up to his neck and earlobes. He licked and kissed Russell behind his knees and up the tender flesh of his inner thighs. Every cubic centimeter of Russell's body tingled with an electric charge, as the older, more experienced man stimulated yet another never-before-tickled erogenous zone. Eliza had no knowledge of these secret buttons. A man knows the mysteries of another man's body and what provokes the greatest exhilaration. A woman can't be expected to be aware of these spots — unless, of course, giving men pleasure is her profession.

Then came the coupe de grâce in the all-star performance of Russell Deacon's premier male lover. David nuzzled Russell's testicles, gently licked and nibbled his scrotum. Then, he plunged Russell's steel-stiff member into his mouth. *Oh, Jesus!* This feeling was beyond blissful; it was transcendent. Being engorged by another man who so clearly loves performing fellatio and who has practiced and refined his skillset over time was a revelation. How David was able to take every inch between his salivating lips and deep into his throat seemed superhuman.

"Ohhhhh, FUCK!" Russell could no longer restrain his appreciation. (He would regret this unbridled exultation the next day over Cheerios, while receiving some very suspicious glances from the other two young interns with whom he shared these unassuming digs. Their unspoken judgment made Russell's hangover and splitting headache that much more difficult to bear.) Digging his fingernails into the sides of that single mattress, and letting out a hound-like howl of satisfaction, Russell experienced a climax like none he'd ever had before. All the muscles in his body went rigid and every molecule of his entire being pulsated with ecstasy. David beamed in the assurance that he had given his youthful bedmate so much pleasure and relief. Had Russell's expert lover been wearing a shirt, the receiver of the blowjob might have pinned a medal of honor to the giver's chest on the spot.

David had introduced Russell to sex with another man in the most gentle, loving, and skillful way. Still, in spite of how glorious that night's encounter had been, this marked the beginning of a period during which young Russell would dig in his heels and stubbornly refuse to acknowledge his truest and most essential queer nature. Russell had been taught that a person was either "normal" or queer; hetero or homo, never the twain shall meet. Yes, it was rumored that some indulgent bohemians "swung both ways." Still, nobody in Russell's world knew that to be anything but myth. The word bisexual was not part of his vernacular, and the disposition "AC/DC" actually delivered an even more derogatory connotation. So, even though Russell had just experienced the optimum sexual gratification of his young life, he immediately made up his mind that he was *no* queer. And logic dictated that, if he wasn't a homo, he had to be 100% hetero. Now, he could check "sex with another man" off his to-do list. He could return to being "normal" with first-hand-knowledge that same-sex sex wasn't really "his thing." He felt a false sense of reassurance, believing he'd gotten all that queer stuff "out of his system" (in the form of one super-intense, absolutely gargantuan cum shot).

And, what about love? Russell asked himself. *Sex had to mean more than mere pleasure, didn't it?* In order for physical coupling to fulfill its highest destiny, it must contain the intimate, unspoken communication that enriches carnality with a divine, spiritual mystery. (As he would discover some decades later, this was a crock of self-manipulative twaddle.) But, since he couldn't imagine ever feeling for David the same way he felt for Eliza, Russell immediately began erasing and denying the ecstasy David had gifted him. Breathing a sigh of relief, Russell locked the memory of that one-night trip to Nirvana in a dark closet at the end of a seldom-trod hallway. Surrendering to queerness for those few hours (and enjoying it) had made him that much more determined to move forward into a 100% normative lifestyle.

"It's just not my thing," Russell informed David the following day. "I was lonely and horny and drunk. I mean, it was okay. But, I'd never do it again." Russell's denial left David wallowing in a sea of guilt and remorse, certain that he must have traumatized a sensitive, arrow-straight young man.

ELEVEN

Having just stepped out of the glare of the midsummer Tennessee sun, it took a full minute for Russell's eyes to adjust to Solario Cantina's dim, neon-lavender ambience. Surveying the dining room, Russell identified David's silhouette, framed in purple light, waving from the furthest corner booth. As he took his first step in his lunch date's direction, Russell's belly gurgled — not from hunger, rather from nerves. He had lain awake for much of the previous night refereeing yet another tug-o-war inside his ever-anxious head. The latest in a marathon series of nocturnal deliberations landed on this conclusion: *More than anyone I know, David would understand.* Yet, Russell remained unsure if he would be able to find words that could pry open that long-locked closet door, while still permitting him to linger inside.

As Russell slid into the faux-leather booth, David took a gulp that nearly finished off his margarita. He waved with one hand and pointed to his glass with the other. "Marghie, this vessel seems to have a leak in it."

"Well," the zaftig, dark-haired server replied, "we'll have to do something about that, won't we."

"We certainly will," David agreed, with a wink.

Marghie then directed her attention to Russell. "Something to drink for you, Sir?"

"An Arnold Palmer?"

"Certainly," she said. "I'll be right back to take your orders."

The conversation stayed surface-deep through the main course. Russell yammered on about his Little League coaching and the stark differences in the personalities of his two sons. David flitted between such subjects as Atlanta's rapid growth, a recent trip to Costa Rica, and his new top-of-the-line BMW coupe. The longer the verbal exchange dawdled in mundanity, the more anxious Russell became, especially since David was so obviously teetering further into inebriation. Then, after a lull of unnerving length, David took a sip from libation number three, and cast his gaze across the table. Russell noticed a quiver in his old friend's lower lip. David inhaled, held his breath for a moment, blinked his eyes several times, then blurted, "I'm sorry, Russell. I am *so, so* sorry."

"What?" Russell was baffled. "I don't understand."

David proceeded to explain that, merely hearing Tess say her husband's name — Russell Deacon — undammed a flood of unresolved guilt. Karma, he had to believe, was at work. Because, as it turned out, Tess's husband was the same Russell Deacon who David — a person of authority at the company for which Russell was interning — had deftly manipulated and ultimately bedded. So, for nearly two decades, David had been wrestling with periodic bouts of remorse, convinced that he must have damaged a vulnerable, straight teenager in some real and substantial way. "I know I don't deserve it," David offered, contritely. "But, could you ever forgive me?"

Russell could scarcely believe the irony of this circumstance. He had arrived for this confab completely flummoxed as to how he might broach the subject of his own same-sex compulsions. David's plea for mercy had just blown the door to this subject from its hinges. Russell released a sigh from the soles of his feet, smiled, and shook his head at this unfathomable turn of events. "You didn't damage me, David," Russell stated, "not at all." David sat back, jowls sagging, puzzlement reflected in his bloodshot eyes. "Really," Russell continued, "that was one of the most amazing nights of my life. I..." He chuckled with nostalgic fondness. "I *loved it.*"

"You mean?" David stammered.

"I just wasn't ready to admit it," Russell said. "If anyone owes anyone an apology..." He shook his head, smiling wistfully. "David, you didn't do anything wrong. You did everything right. You were gentle and caring and... and, you, Mr. Mangold, are a fucking superstar in bed!" David remained stunned, baffled as to how he should feel; happy and relieved, yes. *But what about all that futile, absolutely unnecessary self-flagellation?*

"Is everything alright here? Can I get you gentlemen anything else?" Marghie's check-in might have been awkwardly timed. But, for Russell, it was perfect.

"Yes," Russell said, pointing to David's margarita glass. "I'll have one of those, please. Make it a double."

Lips loosened by tequila, Russell proceeded to out himself to the very man he had misled all those years ago. He detailed the quandary he had gotten himself into: his unrelenting cravings, his chronic cruising, his double life. "Well," David replied, slipping back into his more accustomed role of mentor, "what are you going to do about it?"

Hearing no judgment in the question, Russell answered honestly, from the heart: "I don't know."

"You want my opinion?" David asked.

"Of course." Russell wasn't certain he meant what he'd just said.

"Well, I think..." David spoke slowly, deliberately. "I... think... there just might be an elephant in your house."

"Oh, my god!" Russell was taken aback. "You think Tess knows?"

"I do. Or, least she must have some inkling," David opined. "I mean, she's a smart cookie. And, you can't be married to somebody for... how long have you two..."

"No. I don't think so," Russell interrupted. Tess's recent remark to their son Hank was fresh in his mind, her stalwart insistence that the boy's father was definitely *not* gay.

"Okay," David said, flippantly. "I could be wrong."

"Well, I wouldn't put it that way," Russell countered, making an attempt at kindhearted, but patronizing reassurance.

David, however, had no patience for superficial placation. "So, let me ask you this," he proposed. "What do you think Tess would do if you came out to her? How do you think she'd react?"

"I'm not ready to come out," Russell declared, "to her or to anybody. You're the first person I've ever told."

"Really?" Finding this statement preposterous, David nearly choked on a slurp of coffee. Russell's eyes widened. He pursed his lips to further emphasize his sincerity and affirmed "really" with nod. "But," David demanded to know, "what about all those other guys?" This prompted Russell to go into more explicit detail about his anonymous voyeuristic exploits and his no-contact, withhold-all-personal-information, no-repeat-partner policy. "Oh, Honey!" exclaimed David, adopting the demeanor of a funeral director offering well-practiced condolences to the family of the deceased. "That is so fucking sad."

"Well," Russell divulged, "there actually *is* someone else who knows." He proceeded to fill David in about his ongoing flirtation with Bryan, and the ambivalence that had thus far prevented him from taking the hunky dreamboat up on his fuck-buddy invite.

David laughed and shook his head in disbelief. "This is totally freakin' me out!" he exclaimed. "I'd better have my gaydar re-calibrated."

Russell downed the final dram of his margarita. "Yeah?" he asked. "How so?"

David took a deep breath, exhaled, and looked across the table. "I came here today to grovel to a straight man. I was sure I'd wrecked your life; or, at least, messed you up in some real way. Turns out, you were never straight in the first place. And, it was *my* life that got messed up. Not yours."

"Wow," Russell responded. "Like I said, I guess I should be apologizing to you."

"No," David said. "I did what I did. It wasn't even remotely cool. We do these things to ourselves."

"Okay, yeah," Russell agreed. "But, you *are* wrong about one thing. My life *is* completely messed up. It's an absolute disaster." The reaction Russell wanted to hear was, "No, no, no... you're not a disaster! You're just a confused, flawed human being like everyone else." But, David wasn't one to indulge in such hollow reassurances.

"So, then," David shot back, "being gay is a disaster? Is that what y'all are sayin'?"

Russell suddenly felt like a witness under attack from a combative, shark-toothed trial lawyer. "No, no, no," he insisted. "I wasn't talking about that. Besides, I'm not gay. I'm bi."

"Right. Uh, huh." Russell didn't like David's incredulous tone. Meanwhile, David was growing weary of what, in his opinion, had devolved into yet another wheel-spinning, cliché-riddled conversation. "It'll all come out in the wash," David replied, without a droplet of self-doubt. "It always does." This sounded like something Russell's great-grandmother might have said over a glass of buttermilk. Then, David dug in his heels. "I know Tess pretty well. I probably know a side of her that you may have never seen."

"Okay." Russell reached for his margarita. Disappointed to find his glass still empty, his hand trembled in anticipation. Where was David headed now?

"You need to... No. Fuck that! You *have* to come out to your wife," David insisted, "for her, as much as for yourself." Without a doubt, this was last thing Russell wanted to hear. Worse, it was coming from the last person he ever expected to hear it *from*. A defensive smirk creased his mouth. He was about to shirk the burden of this thorny cloak of reality with a snappy retort, something to the tune of, *Yeah, right. I'll just say it right out loud and everything will be ducky*. Seeing the evasion coming, David cut him off at the pass. "And, when you do — sooner than later, my friend — I honestly don't think Tess will be all that surprised. I predict she'll take it much better than you expect."

Easy for you to say! Self-censorship being one of a master salesman's superpowers, Russell wisely bit his tongue before articulating that thought. After all, David burst out the closet when he was a teenager — with bells on. Yes, he'd weathered his share of bullying and ostracization. But, he'd survived... thrived, in fact. Having lived out-loud as a gay man for 30 years, he couldn't possibly understand how complex and precarious coming out would be for someone like Russell. Russell's entire world — his marriage, his kids, his job, his relations with friends, neighbors, and extended family, even his Little League coaching — revolved around long-established, binary, patriarchal presumptions. Unveiling the truth to his wife would tip the first domino in a chain of devastation. The injury wouldn't stop with the spouse. This would be a multi-vehicle pileup, with no one in Russell's circle left unscratched.

Russell motored away from the restaurant with a mass of toxic turmoil roiling in his belly. His bold gesture had backfired in every possible way. In revelations of this nature, one can never be certain how the recipient of such information will respond. And, by the time the words have been spoken aloud, it's too late. He had entered the confessional of his own volition to acknowledge his sins. *Didn't that count for anything?* Apparently not, when the priest shows the stridency of Harvey Milk and just so happens to be one of your wife's best gay friends. The Celica was laden with penance the man at the wheel was not prepared to pay. In fact, this afternoon's interaction only reinforced the unspoken credo by which Russell had been living: *Honesty is NOT always the best policy.*

From the moment Russell entered the house, something had felt a bit off kilter. Tess seemed particularly vexed, evidenced by her terseness with the boys, as she excused them to their rooms immediately after dinner. Russell was bussing the table when she said, "I need to talk to you about something." The solemn tenor of this announcement sent Russell's heart racing. His mind presumed his worst paranoid fear: *Tess had talked to David. David had taken matters into his own hands and outed him.*

"Okay," Russell squeaked, his voice cracking like a peach-fuzzed eighth grader in the first months of pubescence. "What's up?"

"Diane dropped by today."

"Diane?" Russell asked, ambushed by such an unexpected revelation. "She just showed up? Without calling?"

"Yep," Tess said. "About one o'clock. I was in the middle of fulfilling some orders. The doorbell rang. And, there she was on the porch."

"Diane." Russell needed confirmation that the person to whom Tess was referring was the person he was picturing in his head. Tess nodded yes. "I don't suppose she had a pie in her hands this time," Russell quipped.

Tess, who typically enjoyed engaging in glib repartee, found no humor in this remark. "She told me that Bryan gave her herpes."

"She... *Diane* told you that?"

"Mmm, hmmm," Tess responded. "And, then she told me that Bryan told her that he must have got it from you."

"From m-m-... from me?" Russell stammered. "That's... that's fucking ridiculous! That's absurd!" Blood was rushing to Russell's face. He could hear his rapidly accelerating pulse pounding in his ears. How many times had he daydreamed about initiating lip-to-lip, tongue-to-tongue, and skin-to-skin contact with Bryan? Still, Russell knew this much: it's impossible to contract a sexually transmitted infection in the realm of the imagination. Fantasy sex, as kinky as it might get, is still safe sex.

"Well," Tess elaborated, "evidently, Bryan said that, occasionally, you guys will pick up the wrong pop can in the dugout... you know, drink from somebody else's soda or Gatorade." Russell's enormous sense of relief lasted only as long as his next single, massive sigh. High anxiety was replaced straightway by scathing anger mixed with the excruciating pain of betrayal. Not only had Bryan failed to confess his own transgressions to his wife, he'd dragged Russell into his fabricated account as a human shield. In doing so, Bryan had made his own dilemma even more untenable — Who would have thought *that* was possible? — while implicating Russell as a co-conspirator in the cover-up.

"You know that's ridiculous, right?" Russell pressed his wife. "You don't... you *can't* catch herpes from sharing a drink."

"Probably not," Tess half agreed, "but..."

"Besides, Bryan couldn't have caught it from me anyway... *because I don't have fucking herpes*!" Russell snatched up a soiled plate and ran steaming water over it only to let it go, sending it clanging back into the stainless steel sink. "Oh, my god!" he exclaimed. "This is exactly like that kid on the debate team in high school, Jerry Silberoth. He picked up some skanky chick from Chattanooga at a forensics tournament, came home, gave his girlfriend crabs, then told her he'd got 'em from a toilet seat in a public bathroom."

"Does that mean you have some idea where Bryan might have been exposed?" Russell had waltzed right into this line of interrogation. Of course, he knew precisely how this transfer of pathogens must have taken place. Now, once again, he found himself faced with a decision as to how much of the truth he could, or would be willing to, reveal. So, instead of addressing Tess's very direct question, he attempted to skirt around it.

"I'll get to the bottom of this," he told her. "You can count on that."

"So, there's no chance, right?"

"No chance of what?"

"That you have herpes. Or, that you gave Bryan herpes."

Russell wanted desperately to reassure her by revealing that, three months earlier, in April, he had gone in for a complete STI blood panel and emerged with a 100% clean report. That can of worms, however, had to remain tightly sealed. Still, he *was* able to articulate one truth with confidence: "There's only one way I could have caught herpes, Babe."

"From me, right?" she asked, sheepishly.

"Exactly," he said, twisting his lips into a forced smile. "You don't have herpes, do you, My Love?"

"Fuck you," she said, her pinched expression surrendering to a semi-smile of semi-relief. Russell, however, wasn't feeling any of the same relief. Bryan might as well have been stabbed him in the heart a thousand times with a rusty railroad spike. The irresistible object of Russell's fantasies, the gorgeous, charming Bryan had scapegoated him and thrown him under the bus. And, in his tormented mind, Russell couldn't help but wonder, to what purpose? "Hey," Tess said. From her familiar, suggestive tone, Russell knew where she was going. "Wanna do it?" With verbal communication intractably lodged in his throat, Russell looked at his wife, standing there, still oblivious about his sordid, secretive, second life. *David was wrong about the elephant*, he told himself. If there was a pachyderm in the room, Tess was blind to its presence.

Russell lost it. Tears gushed. He collapsed against the counter top, his entire body convulsing in howls of grief. Tess shuffled over to comfort him. "What?" she asked, placing a gentle hand on his bicep. "What is it?"

"I love you so much," he muttered.

Their hug lasted for a full 90 seconds. As Tess released her embrace, she whispered, "I'll be in bed. Naked." Then, she gave his wet, salty lips a quick, affectionate kiss before padding toward the stairs.

"Okay," Russell responded. Then, as much to himself as to her, he muttered, "I'll be up. Soon as I finish these dishes." A flood of gratitude flowed into Russell's heart. For too long, he'd been looking at his life as an unfulfilled, shambolic dance. All the while, he'd forgotten to consider how much he had to be thankful for: his comely, trusting, smart-as-a-whip wife, two healthy sons, a handsome house on a cul-de-sac growing in value, year after year, a job that provided purpose and paid the bills. And (so far, at least) no sexually transmitted diseases. As he filled the dishwasher, tears continued to trickle down his cheeks. Now, however, they rolled over a pair of smiling, contented lips.

Then, a voice from earlier in the day echoed in his head. David's voice resonated: "It'll all come out in the wash. It always does." Russell pondered, acknowledging the Zen-like truth in this statement. But what, he couldn't help but wonder, was the "it" in this banal, yet never-untrue aphorism?

TWELVE

The anticlimactic fizzle of the Pirates' once-promising season could have been chalked up to several factors. Although Monday-morning quarterbacking can never change the outcome of games already played, time offers clearer perspective on the what-ifs and the if-not-fors that conspired to truncate what was to be Henry "Hank" Deacon's last summer in a Little League uniform and his father's disappointing third and final managerial campaign.

Conspicuous at the time was the abrupt absence of the team's best pitcher and most reliable hitter. Without explanation or warning, Carter simply stopped showing up for practices and games. This left Russell scrambling to adjust his line-up for the penultimate and conclusive games of the regular schedule and a pair of lackluster performances in the playoffs. Bryan was missed as well. But the truancy of this always accommodating volunteer proved to be a mixed blessing for Russell, who had for most of the summer found his helpful assistant's blue eyes and alluring smile a major distraction. Without Bryan there to divert his concentration, Russell should have been better able to focus on making savvy game-time decisions. Instead, Carter and his dad's abandonment of the team only added hot sauce to the simmering emotional stew already bubbling in Russell's gut. The bilious concoction's most active ingredient was anger — anger about Bryan blaming Russell for his herpes outbreak; anger that an egocentric father would, for his own self-preservation, deprive his talented son of a potentially triumphant ending to his Little League experience. But, ultimately, the most barbed anger affecting Russell lay in the vitriol he directed at himself, for his own lack of resolve, his repetitive caving in to lust and impulse, and the increasingly shaky foundation of duplicity upon which this pattern of behavior was constructed.

By season's end, Russell was paddling a teetering raft of self-recrimination across a deepening, now overflowing pool of guilt and shame, and without his manager/coach role to bolster his sense of purpose. This left a sinkhole the size of Yankee Stadium under his already eroding equilibrium. And, hovering ominously over this bleak landscape was an ever-darkening cloud of depression.

Aside from receiving two blowjobs — the first superb, the second less so — Russell had thus far managed to placate his same-sex cravings without touching or being touched by another man. That dam, however, was about to burst. The initial breakthrough came on a Wednesday afternoon in late August. Russell had just completed a particularly disheartening group presentation for a company that served to store and/or shred documents for other companies. Performing his dog-and-pony sales routine for executives was challenging enough. Asking the labor force to voluntarily accept an additional deduction from their paychecks to cover a supplementary layer of insurance demanded the combined tap-dancing skills of Fred Astaire, Gene Kelly, and Sammy Davis Jr.

After fielding a barrage of semi-hostile questions from the company workforce, Russell stepped out of the downtown warehouse into the sweltering late-summer heat. Suffering serious adrenaline crash, it was as though he'd gained 50 pounds in a single laborious step. As he dragged his concrete shoes toward his car, his testicles began to tingle. This familiar, entirely involuntary sensation had been triggered by a sudden realization... that the return route to the office would take him directly past a certain business, one that had been piquing his curiosity for some time. A quick glance at his watch — it was 3:37 — elicited a familiar rumbling in his lower belly. This natural, automatic physical response, in turn, served to cue the internal negotiation and ultimate self-justification upon which a double life relies. Rationalizations passed through his head in the following order: *My work day is basically finished. I really have no pressing reason to touch base at headquarters. Nobody would care if I took the remainder of the afternoon off. And, if anyone asked, I could always say the sales presentation had run longer than expected.*

The building's location, at the junction of two major highways, made The World's Largest Adult Book Store a particularly alluring and convenient stop for horny truckers and business travelers motoring through town. Russell had driven by numerous times on his route to and from sales appointments, chuckling to think that any establishment would tout itself with such an audacious, unverifiable claim. He entered the upper level into a vast, warehouse-sized area housing rack after rack of triple-X videos and DVDs for sale or rent. Through a beaded curtain at the far end of the top floor were 30 or more video booths. A stairway led to the basement level, which comprised a sex-toy shop and two movie theaters, one screening straight porn, the second featuring gay films.

Russell had completed a self-guided tour of the layout when a certain VHS case piqued his interest. Cover graphics for the video *Bears in the Woods 29* depicted a pair of naked fellows, both expansive in girth and exceptionally hairy, engaging in 69 on a blanket, under a massive evergreen tree. As his soldier chubbed in hopeful anticipation, Russell detected a shadow thrown by another person. A quick, over-the-shoulder glance revealed a large, bearded fellow, heavy-set, with a swarthy complexion, hovering approximately six feet away. Russell's immediate inclination was to turn his head to avoid eye contact. As he placed the video case back in its place, the large gentleman cleared his throat suggestively.

Russell swiveled his head to take a second look, this one sustained long enough to discern the real-life bear cocking his head subtly in the direction of the video-booth area. Then, continuing to gaze directly into Russell's eyes, he reached down to touch the crotch of his jeans before pivoting on his heel to stroll casually, hands in pockets, toward the beaded curtain. As the real-life bear reached out to part the curtain, he checked back over his shoulder. Seeing that he hadn't lost his audience of one, he beckoned Russell with a reprise tilt of the head, this one more overt than the first. By this point, Russell's heartbeat was pummeling his rib cage like a prep cook with a meat hammer. He felt dizzy and a tad nauseous. "No," he murmured to himself. "You *cannot* do this!"

"Excuse me?" inquired the cashier, a thin, 60-ish, red-lipsticked woman, with an overly exposed and quite wrinkled cleavage. Russell didn't recall walking from the display racks to the counter. "What can I do ya for?" she asked.

"A roll of tokens, please," Russell heard himself say. His hand, which seemed to have a mind of its own, plunged into his trouser pocket. There, his index finger bumped against the tip of a hardening, bloodthirsty rod. Paper currency appeared in his palm, extended toward the cashier. He snatched up his purchase. No turning back now. Any opportunity for reason or reflection had slipped away. Russell no longer commanded the motor movement of his body. His legs were answering only to their aroused middle brother. This trio of mutineers proceeded to carry Russell back through the beaded curtain and into the dimly lit video-booth area.

Russell's heart was pounding so loudly, he couldn't imagine that it wasn't audible to any ear within 20 feet. A half-dozen other men, in a variety of sizes, skin-colors, and ages, leaned against booths, most of them smoking cigarettes. The bear that had lured him there, however, was nowhere to be seen. As Russell shuffled past one open booth door, a breathy voice came from inside. "Hey." A chill shiver rippled through his shoulders. He stood peering into the open booth, transfixed, as if his shoes had been nailed to the floor. "Come on in," the bear entreated. Russell remained paralyzed. "Really, Dude. I'm not gonna hurt you."

Russell attempted a response but his voice failed. His second effort — "Can we just talk for a minute?" — blurted from his lips at a disproportionately loud volume.

"Jesus!" ribbed one of the loitering smokers, "take it inside, Mary!" Another chuckled mockingly.

Russell found himself standing conspicuously at a three-pronged fork in the road. He could remain a spectacle, a laughing stock, lingering outside the booth, attempting to converse with the man inside. He could skedaddle and made a quick escape. Instead, he picked option number three by taking two brisk strides into the booth. Then, with a shaky, sweaty hand, Russell hastily yanked the booth door closed and turned the lock.

Fifteen minutes later, Russell exited the booth disheveled, with a proverbial euphoric "I just got laid" grin radiating across his flushed face. He didn't care whether anyone else noticed or cared. He was still aglow from the playful roughhouse foreplay and — even with contact limited to hands only — the most luxurious and satisfying cum shot since glorious Blowjob #1. And, unlike the immediate aftermath of that years-ago encounter with David, Russell wasn't attempting to put the whole thing out of mind by quickly depositing it in the bin marked, "Been there. Done that." He was buzzing from head to toe, wallowing in the immersive pleasure this Wednesday afternoon had brought him in the intimate privacy of a video booth at The World's Largest Adult Book Store.

As he strolled out onto the brightly lit main floor, Russell felt weightless. Rounding the corner at the end of the hallway, his shoulder bumped against the shoulder of another man at the top of the stairs. "Sorry," Russell chuckled, still so lost in rapturous reverie that he neglected to glance at the person with whom he'd just collided. Instead, he proceeded to bop blissfully down the stairs. To no one in particular, he quipped, "Maybe I should watch where I'm going."

"Rusty Boy?" the man asked. Russell halted in his tracks on the fourth stair down. Hearing someone say his name was alarming enough. That the voice matched the unmistakable timbre of one particular person, however, abruptly cranked up the alarm to the cusp of panic. That feeling of weightlessness? Gone. Russell was suddenly being yanked down by the gravity of Jupiter. Reluctantly, hesitantly, he turned around and looked up. There on the landing stood the last person in the world he would ever want to run into under such circumstances. "What are you doing here?" Mike Terzian asked. Oddly, Mike's tone wasn't threatening and lacked any hint of the derision Russell had come to expect from the workplace bully. Rather, this inquiry sounded friendly, genuinely curious, almost naïve.

"Well, you know..." Russell stammered, overwhelmed by equal parts embarrassment and incredulity. Most folks, he was thinking, would find it mortifying to encounter a co-worker at an enterprise that peddled porn. Mike, however, didn't appear to be the slightest bit disquieted. Russell's mind, which had, until five seconds ago, been busy replaying the thrill and pleasure of his bear-wrestling encounter, was now scrambling for an answer, one that would explain his attendance in such an establishment, while sounding casual and non-specific enough as to avoid provoking further suspicion. "I've always..." he improvised, "you know, sorta wondered, I guess, about this place."

"Fuckin' hell, Dude!" Mike exuded, as if drooling over the buffet at Golden Corral after a three-day fast. "I mean, this place is awesome!" This same review could easily have come from a 13-year-old kid raving about the grand opening of a new paintball arcade. Russell returned a bemused, pursed-lipped nod. *This clueless dolt,* he ruminated, *has exactly zero awareness of the down-and-dirty activities underway at this very moment, in pretty much every corner of this "awesome place."*

"Looks like you've been having some fun," Mike observed, with a suggestive wink.

Up until now, Russell's post-hook-up bliss had distracted him from devoting any attention to his state of dishevelment. Noticing several damp stains near the zipper of his wrinkled trousers, he quickly pulled his half untucked shirt down to shield the mess from view. "Guess I should tidy up a bit," he said.

"No shit!" Per usual, Mike's quip was boisterous enough to be audible to the entirety of Davidson County.

"Yeah. I was just on my way to the restroom," Russell said. "You know, to..." It didn't seem necessary to finish the sentence.

"Well, Dude," Mike said. "Rock on! And, keep clear of the fags."

"Oh, for sure," Russell answered, forcing a smile, as if cementing the two rival co-workers' newly kindled male bond. Trundling down the remaining stairs, a wave of self-recrimination washed through Russell's chest. Why in the world had he felt obliged to patronize an ignorant, homophobic chauvinist like Mike Terzian? Why had he allowed "oh, for sure" to slip out from between his lips? The utterance of those three syllables left him feeling even more soiled than the pasty stain dampening the crotch area of his trousers.

A minute later, Russell stood staring at a reflection in the men's room mirror. This was someone he scarcely recognized. Hair sticking up and out in random ways — a do Rod Stewart might have spent hours and a gallon of product to accomplish — pale cheeks dotted with blotchy amoebic patches of pink; ears a shade shy of purple; lips severely dry and chapped. Mike had been correct about one thing: Russell most definitely looked like he'd been having some fun.

THIRTEEN

Prior to September 13, 1994, whenever Russell was asked to describe Hell, he was always ready with an answer. "Hell," he'd quipped on numerous occasions, "is being stuck for eternity on the *It's a Small World* ride at Disneyland." However, the afternoon of his younger son's tenth birthday introduced him to an even more torturous picture of everlasting torment. "Hell," Russell concluded after that fateful day, "would be a never-ending child's birthday party at Chuck E. Cheese." A popular purveyor of cacophony, chaos, and cardboard pizza, this enterprise invites children to crash virtual race cars, fire laser beams at slimy alien monsters, and slaughter slavering Jurassic Park dinosaurs. Here, innocent babes inhabit the avatar of their favorite Teenage Mutant Ninja Turtle for the purpose of blowing grotesque, malformed monsters to bits. And, for exercising their most violent tendencies, they are rewarded with tickets redeemable for tacky, plastic trinkets imported from China.

For Russell, the sensory input in this environment was mind-numbing: bells, beeps, squawks, skidding tires, crashes, explosions, garish, clashing colors, and bright, flashing lights, a hundred children howling and screeching; packs of unruly savages streaking maniacally from one game station to another like beheaded chickens, careening into anything and anyone impeding direct and immediate access to the next station on their crazed, improvised itinerary. This, Russell theorized, is where young male humans learn how to exhibit their most obnoxious behavior, where a lad reaps positive affirmation (from parents *and* peers) for his least appealing impulses. In this setting, normal decorum is willingly checked at the door, all etiquette is jettisoned, and absolute insanity comes disguised as fun.

Ultimately, Chuck E. Cheese cleverly serves up its brand of perpetual mayhem to distract from its horrible food. Multi-generations of party attendees weave like ants around 20-foot-long, theme-decorated tables. Guests collide and switch directions like Rumbas in a room populated only by Rumbas. Pimply, purple-polo-shirted staff members weave through the swarm, balancing pitchers of radioactive punch (zero percent fruit juice, laboratory flavored, and dyed the color of Mars). Paper plates featuring the image of the cartoon pizza-chef Pasqually — definitely a blood relative of the Mario Brothers — accommodate peperoni, peperoni, and more peperoni, singed and curled at the edges, resting on a substance with the color of cheese and the flavor of dried spackle, melted upon a crust that tastes like discarded file folders. Dads wearing backwards baseball caps congregate on the periphery, tucking their hands into hoody pouches over bellies that somehow seem to expand another belt loop every year. Moms who, some years ago, gave up trying to lose the baby weight, waddle around in saggy sweatpants and wrinkled tops they yanked off a hanger at Ross For Less, herding packs of sugar-crazed child hyenas, pouring punch, and kissing booboos.

With the birthday table set and the clock ticking down on pizza-and-cake time, Tess dispatched Russell to wrangle Rory and his posse. Russell was pleasantly amused not to find his younger son's contingent engaged in a digitally simulated auto race or a battle in outer space, but huddled around the old-school, mechanical "Pro Baseball" game. Russell stood observing his second-born son taking charge of what appeared to be a lively, enthusiastic tournament, having divided his friends into teams, with each individual player taking his turn "at the plate." Members of the "home team" were howling in collective disappointment over making their third out, leaving the bases loaded in the bottom of the seventh inning, when Rory noticed his father looking on. "Hey, Pops!" the boy called out.

"Pizza's on the table," Russell responded. "Where's your brother?"

"Over there." Rory pointed in the direction of a two-player simulated motorcycle race. Russell was pleased to see Hank and Carter laughing and hooting while leaning their bikes into the turns on the video screen. It had been painful to observe the melancholic effect being forcibly separated from this best friend had on Hank. How, Russell wondered, could he comfort his sensitive firstborn son without tangling an already squirmy pit of vipers into even tighter knots? Hank's unsolicited mention that Carter harbored suspicions about his dad's sexuality added fresh flypaper to an already sticky situation. It was heartwarming to see the two boyhood pals renewing their comradeship. Russell sighed, wishing the whole scenario could be that simple. But this circumstance couldn't be distilled down to the re-burgeoning of an erstwhile pre-teen friendship... because, if Carter was here, Russell had to conclude that the boy's Harpy mother and/or his dishonest, egocentric-but-adorable dad must be close by as well.

Russell redirected his attention to the birthday boy. "Hey, Roar," he called out, "when this game is over, you guys head over to the party area."

Rory sprung to attention, clicked the heels of his Vans sneakers, and gave his father a proper military salute. "Roger, Dodger," he replied. "Copy that."

"And, don't dawdle," Russell said. "Your mother is waiting. I'm gonna drop by the restroom."

No one had provided Russell with a translation book to decipher the symbolic language of anonymous man-to-man hookups. Like a foreigner who learns English from watching American sitcoms, he gradually picked up on the secret codes men like him use to make their interest and intentions known to each other. While such covert signals and cryptic phrases can happen almost anywhere, for Russell, the automatic association of certain olfactory stimuli and the cognizance of ever-present potential made nearly every entrance into a men's public bathroom a somewhat titillating experience. This automatic physical response sometimes came at inconvenient times, thus making emptying his bladder that much more challenging. Russell bellied up, unzipped, pulled out his semi-erect penis, and waited. Thirty seconds had passed, with only a couple of tiny squirts emitting from his constricted urethra.

He was about to give up and shake it off when someone approached the adjacent urinal. "Hey, Buddy," the man said. "I've been looking forward to seeing you today." Russell remained focused on the organ in his hand. There was no need to look up to confirm the person's identity. "I missed you," he said. "How ya been?" The half hard-on Russell had been trying to talk down immediately sprung full-on erect. "My, my, my!" Bryan whispered, leering down at Russell's stiffy. "Looks like somebody missed me, too."

Stowing this ramrod back into a spot only designed to accommodate its more flexible, flaccid state proved to be a trick worthy of David Copperfield. "Fuck you, Bryan!" Russell hissed, as he struggled to yank up his zipper. "You're a fucking asshole. You know that?"

"Wait a minute! Coach, please!" beseeched Bryan, swiveling around, exposing his genitals. "Let me at least explain." Russell stood silent, transfixed on the button head of a circumcised penis peeking out from between a pair of — no surprise — extra-large testicles. Suddenly, in Russell's mind's eye, Bryan's genital region bore a haunting resemblance to a pair of comical "Groucho" glasses, the kind one might pick up in a joke shop. Russell couldn't help himself. He burst into peels of involuntary laughter. "Hey, Dude!" protested a now-embarrassed Bryan. "I'm a grower not a show-er!"

"And I fantasized... for months? About that?" Russell exclaimed, between guffaws, still gazing down in the direction of the very package he had, so often, daydreamed about unwrapping. "Wow!"

Russell was still chuckling to himself as he rejoined the birthday celebration. "What's so funny?" Tess asked. "Where have you been?"

"Men's room," Russell replied, before breaking into yet another spate of titters.

"Carter's here," said Tess. Her smile was warm and maternal. "Isn't that fantastic? Look how happy Hank is!" Hank and Carter had isolated themselves in their own bubble at the furthest end of a table.

"Yep," Russell agreed. "That is fantastic!" Russell took his wife's hand in his and the couple stood side-by-side, observing the festivities.

"Now, it's time to see whose birthday it is today," shouted a teenage mistress of ceremonies, clad in her regulation purple polo shirt, black cap and pants. The young lady's shrill, nasal voice would have been irritating enough at normal conversational volume. Cranked up to maximum intensity, her every utterance threatened to shatter glass. "Who is today's Chuck E. Cheese birthday star?" she screeched. "Step on up!" Rory stuffed the remaining half slice of pizza into his mouth, leapt to his feet, and bounded to the front of the room. "What's our birthday boy's name?" The boy of the hour accelerated his chewing, then stole a gulp of punch from a pitcher before articulating his answer. "How about giving Rory a big round of applause!" urged the MOC. Responding to clapping and cheers, the uninhibited honoree offered a series of immodest bows at the waist and exaggerated blown kisses. Richard Simmons would have seemed reticent and withdrawn next to Russell and Tess's second-born son.

"Now," bellowed the MOC, "who wants to meet the star of the show?" This was a line that invariably got five- and six-year-old party attendees to issue a deafening, unison cheer. Nine- and 10-year-old boys, however, tend to be less responsive to obvious manipulation. "Come on, you guys!" the MOC shouted. "Chuck E. needs to know that you love him!" To gin up enthusiasm, she attempted to initiate a chant... "*Chuck. E. Cheese. Chuck. E. Cheese.*" With only the younger siblings and some of the elderly guests chiming in, Rory embraced the camp-ness of the proceedings by pumping his fist with mock-seriousness and leading the refrain. Within a few seconds, the entire building was quaking with this tri-syllable mantra. Feeling sufficient love from the assemblage to make an entrance, the eponymous rodent, clad in "his" signature purple top with a large, yellow "C" emblazoned on its chest, weaved through the crowd, trading high and low fives with kids and adults alike. "Can you all say *happy birthday* together?" yelled the MOC. "Okay! Happy Birthday on a count of three! One! Two! *Three!*"

By this point, Russell had released his wife's hand and was wadding up shredded napkin fragments, hastily inserting balls of paper into his noise-assaulted ear canals. A distorted polka-derived instrumental piece blasted from shredded boombox speakers, as the MOC and "Chuck E." launched into some loosely synchronized, robotic Hokie-Pokey dance steps. "Repeat after me," screamed the MOC. "I like to party!"

Fist-bumping the air like an Ivy League cheerleader, Rory gleefully led the crowd: "I LIKE TO PARTY!"

The MOC: "At Chuck E. Cheese!"

Rory and his acolytes: "AT CHUCK E. CHEESE!"

MOC: "When I say happy, you say happy! When I say birthday, you say birthday!" Under Rory's exuberant rally leadership, the guests answered calls with responses, until dancing and chanting came to a halt with the MOC's announcement: "It's time for cake! Let's light those candles." Dutiful mother Tess scooted over to unveil the ovular cake, frosted to replicate a super-sized baseball. "Ooo's!" and "Wows!" filled the room as she flicked a Bic lighter across the wicks of 10 bat-shaped candles. "Count down from ten," the MOC instructed, "and we'll all sing together!" As the room resounded with a rowdy, dissonant "Happy birthday to yoooooou," the honoree grabbed Chuck E.'s gloved hand and spun "him" around the floor in a comical, impromptu waltz, much to the amusement of everyone present — with the single exception of Rory's reluctant dance partner.

Before the weary company mascot would be excused to rest up for the next party of the day, the oversized mouse was obliged to pose in a group picture with Rory and his guests. Tess was helping the MOC in her attempt to shepherd sugar-crazed kids into a pose capturable by still camera when Russell observed the situation unfolding at the far end of the table. Bryan was crouched down on his haunches next to his son. By their expressions, both Hank and Carter appeared displeased. Russell observed, as Bryan stood and took Carter by his arm. Carter shook his arm free, refusing to budge. Hank, who now seemed to be on the verge of tears, said something in protest, which Bryan disregarded, while grabbing his son's arm more forcibly. "Ow!" Carter complained. "Dad, you're hurting me!"

By this point, Russell could no longer remain uninvolved. "Hey!" he barked, striding in the direction of the escalating conflict. "What's going on?"

"Stay out of this, Coach," Bryan insisted. "This is a family matter."

"Damn right it's a family matter," snapped Russell. "It matters to my family, too."

Releasing his son's arm, Bryan turned to face Russell. "Can we talk? Privately?"

"It's my kid's birthday party, Bryan," Russell replied. "This is not the time... for, you know... it's just not..."

"Please." Bryan's appeal was barely audible against the canned instrumental overture for the long-awaited main-stage show.

Lights illuminated the front-porch set as an unlikely cast of animatronic characters creaked to life: a chicken with shifty, bugged-out green eyes, a purple hound dog with a banjo on his knee, alongside a robotic Chuck E., whose long snout and two snaggled buck teeth appeared more rat-like than mouse-ish. Completing the ensemble was the aforementioned, mustachioed Pasqually, evidently taking a break from throwing inedible pizza dough to show off his vocal acumen. An overly excited toddler streaked up to pinch robot Chuckie's black-ball nose. Another high-spirited child took this as permission to pry open the chicken's beak. Meanwhile, in spite of the intrusion of these two willful children, Chuck E. Cheese's low-budget twist on Disney's Country Bear Jamboree played on.

Meanwhile, Russell and Bryan had retired to a slightly quieter corner to facilitate communication. "What are they doing now?" Carter asked Hank, who had the better view of their fathers' private confab.

"Just talking, I guess," Hank reported, lifting a plastic forkful of soggy chocolate cake to his mouth. "Oh, shit!" he suddenly blurted. "My dad didn't do anything!"

"What do you mean?" Carter swiveled in his seat just in time to see his father withdrawing his hand from Russell's clavicle.

"He just stood there," Hank remarked.

"So?" Carter seemed confused.

"Look... you said you thought your dad was gay, right?" Hank recalled. "Or, he might be, or whatever."

"Well, yeah," Carter said. "But, I didn't mean it. Not really."

"Your dad just put his hand on my dad's chest, like right *here*." Hank pointed to the place just above his heart. "And, my dad... well, he didn't do anything. I mean, it looked... sorta... gay, I guess."

"Maybe *your* dad's gay," Carter suggested.

"You mean, like *gay* gay? Or, are you saying he's lame? Because they're not the same thing. You know that, right?"

"Whatever, Dude," Carter said, swiveling back to the remainder of his birthday cake. "My mom's a bitch," he stated, as simple a matter of fact.

"Don't look now," Hank said, glancing over his friend's shoulder, "our fag dads are comin' back."

Carter was mid-chuckle when Bryan delivered the order. "Come on, Buddy, we gotta take off. We're late. Your mother's not gonna be happy." Carter looked across the table at Hank. No words were necessary. His dad had just confirmed his appraisal of his mother.

The boys rose to execute their elaborate Pirates handshake. "Good seein' you guys," said Bryan through an unusually unconvincing smile. Russell and Hank didn't respond verbally. And, as Chuck E.'s mechanized quartet entertained the entourage, one father and son watched another father and son trundle off toward the exit.

FOURTEEN

"What's going on, Babe?" Tess closed her book, removed her readers and set them on the bed-side table. Her tone indicated that she wanted a direct, unambiguous answer. Russell lay on his side of the king-sized bed, doing his best impression of a dead man. "Russ,"

she persisted, "I know you're awake."

"I'm tired," he mumbled into his pillow.

"You were acting so weird today," Tess remarked.

"Weird?" he scoffed.

"At Rory's party. The way you were laughing when you came back from the restroom. And then, you got all sentimental and lovey-dovey."

"Our baby boy just turned ten," he grumbled. "Kind of a big deal."

Fourteen years of marriage had taught Tess to pick her battles. She was willing to write off her husband's odd giggling and atypically affectionate hand holding earlier that afternoon. "Yeah, okay," she capitulated, segueing to the topic she really wanted to address. "But, later... what was happening between you and Bryan?"

"Jesus, Tess!" Russell exclaimed. "Do we really need to get into this now?" He was still mulling over a conversation that had shaken him to the core, clueless as to how to feel about what was said during those intense three minutes. But, above all else, Russell was wondering if guys like him, guys who live in glass houses, might be better off keeping stones in their pockets, even though toting a load of rocks makes each step of the trek incrementally more emotionally laborious. And, now, it felt like his exceptionally intuitive — some husbands might say "nagging" — wife was poking at a fresh and very tender contusion.

"I think I deserve to know," Tess persisted.

"You deserve to know?" Russell flopped over to face her. "What do you mean, you deserve to know? I don't pry into your conversations with your friends. Do I?"

"This is different," Tess volleyed, "and you know it."

He did know it. Still, he wasn't about to abandon his fortified position simply for the purpose of indulging his wife's prying curiosity. "I told Bryan to fuck off," he said. "Okay? Are you happy now?"

"Wow!" she said. "Way to go! What else?"

"Jesus!" he exclaimed. "What do you mean, what else?"

"You were talking for what? Four minutes? And that's all you said? Fuck off?"

That Tess had been observing this verbal skirmish from across that frenzied party room with such assiduous attention felt like a violation. It was as though she'd found his private journal in the back of a sock drawer, hadn't read it yet, but was shoving it in his face, demanding, "What the hell is this?" Russell feared that, if he failed to execute his next step with extreme caution, he might have to chop off his own foot to make it out alive. His survival instinct directed him to try a diversionary tactic, in this case, sarcasm. "So, you were timing us with a stopwatch?" For approximately 10 seconds — no one, after all, had a timer on *this* particular conversation — Tess appeared to be stymied. Her eyes revealed that she was wounded, which left Russell feeling feckless. While he was tempted to tell her how sorry he was — about *everything* — he saw a short-term win in his wife's momentary, sorrowful silence. So, he left his apology unspoken.

"Okay," Tess snapped. "You obviously don't want to talk about it." She rolled over with her back to her husband, switched off the lamp, and buried her head in her pillow. "Ya know, sometimes," she murmured, "I don't even feel like I know you anymore." When passive aggression is the weapon of choice, the wife often fires the final shot. But Tess wasn't simply shooting from the hip. Something untoward was simmering beneath the surface of her husband's defensiveness. She was relatively certain that he wasn't having an affair. But the earth was beginning to shift beneath the foundation of a partnership she had always considered rock-solid.

Russell felt the shift, too. But a more urgent concern was occupying his mind. For the next hour, he lay awake, rewinding and replaying the previous afternoon's conversation — or confrontation, depending on how one chooses to frame it — with Bryan. The interchange got off to a contentious start, with Russell castigating Bryan for yanking his son out of Little League. "Do you really think that was fair to Carter?"

"Look, Man," Bryan stammered, "you know I had no choice in the matter."

While Russell wasn't surprised by Bryan's spineless passing of the buck, he recognized an opening, jumped on it, and came out firing with both barrels. "Well, you certainly had a choice when it came to telling Diane how you contracted herpes. And, when it comes right down to it, you also had a choice not to go out and catch that nasty virus in the first place."

"You're right," Bryan conceded. "I've made some really shitty decisions."

While this was exactly what Russell wanted to hear, he was taken off guard by Bryan's easy acquiescence. "Too late now!" spat Russell.

"And I've hurt some folks." The contriteness of Bryan's tone had blunted the sharp edge of Russell's rage. "I'm sorry," Bryan continued. "I really am... to you and my kid and the team and... Dammit! I don't know what to do." By this point, Bryan's baby-blues were pooling with tears. "She's got me by the short hairs," he shared. "If I don't play my cards exactly the way she wants, she's gonna take me for everything I' got."

"So that's all you care about, your precious, fucking money?" Russell was now teetering dangerously on the edge of exhibiting the character trait he despised most: self-righteousness.

"What? Really?" Bryan seemed authentically hurt. "Is that all you think of me?"

"What else am I supposed to think, Man?" Russell demanded. "I mean, you've always had this, like hedonistic... no, what's the word... nihilistic attitude."

"I know that's how I come off." Bryan placed his hand on Russell's chest, partly to steady himself, but also to emphasize his sincerity. "But, inside, I'm... I'm a disaster. I'm losing my mind." Russell found it unsettling to hear another man reveal this level of fragility. But Bryan wasn't finished. He ripped open his chest cavity and yanked out his own beating heart. "I'm gay," Bryan confessed. "You're the only fucking person in my life who knows. I can't have you, of *all* people, hating me. Please, please, Coach. I know I've been a selfish asshole. But I'm begging for your forgiveness. Please. I could really, *really* use a friend right now."

Bryan had just done what Russell had dreaded doing for years. While he was moved, honored even, to be the first recipient of such a personal revelation, Russell was determined to remain stern and resolute. Too, he was surprised by how much he relished being in the driver's seat. To a certain degree, he held this gorgeous faker's fate in his hands. "I'll think about it," Russell replied. Then, remembering how untrustworthy Bryan had proven himself to be, he quickly tacked on an addendum: "No guarantees."

"Thanks, Buddy," Bryan said, as he withdrew his hand from Russell's chest. "I can't tell you how much I appreciate it."

"Better get back to the party." Russell was eager to escape the extreme discomfort of this exchange and return to the solace of celebratory bedlam.

Two vulnerable men were lumbering back in the direction of their sons on four heavy feet when Bryan blurted, "Love you, man."

Russell responded with two caustic words: "Fuck off." That's how he remembered it anyway.

The climate in the kitchen the following morning was unseasonable chilly. That Tess had already made coffee by the time Russell descended the stairs made a statement in and of itself. He had long claimed java as his exclusive domain, from the selection, purchase, and grinding of the beans through the pouring of the perfect blend. Thus, his choosing to not make an issue out of this was equivalent to a white flag of surrender.

"Hmmm. Smells good, Babe," Russell remarked, going for a peck on the cheek, which Tess evaded, simultaneously avoiding eye contact.

"I'm off to yoga," she informed him, while securing the lid on her travel cup.

"On Sunday?" he queried.

"There's a new instructor," she responded, curtly. "I'm gonna check it out."

"I see," Russell responded. He watched his better half scoot through the doorway to the garage and kick the door shut behind her with a heel. Hearing the dull thump of a slamming car door, he uttered the following words to no one: "Guess we'll see you whenever you get home."

Russell plopped down heavily on a patio chair beneath the multicolored awning to sample his wife's brew. Although he felt a quick flash of resentment for being forced to suffer a weak first cup of the day, he quickly found distraction in the sound of his own slurping and swallowing, which seemed amplified, resounding inside his head like spring water in a cave. The quiet following the slurping and swallowing rumbled and shook the ground like a freight train. A heaviness welled up in his chest. His throat constricted. The simple process of breathing in and out suddenly required conscious focus and attention. He felt an overwhelming impulse to stand up and run — somewhere, *anywhere* else — but his lower extremities felt as if they'd been strapped down and anchored to the patio floor. Hearing the familiar burbling of youthful, fraternal banter coming from within the house, Russell glanced over his shoulder. In the kitchen, his two sons were pouring bowls of cereal. This glimmer of normalcy cleared the way for him to take a full breath. Rory, toting a bowl of Frosted Flakes in one hand, waved through the glass with the other. Russell managed a brief, mechanical grin and an almost indiscernible nod of his troubled head. His thoughts were elsewhere.

Bryan appeared to be on the verge of losing everything. The once-magnificent stallion had already been gelded — figuratively, yes, but still — by his wife. In that regard, he had no one else to blame but himself. He chose to marry the woman, after all, presumably having some hint of how superficial, judgmental, and vindictive she tended to be. Getting hitched to Diane was but one in a plethora of, as Bryan himself had characterized, shitty decisions that were now teaming up to push him out onto the plank. Bryan's most unforgivable sin, in Russell's estimation, was being careless and cavalier with his own health and the health of others — including his shrewish spouse. Out of expedience — cowardice, too — the blue-eyed charmer had made the conscious decision to live a lie. What he had no part in choosing, however, lay at the very root of this pattern of questionable behavior: his sexual orientation, his same-sex desires, his innate queerness.

Russell knew he had no right to pass judgment on Bryan, or to criticize any closeted queer person caught up in a similar dilemma. For years, Russell had only revealed his authentic self in furtive, meaningless moments within a shadowy parallel universe, reserving one of the most fundamental parts of his nature for total strangers. Thus far, he had only let two other people in on his secret: Bryan and David. Bryan betrayed their unspoken pact by scapegoating Russell as the source of his herpes. David had responded to Russell's confession in a less-than-sympathetic fashion. This left Russell harboring serious doubts about the trustworthiness of both of his confidants.

Russell's patio mulling abruptly took a paranoid left turn, skipping to that chance shoulder-to-shoulder brush with Mike Terzian at The World's Largest Adult Book Store. *How long,* Russell fretted, *will it take for Mike to put two and two together and come up with queer? Even a dimwitted chauvinist like Mike is capable of drawing a logical conclusion now and then, especially when such persuasive clues land in his lap.* An inevitable next picture appeared on Russell's memory screen... his own reflection in a bathroom mirror, immediately following that fluky top-of-the-stairway collision: spiked, tousled hair, blotchy complexion, disheveled, untucked shirt. But, there was something else in that reflection, something that carried with it an entirely unexpected implication: a dreamy expression of ultimate contentment. In spite of his unkempt clownishness, Russell in the mirror had truly connected with someone. He had, minutes earlier, gaped into that someone's eyes without reservation. That someone had craved and explored Russell's body as Russell had craved and explored his.

Russell wanted to vanish that vision from his mind. But, it couldn't be erased. Eighteen years ago — after that premiere gay-sex lesson from David — Russell had been able to deny how truly wonderful it felt to be naked and unguarded with another kind, affectionate male human. That level of self-delusion, however, was no longer attainable. Russell's bear encounter had infused his soul with essential nutrients. Being with that soft, furry, jumbo teddy was like a nibble from one of those biscuits the Caterpillar gave Alice in Wonderland, chased by a brimming jigger of vitamin B-12. The Russell reflected in that mirror was savoring the aftertaste of a life-giving elixir. Now, he felt starved for a bigger sip. With the bear, Russell had violated one of his own long-standing, self-imposed, personal pledges... the one prohibiting physical contact. He suspected — and worried — that it wouldn't be long before another domino toppled. What principle would be next to fall, his policy of anonymity?

Fantasies Russell had, for years, purposefully put out of reach were now within his grasp. *How much more wonderful,* he mused, *would it be to call your sex partner by his name and for him to respond with yours?* A thrill chill rippled through Russell's shoulders, as he imagined himself and the bear, in the lingering embers of passion, lying together, naked, under sheets and blankets... perhaps even falling asleep in each other's arms.

Russell heard the patio door slide open. "Hey, Daddio. I'm gonna ride my bike over to Finn's. Okay?"

"Okay, Dude," Daddio responded, not making the effort to turn around. He knew his younger son's voice. "What's your brother up to?"

"What do you think?" Rory quipped.

"Right," Russell said, picturing Hank, his face reflecting the glow of the video monitor, joystick in hand, firing lasers at an army of scaly, yellow-eyed monsters. The door glided closed. "Stupid question," Russell mumbled, once again, to no one but himself.

"Doc says she's only a few weeks away from popping," Ed shared. Russell and his bald-pated co-worker were the only passengers in the elevator, on their way up from the basement garage to their third-floor offices.

"I thought Sherry wasn't due till November," Russell remarked.

"You and me both," Ed concurred. "Turns out I must-a knocked her up earlier than we thought. Either that, or the little trollop was diddling her ceramics instructor on the side."

"Yeah," replied Russell, as the shiny metal doors parted. "I seriously doubt that."

"Irregardless..." — one of a dozen or more nonexistent words Ed habitually used — "I'm freakin' pissed." The pair stepped out of the elevator car.

"You're ticked off because the baby is coming sooner than you thought?" Russell was genuinely puzzled. *Ed might be a blowhard and a misogynist. But, there's no question as to how much the dumb jackass adores his kids.*

"Nah," Ed explained. "I'm gonna hafta miss the big shindig in Austin."

"Oh, right," said Russell. Of course, Ed would be conflicted about this. Corporate conventions were custom-made for guys like him. Russell had only attended the annual gathering once over the course of his dozen years with the company. And, in that particular instance, it was an easy three-and-a-half-hour drive down Interstate 40 to Memphis for his induction into the exclusive Million Dollar Roundtable. It hadn't even crossed Russell's mind to register for, as Ed so crassly put it, "the big shindig in Austin." For Russell, company-wide confabs were intolerable. So much ado with so little substance. All that ginned-up enthusiasm for the purpose of revving the sales force into a false frenzy. Russell, who didn't think he needed additional motivation, took personal umbrage at vapid rah-rah group-think exercises aimed at building brand loyalty and comradery. In his eyes, such assemblages oozed with self-congratulation. Too, there was the inevitable excess of drunken revelry and macho backslapping, adults regressing into boneheaded, sophomoric mindsets and behaviors they should have outgrown decades ago — which explained why Ed was feeling so "freakin' pissed" over having to bow out of next month's affair at the Texas state capitol.

"Hey, Dude..." Russell detected the glow of the lightbulb switching on inside Ed's smooth, shiny cranium. "How 'bout you taking my spot?"

"Yeah..." Russell's mouth screwed into a grimace reminiscent of a child anticipating a spoonful of Castor Oil. "I don't think so."

"Come on, Man!" Ed cajoled. "If somebody doesn't take my room, I'm gonna lose my deposit. Do a pal a solid. Your buddy Ed's about to have another mouth to feed."

"Okay," Russell ceded, if only to get himself off the hook for the moment. "I'll mull it over and run it by Tess." What he was actually planning to mull over was a convincing excuse for rejecting Ed's plea.

Alone in his office, it didn't take long for Russell's mental meanderings to veer off and onto an unanticipated side path. Attending the convention, he realized, could very well open up networking opportunities of a less business-oriented, more personal, and far more intimate kind. A two-night hotel stay in a city more than 800 miles away could facilitate the sort of experience that, since his elicit bear encounter, had been invading Russell's reveries several times per day: getting naked with another man, preferably a man with a healthy crop of chest hair and a willing disposition, a man whose name Russell could speak freely out loud and who would respond by saying Russell's name, a man with whom he might even share a bed until the next morning.

Originally, "I'll run it by Tess" had been no more than a stall tactic, an empty, reflexive promise blurted to buy time. After a sufficient number of hours, Ed would assume that Russell had considered the proposition seriously. Office politics being what they are — so often reliant on superficial gamesmanship — allowing an obligatory grace period before begging off would avoid the likelihood of hurt feelings. In reality, Russell hadn't planned to broach the subject with Tess at all.

Now, however, after entertaining the alternative possibilities offered by a three-day, two-night getaway, Russell was actively contemplating various ways to make his case. He spent the drive home concocting a surefire script to convince his better half that his attendance at "the big shindig in Austin" was a good idea.

"I think you should go," Tess said, as if it was no big deal. "I'm all *for* it." His stomach doing flip-flops, Russell's eyes widened, wrinkling his forehead. In preparation to make his pitch, he'd considered every imaginable challenge, much like a collegiate debater would in the days leading up to a major tournament. Tess's immediate acceptance of the idea made those mental calisthenics seem silly. After all, Russell wasn't a timid teenager asking for an advance on his allowance. He should have required neither permission nor justification to attend a company convention. There was nothing whatsoever unusual or conspicuous about the idea. Still, Russell found himself stunned by his wife's response. And, although he did his best to mask his sudden excitement, he was unable to quell the blush flooding into his cheeks.

"What?" Tess asked, coyly.

"I don't know," Russell stammered. "I just..." He was at a loss for words.

"You didn't think I'd let you go. Right?"

"Well," he said, a smile of admission involuntarily blossoming on his reddening face, "it's not... you know... I don't usually..." At this moment, Tess seemed so much more than a wife. She was also a friend, a cohort, a loving, loyal booster. Albeit, she was also a friend who thought she knew him when, in actuality, she really didn't. Russell's heart overflowed with an expanding mixture of emotion: equal parts love for his supportive life partner blended with remorse for the bubble of isolation within which he'd been living for so long. It felt like a five-gallon jug was sitting on his chest. He longed to uncork the vessel, knock it over, and spill it all out, to cut loose and gush the real reason he was so eager to go to Austin... that he was hoping to have a one-night stand with someone he had yet to meet. He wished to be free to confess that, for years now, he'd been a secretive, compulsive, masturbating voyeur, but that standing on the sidelines, observing, and pleasuring himself was no longer enough.

Instead, all Russell could say was, "Thanks, Babe. Ed's gonna be happy about this."

FIFTEEN

"**D**o I smell bad? What's the deal?" The woman's vocal timbre — throaty and nasal in the same utterance — was a clue. Add a certain snide lilt and her identity was unmistakable. This was Russell's fourth Mary Ann sighting of the day. And, it was only lunchtime. Sighting #1 had taken place during the pre-dawn hours, while the two convention-bound co-workers stood in the Delta Airlines check-in line at Nashville International Airport. That interaction comprised brief, obligatory half smiles of recognition. Neither barely awake party felt obliged to devote breathe to a "Hi, how ya doin'?"

The second sighting was equally inconsequential. Having just received his official convention lanyard and swag bag, he was slaloming his way through the teeming lobby outside the Brazos Ballroom. Every "excuse me" and "sorry" fell on deaf ears, as fellow conventioneers were cocooned in their own little universes and/or busy jabbering away with cronies. In the midst of this human ant hill, Russell recognized a familiar face: Mary Ann, immersed in conversation with two rather important-looking gentlemen. Russell's snap presumption — that her acquaintances held some superior status — was based upon the fabric and tailoring of their suits and the purple color of their convention ID tags. Mary Ann appeared to be on familiar terms with them, evidenced by the ease of the trio's ongoing verbal exchange and the manicured hand she casually placed on the forearm of the better-looking, presumably younger of the pair. As Russell drew nearer, Mary Ann sent him a coy, tip-of-the-fingers wave and a saucy grin. Suddenly wishing for invisibility, Russell pretended he hadn't seen her and pushed on toward the entrance to the ballroom to take a seat for the welcome session.

Had he been asked in advance to guess the exact paint-by-numbers script of the morning convention kick-off, Russell wouldn't have missed a lick. Predictably, the festivities opened with a bombastic video, professionally (i.e. expensively) produced and screened at earth-shaking volume. The mini-movie's voice over — Russell was relatively certain the narrator was Kevin Spacey — and visual content recounted highlights from the company's 80-year history, lauded the quality and integrity of its line of products, and updated the workforce as to progress on the construction of an ostentatious new corporate headquarters. This sensory assault was followed by back-to-back, tiresomely redundant welcome addresses delivered by a tag team of department heads. Essentially, the takeaway from this 90-minute, marathon blather fest was, "We're the best company in the entire world, and you are the best of the best because you made the brilliant choice to show up here today." In actuality, the message of the entire morning could have been distilled down to two, vapid, self-congratulatory syllables: "*Yay, us!*"

"Alright!" bellowed the Vice President of Marketing, a tall, gaunt woman, with an angular, geometric haircut and a nose sharp enough to slice ham. "Here he is! The man you've been waiting for! The one! The only... *Jeff Foxworthy*!"

After the obligatory "How's everybody doin'?" patter, the blue-collar comic launched into a series of one-line jabs targeting the sales profession. The raucous nature of the crowd's response proved there's nothing an audience enjoys more than being the butt of a comedian's lowbrow punchlines. After the fifth "... you might be a redneck" joke, Russell rose from his seat, sidled to the end of the row, and commenced legging toward the nearest exit. This early escape facilitated Mary Ann sighting #3. This time she didn't notice

Russell's presence, as all of her attention, and that of her dreamy friend with the purple ID tag was focused, not on the jokester in the spotlight, but on one another. The sexual chemistry between them was apparent.

Thirty minutes later, Russell stood, tray in hand, pondering a weighty decision: to partake, or not to partake of the pasta salad. It was at this moment of indecision that Mary Ann sneaked up behind Russell to say hello by way of an acerbic query: "Do I smell bad? What's the deal?"

"Oh, hey, how're ya doing?" Russell responded. "I wasn't avoiding you."

"Yes, you were," she argued, with a self-conscious titter. "Not that I care or anything." As they grazed their way from coleslaw to Caesar salad, mashed potatoes to baked, and pulled pork to chicken wings, Russell and Mary Ann kept their banter to mundanities. *How's your room? What floor are you on?* That sort of thing. They shared a laugh over the cheap, ill-fitting toupee worn by one of the flight attendants on their pre-dawn Delta flight. Although Russell was dying to find out the identity of the handsome hotshot in the expensive suit, he decided not to pry. Arriving at the desserts, Mary Ann quickly selected a slice of strawberry cheesecake. "Well, all I can say," she remarked, "it's a big relief that you're here instead of Ed."

"You really don't like him, do you." Russell was stating the obvious.

"Do *you*?" she retorted.

Russell was reluctant to say something negative, especially something that might get back to the office. "I can take him or leave him, I guess."

"But, you'd rather leave him, right?"

"Honestly, Mary Ann," Russell answered, an impish smile spreading across his face, "I'd rather the dumb ass just walked off into the sunset, never to return." Giving voice to his unvarnished opinion felt liberating.

"You know what, Deacon?" Mary Ann said. "You're an odd duck. But you're okay."

Russell detected an unprecedented note of earnestness in the woman's voice. He might have taken offense at her characterizing him as odd, had it not seemed backhandedly affectionate, not to mention accurate. *She's absolutely right,* Russell thought to himself, *I am odd... and in more ways than Mary Ann could possibly imagine.* "Even though I'm the most depressed person you've ever met," he quipped.

"You know the old saying," she hinted, playfully.

"I know a lot of old sayings," Russell parried, hoisting a chocolate brownie onto his tray with a pair of tongs. "Which old saying are we talking about?"

Mary Ann's hazel eyes darkened to a shade of brown. Russell noticed an almost imperceptive quiver in her lower lip. "It takes one to know one," she said. Having let her impenetrable protective shield slip, Mary Ann felt the sudden impulse to distance herself. As he watched her strut away, Russell could have sworn she was putting a little extra swing in her shapely posterior for his benefit. There was a certain irony in Mary Ann's evident need to be desired by persons of the opposite sex. That such a strident feminist so frequently and so intentionally summoned up her feminine wiles to gain advantage whenever it suited her seemed a bit unfair. Putting that lovely backfield in motion served as a reminder to Russell that she was in charge and not about to let a peer, especially a male peer, get too close.

Still, Russell detected a thread of connection beginning to solidify between himself and this enigmatic female office mate. And that, should this intuition prove itself correct, would make for an intriguing turn of events.

The remaining Friday agenda offered an á la carte menu of workshop options. Simultaneous seminars retreaded such tired topics as mining for prospects, cold calling, and closing the deal, tricks of the trade that hadn't evolved substantially in centuries. Experience had informed Russell that, at its essence, the insurance game was one based on personal relationships. Once inside the door, the most essential quality the peddler can possess is likeability. Only when a prospect feels comfortable with the solicitor can a sense of trust be burgeoned. And it should go without saying that most prospective buyers are reluctant to open up the company coffers to someone they suspect is there for the sole purpose of selling them a line of goods. Russell knew that getting the combination to the vault begins with asking key questions and listening comprehensively to the answers. Rather than trying to convince the buyer that they need his wares, the successful salesman offers his product as the perfect solution to the client's stated problems. Russell could easily have delivered the convention's keystone address — proposed title: "Be Your Prospect's Superhero."

As Russell's impetus for coming to Austin had nothing to do with re-stoking his motivational fire or refining his sales techniques, he spent his afternoon hours slipping into and out of one workshop after another. With his gaydar antenna raised, Russell visited meeting spaces with names like Trinity, Colorado, Llano, San Jacinto, and Guadalupe. Even prior to entering and subsequently exiting the Rio Grande Room, Russell had begun to recognize the foolhardy nature of such an exploratory mission. With participants seated at long tables or in rows, their attention focused on a facilitator and a PowerPoint projection or, at times, engaged in group breakout exercises, there was little chance of gleaning much, if anything, about any individual, or of detecting some personal trait that might recommend a candidate for a potential one-night stand.

The day's sessions were coming to a close. Russell was standing unzipped at a urinal, silently berating himself for having considered using such a ludicrous reconnaissance strategy to sniff out a potential same-sex partner. "Fucking idiot!" he muttered. Hearing his self-recrimination reverberate off of the tile walls only reinforced an ever-growing feeling of alienation. Still, he couldn't help but chuckle at his folly, as he hovered over the piss basin with his dick in his hand — the very dick he came to the Omni Barton Creek Resort hoping to expose to someone else with a dick. The last echo of the urinal's automated flush was still fading when Russell heard the squeaking hinges of an opening stall door. A large man, convention lanyard dangling from his neck, stepped out of the stall. "Mind sharing what's so funny?" he requested. "I'm so bored, I could really use a laugh about now."

Russell prided himself on his ability to pick up on regional accents. Of late, he'd been developing a keen ear for vocal inflections from the upper Midwest. This fellow's enunciation of the word "laugh" — the vowel sound more akin to how most Americans pronounce "cat" — led Russell to surmise that he either resided in the Chicago area or had spent his formative years near there. "I know," Russell responded. "Shit's a total waste of time." As he applied liquid soap to the palms of his hands, Russell gave his fellow hand washer a quick once over. Approximately six foot two, Russell guessed, two-hundred and forty pounds, give or take five. The man's carriage and broad shoulders suggested that he might have participated in collegiate athletics. His soft, pear-shaped midsection suggested that, since then, he could very well have developed a weakness for deep-dish pizza.

"I mean, what do these dickwads think..." the big man asked, "that we're children?" He seemed delighted to have a sympathetic captive audience for his exasperation. "It's like we've never been on a fucking sales call before."

"Which is exactly why I never come to these things," Russell interjected.

The man, who had finished washing up, was now scrutinizing his reflection in the mirror, trying to tamp down an uncooperative cowlick. "Why'd you come to this one then?" he inquired.

Russell had been taking notice of the thick crop of black hair on the back of the man's hands and fingers. The aroma of bleach combined with the proximity of a large, swarthy adult male triggered an automatic stirring in his groin area. "I'm sorry," Russell apologized, "what was your question?"

"You said you never come to these things," the man said. After bank-shooting his balled-up damp paper towel into the waste bin, he looked at Russell with a goofy, lopsided grin. "And, yet, here you are."

"Yeah," Russell answered, returning a smile. "Long story. Long, tedious story." *Why*, Russell wondered, *is this guy so interested in me? Am I imagining things? Or is there something subtly flirtatious going on here?*

"Can't be any more tedious than the crapolla I've been sitting through for the last three and a half hours," commented the swarthy fellow.

Russell read the man's ID tag aloud. "Giuseppe Gallo. Naperville, Illinois." To compliment his own regional dialect identification skills, he added, "Yep, just as I suspected,"

"Just as you suspected?" Giuseppe Gallo figured out the answer to his own question before he even finished asking it. "Oh, you're clever, Russell Deacon from Mount Juliet, Tennessee," — this, of course, the man was reading from Russell's tag — "I say a couple-a words and, voilá!"

"It's a gift," Russell boasted, in jest.

"I'm impressed," the big man said. "But they got my ID tag wrong."

Russell needed clarification. "So, you're not Giuseppe Gallo from Naperville, Illinois?"

"No, no, no... I mean, yes. I *am* him. Guilty as charged. But everybody calls me 'Guy.' I asked them to put Guy Gallo on the ID. And..."

"They screwed it up." Russell finished his thought. "Well, hello, Guy," he said, extending his newly washed hand for shaking. "You can call me Russ, or Rusty, or Russell... or Dickhead, if that floats your boat."

"Okay then," Guy responded, enveloping Russell's hand in his own over-sized mitt. "Nice meeting you, Dickhead."

As the two men stepped out of the restroom, throngs of conventioneers were filing from the conference rooms into the corridor. "So," Russell queried, "what brings you down here? You know, since you hate these gatherings so much."

"Well, when you've got six kids," Guy joshed, "you'll do pretty much anything to get out of the house."

Russell's nether region immediately stopped tingling. Betrayed by wishful thinking, he'd been tricked into picking up false signals. This super-affable "Guy" was, Russell re-assessed, as straight as a "Guy" gets — extra disappointing, as this swarthy Chicago bear so perfectly matched Russell's physical ideal. The smile Russell muscled onto his mug was insincere, bordering on cynical. "Well, Guy Gallo, from Naperville, Illinois," he said. "Maybe we'll run into each other again over the next day or so."

"If Dickhead plays his cards right," Guy quipped.

"Hey, Deacon!" Russell turned his head. The person calling his name was Mary Ann, legging it down the hallway, accompanied by a talkative gaggle of attractive female cohorts. "We're all going to karaoke at seven," she informed him, as she and her posse swept past. "You should join us."

"Yeah," Russell replied. "Maybe I will." "Maybe" meant that Russell had no intention of even considering showing up. He saw no upside whatsoever to the inevitable humiliation of attempting to carry a tune in a public place or, worse yet, suffering through an evening of drunken, tone-deaf renderings of "I Will Survive," "Eye of the Tiger," and "Friends in Low Places."

"Who's the babe?" queried Guy.

"Our office feminist," Russell informed him.

"She's got the hots for you," Guy opined.

"I seriously doubt that," Russell countered. "Anyway, I'm not remotely interested."

"Really?" the girthy man with the hairy knuckles seemed genuinely surprised and, somehow, oddly pleased to hear Russell say this. "Tell you what," Guy proposed. "If you go, I'll go."

Russell now found himself facing a very real and unexpected dilemma. Tonight would be the first of two precious nights he would have to fulfill his goal. Hanging out with a bunch of rowdy, inebriated, presumably straight insurance associates, all engaged in a degrading activity he'd always considered unworthy of anyone's time didn't seem like the best use of his. And, allowing Friday night to slip away would definitely ratchet up the pressure to make Saturday night count.

"Come on, Man," Guy cajoled. "What else ya gonna do? Sit in your room and jack off to pay-per-view porn? Let's you and me have us some fun."

The bedside alarm clock read 7:52 p.m. It took Russell a full minute to remember where he was... a hotel room at the posh Omni Barton Creek Resort in Austin, Texas. He then realized that, on top of being muddleheaded and disoriented, he hadn't eaten dinner and was in desperate need of a shower. His next revelation was the most distressing one of all: he had been napping away valuable hours that should have been devoted to his quest.

Russell sprang up and off of the mattress, shedding articles of clothing as he scooted from bed to bathroom. He was turning on the shower spigot, when his cell phone rang. It was Tess, concerned that he hadn't yet touched base. Having received assurance that her hubby had reached his destination safely, she requested an update on how day one of the conference had gone. Russell gave her a rosy (almost entirely fabricated) report about the grandeur of the resort, how hilarious Jeff Foxworthy's stand-up routine had been, and the elucidating nature of the afternoon's workshops.

"Are you making any new contacts?" she inquired. The subtext in her question was obvious. Tess had learned the value of strategic networking. And, while Russell knew this was why his wife had so enthusiastically supported his attending the convention, she could have taken a thousand guesses and never touched on the precise kind of networking he had come to Austin to affect.

Regardless, Russell came up with an ideal (and mostly truthful) answer that balanced Tess's need to mouth a silent "I told you so" against his need to terminate the call as quickly as possible. "Absolutely!" he responded. "In fact I'm already late for a meeting with an agent from Chicago. He and I are gonna have a drink and compare notes."

"Great!" Tess exuded. "That makes me very happy!"

"Good. I'm glad," Russell said, ginning up his zeal for her benefit. "Gotta go. Hug the boys for me."

He was hastily pushing the disconnect button on his phone, when he heard, "I love..."

"Shit!" he exclaimed, before ducking under the steamy, luxurious water.

SIXTEEN

Shortly after nine p.m., Russell stood alone on the downtown sidewalk, with a repetitive refrain of self-doubt looping inside his head. The sound of cacophonous revelry spilling out of Ego's Bar was less an invitation to join the Friday-night merrymaking and more a reminder of how alone and out of place he felt. He closed his eyes and inflated his lungs with brisk evening air. On his exhalation, he gave himself a little pep talk: "No turning back now, Russell." He opened his eyes and turned toward the venue's blue door. The first stride was the hardest one. Each subsequent step picked up additional momentum. "You can do this," he self-coached, reaching for the handle.

As he stepped from the cold, inhospitable pavement into the dense, steamy air of the packed club, Russell immediately recognized the strains of Johnny Cash's "Folsom Prison Blues" being rendered in a resonant, flat-toned baritone. "I killed a man in Reno," crooned the man onstage, "just to watch him die." Enthusiastic hoots and hollers resounded off the exposed ventilation pipes tracing across the club's trendy, exposed, industrial ceiling. Russell took note of how the singer's enunciation of the words "watch" and "die" emanated from the back of his mouth and upper cheeks. *This guy might be lamenting a murder he committed in Nevada*, Russell surmised, *but that vocal musculature had definitely been formed in the vicinity of northern Wisconsin, Michigan, or Illinois.* Russell scanned across the room, hoping to locate a familiar visage... specifically Mary Ann. However, as he surveyed the space, his sight line found another face, not nearly as familiar as his female coworker, but still freshly memorable: the man on stage, holding the microphone, belting, "... and I'd let that lonesome whistle... blow my blues away." To the rowdy approbation of the liquored-up crowd, Guy Gallo, clad in a plaid flannel shirt and khakis, handed the microphone to the karaoke host, tossed a diffident wave to his newly won devotees and lumbered down off of the platform.

"Let's hear it for Chi-town Guy, everybody!" bellowed the host. "That was da bomb!"

A trio of college-age girls took the stage next. "Sorority sisters," Russell presumed, chuckling to himself. As the over-served threesome launched into a shrill, semi-unison version of something vaguely resembling Sinead O'Connor's "Nothing Compares 2 U," Russell snatched a freshly vacated stool at the long, hardwood bar and resumed scanning the crowded tables for Mary Ann. The inebriated vocal trio was nearing the end of a sour, slurred performance when one of them abruptly burst into tears and wilted onto the stage floor. There, she sat, sobbing, shoulders roiling, legs splayed, her hardly there skirt now covering even less than it had the moment before her collapse. It seemed evident that the young lady was far more concerned about her shattered, aching heart than her lavender-colored panties being exposed to one and all. Russell wondered if the same break-up that had buckled the brokenhearted girl's knees had also figured into this particular song choice. Then, this sad tableau became even more undignified. As her two girlfriends crouched down to provide aid and comfort, the weeping one thanked them by projectile vomiting onto their legs and shoes.

For the audience — until now, fully enrolled in an evening of alcohol-fueled, escapist diversion — this bilious piece of performance art proved to be an immediate buzzkill. Ego's weekend decibel level quickly attenuated down to the low-frequency hum of a weekday afternoon. An impromptu intermission was declared, allowing an interim takeover of the stage by an employee wielding a mop, bucket, and rags. In the corner of his eye, Russell spied Mary Ann bolting out through the front door, her gal-pal gang hot on the spiked heels of her black-leather, knee-high, fuck-me boots.

By the time Russell exited onto the sidewalk, Mary Ann's contingent was nowhere to be seen. Russell's throat tightened. A heaviness filled his chest. If he'd heard the club door opening, then shutting with a weighted thud, he'd taken no notice. "There you are, Dude!" Startled, Russell turned around. Although Guy Gallo had suggested they convene for karaoke, Russell hadn't come to Ego's for that purpose, in spite of what he'd told Tess on the phone. If he happened to run into "Chi-town Guy," great. If not, no big deal. Now, Russell couldn't remember the last time he'd been this delighted (and relieved) to see a familiar, friendly face. Guy, on the other hand, had been counting on hanging out with his new acquaintance from Nashville. "So glad to see you, Buddy!" Russell noticed the baritone modulating into tenor territory. "Been keeping my eyes peeled for you all night."

Russell could feel the scales of isolation molting from his chest. "Good job on the Johnny Cash tune," he said.

"Oh, you heard that?" Guy smiled and nodded, hoping for more detailed praise.

"It was great," Russell said. "You nailed it. Everybody loved it."

"Well, thanks," Guy said. "Thanks a bunch. That means a lot... coming from you."

Coming from you... What in the world, Russell wondered, *could Guy have meant by that*? They had only met that afternoon... and, only for a few minutes, in a hotel men's restroom, both having escaped the tedium of the afternoon workshops. Did Russell's approval actually mean that much to this jovial fellow from suburban Illinois? *If so, why*? Still, Russell observed, if Guy was equally as inflated with hot air as are most run-of-the-mill peddlers, he'd definitely developed superior acting skills. Russell prided himself on the precise accuracy of his bullshit detector. And this fellow was pushing the needle right past "BS" and pinning it firmly inside the "Sincerity Zone."

Two insurance salesmen, who had met by chance just five hours earlier, now sat side-by-side in the backseat of a Yellow Cab. "Hey. When we get back," Guy proposed, "how about we check out the jacuzzi and the sauna?"

This was, hands-down, the best idea Russell had heard all day. "If the spa's still open," he replied, without hesitation, "abso-freakin'-lutely!" He hid his smile by looking out the window at the lights reflecting on Lady Bird Lake.

It was approaching 11 when Russell entered the pool area to find Guy neck-deep, leaning back, eyes closed, luxuriating in the bubbles, a blissful grin stretched across his face. Russell began easing in, toes first. It took a full minute for his chilled skin to acclimate to the 104-degree water. Finally, fully submerged, he let out an enormous sigh of satisfaction.

"This is the life, right?" Guy remarked. After a minute of luxurious silence, Guy resumed the conversation. "So, Russ... Mind if I call you Russ?"

"I'm pretty sure I gave you permission to call me whatever... Russell, Russ, Rusty. Dickhead, if that's what floats your boat."

"I don't think I know you well enough to do that," Guy said. "But, I'd like to."

"You'd like to call me Dickhead?" Russell was only half joking. "Or, you're saying you'd like to get to know me well enough..."

"Well... that's an interesting question." Guy's foot found Russell's on the floor of the tub. Russell immediately intuited that this game of footsie was not accidental. When neither man withdrew his extremity from contact, their eyes met in silent understanding. The actual dickhead between Russell's legs immediately took its cue to leap to attention. At this moment of unspoken connection, the pool door sprang open. Four middle-aged women traipsed noisily into the pool area, all caped in terrycloth robes embroidered with the resort's logo. The tiled space, which prior to their entrance had been placid enough for quiet conversation, was now resounding with high-pitched jabber. Subjects at hand: husbands, or maybe ex-husbands. Guy and Russell traded lascivious smiles before simultaneously bursting into guffaws. After a good belly laugh, Guy asked, "What do you say we go up to my room?"

Russell's heart was pounding. He responded affirmatively with a nod. "I may have to give it a minute, though."

"Oh, sure. You just got in. I mean... we've got all night."

For Russell, this seemed too good to be true. Was the entire purpose of this weekend's mission about to be fulfilled, effortlessly, like an answered prayer? "I'd be outta this tub in a hot second," Russell elaborated, "except..." He stole a quick side glance to check if any of the ladies were looking. Seeing them still fully engaged in their ongoing chatter, he grabbed Guy's paw, pulled it under the teaming water and to his crotch.

"Oh, Lord!" exclaimed the big man, squinting his eyes and licking his lips. "That's the dickhead I *really* wanna get to know." Without warning, Guy dove into the bubbling water with the grace of a walrus scooting off a rock on its belly. A tsunami wave wafted onto Russell's face and jacuzzi water flooded onto the concrete decking. Russell suddenly worried that this whale-sized man was about to go down on him. Instead, Guy surfaced on the far end of the tub, stood up, leaned his head back like a supermodel posing for a *Sports Illustrated* cover shot, ran his pudgy fingers through his wet hair and shook his head, shedding large drops of water in every direction. As he mounted each stair, the level of the pool diminished discernibly.

Russell wiped the chlorinated water from his bleary, stinging eyes to see the big man poised on the edge of the tub in a wide stance, his carpeted belly suspended over a tiny, black Speedo bathing suit. At that moment, Russell was thinking, *This is, without a doubt, the sexiest man I have ever seen.*

A mismatched pair of barefoot, dripping, swimsuit-clad 40-something men hustled down the flagstone path from the pool enclosure to the main building, tittering like a couple of teenage pranksters under a Halloween harvest moon. The lateness of the hour found the hotel corridor devoid of bustle and clamor, as they stole their way to the elevator. There was nothing unusual or improper or the least bit suspicious about what they were doing. They were, after all, legitimate guests of the resort. But, knowing where they were headed and what was likely to happen when they got there had them feeling like a pair of naughty children making a midnight raid on the cookie jar.

Russell had been groped by men before. Every previous time, his immediate response had been, first, to take a stride back and, if necessary, swat the unwanted hand away. Invariably, these confrontations had been awkward, often resulting in hurt feelings (for the aggressor) and pangs of guilt (for Russell, aware that his mixed signals had probably invited the groping in the first place). Nobody thus far, however, had been as assertive as Guy Gallo. As soon as the elevator car began its ascent, the Chicago bear's right paw was fondling Russell's package, squeezing his rock-hard erection through his wet swim trunks. This time, Russell didn't step away, nor did he put up any resistance. "Wow!" he remarked. "You're really raring to go!"

Guy put his left hand on Russell's cheek, looked down into his eyes, and said, "It's not often that I meet a Russell." A unique blend of emotions resounded in the big man's voice: equal parts carnal desire and sincere gratitude. It was as though Chi-town Guy had tapped into a state of being Russell had always suspected might be attainable but, for him, would forever remain out of reach.

Inside the room, Guy wasted no time. Pinning the smaller Russell against the door, he dropped to his knees and proceeded to tug Russell's swimming togs down to his ankles. Russell did his part by stepping out of the still-damp trunks, and sweeping them aside with a big toe. Fantasy and reality were uniting as one. Russell had only dreamed this scenario. Now, he was completely naked in the presence of another grown man, under the implicit understanding that they were about to engage in consensual sex. Something of concern occurred to Russell. "You're clean, right?" he asked.

"Of course," the man on his knees responded. With this utterance, Russell felt Guy's hot tongue and breath tickle his genitals. The big man proceeded to nibble eagerly but gently at Russell's scrotum, which sent electric currents of arousal rippling up through Russell's belly, chest, and shoulders.

"Because," Russell insisted, "I can't risk... you know, I can't be catching something and taking it home... OH, MY FUCKING GOD!" The Chicago bear was deep throating Russell. "How do you *do* that?"

"Shhhh!" Guy shushed. "Just enjoy it." Once again, Russell's entire eight inches disappeared within the man's mouth.

"I am," Russell insisted. "I'm... My god, you're really good at this."

"And, you," Guy responded, now licking the shaft, "have a beautiful cock."

"A match made in heaven, I guess." Russell wasn't one to talk during sex. This situation, however, felt different. Part of his chattiness was born of nerves. It was also a way of staving off premature ejaculation. He was feeling genuine passion for this jumbo-sized, woolly Midwesterner. Should he spill his load too quickly, Russell worried that his feelings might change, that he might even feel the urge to beg off and run. He hadn't, after all, come all the way to Austin for a cum-and-go, wham-bam-thank-you-man encounter. The man delivering the blowjob gagged loudly. "I'm sorry," Russell said.

"No worries," Guy reassured him, "I love it. I want every inch of this gorgeous thing." The big man climbed to his feet, took Russell by the hand, and led him to the bed.

"Don't you want to take off your suit?" Russell queried.

Guy looked down at his yet-to-be-removed Speedo. "Oh," he said, "it's not important."

"Come on! I came here to get naked with you!" Russell slipped his fingers inside the sides of the tiny, tight swimsuit, pulling them down over the man's thick thighs. What he saw between those stout legs was surprising. Not only was Guy's penis on the small side, it was still flaccid.

"Like I said, it's not important." A sad, apologetic grin crept across Guy's lips. "I take a statin. For my blood pressure."

"Do you ever get hard?" Russell inquired.

"Sometimes," Guy confessed. "But never for long. I like to have my nipples sucked and pinched, if you really want to, you know... get me aroused. Mostly, though, I just love sucking dick."

"Well," Russell responded, with a smile, "I love fondling and sucking hairy man boobs."

"So, you were right," the big man chuckled. Russell's bemused expression begged for clarification. "We *are* a match made in heaven."

Russell pushed Guy back onto the bed, splayed his big legs, fell on top of his barrel chest, and kissed him on the lips. "Thanks for inviting me to your room," he said.

"Hey," Guy responded, "like I said, it's not often that I meet a Russell."

"And, I've *never ever* met anyone like Giuseppe Gallo."

Russell awakened to the sound of the toilet flushing. Guy shuffled out of the bathroom yawning, still clad in nothing but his triple-XL birthday suit. Although the pair had spent the entire night bound in man-on-man intimacy — Russell, for the first time in his life — neither of them had reached their climax. Instead, both men had felt an immutable, visceral yearning to fuse together into one quarter-ton, amoebic blob of human nerve endings.

"Good morning, Sunshine," crooned Russell.

"What happened to 'Sugar Bear'?" Guy pretended to pout, as he slipped back under the covers to spoon his cool belly against the warmth of Russell's backside.

"I've decided that Sugar Bear is your nighttime nickname," Russell teased, sleepily.

"I see," Guy said, exhaling warm, moist breath into Russell's ear. Russell's soldier immediately responded in the only way it knew how. The bear's paw was immediately drawn to it as if the erection had its own gravitational pull.

Russell felt a gurgling in his abdomen. "Hey," he began, "this may sound kinda weird..."

"I'm listening."

"Okay," Russell said. "How do I put this? Guess I'll just say it." Sudden nervousness only increased his level of arousal. He swallowed hard for courage. "Wanna watch me jerk off?"

"Damn straight I do," affirmed the big man. "Pun intended... or *not* intended, whichever way you take it."

Noticing something hard poking him just below his buttocks, Russell reached his hand down to investigate. "What have we here?"

"Well," Guy answered, "I haven't taken my lovastatin yet."

"So, that means..."

"We'll see. Sometimes I'm good for five, maybe ten minutes."

Russell rolled over on his back and threw off the covers, exposing his lower extremities. Looking into Guy's watery brown eyes, he removed the big man's hand from its fluffing duties and filled his palm with saliva. Guy took the cue to kick the covers off of his side of the bed. Russell looked down. The appendage that had appeared so meek and miniscule seven hours ago now stood stout, solid and fully erect. The two men lay side by side, calves entwined, observing each other as they shamelessly pleasured themselves.

"Oh, God!" The big man exuded the surprised delight of a man gazing upon a winning lottery ticket. "I'm gonna cum!"

Guy's boyish joy inspired Russell to summon up his coaching skills. "Go for it, Baby! Blow your wad!" As milky white spunk shot onto Guy's stomach, he growled, as if doing his best impression of the bear he so resembled. "Oh, yeah!" Russell exclaimed. "Now, it's my turn." Guy smiled dreamily as Russell closed his eyes and quickened his stroke. Russell came with a moan that rose from deep within the center of his core. It was physical *and* metaphysical, erupting simultaneously from gut and soul. Just when he thought he couldn't possibly experience any greater bliss, Guy's lips met his, and they feasted on each other's tongues like two ravenous prisoners breaking a monthlong hunger strike.

"So, does your wife know?" Russell was toweling off. Guy had just stepped into the shower.

"That I'm bi?" the big man asked.

"Yeah," Russell was unsure how to broach the subject, or whether bringing it up was even allowed. "Or, you know, that you do this sort of thing... like when you're at a convention, or whatever."

"She knows."

Guy's blasé matter-of-factness sent a pang of envy through Russell. "So," he continued to pry, "you tell her about it? Or..."

"Not exactly," Guy responded. "But, she knows... or, let's say, she probably assumes."

"And, how does she feel about it?"

"We have a certain arrangement."

"What kind of arrangement?"

Guy's tone turned impatient and dismissive. "Look, Man. You and me... we had a good time together. It was fun. But let's just leave it at that. And let's just keep our wives out of it. Okay?" Russell felt wounded, as if he'd gotten a sharp slap on the back of the hand from Mommy while attempting to purloin a handful of Cheetos too close to dinner time. However, that brief sting was quickly replaced by a sense of relief. He'd achieved his goal, having enjoyed the exact experience he'd come to Austin in search of. And, it had not been a disappointment. In fact, one night in bed with this Chicago bear turned out to be far more fulfilling than he could ever have expected. Now, his comrade in this secret alliance was assuring him there were no strings attached. He was free to walk out of this room without looking back, which had to be the best outcome possible.

Guy was still in the shower reprising Johnny Cash as Russell wriggled his cool, still-damp bathing togs up over his knees. He patted the sheets goodbye, inhaled deeply, rose to his feet, exhaled, pulled the trunks up the rest of the way, and sneaked quietly to the door.

SEVENTEEN

When Mary Ann emerged from her room shortly after eight a.m., what she witnessed seemed particularly intriguing: Russell slipping stealthily into the sixth-floor hallway, still clad only in a bathing suit. This, in and of itself, would not necessarily have aroused suspicion, except that Mary Ann distinctly recalled Russell informing her that his room was on the fifth floor. She remained a silent, stationary fly on the wall observing, as he scooted, barefoot, shirtless, and oblivious to her presence, to the far end of the hall and into the stairwell.

"Hmmm," she murmured to herself, securing the strap of her valise on her shoulder and taking an intentional stride toward the elevator. She was about to pass the room from which Russell had just exited when its door abruptly reopened. Guy Gallo, still dripping from the shower, stepped out, gripping a bath towel that, due to his bulk, only partially draped his most private parts. For Mary Ann, who by now had picked up considerable forward momentum, the big man's sudden appearance necessitated a spontaneous one-footed, sideways hop to circumvent this imposing, nearly naked, human road block.

"Excuse *me*," she exclaimed. Guy, however, paid her as much attention as he would a fluttering moth — being, as he was, far more intent on surveying the entire length of the hallway, hoping to catch sight of last night's now-vanished paramour. As the elevator door slid open, Mary Ann was having a private chortle over a fresh and quite delightful awareness: Russell Deacon — perfectly predictable, impossibly dull Russell Deacon — was evidently a lot more interesting and complex than she had previously assumed.

Meanwhile, the subject of Mary Ann's private musing was entering Room 517 wearing nothing but his slightly damp swimming trunks and a dreamy grin born of post-sexual gratification. Upon seeing the blinking red message light on the bedside phone, his facial muscles automatically surrendered to gravity and his grin drooped into a grimace.

The previous evening, upon departing the room for the jacuzzi, Russell had made the conscious decision to leave his mobile phone behind — primarily to prevent the device from falling into the hot tub, but also to avoid having to answer an inconveniently timed call from home base. Although he'd traipsed down to the pool building still fixated on the idea of spending the night in bed with another man, he hadn't any realistic expectation of this aspiration being immediately realized. That the bed in his ideal vision might be in the other party's room hadn't even occurred to him.

His Nokia 2110 was not the only thing Russell had expelled from his mind. Any thought about Tess and the boys had also been set aside. For 10 consecutive, blissful hours, an all-consuming, almost magical bonding with a cuddly insurance salesman from Illinois had temporarily shorted out all strands of connection to Russell's real world in Tennessee. That flashing red light, however, was a signal that the real world hadn't forgotten about him. He picked up his cell phone with a trembling hand, only to discover notifications for five voicemail messages left at various hours of the night, all from the 615 area code.

Every worst-case scenario Russell could imagine flashed through his head: Perhaps his father-in-law's Parkinson's had taken a negative turn; or, worse yet, the old man had suddenly succumbed to that degenerative malady; or, Tess's mother had a stroke. *Fuck!* He shuttered at the specter of Rory having a bicycle accident or Hank getting pounded by school bullies. Whatever Tess was calling about, Russell was certain, must be serious. In the midst of these anxious speculations, his mind clicked into self-defense mode. Inventing a believable explanation for not answering the cell phone would be simple enough: dead battery, left it at a restaurant... any number of extemporaneous yarns would do the trick. Coming up with a credible reason why he hadn't been in his room for the entire night would require a far more inventive song and dance, a routine he would have to compose and choreograph on the spot, with a sleep-deprived brain.

However, he didn't have a single minute to collect his thoughts, let alone concoct an alibi. The bedside phone rang with such voluminous brashness that he nearly jumped out of his bathing suit... *and* his skin. Russell stood there, frozen in place. Finally, after three prolonged, ear-splitting rings, he reached down for the receiver. The hand set might as well have been a fifty-pound dumbbell as he hoisted it to his ear. On his first attempt at uttering a "Hello," his voice failed. He fought the constriction in his chest to draw a deeper inhalation. "Hello," he eked, "this is Russell Deacon." Although he was relatively certain who was on the other end of the line, he thought answering in a business-like manner might throw her off.

"Russ?" he heard Tess exclaim. "Oh, my God, *finally!*"

"Hey," Russell responded. His weak attempt at sounding affable and nonchalant was negated by gritted teeth. "Look, Babe, sorry..."

She interrupted. "You can apologize, or explain, or whatever later. I have some not-so-pleasant news." In her frantic exhaustion, Tess's voice sounded as froggy as Russell's. "And, I thought you'd want to know."

Russell sat down heavily on the edge of his still-made bed, dreading what he was about to hear. "Of course," he replied, "what's happening?"

"I couldn't sleep last night," she began, quite obviously starting to cry.

"Is it your dad?"

"No, Dad is good. Well, he's not really good. But, you know what I mean. He's the same. Which is not good. Anyway, nothing's changed." For a second, Russell breathed a little easier. Ever since his father-in-law's diagnosis, he'd been fretting the inevitability of having to be the stouthearted, unflappable rock for a wife grieving the passing of her beloved, doting, but pompous and overbearing father. "David called," Tess sputtered.

Russell's heart re-accelerated. "David?" he queried. "*Atlanta* David?"

"Yes," she said. Crying had now segued into sobbing. "Your friend and mine. David." Ever since their ill-fated lunch, Russell had worried that David might out him to Tess. Like the iconoclastic Harvey Milk, David was an uncompromisingly proud and strident gay man, and not one to suffer fence sitters. The idea that any man would remain married to a woman while acting out in secret with anonymous partners was intolerable to him. That the unwary spouse in this particular dance of deception happened to be both friend and protégé made such duplicity even more objectionable. Add that posture to those years of needless guilt David had suffered, due to young Russell's denial of his sexuality, and only one conclusion remained: *Tess is distraught because David let the queer cat out of the bag.*

Up until this moment, Russell had managed to postpone thinking seriously about coming out. When and if he should ever decide to leave the closet behind, he reasoned, it would be far enough into the future to give him more than adequate time to plan what he might say to control the narrative and ease the blow. Now, assuming he was reading the present situation correctly, he was left with two choices: either face the music and choke down a very jagged pill or make a last ditch attempt at tap dancing his way around it. "Look, Babe, I..." Russell stammered, "... can we talk about this later? David can be..."

"He has AIDS, Russ," Tess blurted through her tears. "David is dying!"

The relief Russell felt upon hearing about an old friend's fatal disease was natural and, at the same time, heartless. "Oh, God!" he exclaimed, faking concern, while singing a silent hallelujah. "That's... fucking horrible!"

"He's in the hospital; intensive care," she elaborated. "I want to... I *need* to go see him."

"Do you want me to come home early?" he offered. "I can see if I can change my reservation. It might cost a pretty penny, but..."

"How can you think about money at a time like this?" she sputtered. Serendipity had already stepped up, allowing Russell to have the exact experience he had come to Austin for. Now, his wife was handing him a perfect excuse to make an early exit. Not only would it free him from the tedium of a second convention day, catching a Saturday flight home might also serve to avoid a potentially awkward day-after encounter with the Chicago bear. But hearing the pain in his wife's voice smothered those self-serving, self-interested thoughts under a wet blanket of self-recrimination. He had, after all, spent the previous night indulging in fleeting, sensual pleasure, in defiance of his marriage vows. Meanwhile, his life partner of 14 years, the mother of his two sons, had been pacing the floor, fretting over this dreadful news, unable to reach the one person in the world she believed was capable of sharing her distress. "It's only a four-hour drive," Tess reasoned aloud. "I can take the boys. Or, they could stay with friends. We'll work it out."

"Are you sure, Babe?" he responded, "because..."

"No. There's no need for you to disrupt your trip. I mean, you must have been completely beat last night. You didn't even hear the phone!"

"Well, yeah." Russell felt like a fish that had been snagged, netted, and gasping for oxygen, only to be tossed back into the lake. Was she actually letting him off the hook without his having to scramble for a plausible explanation? "I guess I must've been dead to the world." There was a lengthy pause, during which Russell experienced a myriad of conflicting emotions, none of which were particularly self-assuring. He had entered his room five minutes earlier buzzing with warm, bubbly elation. He'd only just discovered (or perhaps reaffirmed) a part of himself that, for all of 10 hours, felt real and right. With the ring of a phone, reality had barged onto the stage and slapped him across his dopey face, as Cher did to Nicolas Cage in the movie *Moonstruck*. *Snap out of it, you fool*, reality demanded. *You thought your life was complicated and unwieldy before? I seriously doubt you're at all ready for the rollercoaster ride you just bought a ticket for.*

"Okay, well..." Tess's voice sounded slightly less upset. "I just thought you should know about David."

"That really sucks." Russell felt like a dolt for stating the obvious. But his head had turned into a junk drawer. Better, more comforting words were tangled up in the clutter. "About David, I mean." Just then, a semi-optimistic thought sparked in his head. "But, we shouldn't lose all hope. They've got those pharmaceutical cocktails. They say Magic Johnson is doing really..."

"That's how he lasted *this* long," Tess interrupted, once again losing grip of her emotions. "David's been taking AZT. For several years. But, once the cell count falls low enough..." She was unable to complete her sentence.

"I'm sorry, Babe," he said, wishing he were there to take her in his arms and assure her that everything would be alright. "I didn't know."

"Well," she snapped, "now you do." These four words, so economically chosen, seemed intentionally targeted to strike Russell in the heart. Years of practice had honed Tess's aim and made the timing of her ambush exact. This left Russell staggered by her arrow. But she didn't stop there. She knew precisely when to twist the shaft. "And, that's why I've been trying all fucking night long to reach you." By now, Russell was feeling lower than a sunbathing snake. "I mean," Tess continued, "the news may be horrible. But it's even worse being left in the dark." She paused ever so briefly before launching her final sortie. "You may not see it that way. But that's how *I'd* feel about it if I were you."

"Definitely." That's what Russell said. And, he was sincere when he said it. Tess, however, had no idea what that single word of agreement actually meant to the husband she had long trusted without a shred of doubt. He, after all, had been leaving *her* in the dark for some time, and doing so guided by a totally antithetical axiom: *What she doesn't know can't hurt her.*

Russell was just beginning to wrestle with an internal predicament he couldn't have anticipated. Until recently, closeting this private part of himself only served to enhance the anticipation and thrill of each impulsive quest for pleasure. He loved how his attraction to persons of the same sex felt so deliciously naughty. Getting away with being a bad boy provided nearly as much of a charge as the sensual enjoyment itself. Russell seldom found his private yearnings shameful. But, when he did, his shame was no more than a minor irritation, something he could shoo away with less effort than it would take to wave off a pesky fly. Refusing to be constrained by heteronormality, he preferred to think, made him special, exceptional, even superior, far more evolved than your straight average Joe. Too, Russell's queer curiosity was the only piece of his life he could call his and his alone. It was the single aspect of his day-to-day existence that didn't ask him to put his family, his job, or the Little League team first. Being selfish in the shadows was a gift he gave himself. If those forays into taboo territory constituted a crime, he rationalized, it was a victimless one. If he had been guilty of anything, it was the offence of dishonesty. But what human hasn't resorted to fabrication under certain circumstances? And, when someone does engage in deception, it's often to protect someone else from having to deal with an unsettling reality. In Russell's mind, what he'd been dishonest about came with far greater benefits — not just for him, but for anyone who might be affected — than any damage his habitual prevarication could possibly cause.

Last night, however, had unveiled a new wrinkle. Being naked with Guy Gallo hadn't felt the least bit naughty or bad or wrong. On the contrary, it felt completely right. So, what Russell had justified for so long as a harmless side interest, a pressure valve to let off steam, had now morphed into something that could no longer be so easily placed under the playful heading, "guilty pleasure." It was beginning to dawn on Russell that the secret he'd kept so neatly tucked out of sight had always been loaded with different, far greater risks than he'd ever allowed himself to imagine. So, while common parlance blithely demands that a secret can and must be kept, the real truth was becoming clear: Russell's secret had actually been keeping *him*. This cover up had never been about what he'd so frequently been driven to do. It was about the real reason he'd been driven to do those things. It was rooted in who he really was: a queer man who had yet to fully inhabit all of himself. This realization was both overwhelming and terrifying.

Russell's dilemma comprised other complexities as well. Lines in the sand he'd deliberately drawn for his own protection — and for the safety and well-being of his wife — had now been obliterated. Feasting on sweet, succulent, forbidden fruit that, for years, Russell had purposefully placed beyond his reach, meant that he was no longer the master of his cravings. This clumsy puppy of a secret he'd always managed to keep crated, or at least on a short leash, was growing too big and muscular to be confined or restrained. Now, he had a snarling, feral creature on his hands, a beast he feared was becoming too powerful and too ferocious to control.

"I'll let you know when I get to Atlanta," Tess said.

"I hope so." Russell's utterance passed his lips in little more than a whisper.

"I love you."

"I love you, too."

"Sometimes I wonder."

"Never doubt it." This, he said, more to bolster his own confidence than to reassure hers. "Hug the boys for me."

"Sure, Babe. Will do."

EIGHTEEN

As Russell squeezed himself down the aisle of the Douglas MD-11, every step seemed heavier than the one before. He was looking forward to retreating back into the familiar ecosphere of hearth and home. By contrast, the notion of reporting in to the office painted a less rosy picture. First, he would be called upon to address the staff in summary of his convention experience. That he'd avoided participation in 90% of the programmed agenda would make delivering such an account equivalent to writing a comprehensive book report based entirely on a hastily scanned CliffsNotes distillation of a tome he'd never opened. He was dreading another inevitability as well: suggestive winks, heavy-handed back slaps, and relentless cajoling from Ed and Mike. He pictured the Neanderthal duo conspiring a tag-team assault to badger "Rusty Boy" into revealing any and all juicy scuttlebutt from the Austin shebang.

After stowing his carry-on in the overhead compartment, Russell settled into his assigned window seat and proceeded to inflate his travel neck pillow. He was attempting to get the air pressure just right when a plus-sized woman wedged herself into the middle seat. It was uncomfortable enough to have her sweaty left arm and shoulder pushing against his right arm and shoulder. When she kicked off her shoes, Russell found himself struggling to breathe and beginning to feel queasy.

"Ma'am, do you mind if we trade seats?" The rotund woman with the stinky feet looked up to see Mary Ann hovering above. "I have an aisle seat over there," Mary Ann informed her. "If you don't mind, I'd like to sit next to my friend." As his erstwhile seatmate gathered her things, Russell felt somewhat conflicted. Not being forced to sit beside this over-sized, exceedingly aromatic person for the duration of the flight was a definite positive. However, he wasn't so sure that sitting next to Mary Ann would be worth the tradeoff. He'd been planning to catch some shuteye on the flight. Too, hearing Mary Ann referring to him as her friend triggered immediate suspicion.

"I hope you don't mind," Mary Ann said, clicking her seatbelt.

"Are you kidding?" Russell whispered. "I definitely owe you for that."

"No, I mean, about the 'friend' thing," she clarified.

"Well..." Russell was wondering where this conversation was going. "That was kinda strange, I guess."

"How so?"

"Look..." Russell spoke haltingly. "How do I put this? You're... kind of a tough nut to crack."

Mary Ann wasn't one to take offense or pussy foot. She got right down to brass tacks: "Right. But would you like to be friends? Or, at least, be more friendly?"

What is a person supposed to say in such a circumstance? While Russell wasn't certain that Mary Ann was trustworthy, he couldn't help but feel flattered. After years of being intimidated by this woman, she seemed to be suggesting a closer, less guarded relationship. He'd always found her fascinating; but only from a safe distance. Too, he hadn't decided whether he actually liked her, let alone that he wanted her as a friend. Then again, Russell didn't have many close friends. And, someone caring about him — other than his wife and his sons — couldn't possibly be a bad thing. *Or, could it?* "That's an interesting proposition." Russell intended this answer to be diplomatic, not flirtatious.

"Well," she retorted, "I hope you don't think I'm propositioning you."

"No, no, no, no..." Russell stammered, his cheeks and forehead flushing red. "I was just... maybe I..."

"I'm kidding," she said, with an assured, apologetic chuckle. She placed her perfectly manicured fingers on his forearm. "You can relax."

"Okay." What he really wanted to do more than anything was kick back and rest. Still, this repartee was compelling. "But what are you kidding *about*?" he asked. "Being friends? Or... you know, the other thing?"

"Oh, my God!" she exclaimed, half seriously. "You are hopeless!" Mary Ann picked up the *Sports Illustrated Magazine* from her lap and began rifling through the pages so quickly Evelyn Wood would have been incapable of gleaning any comprehensible meaning from the printed material.

"The answer is yes." Russell articulated this statement the way one does to prevent a conversation from ending, by saying what one thinks the other person wants to hear.

"Mmmmm, hmmmm," she mumbled, her eyes now fixed on a vivid, full-page photo of Scottie Pippen dunking a basketball. "Yes, what?"

"To the friends' thing," he clarified. "That actually might be cool."

"Okay," she teased. "We'll see."

This, Russell decided, might be a good time to change the subject to something less personal. "I didn't know you were into basketball."

"Well," she quipped, "keep your eyes open, Buddy Boy, you may find out all sorts of things."

"D'you think Jordan is gonna come back?" One of the most talked about sports stories of the day surrounded Michael Jordan's early retirement from the Chicago Bulls in pursuit of what turned out to be a short-lived, less-than-stellar minor-league baseball career.

"Sorry," she replied, sardonically, "I left my crystal ball at home."

"Are you a Bulls fan?"

"Nope."

"Okay."

"I'm more into college hoops," she revealed.

"Cool." Russell was pleased that Mary Ann had brought up a subject of common interest. "I've got season tickets for the Vandy games."

"Whoa, Dude!" she said, with sincere interest. "That's way cool."

"They're in the nosebleed seats. But Memorial Gym is such a blast."

"I know," she said, matter-of-factly. "I used to play there."

"Come on!" Russell felt certain she was toying with him. "You can't be serious! You played there?"

"Yep," she affirmed. "I played back-up guard for the Lady Commodores from eighty-two through eighty-five."

"No way!" Mouth agape, Russell was both blown away and incredulous.

"Way," Mary Ann contended, a la Mike Meyers in *Wayne's World*.

"I don't remember anyone named Mary Ann on those teams," he said. Then the bulb in his cranium ignited. "Mare Morgan! You're Mare Morgan?" Confirmation came in a slight nod of Mary Ann's head. Then, she provided conclusive proof by gathering her hair in a fist and pulling it back into a regulation white-girl, collegiate-athlete ponytail. "You were freakin' instant offense," Russell effused, "like an automatic three-point machine!"

"Glad somebody remembers," she said, appreciatively.

"You didn't play much 'D' though, did you."

"Hey, I'm only five-five," she protested. "Cheryl Littlejohn was six-three. Dawn Marsh and Sherry Bostic could run rings around me. For a short, slow, white girl, I think I did okay."

"Mare Morgan," Russell uttered his inner thought aloud. "Wow! I... can't believe it."

"So, enough about me," Mary Ann said, suggestively. "Let's talk about you."

Wow! A woman of accomplishment wanted to be his friend and was expressing sincere interest in his personal history. "Well," Russell began, "I was born in Topeka, Kansas. My parents..."

Mary Ann stopped Russell's aural biography in its second sentence with a "Blah, blah, blah..."

Russell presumed she was toying with him again. "Yeah," he confessed, "it's a pretty boring story. Nice guy gets good grades, wants to play baseball but stops growing in ninth grade, gets beaned by a fastball, becomes scared of the ball, can't hit the curve, goes to college, graduates, becomes an insurance salesman, falls in love with a nice girl. They get married and pop out a couple-a kids..."

"That's all very interesting. But, what I really want to hear about is..." She paused for dramatic effect. "How was your convention?"

This question didn't compute. Why in the world would Mary Ann have any interest in Russell's convention experience? "Is that really what you want to talk about?"

"It is, yes." Having no idea where to begin, Russell sat, blinking his eyes and clenching his jaw. "Did you meet any interesting people?" she probed.

Russell's neck stiffened. *Why would she be offering this prompt?* "Did I meet any interesting people?" he responded. "At an insurance convention? That's kind of a contradiction in terms, sort of a, whatchamacallit, oxymoron, doncha think?"

"Whoa... somebody sounds just a little bit defensive." Her observation was spot on. If he'd been more in command of his faculties, Russell might have countered by asking her a similar question: *Who was that way-too-handsome dude in the expensive suit with the purple ID tag?* But, his weary brain was too sluggish to go that route.

"Look," Russell managed. "I'm, I'm... I'm sorry. I'm like... really tired."

"Well, then..." she snapped, with evident condescension. "We'll just let the little boy take his little nappy."

"Thanks," Russell said, pushing his seat back, positioning his neck pillow and closing his eyes. "That's very nice of you."

"That's what friends are for."

"Mare Morgan," Russell mumbled, as he drifted off, "I can't freakin' believe it."

Mary Ann chuckled to herself. Determined to unravel the mystery of why Russell had emerged nearly naked from another man's room Saturday morning, she was already brainstorming her next scheme to get him talking.

Although the flight had been brief and relatively free of bumps, Russell was suffering a bit of jetlag on top of the fuzzy-brained malaise one often experiences after waking up from an afternoon snooze. He descended the escalator, surrounded by airport clatter and rush. At the bottom, he plodded heavily past the baggage carousels, intent on catching a shuttle ride home.

"Hey, Deacon!" He stopped to follow the sound of Mary Ann's voice and located her dragging a Louis Vuitton Pullman suitcase from the luggage carousel onto the polished concrete floor. "What took you so long, Slowpoke?"

Russell recalled being awakened, still belted into his seat. "Sir." The flight attendant's baritone voice was soft and gentle. "Wakey, wakey. Time to rise and shine." A toothy smile made a vivid first impression. Not only was the plane stationary and devoid of engine noise, he seemed to be the only remaining passenger in the coach section. A clean-up crew was busy, tidying up the aircraft for its next scheduled trip.

"Oh, jeez!" Russell mumbled, wiping a blob of drool from his chin.

"You were sacked out," the flight attendant informed him. "Welcome to Nashville."

For a moment, Russell felt like a princess in a fairy tale, having been brought out of a spell by the kiss of a handsome prince. Except, unlike storybooks he'd known as a child, there was no kiss, and this dream interrupter had ebony skin, thick, wet lips, and deep brown eyes. "Thank you," — Russell took notice of the name tag pinned to the jolly fellow's ample, uniformed chest — "Jamal."

It was suddenly evident to Russell that something inside him had changed. He was looking into the eyes of another man with new eyes of his own, eyes that automatically x-rayed through skin-deep features in search of soul-deep substance. At close examination, Jamal wasn't exceptionally attractive. There was a gap between his front teeth, his cherubic cheeks were pock-marked and his chin was on the weak side. But, Russell found something entrancing in his smile. He felt a sudden impulse to lay a lip lock on this mysterious stranger. But, he restrained himself. For an eternal five seconds, the two men gazed at one another. The flight attendant was the one to break the silence. "We have to..." he began.

"Absolutely!" Russell extended his right hand. "Russell, by the way." Jamal's palm was as cushy and comforting as his voice.

"Nice meeting you, Russell." Jamal straightened up and took a single stride toward the galley before stopping and turning around. "Maybe we'll cross paths again."

"I hope so." Russell wasn't absolutely certain he'd said this out loud. The flight attendant smiled and strutted off to finish up whatever final tasks remained.

Russell hadn't anticipated "again" happening so soon. As Jamal appeared on the down escalator, Russell's heartbeat accelerated. Instinctively, like a ragamuffin child about to meet the mayor, he licked the heel of his hand and attempted to push a shock of disheveled slept-on hair back from over his ear. From across the expanse, Jamal pranced toward Russell like a black stallion after winning the Kentucky Derby. Self-consciously, Russell avoided staring, directing his sight line toward anything but the approaching flight attendant. As Jamal swept by, pulling his carry-on bag, Russell couldn't resist giving him a quick glance, long enough to catch a wink in his direction so subtle that it would have been indiscernible to anyone but him.

Is this how it's going to be from now on? Russell wondered. In the past, he'd shared meaningful eye contact with many men. But, those unspoken messages were simple and puerile: *I'm interested in getting it on... now, no strings attached. Are you in*? But, in Austin, Russell spent an entire night with another man, during which the shared currency had been much more than touch and saliva. Names and deep intimacy were exchanged as well. From this juncture forward, eye-language would be taking on new dimensions of potential import. Russell would no longer be playing a simple game of pong. He was now engaged in a far more complex game of three-dimensional chess, with each move leading to a nearly infinite number of possible outcomes.

"He's no Denzel Washington," joshed Mary Ann, "but I could pretend if the room was dark enough." Mary Ann had sidled up next to Russell, who was standing, stone-still and lost in pensive contemplation, observing the flight attendant glide gracefully through the revolving exit door.

"Shit!" Russell responded, clutching his palpitating heart. "Don't sneak up on me like that!" In spite of having been so abruptly shaken from his trance, Russell couldn't stop gawking at Jamal who was, by now, crossing the street. As the subject of his fascination disappeared into the parking structure, the wistful sigh he emitted only added fuel to the notion Mary Ann had been formulating for the last day and a half.

"Just kidding, of course," she said, yanking her luggage toward the exit. "That one would much rather fuck you than me." Although Russell hoped she was right, he was not about to reaffirm such an insensitive quip. Oddly, although he had always felt umbrage upon hearing derisive statements like this one — more often uttered by ignorant, insecure persons of the masculine persuasion — this was the first time he'd ever taken such a remark personally. He had felt a connection with the subject of Mary Ann's mockery. Too, a recent overnight with the Chicago bear had put him in closer touch with his own queer identity.

Out on the sidewalk, Russell started toward the shuttle stop. Mary Ann, however, would have none of her "friend" having to pay for what she characterized as "a lonesome, bumpy ride home in a short bus."

"I really wouldn't want to take you out of your way," Russell responded, before gratefully accepting her offer. Although she hid it well, Mary Ann was elated, having successfully commandeered an extra 25 minutes for additional poking and prying.

"I feel bad..." Mary Ann confessed, as she merged her Beamer into Interstate traffic, "... about what I said about the flight attendant. I hope you weren't offended."

"Why would you think I'd be offended?" Although Russell *had* taken offense, even personal offense, this evasion was primarily about dissuading any insinuation Mary Ann might be making regarding his sexuality.

"Well, I'm glad you weren't." This assumption was a way of assuaging her own guilt. "I usually try to be more sensitive about these things. Live and let live... that's what I always say."

"Hmmm..." he teased. "I can't recall ever hearing you say anything of the kind."

"Well, you know what I mean." There was a slight tone of defensiveness in her voice. "I'm not... you know... one of those people."

"You're not a homophobe," he stated.

"Exactly. Thank you." This exchange was not going how Mary Ann had imagined it would. Theoretically, she'd surmised, opening the floor to a gay theme might make Russell more comfortable about revealing the spicy details she so desired to extract. Her prompt, however, had completely backfired, placing her square in its crosshairs — a stressful posture for someone whose comfort depended upon maintaining maximum control in every situation. Hoping to regain the upper hand, she tried a different approach. "So, how was life on the fifth floor?"

Russell pondered this for a few seconds, unsure where she was going with what, on its face, seemed a completely innocuous line of questioning. "Fine, I guess." Mary Ann deliberately left a chasm in the dialogue, which Russell couldn't resist filling. "Probably not much different than any other story in the hotel. Nice view of the golf course and a bunch of fat cats with putters, waddling around in pastel pants. What floor was your room on again?"

"Six," she said, "... six-thirty-four." The realization that Mary Ann had been only a few doors down while he and Guy Gallo were indulging in naked intimacy sent a jolt of paranoia through Russell's entire body. *There was no possible way she'd seen or heard something.*

Or, was there? "I really wish you'd joined us for karaoke on Friday night," Mary Ann said.

"Yeah, I took a nap," he responded, relieved by the spontaneous change of subject. "By the time I woke up, it was too late."

"There was this guy. An agent. Big dude. From Chicago, I think." With every detail, Russell's level of discomfort ratcheted up another 10 notches. "Anyway, he did Johnny Cash. The whole place went berserk. In fact, I think you may have met the guy."

"Guy Gallo." Russell didn't see much upside to pretending he didn't know who Mary Ann was talking about. After all, she'd seen the two of them standing side-by-side in the hotel corridor, outside the men's room, that very Friday afternoon. Russell's nether regions awakened at the muscle memory of the Chicago bear's warm, furry torso. "Funny man," he remarked. "Really likeable." The next pause was pregnant with twins. "Not that I know him all that well or anything."

"Well, he's not just funny. The dude can sing, too. You really missed an amazing karaoke performance." Russell hadn't missed Guy's performance. In fact, he remembered it vividly, just as he recalled witnessing Mary Ann, in her knee-high, fuck-me boots, leading a column of gal pals in a hurried exit from Ego's — this all before he'd had a chance to let her know he'd arrived; then, shivering in the frigid, October wind, feeling lonesome and forlorn, and Guy Gallo, in his plaid Pendleton shirt, coming to his emotional rescue.

As the BMW exited the Interstate, Russell chuckled to himself. If Mary Ann had been that impressed by Guy Gallo's Johnny Cash impression, he could only imagine how awed she might have been by the big man's midnight sausage-swallowing demonstration. The triple-XL-sized agent from Illinois was a man of many talents, several of which, if Russell had his way, Mary Ann would never find out about.

"What?" Mary Ann pried.

"Oh, nothing," he answered, "just a private thought."

"Nothing you can share with a friend?"

Russell saw this reprisal of the friend theme as his opening. "I tell you what," he proposed. "You fill me in about that too-good-lookin' young exec in the sharp suit first. And, maybe..."

"Noah Shapiro?" she interrupted. "What do you want to know? V.P. of corporate communications. Lives in Des Moines. Married. Wife's name is Alice. Three kids."

"You two seemed pretty cozy. Just sayin'."

"Okaaaay." Rather than ending the word, she let the vowel sound fade away. "So, what are you getting at?"

Although Russell couldn't tell if she was attempting to make light of this surprise left turn in the conversation, if she might be losing her patience or, perish the thought, was growing angry. Regardless, curiosity trumped discretion. "Could Mare Morgan" he inquired, "be a homewrecker?"

Something happened, something Russell could never have anticipated, let alone imagined witnessing. Mary Ann's steely countenance, her feminine power mask simply vanished. The hurt in her eyes was evident. Her mouth drooped into a forlorn frown. Tears collected in the corners of her eyes. Russell had discovered a heretofore unseen button, the one that lifted the curtain. The Unbreakable Mare Morgan was a real, flesh-and-blood, human woman who, if Russell was reading the tea leaves correctly, was hopelessly in love with a married man.

The vehicle sat idling in the driveway of the Deacon residence. "I'm sorry," Russell said. "I was completely out of line."

Mary Ann blew her nose, wiped her cheeks with a tissue, and forced a smile. "Well, at least I don't have to come home to a spouse and pretend something didn't happen."

"Right." In this context, precisely what Russell had just affirmed was strangely elusive, even to the man giving his agreement breath. If

Mary Ann's declaration had been intended literally, without irony or subtext, Russell's concurrence was equally direct and unambiguous in its connotation. But, if she was actually suggesting that, unlike her, Russell was returning from the convention weekend harboring a secret he would have to hide from his wife, the word "Right," although entirely appropriate and sincere, was also an admission that he was about to reenter a world of deception.

"Thanks so much for the lift," Russell said, as he yanked his suitcase out of the back seat. Mary Ann's reply was a bloodshot glance in the rearview mirror. He shut the door. As soon as Russell had cleared the path of the vehicle, Mary Ann lost no time, backed out, and drove away.

NINETEEN

"Look, Dude," Ed persisted, "all I'm saying is... come on, you can tell Uncle Eddie."

"Sorry, Bud," Russell insisted. "I'm not going there."

Ed was not ready to take no for an answer. "So, what you're saying is, you don't kiss and tell."

"If I kissed, I wouldn't tell *you*," Russell volleyed. "And, if I didn't, it's none of your damn business. Simple as that."

Ed drew so close Russell could feel the man's breath on his neck, and dialed his voice down to office-gossip volume. "Okay, then," Ed pried, "what about Mary Ann? I bet that horny little tart hooked up. Probably with some butch dyke from San Francisco."

"Finally! Something I *can* tell you about." Russell enhanced this tease by affecting a knowing grin.

"Now we're talkin'!" Ed rubbed his hands together greedily, adopting the posture of a Labrador retriever awaiting a treat for being such a good boy.

Russell leaned in. "Yeah," he whispered, as if he was about to grace Ed with the secret of all secrets. "That definitely didn't happen."

"Fuck you, Russ!" Ed fumed, executing an exasperated about-face and stomping out of the breakroom.

From Russell's first post-convention stride out of the elevator, Mike — then Ed, then Mike, then Ed again — had been badgering him mercilessly. Consistent with their mutual inclination to place odds on any variable outcome, Dumb and Dumber had made a wager as to which of them would be the first to glean even the tiniest scrap of dirty laundry from the prior weekend in Austin.

Russell locking his secret away in solitary confinement had thus far provided security for the secret. But that policy came with consequences he hadn't foreseen. Internalizing the truth for any extended period of time eventually becomes toxic for the internalizer. If an incarcerated skeleton is never freed to amble into the sunshine, it begins to fester and emit a rank odor. Russell's best-kept skeleton was busily plotting to tunnel out of its underground cell by whatever means necessary. And, should its jailer continue to deprive it of fresh air, the prisoner might have to resort to even more desperate measures, like burning the jailhouse down. The round-the-clock vigilance required to keep his secret from exposure was slowly but steadily ripping Russell in two. Day by day, one stitch at a time, the curtain dividing one side of his double life from the other was coming apart at the seams. This disintegration wasn't due to any external force. As in one of those classic horror plots, the real threat was coming from inside the house.

Two steps into the hallway, Russell put on the brakes to avoid a collision with Mary Ann. "I was just looking for you," she said. "How about you and me catching some lunch?"

"Are you sure that's a good idea?" asked Russell, attenuating his voice to thwart the eavesdroppers. "Mike and Ed are already kinda jumping to conclusions."

"Let their tiny, little monkey brains go ape shit," she jested, before breaking into a familiar Bonnie Raitt refrain: "Let's give 'em somethin' to talk about," replete with finger snaps and wiggling booty. Witnessing this heretofore hidden happy-go-lucky side of Mary Ann's personality, Russell broke into spontaneous laughter, prompting her to laugh in response. After two years of keeping their distance, these coworkers were discovering a pleasant fact: they genuinely liked each other. *Go figure*, Russell was thinking. Mary Ann's offer of friendship was actually becoming real.

"Wow," Russell remarked, "I never knew places like this existed in Nashville." He was sitting across from Mary Ann, at a long, functional, wooden table. The remainder of the bench seats at the table were occupied by strangers. Russell's eyes shifted around the room. "Where did all these weirdos come from," he kidded, "a Topanga Canyon time warp?"

"Yep," said Mary Ann. "It's a whole different planet outside the meat 'n' three world." This, in reference to the plethora of casual, cafeteria-style eateries catering to Music City's more carnivorous lunch crowd.

The pungent aroma of steamed vegetables and brown rice wafted up from Russell's plate. He sampled a bite, allowing his taste buds to luxuriate in the natural flavor. "My God!" he exclaimed, "this is *so* good!"

"I come to Country Life at least once a week," said Mary Ann, "sometime twice."

"I can see why." Russell savored a second bite. "I bet you don't see many people from the office here."

"Never," she said. "Sometimes I run into someone I know from Vanderbilt, a professor, maybe... or someone from the athletic department."

"Right, 'cause it's right next to the campus."

"This was the original Home Economics building."

"But the university doesn't run it now," Russell concluded.

"Nope. The restaurant is a co-op, I think," Mary Ann recalled. "It's actually run by some religious cult."

"Hallelujah!" Russell responded. "Maybe this food tastes so good because they sprinkle it with Jesus powder."

"As often as I eat here," kidded Mary Ann, "if they cooked with heavenly spices, I'd be standing on a corner with a bullhorn by now, spouting scripture, trying to convert the unwashed masses."

Russell was chuckling and chewing when his gut did a somersault. Several tables over, one particular face looked eerily familiar. Unable to put his finger on the person's identity, he found it impossible to cease his staring. And, the more he stared, the more unsettled he became at not being able to place the man's visage. Over the years, Russell had shaken countless hands, particularly in his capacities as insurance purveyor and Little League coach. Maybe this fellow had coached a rival team. This hypothesis made enough sense that Russell's digestive system began to settle down. Then, like the whack of Oral Roberts' palm to a believer's forehead, it hit him. The site of their meeting wasn't an office building or a baseball diamond. Their initial (and every subsequent) encounter had taken place in the men's lavatory next to the Centennial Park duck pond.

Although the majority of men who cruised the park bathrooms willingly played by a certain set of unwritten rules, a few were overly aggressive. The gangly man presently finishing a plate of vegetarian grub was, from Russell's experience, the worst of the worst. His pattern of behavior was so insolent, in fact, that Russell had learned to simply drive on when the man's vehicle was parked outside the cinder block structure. Russell's shoulders spasmed as he recalled one particularly disquieting happenstance involving this nervy fellow. "What's going on?" Mary Ann inquired, looking up from a forkful of eggplant.

"Oh, sorry," Russell said, his eyes still fixed on the gangly man, now rising from his seat. "I thought I recognized somebody."

"You never know who you're gonna see in a vegetarian restaurant, right?"

"Right," Russell concurred. "But, I don't think it's who I thought I was, after all."

By then, the gangly man was approaching the table on stork-like legs. He, too, must have identified something familiar about Russell. "Hey, how're you doin'?" he asked, in a casual baritone.

Russell's face flushed crimson. "Good... good..." he stammered, barely looking up.

"All right, you take care now," the man said, continuing toward the exit.

"He seems to know you," Mary Ann observed.

"Yeah," Russell agreed. As he loaded his fork with rice and veggies, he pursed his lips and shook his head. "Weird." Eager to change the subject, Russell blurted the first thing that popped into his head. "Heard anything from what's his name... Noah?"

Mary Ann cocked her head and squinted her eyes, as if she was appalled that a friend would intrude into such sensitive territory. "Oh, you had to go there, didn't you..." Russell held his breath. It was unclear whether she was being glib, pretending to be hurt, or if he'd carelessly poked an open wound. It was becoming apparent that part of a friendship with Mary Ann involved being left dangling in emotional limbo on a regular basis. The joyful smile blooming across her face allowed him to exhale. "He's coming to town," she squealed, like a giddy high-school girl who'd just been asked to the prom by the most popular boy in the class. "... In two weeks! I'm so excited!"

"He's using you, you know." Russell seldom articulated such candid opinions out loud. For his own self-protection, he prepared to dodge a hurled fork.

"I know," she admitted, "But, I'm using him, too. It all comes out in the wash."

"I get it," he said. And, he did.

"Do you?" she challenged. "You're married. What could you possibly know about such arrangements?"

"Oh, I'm probably a lot more worldly than you think." This was an ill-considered stab at making himself more interesting to someone who, in his eyes, always seemed beguiling and mysterious. Russell immediately regretted casting a bated hook into the lake. It was bobbing just under the surface, and he was hoping she wouldn't bite.

"Really…" These two syllables were not punctuated with a question mark. It was Mary Ann's way of saying, *Okay, tell me more.*

For a moment, Russell allowed himself to imagine how liberating it would feel to throw open the cell door and expose his truth to someone in his real world, someone sympathetic and non-judgmental. Among his friends, Mary Ann was, by far, the most likely to listen with dispassionate empathy. He couldn't imagine her thinking ill of him for following his natural inclinations. It took every bit of what was left of his resolve to not utter what he so desperately longed to say. Rather, instead of taking that imagined trust fall, he deftly changed the subject. "Mike and Ed have been stalking me like a couple of hungry hyenas. They can't stand not knowing whether anything sordid went down at the convention."

"Fuck those assholes!" Mary Ann exclaimed. "Ooops, sorry about that." Her apology was not for her profane outburst, but for the splotch of eggplant that had just flown from her mouth onto Russell's placemat. "But, really," she reiterated, "*fuck* those assholes."

"Well," Russell said, "Rest assured. Your secret is safe with me."

"*My* secret?" she inquired, raising her eyebrows. "What about yours?"

Russell's heartbeat fluttered. He wasn't at all sure where Mary Ann was going with this. He did know, however, that she had just provided him with the perfect opportunity to lift a boulder off of his chest. Instead, this question only served to re-activate a hard-wired survival response. "If I *had* a secret," he responded, "I'd sure as shit keep my yap shut about that, too."

"Yeah," she said. "You're good at that, aren't you."

"Good at what?"

"Keeping secrets," she clarified. "That's one thing I'm pretty sure we have in common."

Russell's jaw dropped visibly. He hoped the smile spreading across Mary Ann's face was an expression of affinity. But, there appeared to be a little bit of "gotcha" in the upturned corners of her mouth. As so often happened with this woman, Russell was unable to get a clear reading. Feeling unmoored and exposed, he dug in his heels a little deeper and continued his duck and weave. "If that's your way of complimenting my discretion," he countered, "I appreciate you saying so."

"No," she countered. "I was talking about keeping secrets... you know, your own, personal, *worldly* secrets." Russell stopped chewing. Why had he used the word worldly in the first place? "Tell me about Johnny Cash from Chicago," she probed. "What's he like?"

It took two gulps of peach tea for Russell to choke down the half-masticated lump in his mouth. "Well, really..." — the discretion he'd just boasted about was being put to the ultimate test — "I barely met him." Then, a pertinent detail occurred to him. "Oh, oh... he did tell me that he's got six kids." If she was harboring suspicions, Russell thought mentioning the big man's baby-making prowess might put her off the scent.

"Six kids? Jesus!" she remarked. "Dude must have a high sperm count."

"Or," Russell cracked, "he should stop buying cheap condoms."

"That's good!" Mary Ann replied, laughing aloud. "So, tell me, how does a man with that much belly even see down there to put on a condom?"

"God, I never thought about that!" Russell sputtered, joining her in peals of mirth. "Maybe he just keeps getting the damn things on wrong." By now, to the evident annoyance of nearby diners, the two guffawing friends had tears of merriment streaming down their faces. It took an entire minute for their unbridled hilarity to calm. Mary Ann exhaled a massive sigh, only to be overtaken by a series of final titters. They sat, smiling at one another across the table through tear-blurred eyes.

"I don't remember when I've had this much fun," noted Russell, as he dried his cheeks with a paper napkin.

"I know," agreed Mary Ann. "I haven't laughed this hard in years."

"Russ?" It was another voice, a third voice. The bony, angular woman addressing Russell hovered over the table, holding a tray.

"Oh, hey" he said. "Fancy meeting you here."

"That's exactly what I was about to say," the woman remarked, forcing a pinched smile. "I didn't know you were a vegetarian."

"Well, I'm not," he retorted. "But, with food this good, I'm considering converting." There was an uncomfortable several seconds of silence, as the woman lingered, her shifting eyes making the overt inference that, at this juncture, it would be appropriate for Russell to introduce her to his lunch date. In most any professional setting, Russell considered himself a master of introductions. This situation, however, was neither totally professional, nor was it purely social. His relationship with Mary Ann was rooted in business, yes. But, evidenced by the jollity they'd been sharing, it seemed evident that she was someone whose company he enjoyed.

Mary Ann, who evidently had a sixth sense for such awkward impasses, seized the initiative. "Hi, I'm Mary Ann," she offered, extending her hand. "Russell and I work in the same office."

With her hands busy balancing her lunch tray, the hovering woman could only manage a nod. "Nice to meet you, Mary Ann," she responded, shooting a squinted side glance at Russell. "I'm Judith. Tess and I... we serve together on the PTO. My daughter Heather is in Mrs. Callahan's class with Rory."

"I see." The patronizing tone in Mary Ann's voice hinted that she was already growing weary of hearing details about which she had zero interest.

"Well," Judith said, "I don't want my food to get cold."

"I'd ask you to join us," said Russell. "But..." He gestured toward his nearly empty plate.

"Yes," Judith observed, "you folks are finished." At that moment, a waving hand caught Judith's eye from a few tables over. "Oh!" she said, happily, "I see a friend!" Russell heard the relief in her voice. *Probably not simply because she won't have to dine alone*, he surmised. *Running into a friend's husband having an enjoyable lunch with an attractive, stylish, female colleague has to be somewhat discomfiting as well.* "Well," Judith said, "say 'hi' to Tess for me."

"Will do," Russell responded, with artificial good cheer. As Judith shuffled off to join her friend, Russell leaned across the table. "Thanks for that," he whispered. "I completely forgot that woman's name. I would have introduced her to you as Debbie."

Hilarity revisited Mary Ann. Judith looked back over her shoulder with the pained self-consciousness of someone who suspects they've become the butt of a joke. Russell, jaw clenched in a fixed grin to hold back his own laughter, gave her a wave. As soon as she turned back around he, too, once again surrendered to unrestrained glee.

The scheme had been hatched on the brief ride back from what had been, at least for Russell, a surprisingly pleasant meal, augmented by lively, enjoyable conversation. Mary Ann, at the wheel, had been reprising Bonnie Raitt's "Let's Give 'em Something to Talk About." Having rendered all the lyrics she could withdraw from her memory bank, she ended her a capella rendition to suggest, "What d'ya say we dangle a big juicy carrot for Mike and Ed to chase after."

"Are you saying what I think you're saying?" Russell wondered aloud.

"Why not?" she said. "Those piggies are always eager to wallow in the mud."

"But, nothing specific, right?" While Russell was reluctant to put any real meat on the rumor bone, sowing a few seeds of speculation sounded like oodles of fun. Too, it might sidetrack any notions Ed and Mike might be having about his sexual orientation.

"No. Of course not," Mary Ann confirmed. Russell's hand meeting hers in a high five — the first time he'd ever made physical contact with Mary Ann — induced an odd sensation. A split second of palm on palm reaffirmed that this icy-veined superwoman was constructed out of flesh and blood after all.

Russell and Mary Ann emerged from the elevator, mid-chat. "When that happens," Mary Ann was expounding, "you've just gotta locate the exact, perfect spot and apply just a little more pressure."

"Would that be steady pressure?" Russell inquired with mock seriousness. "Or, are you talking side-to-side pressure?"

"Mix it up," she advised. "A little of both. Whatever's working. Just pay close attention to the silent signals."

"Body language," Russell assumed.

"Exactly," she responded.

"That's really good food for thought," Russell said. "I'll keep working on it."

"But don't get me wrong." Mary Ann cranked up the volume to ensure she would be overheard. "I enjoyed it." Then, her voice adopted a slightly suggestive tone. "I really did."

"Let's do it again," Russell proposed, "soon."

"You just say the word." Mary Ann peeled off, pointing the toes of her spike-heeled boots in the direction of her office.

Mike Terzian stepped out from the breakroom into the hallway, just in time to witness Mary Ann's compact frame disappearing around a corner. "Fuck that little faggot Deacon!" he muttered, ferociously. "There's no way he's tappin' that."

TWENTY

By the time the final eulogist mounted the lectern, tributes and reminiscences had been underway for nearly two hours. Frequent gurgles from down below suggested that Russell's empty stomach was beginning to digest itself. Tess placed her hand on Russell's midsection, as if to instruct the volcanic juices within to calm themselves.

"What can I say about David Mangold," the speaker began, "that hasn't already been said this afternoon?" Tess recognized the fellow at the microphone as a key member of the core relay team that kept 24/7 vigil at David's bedside during his final weeks. The group's co-responsibility was to provide as much comfort for their dying friend as possible. This task not only included making sure David was sufficiently hydrated and taking his meds but also involved providing an adequate supply of off-color insults. She was uncertain of the man's name. *Freddie maybe? Or Teddy?* Then, thankfully, it came to her: *Edward! Yes!* Quick-witted and, like all of David's friends, fastidious of dress and grooming, Edward's eyes twinkled as he shared recollections about one of the Atlanta gay scene's most memorable characters.

"David was, among other qualities, snarky," Edward continued. "His tongue was as swift and sharp as it was merciless. And, we loved that about him."

"Most of the time," called out a voice from the crowd, triggering yet another spate of laughter.

"Let's just say," Edward said, "no one was spared from his infamous cutting sense of humor. But, underneath that tough,

I-could-give-a-shit shell, there was a soft, marshmallow heart. David cared deeply about people and wanted, more than anything else, to affect others in a positive way. If he thought there was any chance that he'd actually wounded someone, he would be wracked with guilt. He couldn't rest until he made amends, till he made things right. One night — we'd had a few libations — David shared a regret he'd been carrying around for decades. It happened way back when he was a young, hotshot exec at the P.R. company he co-founded, GRMN8. He'd grown particularly close to a young summer intern. A summer crush. Who hasn't had one of those, right?"

Russell squirmed uncomfortably in his seat as Edward proceeded to fill in the details.

"Well, evidently, David misread the signals and pushed things a little too far. Particularly awkward... because, *uh-oh*! The young buck turned out to be straight. Over time, David lost touch with him. Most people would have forgotten about it, or at least forgiven themselves. But David was sure he'd caused this guy some serious trauma. He was still experiencing remorse about it all these years later. Then, earlier this year, David happened to run into the guy. A coincidental friend-of-a-friend thing. So, David took this opportunity to finally apologize. And, the guy laughed it off. He hadn't been traumatized at all. So, David had been torturing himself needlessly for years. That's the kind of caring person David Mangold was. He just didn't want anyone to know he was such a softy. So, fuck you, David. I really would have preferred to go on assuming you were just a shallow, selfish, sarcastic bitch. But, no... you had to go and reveal your tender side to me. Well... I love you anyway. And, I'll miss you... so, *so* much. Thank you."

The memorial ended appropriately with a moving performance of "Somewhere Over the Rainbow" by members of the Atlanta Gay Men's Chorus, resulting in copious, unrestrained weeping and nose blowing.

The reception was held at a popular gay night spot. Ten hours earlier, buff, sweaty young studs in spangled jockstraps had been gyrating and twirling across this dance floor to bottom-heavy house beats. Now, a neat, well-heeled group of men, uniformed in Banana Republic and/or J. Crew, along with a handful of women — including Tess and David's sallow, bespectacled sister, Eileen — were browsing a series of abundant buffets. It was an opulent spread, one worthy of the honoree, who was, as Mick Jagger rasped, expressing sympathy for the Devil, "a man of wealth and taste."

Russell was glopping comfort food onto his plate, when Tess took him by the elbow. "I want you to meet somebody," she said. Russell turned around to find himself face-to-face with the memorial tribute's final speaker. "Edward," Tess said, "this is my husband, Russell."

"So nice to meet you, Russell," Edward gushed.

Still rattled by the anecdote with which this man had closed his eulogy, Russell uttered a tentative, "Nice meeting you, too."

"Tess informed me that you interned under David at GRMN8," said Edward. "Such a coincidence."

"Well, yes, yeah..." Russell stammered, nervously. "To be absolutely accurate, I didn't intern directly *under* David. I mean, of course, I *met* David that summer..."

"How could you *not* have met him, right?" Edward effused, with a wink only slightly less overt than Eric Idle in a *Monty Python* sketch.

"Oh, he always made his presence known," Russell concurred. "But I made copies and fetched this and that for all the suits in that office."

"Of course." Edward expressed his understanding with an exaggerated nod. During the brief, unsettling pause that followed, Russell noticed the impish twinkle in Edward's eyes being underscored by a subtle, knowing grin. "Well, I just wanted to meet Tess's better half," Edward stated. "We all appreciated her so much... you know, when David was..." Raw grief prevented him from articulating the obvious. "Too bad you didn't have a chance to say goodbye. I'm sure it would have meant a lot to him."

"I was at a company convention," Russell attempted to explain. Edward, however, was being pulled aside by a writer from *The Georgia Voice*. The reporter's demand, however, didn't prevent Edward from sending Russell a quick side sneer that said it all. David, Russell was certain, had told Edward the whole story, chapter and verse.

As Russell swiveled back to the safe, uninquisitive passivity of baked beans and potato salad, Tess said, "Guess I'll get us a table. And a drink."

"Okay, Babe. Thanks. Make mine a double." This, Russell tossed over his shoulder. Otherwise, Tess would surely have noticed that her husband's face had flushed to a shade of red more commonly associated with fire engines.

Plate filled, Russell sidled through the crowd, eyes peeled for his wife. Initially, he felt flattered by the flirtatious leers, suggestive grins, and head-to-toe perusals he received from several of the attendees. This was a fraternity where he assumed, under different circumstances, he would be accepted for his whole true identity. Instead, because he was still under long-term contract, playing the part of the straight, married man in an open-ended run, he felt trapped in a living limbo. He wondered if his true self would ever actually belong anywhere. A sense of isolation descended, as if a clear sack of warm Jell-O had been slipped over his head. He was present; and, yet, he wasn't. He felt the urge to approach some random fellow and say, "Hi, I'm Russ. I'm queer, too." But, instead of melding effortlessly into this flaming fraternity, he felt like a party crasher, an interloper, a mute, invisible spy from No Man's Land.

Russell plopped down heavily in the chair next to his wife. He lifted the tall tequila sunrise she'd ordered for him to his lips and drained the glass dry in three quick chugs. Tess, fully engaged in affable conversation with another couple — a man and a woman, presumably straight — hadn't noticed. "I'll be right back," Russell muttered, rising to carry his empty glass toward the bar. By the time he returned with a refill, he had downed two more. The drink in his hand would be his fourth in less than 10 minutes, with cocktails one-through-three having been imbibed on an empty stomach.

"Russ coaches Little League," Tess was informing her new acquaintances.

"Those were the days," Russ mumbled acerbically, gnawing flesh from a chicken wing. "Damn! So *HOT!*"

"Oh, yeah!" It was the male partner from the other couple speaking. "Those wings'll getcha! That Buffalo sauce is on fire!"

"Is that what this is?" The grimace on Russell's face revealed the severity of his pain. "I thought it was barbecue. Jesus!" Russell snatched up his drink and slurped down half of it in one desperate gulp. "Hoowee!" he exclaimed. "My mouth is burnin' up. I'm sweatin' bullets. And, now... I gotta pee."

Russell was unzipping at the urinal, when he overheard some shuffling feet and whispers coming from a toilet stall. A picture formed in his mind of what was likely happening behind the stall door, sending the attention order to his always-on-call soldier. Erection in hand, Russell remained still, focusing his aural sensors on whatever noises might emit next from the bathroom-stall hook-up in process. His heartbeat pummeled his chest as 10 excruciating seconds of quiet ticked past.

"Helloooo!" A fey, high-pitched voice chimed out. Russell's throat produced an involuntary squeak, like the sound a newly inflated balloon makes when you're attempting to tie a knot in its neck.

"We know you're there..." The second voice was manlier, deeper in pitch. Blood was rushing out of Russell's head and into his excited lower extremities. He felt faint. He lobbed saliva into his hand and began stroking himself, placing the palm of his idle hand on the wall for balance.

"Wanna join us?" inquired the fey voice.

"Shut up, girl! You're so *bad*!" This admonition from the manlier voice was followed by giggles in two-part counterpoint.

"No," Russell managed, mid-stroke, feeling the urgency to finish before someone else entered the restroom. "I'm good."

"I'll bet you are," quipped the fey voice. "How good *are* you?"

"Right now," Russell reported, "excellent." Had he wanted to postpone his ejaculation, he couldn't have. "Oh, Jeeezus!" Russell's wail of pleasure was still echoing off the tile, when he heard...

"Wow!" Russell had only just met the man. But seven minutes of listening to Edward's memorial testimonial made his voice recognizable in a single syllable. "What's going on *here*, Russell?"

"Russell?" the manly voice remarked from the stall. "That's my brother's name."

"Are you cute, Russell?" queried the fey voice. "You sound cute."

"Cool it, ladies," Edward commanded, by now standing shoulder-to-shoulder with Russell at the adjacent urinal. "He's straight. *And*, he's married. To a woman."

"Oh, sure," the fey voice responded. "All the straight, married guys get turned on when they hear a couple-a fags getting it on in a bathroom stall."

"Is that true, Russell?" Edward's shock was entirely fabricated. He'd borne first-hand witness to Russell's self-gratified outburst. And, now, smoking-gun evidence was poking out from Russell's unfastened trousers. "Was I wrong? Tell me you're straight." Edward's manner had shifted to direct, unabashed confrontation. Focusing on the wall to avoid eye contact, Russell crammed his still dripping soft-on back into his pants, zipped up, and flushed. "Tell me you're straight, Russell," Edward goaded, "you know... like you told David." Russell squeezed liquid soap onto his hands, cranked the faucet, and began scrubbing. "I wanna hear you say it!" Edward hissed.

"Hey!" the fey voice called out. "Cool it, you guys!"

"David knew," Russell said, his hooded gaze still directed down at his sudsy hands.

"He knew what?" Edward demanded, zipping up his pressed khakis, and flushing the urinal. "What exactly did David know?"

"That I'm not... that I'm not exactly straight." Russell's eyes met Edward's in the mirror.

"And what, pray tell, does *that* mean?" Turning his back, Russell snatched a paper towel and began drying his hands with an overabundance of focus. "I'm all ears, Russell," Edward pressed. "What exactly does it mean to be not exactly straight?"

"Look," Russell responded, "I don't know why I have to answer to you..."

"You don't..."

"Or, anyone else, for that matter..."

"The only person you have to answer to is yourself!"

Russell had forgotten to breathe. His oxygen deprived lungs spasmed to draw a deep breath. He exhaled loudly. A dozen thoughts raced through his mind in a matter of seconds. He wanted to call Edward out for spouting a lazy cliché barely worthy of a Hallmark Card: *The only person you have to answer to is yourself*? Excess alcohol had Russell's head spinning. Having just ejaculated, his knees were weak and rubbery. At this fraught moment in time, all he wanted was to get as far away from this place as quickly as possible, to escape further accountability — to Edward, to David, to the gay community, and to himself. He took a stride toward the door, but

Edward stepped in his path. "Look, I'm having a really rough day," Russell said, attempting a conciliatory smile.

"Oh, poor baby!" Edward mocked. "David had twenty years of bad days because of you. And you expect me to feel sorry now because you're a little bit uncomfortable?"

"Come on, Man," Russell pleaded. "Let's just let bygones..."

"No! I wanna know..." Edward was literally yelling. "What does not exactly straight mean? Have you told your beautiful, trusting wife that you're not exactly straight?"

"I told David."

"Oh, yeah! Good for you! Two decades too late. Let's give Russell a gold star! You know what, Russell? David despised you for that. Did you know how outraged he was?"

Until that Opryland lunch, seven months earlier, it hadn't occurred to Russell that what he and David had shared during that long-ago summer was all that important to David. Russell was two months shy of 19 when he received Blowjob #1. His experience with sex and romance was minimal. And, when it came to same-sex relations, he was a total virgin. To him, that fateful night, although significant and unforgettable, was nothing more than self-indulgent, no-strings-attached play. This supposition, as it turned out, was entirely misguided. But, to Russell — who, in spite of his attraction to persons of the same-sex, had only ever felt romantic love for cis-gender females — it seemed perfectly logical. Sex for a guy, Russell had come to believe — gay, bi, or straight — was, first and foremost, about getting off. Sure, intimacy and affection (or even love) might add icing to the cake. But the cake was still delectable without frosting. This preconception made David's less-than-empathetic reaction to his coming out confounding, even hurtful. However, as Russell was just beginning to realize, it wasn't David's lack of empathy that was at issue. It was his own. He hadn't considered David's feelings at all. "I guess not..." Russell admitted, sheepishly.

"Then," Edward admonished, "for David to find out that, not only did you lie to *him* back then, but you'd been lying to his friend — your wife! — all these years, too?" So, evidently, David's anger was not solely about all those years of needless guilt. His resentment was doubled because someone else he cared about was also being victimized by Russell's ongoing deception. In retrospect, David would have been far more content and accommodating had Russell simply accepted his long-overdue apology graciously, while continuing to maintain his straight-man ruse.

Russell and Edward stood nose to nose, Edward providing the only impediment between Russell and the escape he so desperately longed to make. For a split second, Russell felt a powerful impulse to disarm this human blockade by grabbing those angular cheeks and planting a sloppy, wet kiss on Edward's thin, snarling lips. Instead, Russell's lizard brain instructed his hands to exert a forceful shove against Edward's sloping shoulders. His nemesis proved to be less moveable than Russell — drunk as he was, and unstable of foot — had anticipated. Edward's retaliatory slap took Russell by complete surprise. The sting on his cheek triggering a fit of rage. Thankfully, his attempt at throwing a punch was thwarted by a peacemaker.

"Let's give it a rest, ladies." The fey voice certainly didn't match the man. He wasn't tall. But his shoulders were broad, his pecs were toned, and his tatted biceps and forearms were well-developed. With minimal effort, Fey Voice was able to grasp Russell's arms from behind and pull him back and away from the escalating conflict.

"Fuck you, Russell, you slimy piece of dog shit," muttered Edward, as he approached the sink to wet his hands and splash water on his flushed-pink face.

Tess was appalled. Russell's uncompromising insistence on an immediate exit had deprived her of the chance to make her rounds, distributing tearful goodbyes and farewell hugs. And now, she was standing on the sidewalk, in the twilight of a November Sunday afternoon, watching her over-served husband on his hands and knees spewing orange-tinged vomit into the gutter.

The buff, fey-voiced, bathroom interventionist emerged from the club on the arm of his funeral date — *not*, it should be noted, the manlier sounding hook-up from the bathroom stall. Spying Russell's plight, Fey Voice expounded, "Oh, my, Russell! Honey, you *are* having a bad day."

"Wait! How do you know this guy?" queried Fey Voice's date.

"Long story, Honey. We'll save it for later." Fey Voice turned his attention to Tess. "You must be the wife."

"Tess," she informed him, bewilderment now piling on top of the disgust she'd been feeling 30 seconds earlier.

"I'm *so* sorry," Fey Voice said with super sincerity. Tess wondered: *Is this guy apologizing? Or, is he sympathizing? And for what reason?* "Is there anything I can do to help?" Fey Voice inquired. This offer was interrupted by a punch to his shoulder from his date. "Ow! For the love of Dorothy! What was that about?"

"Can't you just let these people deal with their own crap?" complained his date, while tugging at his arm. "You're always butting into everybody's business. Let's go." Fey Voice looked at Tess, as though he needed her permission to leave.

"We're fine," Tess declared, although it was crystal clear that her stab at reassurance was pure pretense. "But thank you so much for your kind concern."

Russell slept from Atlanta to Chattanooga. Although the autumnal temperature was plunging into the low 40s on the Fahrenheit scale, Tess had kept the side windows cracked open for the entire two hours to dissipate the stench of stomach bile, tequila, and partially digested Buffalo sauce emanating from her unconscious husband's clothing and shoes. A chill spasm awakened Russell as Tess pulled into a Shell Station for a pit stop.

"Take your shirt off," she demanded.

"It's fucking freezing," Russell whined.

"You smell like puke."

Russell looked down. The blotches of ochre on his chest looked like a preschooler's finger painting. "Shit," he mumbled, removing the offensive garment. At that point, he noticed the dark mark of dried semen that had seeped through the crotch of his trousers. Tess snatched the shirt and kicked open the driver-side door, allowing a frigid blast of wind to blow through the vehicle. By this point, Russell's teeth were chattering, and his entire body quaked with hypothermic tremors. "Pretty sure there's a blanket in the back," she snapped, before giving the door a furious, frustrated slam.

Trembling like a blue-skinned toddler who'd just emerged from too long in a backyard kiddy pool, Russell watched through the window as his incensed wife stuffed his soiled shirt into a trash can before entering the mini-mart. For some unexplained reason, he felt compelled to flip down the sun shield and slide open the make-up mirror. There, in unforgiving, close-up detail, he saw the sad, red-streaked eyes of a pathetic, extremely unpopular man. David had gone to his final reward despising him. Edward seemed intent on keeping his late friend's animus alive. And, having succeeded spectacularly in ruining the memorial for his wife, he'd provoked her ire as well. Pretty much everybody hated Russell. And now, Russell loathed himself as well. "Asshole!" he hissed at his own, scruffy, tousled reflection. "Fucking *ASSHOLE!*"

He flipped the sun shield back up, wishing it were as easy to erase his own existence as it had been to hide his mirrored image from sight. He was grappling for the door handle when the passenger door flew open. Suddenly, he found himself tented by a car blanket. "There," Tess growled, "wrap yourself up. You look like a frozen turd."

TWENTY-ONE

"**I** really don't think I'm being unfaithful." Despite the obvious delusion reflected in this statement, Russell meant it. That is how skillful he'd become at the uniquely human art of compartmentalization. Mary Ann, having gone toe-to-toe with her share of double-dealing men, was equipped with an infallible bullshit detector. But, to be real, it would hardly have taken a pair of X-ray specs to see through her friend's attempt at dodging accountability for his obsessive behavior. "I mean... I've never cheated with another woman," he emphasized, before taking another bite of rice and vegetables.

"Well, good for you," Mary Ann cracked, eyeing a forkful of eggplant, then deciding she'd had her fill and placing the utensil back down on her plate.

"Really," persisted Russell. "I think it's actually good for my marriage. It's like... like a steam valve, a pressure release. It makes me a better husband."

"You've been cheating on your wife," Mary Ann countered. "Get fucking real." Russell sat speechless. He was genuinely shocked to hear such blunt language coming from his new (and possibly only real) friend. "And, you know what?"

"What?" Russell's irritation was showing. He'd endured more than enough lecturing already.

"You're going to have to tell her."

"Fuck!" squawked Russell. "No way. I can't... Really? Why?"

"Yes, really," Mary Ann replied. "Why? It's simple. She deserves to know." Russell's heart sank, as the un-masticated food in his mouth suddenly became dryer than two-hour-old bubble gum.

This interchange had begun on the route from the office to Country Life organic vegetarian buffet, where Russell and Mary Ann had been lunching on a weekly basis. "You look glum, Buddy," Mary Ann observed, as she steered along West End Avenue. "What's going on?"

"No," Russell responded, modulating his voice upward in pitch. "I'm good." His stab at cheeriness was unconvincing.

"No, you're not," she contended. "You're depressed. You can't bullshit a bullshitter."

Russell's heartbeat quickened. He swallowed hard, as he armored himself. "Can I tell you something?"

"Of course. Anything."

"Look," he said, "if I tell you this, you can*not* tell anybody else."

"Oh, boy!" she snickered. "Here it comes. Russell's dirty little secret."

"Never mind." Russell swiveled his neck to take a vacant look through the passenger side window.

"Wait!" protested Mary Ann. "You can't just dangle a juicy nugget out there and then yank it away!"

"You don't seem to be taking this seriously," grumbled Russell.

"Well," she said, softening her tone. "I'm here to listen. You can confide in me. I hope you know that. And..." She patted his hand with platonic fondness. "... about *that*, I *am* dead serious."

"I'm bisexual," he blurted. "There. I can't fucking believe I said it."

"I thought so." Mary Ann's smile was smug.

"You *thought* so! What?"

"Yep." Mary Ann proceeded to reveal that, from her earliest days at the company, she'd suspected that Russell was harboring a secret of some kind. Then, in Texas, she'd seen him emerge from Guy Gallo's room in his swimming trunks at eight a.m. "That's when I finally knew for certain that you were worth getting to know." While she meant this as a compliment, it was a backhanded one at best.

"You are one strange, sick person, Mary Ann."

"Oh, come on," she retorted. "You know I've got absolutely nothing in common with the ladies in that office. And you obviously have more depth and character than any of those other dipshit company clowns."

"Thank you." Tears were welling up in Russell's eyes. It was as if the anvil he'd carried around for decades had been lifted from his shoulders. At long last, he'd voluntarily revealed his true nature to a friend, someone with whom he'd never been sexually intimate, nor would ever be. Unveiling his secret was something he'd been dreading for years. And, yet, saying it out loud had gone so much smoother than he could ever have hoped.

A half hour later, however, sitting on a hard bench at a long, communal, wooden table, Russell's digestive juices had turned sour. Mary Ann was not judging him negatively for his sexual orientation. She was, however, expressing a strong, unambiguous opinion regarding his willingness to keep his wife in the dark about it. Russell, on the other hand, didn't like what he was hearing one little bit, nor was he willing to receive such unwelcome feedback constructively.

Suddenly, Russell remembered something he'd put out of his mind for the benefit of his own emotional equilibrium: a similar moment, at a similar time of day, over lunch, and shortly after he'd confessed his same-sex attraction to another person. "It's probably the elephant in the room," David Mangold opined. "If Tess doesn't know, surely she's had inklings. Just tell her. What've you got to lose?" Only a comfortably out gay man could make such an assumption. Only a person unencumbered by the responsibilities of parenthood could so cavalierly dish out such advice. Russell remained convinced that David's conjecture was off-base, that Tess hadn't a clue about his secret. Or, if she did, she was cramming any and all qualms inside a dark closet of her own design.

The real elephant in the Deacon household, according to Russell, was that his wife's life was a grand performance. And, from his front-row seat, she wasn't that skilled an actor. Yes, she played the role of vibrant, charismatic Tess Deacon with panache. The trick to this artifice, however, lay in her ability to see any individual as the person she wanted them to be, while blindfolding herself to their messier, more problematic character traits. This singular talent enabled her to pretend she liked everyone as much as she fully expected everyone to like her. Through Tess's finely ground, self-warped lens, her husband's character was beyond reproach. Therefore, it naturally followed that their life partnership must also be exemplary and enviable. And, because she put so much stock into projecting an impeccable marital aura out into the world, the world reflected that same image back. From the outside, Russell and Tess comprised the perfect couple. Maintaining this unblemished image placed constant stress on Russell, to leave his wife's precious mirage undistorted, while meeting the expectations of outside world as well. His coming out to Tess would be disillusioning enough for her. But, the collateral damage caused by such a revelation would be widespread. In one fell swoop, Russell raising the curtain on his truth would obliterate his wife's core worldview, while destroying an entire social circle's ideal of the ultimate spousal partnership.

As Mary Ann shuttled him back to the office, Russell continued to cling to the flimsy, self-serving theory that his closeted identity and his compulsive side interests were healthy and beneficial for his marriage. And he would continue to straddle his dual identities for as long as he could get away with it. That was that; he had no other choice.

The number of friends who now knew Russell as his whole, authentic self could be counted on one hand, with a digit to spare. David was no longer living. Two others — Bryan and Guy — were entangled in the various intricacies of their own queer journeys. The fourth, Mary Ann, had been unabashed in her criticism of his ongoing facade. Feeling more isolated than ever, Russell was convinced that no one could possibly understand the quandary in which he found himself — married to a woman, the father of sons, passing as straight, yet bisexual and closeted. Still, the gnawing hunger for same-sex connection remained unabated.

One late Friday afternoon in mid-December, Russell exited a Fourth-Avenue business from what had been the week's final scheduled sales call. On numerous occasions, he had motored past the expansive, fenced-in deck of Ynonah's Saloon, invariably casting wistful side glances at the marathon party within. This evening, he found himself shuffling by the rollicking gay haven on foot. The nearer he drew, the more the four-on-the-floor house-music vibrated the sidewalk beneath his feet and the more audible the happy-hour revelry grew. His mixed emotions were at odds: an aching envy for these men and their freedom to commune and embrace one another in public fighting an urgent impulse to circumvent the place as rapidly and invisibly as possible and escape into the safety and security of his wholesome family cocoon.

Russell couldn't resist stopping to scan the crowd on the deck, where men of every age, race, and body type appeared to be having the time of their lives. Suddenly, his heart nearly stopped. He hadn't seen Bryan since that disquieting meltdown at Rory's birthday party three months earlier. On that occasion, the remorseful cad had laid his heart at Russell's feet in a plea for compassion and forgiveness. Russell had left Bryan's appeal on a "we'll see what happens" basis. Nothing in the interim had happened to change the up-in-the-air status of their fitful friendship.

Third-hand chatter had informed Russell about Bryan and Diane's separation. He'd intended to reach out to make sure Bryan was okay. But, as often happens in life, Russell found excuse after excuse to postpone that friendly check-in. Now, it appeared that any worry he might have felt had been for naught. There stood Bryan, in a circle of guys, radiating that irresistible smile, blue eyes twinkling, a tallboy of Pabst Blue Ribbon in one hand, his other arm around another man's shoulder. By all appearances, Bryan had landed solidly on his feet and was fully embracing his new out-gay life. Russell was exhaling a covetous sigh when Bryan's baby blues fell upon him. Embarrassed, Russell quickly averted his gaze and commenced legging it the half block to his parked Celica. He had just put the car in gear and was about to pull out when he looked up to see Bryan standing directly in front of the vehicle, hands and arms extended out to the side in a posture that asked, "What the fuck, Dude?"

The smile Russell manufactured might have been borrowed from Wiley Coyote, in the moment of realization that gravity is about to send him plummeting to the canyon floor below. Resigned to the reality of this serendipitous circumstance, Russell switched off the engine and stepped out of the vehicle.

"Coach!" Bryan exuded. "What's happening? It's been forever! I missed you." Other than some playful, surreptitious, under-the-table groping at a family dinner party, Russell and Bryan had never gone beyond a handshake. The intervening months of open gay interactions had accustomed Bryan to prolonged hugs with men, as well as kisses on the lips. Russell hesitated at first, but then allowed the hug. Much to his surprise, it felt so natural and nurturing that he, not Bryan, was reluctant to release the embrace. Bryan took this demonstration of affection as a cue for a kiss on the lips. Russell panicked and turned his head at the last second so that Bryan's puckered lips landed on his cheek.

"Come inside," Bryan insisted, laughing at the slapstick clumsiness of this fumbled smooch. "I want you to meet some people." Russell had assumed this chance meeting called for some brief chitchat outside, on the sidewalk — about life in general, kids in particular. Instead, Bryan was hurdling past small talk and offering to chaperone Russell into a gay bar. Russell's first emotional response was relief at not having to explain why he'd been keeping his distance these last several months. Next came the buzz of excitement at having just received an invitation to experience his first total immersion, sans wife, into the queer community. Russell's soldier quickly endorsed this idea by chubbing up. As Bryan led him up the stairs onto the entrance landing, Russell covertly slipped off his wedding ring and tucked it into the watch pocket of his trousers.

As had happened during the reception following David's memorial, Russell was greeted by suggestive smiles and lustful leers. Sidling through the shoulder-to-shoulder crowd, it seemed evident that the dress code was out of sync with the season. Even on the cusp of winter, on an unheated outside deck, gay-happy-hour fashion still featured tight, torso-hugging T's, tank tops, and leather vests over bare, hairy chests. Russell's sport coat, shirt, and tie seemed woefully out of place. Approaching Bryan's circle of friends, he was feeling conspicuous and tragically unhip.

Russell's head swam as Bryan rattled off names and barbed quips about each individual in the group. As Bryan volunteered zero background for who Russell was, how the two had met, and what their relationship meant, the curious bunch was left to bombard the newbie with queries — what Russell did for a living, where he grew up, where he lived, etc. One question, however, wasn't asked. No one inquired about Russell's sexual orientation. The presumption seemed to be that, because he was friends with Bryan and had shown up at Ynonah's for Friday happy hour, he must be queer. For that reason, in spite of his conservative attire, Russell began to feel more at-ease.

That comfort level, however, was dashed upon Bryan's return from the bar with two PBRs. When Russell reached out with his left hand to accept the frosty can, one of the fellows made an observation. "So, Russell," the man asked, "are you still married?" Russell looked at the pale circle on his ring finger where, for nearly a decade and a half, his wedding ring had shielded his skin from the sun. The jig was up. Either he was attempting to hide the fact that he was still married or he and his spouse were freshly separated. The group's banter came to an abrupt halt and all eyes turned to Russell for his answer.

"Yes," he replied. "Fourteen years now. Tess and I have two boys, ten and twelve."

"Russell and I met coaching Little League," Bryan explained. "Our sons were on the same team."

"Oh, that's fabulous, Russell!" exclaimed the inquisitive one. "You should join our softball team! There's a poster on the bulletin board outside the restroom with all the info."

"Sounds great," said Russell, thankful he hadn't been automatically shunned and excommunicated from the group for the sin of having a wife and kids.

"My eleven-year-old plays soccer," another man shared. "He loves it. I just wish I could give him more help with his game. I'm hopeless when it comes to sports."

"Oh, but Honey," remarked his companion, "you sure know how to juggle a pair of balls." With the boisterous laughter that followed, the repartee was diverted away from Russell and put back into the more familiar realm of naughty double entendre and affectionate insult. As a cascade of snappy barbs flowed freely, Russell removed his sport coat, unfastened the top button of his shirt and loosened his tie.

Russell was standing outside the restroom examining the recruiting poster for the aforementioned softball team, when he encountered another familiar person. At first, he couldn't place this individual's exact identity or the circumstances under which they'd met. One thing he did know for certain: he felt a strong attraction to this man.

"Thinking about joining the team?" a resonant baritone voice asked. "We're actually pretty good."

Russell looked up. The large man standing next to him had shiny black skin. His cheeks were slightly pock-marked and his chin was recessed, almost non-existent. When he parted his ample lips in a smile, Russell noticed the gap between his front teeth. "Oh, my!" Russell exclaimed. He suddenly felt as if his earlobes were on fire.

"What?" the large black man wondered aloud. "You don't think a gay softball team can be competitive?"

"No," Russell replied. "I know you. We've met."

"Really? Are you sure?" As a flight attendant, the man couldn't possibly be expected to remember every individual passenger. Still, he had made an indelible impression on at least one of the travelers he'd served.

"Your name... let me think..." Russell recalled, "is Jamal. Right?"

"Correct," Jamal confirmed. "You look vaguely familiar. Where did we meet?"

"Wakey, wakey," hinted Russell.

"Well..." Jamal seemed even more baffled. "I hope you're not suggesting that we slept together. Because I'd remember that if..."

"No, no, no!" Russell interrupted.

"Oh!" Jamal exclaimed. "I remember now. Austin to Nashville. You were sacked out. You were so adorable. I hated to wake you up."

"I thought you were adorable, too." As Russell offered his hand for shaking, he reminded Jamal of his name: "Russell."

Rather than grasping the outstretched hand, Jamal opened his soft, powerful arms and pulled the smaller man against his ample torso. "Russell. Yes," he said, as if the circumstance of their meeting was coming back to him in vivid detail. The chemistry was palpable. Both men felt it.

"So, you're on the team," Russell assumed.

"When my flight schedule permits."

"You look like a slugger," Russell observed. "Are you... a slugger?" With this question, the conversation had crossed the line into overt flirtation.

"Well..." A shy smile blossomed across Jamal's full lips. "I've been known to hit a home run... or two... in a game."

"How about *off* the diamond?" Russell could scarcely believe he'd grown bold enough to go here. "Are you hitting any homers in your love life?"

"Oh, I do alright," Jamal said, with a wink. "But, lately, I've been in a bit of a slump."

"Hmmm," purred Russell, placing his hand on Jamal's chest, licking his lips, and sending him a heavy-lidded look. "I've got a lot of coaching experience. So, if you ever need some help... with your stance, or your grip, or your swing, I'm open to giving you some pointers." The pause in conversation that followed was thick and heavy enough to slice with a knife.

"Who are you here with?" inquired Jamal.

"Oh," Russell answered, "a friend. In fact, he was my assistant Little League coach last summer. Come to think of it, he'd be a great addition to the team as well."

Jamal was following Russell through the crowd when Bryan saw them approaching. "Jimmeeeee!" he rasped. Russell observed Jamal and Bryan's easy embrace and kiss on the lips with a twinge of jealousy. Of course, charming, gregarious Bryan would know tender, irresistible Jamal. How well they knew one another was another question.

"I'm so glad you met Jimmy, Coach!" exclaimed Bryan.

"Actually," Russell said, "we met back in October. I was out cold after a flight. And, Jamal was the handsome prince who awakened me."

"With a kiss, I hope," one of the others quipped.

"Unfortunately, no," Russell responded. "But, when I opened my eyes and saw that gorgeous face, I had to stop myself from grabbing those cheeks and laying a wet one on his luscious lips."

"Sounds like you've got some housekeeping to do, Russell," another man offered.

"Sorry?" The subtext of this remark had gone over Russell's head. Then he noticed the man's eyes, directed toward the pale circle of skin around his ring finger. "Oh." Russell's vocal tone flattened out, as a shadow fell over his lightened heart. "I getcha." It was acceptable to still be married and living with his wife and kids. Less acceptable, apparently, was a married man actively courting someone committed completely and wholeheartedly to a gay life.

Russell found himself visited by fresh qualms. Was the acceptance he'd been feeling amongst this bunch no more than an illusion? Feeling a sudden urge to distance himself from scrutiny, he abruptly begged off with a couple of tentative hugs — still no kisses on the lips. A few minutes earlier, he'd felt like he belonged. Now, the still-married, still-closeted, bisexual man was once again feeling alienated, lonely in a crowd.

TWENTY-TWO

"What's this?" Tess was showing Russell a business card. "Is this important?" Next to the photo of a smiling, gap-toothed Black man was the contact information for Jamal Abdoulaye Diallo, Senior Flight Attendant, Delta Airlines.

Russell, his heart skipping every other beat, made his best attempt at appearing nonchalant. "Where'd you find it?"

"In the pocket of your grey sport coat."

In the insurance game, the daily exchange of business cards is as common as breathing in and breathing out. Still, as Russell received this palm-sized paper rectangle from his wife, he was blushing and his fingers trembled. Jamal, he assumed, must have slipped his contact information into that jacket pocket prior to Russell's exit from Ynonah's Saloon. "Thanks, I've been looking for this." This was a lie. He couldn't have been looking for something he hadn't even known was in his possession.

"Potential client?" Tess inquired.

"Delta Airlines," he said, raising his eyebrows and tilting his head for emphasis. "Could be huge."

"No wonder you're so excited."

"What do you mean?"

"Well, your cheeks are all flushed, and you're all fidgety."

"Well, the guy's just a flight attendant. But... he claims to know some of the big, mucky-muck decision makers."

Ever the supportive spouse, Tess gave Russell a peck on the cheek. "Go get 'em, Tiger," she said, before traipsing back into their shared walk-in closet.

Of course, Russell's involuntary emotional response upon seeing Jamal's card had nothing whatsoever to do with selling insurance. This, he had to believe, was an explicit invitation. From the moment his sleepy eyes first beheld Jamal's face, he'd felt undeniable attraction. The card appearing in his jacket pocket provided solid evidence that Jamal would be receptive to further contact. This unspoken message was as clear and enticing as a certain game of footsie initiated by Guy Gallo beneath the bubbling waters of an Austin jacuzzi. The ball was in Russell's court. All he had to do was pick up the phone and dial.

Russell's overactive imagination immediately began painting erotic scenarios. However, as exhilarating as those mental pictures were, the possibility of hooking up with Jamal also came fraught with complications. The what-ifs were myriad. *What if they started having deeper feelings for one another? What if one had deeper feelings than the other? What if they failed to click physically?* Worse yet... *what if Jamal turned out to be HIV positive?*

Still, for Russell, reason never held much sway in circumstances where the real potential for male-on-male sexual contact was within reach. He knew that, in short order, he would be dialing the number on this card. Actually, he figured, it would be impolite if he *didn't* call. Now that Jamal had put his cards on the table — by slipping his card into Russell's pocket — it was not a matter of whether but, rather, a question of how soon.

Russell sat at his office desk in a stupor. Monday mornings were typically dedicated to the weekly staff meeting, after which he would sort out and prioritize his leads, in preparation for a marathon afternoon of cold calls. During this morning's company confab, he'd found concentration impossible. His only victory was that he'd somehow avoided dozing off for more than a few seconds. Now, with a printed list of prospects' names and phone numbers swimming in front of his bleary eyes, he could think of nothing else other than a certain large, ebony-skinned man. He pulled Jamal's business card from his shirt pocket and placed it next to the tip sheet. He'd already made his pitch to Jamal. The card told him that he'd made the sale. His next logical move was to close the deal.

He dialed the number. Five rings seemed like a hundred. "Hello, this is Jimmy," the outgoing message began. "I'm probably thirty-thousand feet above Terra Firma right now. Please be so kind as to leave me a detailed message after the beep, and I'll call you back as soon as I get my feet on the ground. Thanks for calling. And have yourself a blessed day!" At the sound of the beep, Russell felt a sudden jolt of panic. He hastily slammed the receiver down on its dock and yanked his hand away, as if the phone had transformed into a slavering Gila Monster.

Have yourself a blessed day! That's Christian talk! Hearing Jamal speak this phrase had tossed yet another random ingredient into a simmering pot of anxiety soup. Imagining getting to know this hunk of a man better had become Russell's primary obsession. But he'd had his fill of *Bible*-thumping — albeit well-meaning — acquaintances intent on saving his immortal soul.

Russell — a lapsed Episcopalian since middle school — had sampled three local churches over the previous 10 years, all at the behest of friends or neighbors determined to spread the good news about Jesus. However, his motivation for attendance was less about finding religion than about meeting and cultivating potential new clients, engendering good will, and procuring referrals. So, once he'd squeezed the lowest hanging business benefits out of a congregation, he found it challenging to muster up sufficient faith to return to those same pews Sunday after Sunday. Russell would have considered it a blessing if all the residents of Middle Tennessee took a permanent break from instructing him to have a blessed day.

Russell emitted a breathy "whoof!" in relief. This spanner in the works gave him an ideal excuse for not making the call. He felt charged with a shot of adrenalin, as if he'd dodged a bullet. Five words in an outgoing answering-machine message had made the immediate future far less fraught with confusion, uncertainty, and potential guilt. He chuckled cynically to himself, spun Jamal's business card into his trash can, and returned to perusing his list of leads. However, that smiling, gap-toothed photo kept looking up at him, as if Jamal was still insistent on distracting him from his normal routine. Russell pushed his chair back, rose to his feet, and headed toward the breakroom for yet another cup of coffee.

"Oh, good!" the woman on the stepladder exclaimed. "A man!" By Russell's guesstimation, Ruby, from Admin, was closing in on 60. Barely five-feet in height, and round as a boulder, she was one of the few employees who'd been with the office longer than Russell. Ruby frisbeed a package of pushpins in Russell's direction, which he managed to snag in flight. "Can you open that for me?" Ruby asked. As she did every December, Ruby had taken it upon herself to adorn the lobby and common areas of the office with festive Christmas décor. This morning, she was hanging a strand of gold-tinsel garland the length of the hallway.

Russell found that the clear, vinyl box was resistant to any and all efforts to break its seal. "Harder than it looks," he noted.

Ed popped out of his office. "Here, let me do that," he demanded smugly, grabbing for the uncooperative container. Russell impulsively decided to engage in a game of keep-away. Swiveling deceptively, he extended his arm to keep the pushpins out of Ed's reach.

"I've got this, Ruby," Russell said. "I will go to my grave to prevent Ed Stengel's grubby paws from soiling your precious Yuletide tacks."

"I said, 'Oh, good, a man!'" Ruby remarked, as her chubby arm grew heavier from holding up the garland at the desired height. "You're not men. You're a couple of little babies."

"Gimme that, asshole!" Ed growled, finally getting a grip on the contested package. Ed yanked. Russell held on. The recalcitrant seal cracked open, sending hundreds of push pins scattering onto the hallway floor.

"God damn it!" shouted Ed, as if genuine tragedy had befallen the office. "Now, look what you did, you dick!"

Russell, however, was finding hilarity in this absurd outcome. "See, Ruby..." he said, between guffaws. "You sure picked the right guys for the job."

"Yeah, right," Ruby responded. "You two can both go fuck yourselves." By now she, too, was tittering at these sophomoric, boys-will-be-boys shenanigans.

Russell picked up several push pins from the floor and handed them up to her. "Honored to be of service, M'Lady."

"Grab a broom, Dickwad!" Ed ordered Russell. "You're cleaning up this mess." By the time Russell had returned from the supply closet, Ed's face and hairless pate had flushed redder than Santa's coat, from stooping down to gather errant pushpins. "Ouch! Damn!" he exclaimed. "Those little buggers are sharp!"

"Here," Russell offered, extending the dust pan. Ed opened his fist with evident disdain, and dropped a dozen pins noisily into the trash can in his other hand. At this point, Russell noticed Jamal's card at the bottom. Suddenly the situation wasn't so funny anymore. "Did you go into my office, Ed?" queried Russell.

"What about it?" Ed snapped back. "A trash can is a trash can."

"You were trying to poach my leads, weren't you."

"Don't be ridiculous!"

"What's this, then?" Russell reached into the trash can and fished out Jamal's card.

"Is that how you file your leads these days, Rusty Boy?"

"Stay the fuck out of my office, Ed!"

"Sorrrrreeeeey!" mocked Ed. He looked up at Ruby, still busy with her decorating. "He's afraid I'm gonna steal one of his boyfriends."

"What did you say?" Russell demanded.

"Well, I wouldn't put it past ya," Ed teased. "Looks like the kinda guy you'd fall on your knees for."

"Because why?" Russell fumed. "Why, Ed? Because he's Black. Is that what you're saying?"

"I bet that boy's got an impressive Johnson," Ed jabbed. "You know what they say... once you taste dark meat, you never go back."

"What if he *was* my boyfriend, Ed?" By now, Russell was delirious in his fury. "What would you say then? Huh?"

"Look," Ed stammered. "I was just kidding. You know me, Russ. I'm a lover, not a hater. I love everybody."

"Everybody... except Black people and faggots!"

"Hey!" The abrasive, high-pitched holler came from the far end of the corridor. Russell turned to see Mary Ann standing, hands on hips, her squinted eyes shooting lasers the length of the hallway. "You guys wanna keep it down? Some folks 'round here are trying to get some work done." Russell and Mary Ann locked eyes for a full five seconds until she surrendered the staring contest and strutted back into her office.

"So," Ed inquired, "why would you toss your boyfriend's card into the trash can?" He was only half joking.

Russell held the card up six inches from Ed's eyes. "Did you bother to read the card, Ed? Delta Airlines. Ring a bell?"

"So sweet," Ed teased. "Rusty Boy fell in love at thirty-thousand feet."

"You got it, Ed! I joined the queer mile-high club on the way back from the company convention. Ask Mary Ann about it. She was there. She'll recap the whole story..." Once again, Russell had bated Ed with an irresistible set-up line. Then, with pristine timing, he popped the balloon. "... about how I slept the whole way back from Austin." Russell seldom displayed this side of his personality, so vehement and uncompromising.

"Look, Russ," Ed explained, "you know I was just giving you a hard time."

"Sure you were," retorted Russell. "And, next, you're gonna tell me you were just giving gays and Blacks a hard time, too."

"Come on," Ed protested. "You know I didn't mean it that way."

"No, I don't. And I don't appreciate your racist, homophobic horse shit. It's not clever, or remotely funny. And, I won't stand for it. Capeesh?" As Russell waited for Ed's response, he felt a rush of pride for having spoken out, standing up against his co-worker's micro aggressive bigotry. "Capeesh?" he repeated, demanding a response.

"I hear ya." While it was clear that Russell was sincere, Ed's reptilian brain was incapable of understanding how this accusation specifically applied to him. Thus, this was less an admission of his own intolerance and more an effort to affect a temporary ceasefire. As Ruby continued draping the garland, Russell and Ed finished picking up the remaining push pins in silence.

Immediately following the rowdy Secret Santa gift exchange, Tess's rendition of "Have Yourself a Merry Little Christmas," accompanied by roly-poly Ruby on the Casio keyboard, had become an annual office Christmas-party tradition. Tess thrived in social situations. The more attention she drew to herself, the more comfortable and alive she felt. Although she exuded a natural allure, she was never content to depend solely on her personal magnetism to draw the attention she craved. As soon as she entered a room full of people, she would immediately crank up her vocal decibel level, while punctuating her every statement with overly dramatic gestures.

Russell had long ago grown weary of this. Secretly, he disdained the over-the-top manner with which Tess gushed over another woman's outfit, her haircut, or her chic glasses frames. Even more irksome was the way she would touch another man's hand or forearm and laugh boisterously at his lame jokes. Russell had suffered this conduct for years without comment, in part, because everyone else seemed to find Tess so charming. Still, he wondered if any of them could see through his wife's pretense or if they ever found her social persona overwrought or irritating.

As Tess took her bow, Russell stood at the back of the room, a glass of punch in hand, while the office staff, their partners and spouses clapped, whistled, and hooted their appreciation. Bill Gates could have delivered a brilliantly insightful 20-minute keynote address. But, if Tess sang one song, that's all anyone would be talking about for the remainder of the evening and her cameo cabaret act would be mentioned with gushing admiration for months afterwards.

"She's incredible!" raved Martha from the underwriting department. "You're one lucky guy."

"Yep," Russell agreed, through gritted teeth, "she's incredible alright."

So, as the evening wore on, it seemed odd to Russell that Mary Ann was spending so much time in one-on-one conversation with Tess. He would have assumed that Mary Ann, of all the women in the office, would see right through Tess's skin-deep façade. Still, every time Russell surveyed the gathering, he'd locate Mary Ann and Tess off by themselves, one riveted on whatever the other was saying. So, the one person in the company to whom Russell had come out — and the office's most uncompromising feminist — was becoming increasingly familiar with the very person Mary Ann had insisted most deserved to know about Russell's heretofore closeted identity and chronic infidelity.

Finally, after meandering from clique to clique, enduring conversations about kids applying to private schools, riding lawn mowers, and the Tennessee Vols' upcoming Liberty Bowl contest versus Maryland, he'd had his fill of playing the wallflower. Russell shuffled over to Tess and Mary Ann, who had commandeered a pair of chairs by the windows overlooking the courtyard. "You two ladies seem to be getting along better than Thelma and Louise," he observed. "Having your own private party, or what?"

"Hi, Babe. Mary Ann was just telling me about her trip to Austin," Tess reported.

Russell locked eyes with Mary Ann. "You mean *our* trip, right?"

"Okay, yes," Mary Ann confirmed, "we did take the same flights there and back... But our convention experiences were quite different."

"Can't argue with that," Russell concurred, his eyes still fixed on Mary Ann, as usual, making a fruitless attempt at reading her mind. "I don't suppose you mentioned anything about our weekly vegetarian lunches at Country Life."

"What? No." Tess was knocked back by a sneaker wave of jealousy. In the last 30 seconds, she had been bushwhacked with two new — to her, important —items of information. Not only had her husband and the intelligent, stylish, fascinating woman with whom she'd been conversing for the last two hours flown to and from Texas together, they'd also been having lunch on a weekly basis. *What could they be talking about? Certainly not marriage and children. Mary Ann was single and had no kids.*

Having a strong inkling as to what Tess was thinking, Russell deftly changed the subject. "Did Mary Ann tell you that she played hoops for the Lady Commodores?"

"Really? Wow! Amazing!" Tess immediately felt silly for questioning the solvency of the marriage she preferred to think was absolutely perfect. This was a simple, easy calculation. That Mary Ann had been a collegiate athlete incrementally increased the probability that she was a lesbian, which, in turn, explained why she was unmarried and childless. "Well," Tess said, a smile of relief blossoming across her face, "you two must have a lot to talk about."

"We'd better hit the road, Kiddo," Russell suggested.

"Really? Shoot!" Tess protested. "I don't remember when I've had such a good time."

Maybe it's because you haven't been working so damn hard to be the center of attention. Russell didn't say it. But that's what he was thinking. He directed his attention back towards Mary Ann for an obligatory explanation. "Gotta get back and make sure those little rascals haven't burned down the ranch house."

"Time flies when you're having fun," Tess exuded, as she rose to her feet. "Maybe you guys will let me crash your next veggie lunch date."

"That would be great." Mary Ann said this purely out of courtesy, as she and Tess hugged. Then, to assuage Russell's concern, she put a buffer zone between the present and any future three-way lunch. "Maybe sometime later in the new year."

Russell and Mary Ann exchanged knowing glances. "See ya 'round campus, Pal," Russell said, with a casual salute.

"Copy that. Y'all drive safe now," advised Mary Ann.

TWENTY-THREE

For Russell, driving in peaceful silence provided a welcome respite from the cacophonous, alcohol-lubricated vigor of the office Christmas party. They were approximately halfway home when Tess disturbed the quiet. "Didn't you tell me that you didn't like Mary Ann?"

"Well..." Russell responded, "I doubt that I said *that*, exactly. She's always kinda kept a wall up. Before Austin, I didn't think she liked men much."

"What do you mean, before Austin?"

"Oh," Russell stammered. "I thought that was what you two were talking about." The "that" to which Russell was referring was Mary Ann's unrequited crush on a certain dashing and very-much-married company executive.

"What? No," Tess clarified. "She was telling me about going out with the girls for karaoke and some woman executive she admires. Stuff like that."

"Shit!" Russell hadn't intended this four-letter word to be audible. His profane utterance was born of a disquieting realization: he had blundered into treacherous territory and was teetering on the edge of betraying Mary Ann's confidence. And now, he was caught between remaining loyal to a friend and being transparent with his wife. "I probably shouldn't have said anything." This, he would soon learn, was an understatement.

Russell's atypically evasive demeanor set Tess's imagination spinning out of control. For two years, her husband had presumed that this woman, Mary Ann, didn't like men. Then, he and this woman, Mary Ann, flew together to a convention in another state.

213

And there, he became convinced otherwise. Before tonight, she'd never entertained a single, serious doubt about her husband's fidelity. Her imagination had been programmed to paint the rosiest picture by default. Now, the colors on her mental palate were becoming muted and muddled.

It's amazing how frequently it happens, even within the most loving, trusting relationships. One partner will say something with purposeful intention, thinking they've expressed themselves with absolute clarity and the other partner will hear those same carefully chosen words as if they mean something else altogether. Should that misconception remain unaddressed and unrectified, the two individuals in that relationship will proceed from that point of departure under two very different, sometimes even completely opposite realities.

"Are you..." The words stuck in Tess's throat. There she was, needing to know the truth but dreading hearing it. A rogue tear drizzled down her cheek. She took a deep breath, cleared her throat, and started again. "Are you... are you having an affair with Mary Ann?"

"What?" This question, coming from the warning track at the furthest edge of left field, caught Russell totally unprepared. "Oh, my God!" he sputtered. His laugh to follow was purely out of disbelief. "Is that what you're thinking?"

"Well, then, Russell..." Tess seldom called him by his whole first name. So, when she did, he knew she was dead serious. "What the fuck is going on?"

"What do you mean, what's going on?" Russell knew that shouting at his already distraught wife would only make matters worse. But he was flailing in his exasperation. "Nothing! Exactly fucking nothing! *That's what's going on*!"

The Deacons rarely bickered. And, when they found themselves at odds, the issue was usually trivial enough that one of them could let down their defenses and seek out a dab of humor to keep the impasse from blowing out of proportion. As a couple, they were rank amateurs when it came to the brutal blood sport of life-or-death spousal combat. Tattling details about Mary Ann's untenable romantic predicament would have soothed his troubled wife's concerns; but not without revealing information shared with him in confidence. To exacerbate his quandary, he was still depending on Mary Ann to keep *his* big secret. And, as far as he was concerned, that was a bomb of immeasurable destructive power. Adding to those factors, Mary Ann had been pressuring Russell to face the music, man up, and come out to Tess. If he couldn't be forthright with his wife about his own secret, he certainly had no right to dish the dirt about someone else's personal love life.

"Pull the car over," Tess demanded.

Concentrating on his driving, Russell hadn't noticed that his wife's complexion had gone greenish pale and beads of perspiration were bubbling on her forehead. "Babe, we're almost home."

"Pull the car over!" she repeated. "NOW!"

"Look, there's no need to be dramatic. His tone had shifted from peeved exasperation to patriarchal condescension. "We're on the Interstate. When we get home, we'll hash this out."

Tess had been sensing the rapid onset of a migraine since the beginning of this conversation. Now, she was losing the struggle to stifle the queasiness in her belly. The eruption came blasting from her mouth and nose with the intensity of a city fire hydrant on a steamy August afternoon. Jumbo shrimp, Camembert, water crackers, raw carrots, celery, and sweet peppers, mixed with shortbread, chocolate truffles, white zinfandel, and bitter digestive acids painted the dashboard, glove box, and the interior of the windshield with a multi-textured, three-D coating. If it weren't for the horrific odor, one might guess that Russell had transformed the interior of his

Celica into a mobile science-fair project, a paper maché replication of the rugged, reddish surface of Mars.

Russell said the only thing one can say in such a circumstance: "Fuck!"

"I tried to tell you..." That's all Tess was able to articulate before the second projectile blast. That she was speaking to Russell when it occurred made him its next target. By now, the entire front seat area, as well as the driver, had been spackled by the contents of Tess's stomach. Tess couldn't help herself. The sight of her barf-splattered husband motoring down the Interstate was too comically absurd. Russell's immediate response to her laughter was a savage, squint-eyed scowl. When she hiccupped loudly, he suddenly recognized the absolute ridiculousness of this filthy, foul-smelling, mobile tableau.

Their shared laughter might have provided a temporary pressure valve for the tension. But, levity alone couldn't stave off the debilitating pain pulsating behind Tess's eyes. At home, as he had so many times before, Russell prepared the treatment regime. He trudged up the stairs, a damp, cold washcloth in one hand, the syringe in the other. After administering the injection of Imitrex, Russell pulled a chair to his ailing wife's bedside and began running his fingernails gently up and down the soft skin on the inside of her arm.

"Tell me a story?" Tess requested.

"Which one do you want to hear?" he whispered. "The one about the princess?"

"Yes," she said, adopting a high-pitched, childlike voice. "I like that one. It's my favorite."

No one but Russell ever saw the shadowy side of his wife's relentlessly cheerful, bubbly, outward-public demeanor. Observing her spending so much conscious energy and effort on being liked and admired by everyone in her world, he surmised that her constitution needed to balance the ledger on a periodic basis. To purge the bottled-up human vulnerabilities she so persistently kept hidden, her body resorted to occasional bouts of unbearable pain and nausea. Sometimes, she would be confined to her bed for 72 hours at a stretch. Over the years, Tess had called upon Russell not only to be her nurse maid, but to provide distraction from her agony. He fulfilled this role by concocting elaborate, twisted fairytales which, in their telling, gave the sumatriptan adequate time to filter into her bloodstream. With some arm tickling, hair stroking, and fresh, cool compresses over her eyes and forehead, she would eventually cease her writhing and moaning and drift off into merciful slumber.

Russell was in the garage, giving the interior of his car the finishing touch with Armor All. After getting sporadic sleep, mostly due to his on-call nursing duties, he'd devoted the first hours of the morning to the unenviable task of swabbing the dashboard and upholstery with rags soaked in Dawn dish soap.

"Hey, Dad..." The boy's voice came from the door to the kitchen.

"Yeah, Hank," Russell responded wearily, "I'm kinda busy right now. What is it?"

"Mom told me to tell you that she's hungry."

As a seasoned veteran of the migraine-recovery process, Russell knew exactly what this meant. "Hank," Russell responded, "you know how to make ramen. That's what she wants. Make some ramen for your mother."

"She said she wants you to do it," the boy insisted.

"Oh, for Chrissake!" exclaimed Russell. "Tell you what. Fill a pan with water and put it on the stove. I'll be in in a few minutes to finish the job."

"I'm like in the middle of a game," the boy protested. Russell wondered what sort of values he had imbued in his progeny. Could

Hank actually feel, even for a moment, that some virtual computer battle was more important than the minimal effort it would take to provide his suffering mother with some boiled noodles? Could the youngster possibly believe that mowing down imaginary aliens deserved precedent over whatever domestic chore Dad had undertaken on a Saturday morning? Russell communicated his paternal disapproval with a precisely aimed leer of intense ferocity. The boy responded by shrugging his shoulders. "Okay," Hank capitulated. "But don't forget there's a pan on the stove, Daddio." Because, of course, the short-sighted, self-serving little twit couldn't be bothered to pause his game a second time and check himself.

As Russell tore open the package and slid the brick of dried noodles into bubbling water, he took stock of a life that seemed wholly out of balance. His present existence was lacking in substance, authenticity, and fulfillment, while being overly abundant in pretense, frustration, and compromise. His life partner was starring in a self-authored play. Yes, Russell played a significant role in that marathon production. But the costume she provided severely restricted his freedom of movement, while chafing his sensitive skin. The eldest of his two sons was an entitled ingrate, while the younger, having been blessed with considerable native charm and savvy, was in danger of growing up to be a manipulative scoundrel. His job had become routine. Russell's co-workers, with the single exception of Mary Ann, fell into one of two equally unappealing categories: superficial dolts, or vapid robots.

The rotting cherry topping this sad sundae was that his internal life was being ripped apart by unrelenting same-sex desires and fantasies, most of which currently involved falling to his knees before a certain dark-skinned, gap-toothed, senior flight attendant. And kneeling, in the context of this constant craving, had less to do with offering up a prayer than with a prayer being answered. If this long-running, real-life soap opera continued as scripted, he wasn't sure it was worth getting up every day to recite the lines he'd been programmed since early childhood to memorize by wrote. But here's what Russell had yet to acknowledge: He had actually volunteered for the role he now found so ill-fitting and smothering. No, he hadn't been conscripted into a normative life. He'd signed up for it... in *ink*!

Twenty-five years ago, at 19, Russell was given a chance to explore an alternate path. David Mangold handed him the map and invited him to tag along. But, after a brief and pleasurable stroll along the scenic route, Russell pretended he didn't care for the view and turned back. So, conflicted by private, personal feelings he wasn't prepared to comprehend, let alone accept, Russell intentionally rejected the road less taken and rushed over to fall into lock step with the Main Street parade. The farther one has traveled down a chosen pathway, the more difficult a course correction becomes. And, at this juncture, Russell was incapable of seeing any alternative outcome that wouldn't leave scorched earth in its wake.

"Soup's on," Russell announced, as he stood over his ailing wife's bedside balancing a tray.

"Oh, thank you, Babe." Tess's voice was hoarse and weak. "You're the best."

"Really?" Russell asked, as he helped rearrange the pillows for her to sit up. While he liked hearing his wife say so, Tess's praise was cheap. She distributed superlatives like Halloween candy to whomever rang the bell. In the end, her liberal pandering rendered her appreciation meaningless. Russell guessed it was better than having a chronically dissatisfied spouse, who bitched, belittled and disparaged; but barely.

"Will you sit with me for a few minutes," she asked, before blowing on a spoonful of broth to cool it down.

"Sure." The air in the room was heavy with moisture from 10 consecutive hours of Tess's exhalations. "How would you feel if I just cracked open the window a half inch?"

"It's winter, Russ," she chuckled. In her mind, he might as well have asked if she wanted him to poke her repeatedly with a needle or slip a rabid weasel under her covers. "You want me to freeze?"

"Yes," Russell snapped. "That's exactly what I want... for you to freeze." Tess's furrowed brow revealed how hurt she was by his sarcasm. "I'm actually in the middle of doing some work in the garage," he continued. "So, if you don't mind..."

"Oh, God, the car!" she exclaimed. Last night's projectile-barfing episode returned in a vivid flashback. "Is it really bad?"

"I'm almost finished," Russell said, deliberately avoiding the ugly details. "A few hundred more swipes of Armor All, and it will be good as new."

"I'm sorry." Her apology was more rooted in embarrassment than contriteness.

"Anything else you need? You know, before I..."

"A kiss?"

"I think I can comply with that request," Russell said, summoning as much gallantry as he could muster. As his lips drew close to hers, the smell of rancid, acidic halitosis wafted into his nostrils. Although he had to fight a guttural gag reflex, he knew better than to say anything about it. Throwing up all over the car had been humiliating enough for Tess. Sweating and writhing in pain all night had left her hair so disheveled and matted, Sid Vicious would have looked kempt by comparison. The cords on her neck protruded, making her appear 20 years older than she had at last night's Christmas party. After holding his breath through a one-second peck on the lips, Russell beelined to make his escape.

"I love you," Tess said, sweetly.

Reaching for the door handle, Russell eked out an "I love you, too." Only when he'd reached the hallway did he dare to inhale again.

Russell first encountered clinical depression during a disillusioning freshman year of college. Thoughts of ending his life arrived during his sophomore Fall semester, not long after that unforgettable summer interning for GRMN8 Public Relations. Russell had never connected his mental-health descent with the night David Mangold so skillfully popped his queer cherry. Rather, he blamed the dark times that followed on two other factors: his girlfriend's parents forbidding her from seeing him after a pregnancy scare and his self-medication with drugs and alcohol. However, he'd gotten over that teenage heartbreak decades ago. He'd fallen in love and partnered with Tess. Booze had become something he could take or leave. And he couldn't recall the last time he'd taken any drug stronger than a Motrin. Those earlier explanations for his chronic melancholia could no longer explain away the enduring gloom.

Four months earlier, inside a certain sixth-floor hotel room in Austin, Russell gave himself permission to be his whole, complete self. That night, he'd experienced genuine happiness. He felt no guilt or regret for the act of getting naked with another man. Consistent with his defense of any number of previous same-sex encounters, he believed that spending a blissful night with the Chicago bear was a benefit to his own mental and emotional health and a boon to every aspect of his life, including his marriage. He was honest with himself about one thing: his craving for male sexual contact. But, he had yet to be forthright with his wife about who he really was, what he really needed, and what he'd been doing in the shadows for years to fulfill that need.

With the new year (1995) underway, Russell found himself feeling increasingly unmotivated and lethargic. Simply getting out of bed was a chore. Mundane tasks like taking a shower, brushing his teeth, putting his dirty socks and underwear in the hamper all seemed to require an inordinate amount of effort. He'd sit in his office for lengthy periods, staring blankly at his desk phone. Lifting the receiver to his ear and dialing the first cold call of the day seemed as impossible as hoisting Andre the Giant above his head to deliver the behemoth a body slam.

At the sound of knuckles tapping on his office door, Russell's shoulders tensed and his face scrunched into a wince. Mary Ann peaked in. "Hey, Grumpy."

"What's up?" Russell managed, attempting to lift his drooping jowls into something resembling a smile.

"You gonna sign up for the softball team?"

"I didn't know anything about it."

"Well, we could really use you," Mary Ann said. "There's a sign-up sheet on the bulletin board."

Two months had passed since Russell had taken a gander at a comparable list of names during Friday night happy hour at Ynonah's Saloon. He vaguely recalled feeling very much alive that night, pleased to be counted, if only for an hour or so, amongst a confluence of quick-witted, queer peers. What, he wondered, had happened since that evening, that he had become so disconnected with the vibrancy, the essence of being alive? He scanned across the horizon into his immediate future. Nothing seemed worthy of looking forward to. An aching welled up inside his heart. He wanted to be excited again. He longed to recapture that lost feeling of acceptance and belonging. He needed to find a new sense of purpose.

A pen dangled from a string attached to the sign-up sheet. Russell snatched it up and printed his name on the next open line, right below Mike Terzian.

TWENTY-FOUR

For a newly assembled insurance-office softball squad, the Premiums showed real promise. Certainly, the team lacked the brute, barrel-chested batsmanship displayed by the team from Sharp Transport or the airtight defensive acumen of the Roscoe Brown Plumbing lineup. But, with few exceptions, the field positions were filled with competent players. Several of his co-workers, to Russell's pleasant surprise, showed some natural athleticism.

Mary Ann was steady and fearless at second base. Mike was proving himself to be surprisingly quick and coordinated at the hot corner. He had a strong, accurate throwing arm and, when he managed to make contact, wielded his aluminum bat with power. Russell covered a lot of real estate at shortstop and, although challenged initially at the plate, was beginning to acquire the requisite patience and timing to turn a slow, high-arching pitch into a line drive. Ed wasn't swift afoot, but he was proving relatively reliable in center field. With her ovular shape, Ruby was born to play catcher, a position in slow pitch that, for the most part, amounted to knocking down or fetching a bounced ball and lobbing it back to the pitcher. She loved being in the center of the action and, more than anything, trash talking and taunting opposing batters.

The Premiums' secret weapon was Billy Fitch. The new guy in the mailroom was 25, six-foot-three, wiry, and could play any position on the field. When he wasn't lobbing spinners from the mound, Billy was a crackerjack first baseman and performed superbly in the outfield, too. And, once he reached base, which he did with frequency, he was aggressive, crafty, and deceivingly fleet on the base paths.

Co-managing the Premiums (with Mary Ann) had supplied Russell with a much-needed project to lift him out of his doldrums. He was a natural, experienced coach, a role he relished and a responsibility that was already earning him additional respect and prestige in company corridors. And spending time together in the fresh Spring air was boosting employee comradery inside the office as well.

Russell was particularly nervous about the third game on the schedule. Certainly, he cared about the team notching its first victory. However, as he dragged the canvas equipment bag from the trunk of his Celica, the flock of butterflies tickling the lining of his belly weren't about numbers displayed on a scoreboard at the contest's end. Russell's anxieties on this early April afternoon reflected concerns of a less competitive nature.

"Hey, Coach! Longtime, no see!" Russell turned around to be greeted by that familiar, winning smile and those clear, Paul-Newman-blue eyes. "Put that sack down," Bryan insisted, "and give an old pal a hug." Russell hadn't embraced another queer man in nearly five months. He'd almost forgotten what it felt like; and it felt like coming home. Lingering, chest to chest with Bryan, stubbled cheek to stubbled cheek, Russell was reminded of an essential nutrient, one he'd been depriving himself of for far too long.

"Okay, you guys. Get a room." The wisecrack came from Mike Terzian. Immediately feeling self-conscious, Russell released the embrace, and took a step back.

Having spent considerable time in the closet himself, Bryan immediately picked up on Russell's discomfort. He stretched his hand out toward Mike. "Bryan Bradley," he said, instinctively deepening his voice. "My son played on Coach's Little League team."

"Coach?" To whom, Mike wondered, was Bryan referring. He was even more puzzled as to how a guy wearing a pink and purple jersey adorned with the logo of a local gay bar could have fathered a son.

"I coached Little League," Russell explained. "The Pirates. Bryan's kid, Carter, was one of our star players. Bryan was a big help... as a volunteer."

Mike stood stationary, working his jaw muscles, leering down at Bryan's still-extended hand. Seeing that the man in the queer-bar colors wasn't going to retract his tactile greeting, Mike reluctantly accepted the handshake. From his expression, it was clear that he hadn't anticipated the strength of Bryan's grip. The momentary pain in his knuckles left him even more baffled.

It was then that Russell spied another familiar fellow lumbering across the parking lot, pounding his ham-sized fist into a weathered mitt. The look in Jamal's eyes suggested that he was focused, preparing himself mentally for competition. The big man's only acknowledgement of Russell comprised a subtle smile and a quick, almost indiscernible wave. Russell's gut response was conflicted. While he was relieved that Jamal hadn't rushed over for what would have surely been another embarrassing male-to-male hug or, heaven forbid, a kiss on the lips, Russell couldn't help but worry that Jamal's indirect snub might have something to do with his failure to dial the number on the business card Jamal had so stealthily slipped into his jacket pocket. Still, the proximity of this imposing, dark-skinned hunk sent Russell's heart racing. His knees went wobbly and he felt faint.

Taking note of Russell's light-headedness, Bryan gallantly took his friend by the elbow to steady his balance. Witnessing yet more male-to-male physical contact served to reinforce Mike's growing suspicions about the relationship between "Coach" and his helpful "volunteer." Still, certain factors seemed incompatible. How, Mike pondered, could two fathers, one with a vise-grip handshake, the other so knowledgeable about sports, be light in the loafers? Then again, how could a couple of hetero dudes be this comfortable with physical intimacy, especially right here in public? It didn't add up.

It was the top of the fifth inning with the teams locked in a six-six tie. Russell and Mary Ann had just pulled off a perfectly executed double play. With two outs and the bases empty, Jamal walloped Billy's pitch into deep right-center field. Unaware that Ed had fielded the careening orb cleanly off of the fence before firing it to Mary Ann, Jamal found himself caught in a pickle between second and third. He toyed playfully with Russell and Mary Ann, sprinting to and fro to avoid getting tagged, in the hopes that an errant toss or a dropped throw would allow him to reach base safely or, optimally, round third to score the go-ahead run. Growing short of breath, Jamal reversed direction for the nth time, only to encounter Russell, ball-in-glove, standing directly between him and third base. Unable to stop his momentum, Jamal plowed his 240-pound girth into Russell's 165. Amazingly, although he hit the ground hard, Russell held onto the ball.

"You're OUT!" bellowed the umpire. Jamal stood, hunched over, wheezing, hands on his knees. Meanwhile, Russell was lying stationary in the dirt, staring up blankly at the dusky sky. His shoulders twitched, and a clicking sound emerged from his throat, as he struggled to draw air into his lungs.

Mary Ann rushed over to her prone teammate. "You okay, Buddy?" she asked. Observing Russell's glassy, clouded eyes and inability to speak or breathe, she shouted. "I think he might be seriously hurt."

Jamal, still gasping for breath himself, nudged Mary Ann aside and kneeled down beside Russell. Fortunately, flight attendant training had prepared him for such emergencies. He inserted the thumb of his right hand over Russell's bottom teeth and tongue to prop open his mouth and clear his windpipe, then pinched his nostrils closed with the fingers of his left. Jamal whispered softly, "I'm so sorry, Honey. But you're gonna be alright. I promise. Jimmy's gonna take good care of you." Jamal placed his mouth over Russell's and exhaled steadily, forcing air down into Russell's malfunctioning pipes. Russell's chest rose in response, followed by a slow release of air that sounded like a squeaky door in a haunted house. Russell's eyes, however, remained glassy and clouded and his skin was beginning to take on a blueish tint.

"I bet his peepee gets hard when he does that." This highly inappropriate remark went from Ed to Mike, as they stood on the edge of the outfield grass kibitzing the emergency treatment.

Mike chuckled and raised his hand in the air for a congratulatory high five. "Watch out, Rusty Boy," he heckled. "If you're not careful, you're gonna have a second tongue in your mouth."

Bryan, who had sprinted onto the field out of concern, fired a beady eyed stare at Dumb and Dumber. "Are you fucking kidding me?" Bryan shouted, taking a stride toward Ed and Mike. "Did you assholes actually say what I just heard?"

"Oops," Ed responded, mockingly, "Sorry. Guess we must-a hurt somebody's tender little feelings."

"What kind of an idiot are you?" Bryan demanded. "A man's life could be in peril! And, what are you doing? Standing there cracking asinine, homophobic jokes?"

"Look," Mike said. "There's no reason to make such a big deal about..."

"Fuck you, Dude!" Bryan rasped.

"Don't get your panties in a wad, Nancy." As usual, Ed was unable to resist putting his innate obliviousness on full display. Bryan balled his fists, tilted his head forward, and took two bullish strides toward Ed and Mike. The sound of Russell taking a loud gasp of air stopped him in his tracks. Bryan turned to see the fog clearing from Russell's eyes.

"What happened?" Russell rasped. Players from both teams burst into spontaneous applause, accompanied by whistles and cheers. With obvious reluctance, Ed and Mike were last to join the celebration, a smirking Ed doing so in an ironic slow clap.

Jamal's eyes were filled with tears as he put his hands on Russell's shoulders, gently restraining him from attempting to sit up. "Better safe than sorry," he said.

Russell looked up at the face of the man who had nearly knocked him into the next world. A warm wave of love flooded into his heart. "I had no idea..." he managed.

"You had no idea of what?" Jamal asked.

"That you were so... so competitive." An adoring smile spread across Jamal's cherubic countenance. The deep belly laugh to follow came partly out of relief that he'd been able to revive Russell and, partly, because he found Russell's quip both endearing and genuinely hilarious.

The sirens, faint at first, increased in volume, as a pair of EMT vehicles sped toward the park. By the time Tess arrived, Russell had been lifted onto a gurney and was being wheeled toward the rear hatch of the waiting ambulance.

"Oh, my god, Babe... are you alright?" demanded the worried wife.

"What are you doing here?" Russell wondered aloud. "Who called you?"

Russell got his answer when Mary Ann wrapped a comforting arm around Tess's shoulder. Initially, he was filled with deep sense of gratitude that she had thought to alert his wife. That, he assessed, was exactly the kind of thing a good friend would do. Then, it reoccurred to him that Tess had weaseled her way into a friendship he had considered his exclusive domain. With his wife in the mix, the private confidences he and Mary Ann had shared put both of them in the prickly position of having to betray at least one of two sacred bonds. As the paramedics hoisted Russell into the back of the ambulance, he felt like he was the one caught in a pickle with no safe base in sight. And, as had just been proven, a pickle always ends badly for someone.

"We'll see you at the hospital, My Love." Tess's promise was more for the benefit of onlookers than it was for Russell's solace, her way of meeting expectations by assuming the guise of the faithful, dedicated spouse. As Tess gave Mary Ann a hug of gratitude, someone she hadn't seen in a number of months appeared in her sight line. Waiting patiently, like an admiring fan at a meet and greet, he was holding a baseball mitt and a cap. Feeling Tess pulling back, Mary Ann stepped aside. Tess squinted her eyes, attempting to make sense of the person standing in front of her at this particularly dramatic moment in time. "Hey," Tess addressed Bryan.

Bryan took a step forward, extending the mitt and cap. "These are..."

"Russ's." Tess completed the sentence.

"Right." Bryan nodded. Neither he nor Tess had a clue what to say next.

"Okay, then," Tess said, finally breaking the silence. "Thanks."

"Don't mention it," Bryan responded.

Tess's ingrained sense of decorum nagged at her. According to the norms of everyday human interaction, this would have been her cue to inquire how Bryan was doing, maybe get a quick update on Diane and Carter. In spite of her having spent the last eight months despising him for lying to his wife and scapegoating her husband, she still craved the man's respect and admiration. "Well," she said, "have a nice day." As she turned to walk toward the parking lot, she felt a rush of self-esteem for having resisted the urge to engage in small talk with someone she no longer considered worthy of her attention. She hadn't planned to say it. It just slipped out in a barely discernible murmur. "Asshole."

Bryan understood the woman's resentment. And, in his heart, he wanted to apologize. But, knowing this was neither the time nor the place, he held his tongue. "So, how 'bout we call it a draw?" he called out to the players on the field. "What d'y'all say?"

"As we suspected, we're looking at a pneumothorax, and a pretty serious one." The attending physician didn't look old enough to have graduated from high school, let alone medical college.

"What does that mean exactly?" Russell asked groggily, propped up in his hospital bed, wincing from the pain of each inhalation.

"Well, there are four fractured ribs. And, unfortunately, one of them pierced your left lung."

"But, I'm gonna be okay, right?"

"Of course," the doctor said, smiling for all of two seconds before re-knitting his brow in an intentional effort to add weight to his prognosis. *I bet he practices that expression in the mirror*, Russell was thinking to himself. "Usually this type of injury heals in six to eight weeks. But, just to be safe, we'll need to keep you here, at least overnight, maybe longer, for observation. Anything can happen. And, if something should take a turn, it's better that it happens here in the hospital."

"Well," Russell groused, "that doesn't sound good."

"Abundance of caution. We want to be safe. Okay?" He might have been a rookie, but the pink-cheeked doc knew that a more reassuring tone would get him out of the room quicker and on to the next stop on his rounds. "But, don't you worry. We're going to take good care of you. Any other questions for me?"

"Will he have to do physical therapy?" Tess piped in.

"That's not my call," the doctor answered. "An O.T. will be swinging by in the morning for a preliminary evaluation."

"So, that means he won't be released tomorrow," Tess assumed.

"Let's just take it one day at a time," the youthful physician suggested. "We'd rather not make promises we can't keep."

Tess pulled up the guest chair as close to Russell's bedside as possible. Now, she felt free to say what was really on her mind. "It was strange seeing Bryan out there."

"Oh, yeah," muttered Russell, "I'll bet."

"So, he's gay now?"

"Yep." Russell pondered for a second. "Well, he's always been... you know."

"Sure," Tess responded. "But, now he's like really gay-gay, like full-time."

"Correct," Russell affirmed, feeling a momentary pang of envy. "Bryan Bradley is out."

"Did you know before?"

"Did I know what before?" Russell knew exactly what she was asking. He was stalling to formulate a believable answer.

"That he... you know... that he liked guys."

Russell found no pleasure in lying to his wife. Still, he felt little compunction about withholding certain selected details. That, in his mind, was more about discretion than prevarication. But his wife had just posed a direct yes-or-no query, which presented a far more stark ethical challenge. This, he decided, is when a half-truth might do the trick. "I kind of had some inklings," he admitted.

"Well, I sure didn't pick up on it," Tess said, contemplatively. "What made you suspicious?"

"Carter said something to Hank."

"No kidding!"

"Surely I told you about that."

"Not that I remember. And, that's something I think I would... Wow! That's really interesting." Thinking how fortunate she was to have such a steadfast partner, she gazed at her presumably straight husband through adoring eyes.

"And," Russell pointed out, "that's probably how he caught Herpes."

"Oh, my god!" Tess exclaimed. "Was he? Do you think he was... you know, like going behind Diane's back, getting it on with... with other guys?"

"It happens." This, Russell knew, was the understatement of the year.

"That's disgusting! That's just... I can't believe that a man would... I don't know what to say. The bastard not only cheated on his wife, he was playing fast and loose with her health, too?"

"But he didn't cheat on her with other women." Russell wasn't defending Bryan. He was patting himself on the back that he'd always reserved his own indiscretions for persons of the same sex.

"Come on!" Tess laughed. "There's no way you think gay sex outside of marriage isn't cheating."

"It's different," he offered, more to reassure himself than to convince her.

A new voice piped in. "Oh, I'm sorry. I didn't know you had a guest." With the conversation slipping into such precarious territory, Russell found this interruption particularly well-timed. The apology was coming from the large Black man standing in the doorway, clutching a bouquet of Spring flowers, and wearing the colorful jersey of the softball squad from Ynonah's Saloon. "I should have called," Jamal said, contritely.

Tess not only recognized this person, she remembered being concerned about him. Russell's ambulance had just pulled away from the ball diamond with its blue and yellow lights flashing. She was trudging through the gravel parking lot toward her parked SUV when she heard a man mumbling to himself. There, sitting behind the wheel of a parked Mazda Miata, rag top down, was the man who now stood in the doorway of her husband's hospital room. She recalled the *Bible* laying open in his passenger seat. Head bowed, hands folded, fingers intertwined, tears streaming down his bulbous cheeks, he appeared to be praying.

"I'll come back at a more convenient time," Jamal said, turning to leave.

"No, no, no..." Tess insisted. "Come in."

"Really?" Jamal asked. "Because I don't... I feel like I'm..."

"What lovely flowers!" Feeling a jolt of maternal anxiety about having left the boys alone at home over the hours required for Russell to go through comprehensive X-rays and a head-to-toe MRI, and then wait for a diagnosis, Tess was ready to be relieved at Russell's bedside. Mary Ann had dropped by earlier, but only for a half hour.

"I just thought, that's what you do..." Jamal said, extending the bouquet toward her, "you know, when you visit a friend in the hospital."

"You two are friends?" Jamal's use of the word piqued Tess's curiosity. "I'm Tess, by the way. Russ's wife."

"Jimmy," Jamal said, "the guy who knocked your man out and put him in that bed."

"I figured," Tess responded. "Russ should have known better and stepped aside when he saw you coming."

"That's for sure," jested Russell. "If I had the chance to do it again, I would definitely make a wiser choice." Stabbing pain preventing him from laughing at his own quip.

"Hmmm..." Jamal's pain was rooted in guilt. "Like it was *your* fault. I... I honestly don't know what got into me. I feel horrible about this, Russell."

"It's okay," responded the woozy man in the hospital bed. "Water under the bridge."

Tess was sensing an ease in the banter between her husband and this visitor. Jamal had characterized himself as Russell's friend. The Russell she knew tended to be more staid and businesslike with men he didn't know well. Plus, there was something strangely familiar about this man's visage. Although she couldn't put her finger on it, she *had* seen Jamal's face before... on the Delta Airlines business card she'd retrieved from her husband's jacket pocket.

Tess, who much preferred to think happy thoughts, especially when it came to her marriage, actively began discrediting her own suspicions. Perhaps, she reasoned, the painkillers had tenderized her husband's natural outer shell. Certainly, it made perfect sense for someone who'd caused another person injury to call on them in the hospital, regardless of their level of friendship. Finally, her always-positive outlook concocted another plausible theory for this evident familiarity: that simply taking the field of play on opposing teams must automatically create a fraternal bond.

"Look," Tess pointed out, "it's late. I left a pair of untrustworthy hooligans at home. I'll just let you guys talk about whatever guys talk about when wives aren't around." She leaned down and gave Russell a peck on the cheek. "Feel better. Love you." She cocked her head in Jamal's direction. "And stay out of this guy's way."

Truly, the last thing Russell wanted was to steer clear of Jamal. "You've got the list, right?" he asked.

"Yep," Tess responded, scooting toward the door. "I'll be back in the morning with your care package. Nice meeting you, Jimmy."

Russell and Jamal listened to Tess's footsteps become less pronounced as she traipsed her way down the corridor toward the elevator. "She seems nice," observed Jamal.

TWENTY-FIVE

Russell should have been devoting his full attention to his younger son. Rory's tongue was barely keeping up with his own rapid-fire description of a skateboarding trick he'd been practicing. The boy's father, however, was finding it impossible to focus on this frantic, scattershot report. His opioid-muddled mind was stuck in a replay loop. One specific recollection was indisputable: Jamal had definitely visited his hospital room the previous evening, as evidenced by the colorful Spring flowers on the window sill. Another delicious memory remained somewhat murky and might have been a hallucinatory side effect of the Morphine drip.

Laying prone in his hospital bed on a Sunday morning, Russell watched his kid's lips move, hearing every third word, and nodding his head as if he was keeping up with the narrative. He re-ran the previous night's scenario for the dozenth time. Tess had departed for the evening. After locating a hospital urinal to serve as a make-shift flower vase, Jamal hunkered his hulky frame into the bedside chair. They'd engaged in small talk, mundane stuff: Jamal's upcoming flight assignments, the weather, some pertinent observations and opinions about masculinity. Jamal apologized yet again for his impression of a human bulldozer on the base path between second and third.

"Stuff happens," Russell responded.

"Is there anything I can do to make you more comfortable?" Jamal inquired. Although he hadn't intended to suggest anything of a sexual nature, both men picked up on that innuendo. A palpable sexual chemistry was permeating every air molecule in the room. They spent an entire minute ogling one another, taking turns sighing. Although the lust Russell felt was familiar, it came with an additional component, something more all-consuming than carnal desire. This lighter-than-air giddiness was a rush he hadn't felt in many years — thrilling and, at the same time, confusing and scary — an electric charge that, previously, had only been stimulated by persons of the opposite sex. Russell was experiencing the initial shivers of burgeoning romantic love — this time, for another man.

Russell's sight line shifted down toward the obvious tenting of his bed clothes. Jamal's attention followed. "Oh, my!" the visitor exclaimed, eyes widening, as he demurely bit his lower lip. Jamal's George Takei impression inspired titters, a mixed blessing for Russell, as laughter only reignited the flame within his throbbing rib cage. This prompted Russell to ask Jamal to press the button, releasing another drop of Morphine into his vein.

From this point, Russell's recall became fuzzy. Had he drifted off? Had the conclusion of this plotline been merely a drug-induced projection of desire in the land of nod? Or, had Jamal actually slipped his large, soft hand under the sheet to stroke his erection? And, upon reaching his ultimate release, had Russell actually made animal noises loud enough to alarm the nursing staff?

"Next," Rory expounded, "I'm gonna try a double-kick flip."

Hank was leaning against the far wall, hands plunged into the pockets of shorts baggy enough they could have accommodated both brothers. He expressed his boredom with a yawn. "I don't think he's listening," the older boy remarked. "Dude's on drugs."

"I am *too* listening!" Russell contended. This was untrue. Rory had been jabbering about skateboard tricks. That was the sum total of his semi-delirious father's comprehension.

A brisk knock presaged the door swinging open. The morning shift's attending physician, a woman with short, poodle-like, salt-and-pepper hair, no more than five feet tall and all of 95 pounds, scooted in on a pair of pink-canvas Converse high tops. Tess, who'd been getting the lowdown outside in the hallway, was on the heels of the diminutive doc's sneakers.

"Time to get you packed up!" Tess announced, cheerfully. "We're takin' you home!"

"'Bout freakin' time!" grumbled Hank.

"Let's not be hasty," the doctor cautioned. This was her cue to issue an obligatory litany of warnings and instructions, a laundry list of dos and don'ts.

Hank butted in. "Can I get a snack? Is this gonna take a long time?"

"No, Hank," Tess responded. "We need to pay attention to the doctor... so we can take good care of Dad when we get home."

"Whatever," Hank muttered.

The doctor paused to direct a glower in Hank's direction, as if to ask his permission to proceed. Hank sneered and averted his eyes toward the window, to watch the slow parade of flat, grayish-white clouds drifting across the sky. The doctor took the next moment to make eye contact with Tess in a wordless statement of sympathy for a mother who, she assumed, must deal with such puerile recalcitrance on a daily basis.

Climbing out of Tess's SUV was slow-going for Russell. "Easy does it," Tess cautioned, taking her husband's hands as he adjusted his balance, in preparation to step down from the runner. Russell emitted a squeal of pain as his stockinged foot landed on the unforgiving concrete garage floor. By this point, Hank had already rushed into the kitchen, snatched a canister of Pringles from the pantry and a Dr. Pepper from the fridge and was beelining it to the living room to resume slaying alien enemies in the digital world. Rory was toting his skateboard, helmet, shin guards, and elbow pads out into the sunshine. Russell stopped for some La Maze breathing to subdue the stabbing pain in his side.

"How late did Jimmy stay last night?" Tess inquired.

"Honestly, I don't really know," Russell said.

"What do you mean?" Tess was supporting Russell as they shuffled in a sloth-like sack race toward the door to the kitchen.

"Well, I must have drifted off. Because I don't remember him leaving."

"Did you know him before?"

"Before what?" Russell didn't much like where this interrogation was headed. Should the dialogue continue on this trajectory, some level of prevarication would be required.

"Did you know him before the game yesterday?"

"Why is that important?" This was a blatant attempt to evade giving a direct answer.

"Oh, I don't know," she said. Russell winced as he lifted his foot onto the cement step to the kitchen door. "Oooo, you okay, Babe?"

"Just a lot of pain. Nothing to worry about." Russell welcomed any opportunity to repeat his favorite line from *On Golden Pond*. In this instance, the wry post-heart-attack complaint uttered by Norman Thayer Jr. to his concerned, attentive spouse seemed particularly appropriate.

"Can I fix you some tea?"

"Sounds good." Russell was hoping Tess had lost track of the subject at hand. But, as he slowly and painfully lowered himself onto a chair at the kitchen table, she resumed where she'd left off.

"You guys... you and Jimmy... you seemed very comfortable with each other right off the bat."

"Pun intended, I presume," Russell joshed.

"Pun?" Tess pondered for a moment. "Oh, 'off the bat.' Right. Nope. Pun entirely accidental."

"See!" Russell teased. "You're not so humor-deprived after all. You just don't get your own jokes sometimes." By shifting the focus of the conversation to Tess, Russell had successfully diverted the line of questioning away from last evening's night visitor.

"Who says I'm humor-deprived?" Tess wasn't sure whether she should take offense.

"Certainly not me," Russell quipped. "I consider my wife to be a million percent funnier than a short bus packed with clowns."

"Oh, now I'm a clown? Is that what you're saying?"

"I said nothing of the sort. You said it. I just heard you."

"No sense in arguing with you, Babe," she said, dipping a bag of mint chamomile into a steaming mug. "We'd better start weaning you off those pain pills ASAP. I think they're making your brain even wackier than usual."

For Russell, having protracted time to sit and ruminate seldom led to a positive outcome. When left idle, his mood was naturally inclined to drift to the shady side of the street. With pain meds limiting his ability to focus on a single train of thought for more than a few seconds at a time, he was finding it impossible to absorb, let alone enjoy reading, the written word. Even a half-hour television sitcom required more concentration than he could marshal. He tried a classic rock station on the clock radio. But every other song seemed so shrill and banal, the playlist only ended up making him angry. Public Radio featured repetitive segments throughout the day. And exposing himself to the same bad news over and over again only darkened his mood.

This led to spending hours reclining in bed, staring up at the ceiling fan, and stewing about his lot in life. Every so often, one or more of his body parts would complain, necessitating yet another positional adjustment. And each attempt at relieving the pressure on one section of his back, or hip, or shoulder would set off a chain of unpleasant physical responses, invariably beginning with stabbing pain and difficulty drawing a breath. Once settled in what, for the moment, felt like a more comfortable posture, the itching would begin... on the back of the calf, behind an ear, the crown of the head, an ankle, the base of the rib cage, a spot on the clavicle. At minimum, he spent an hour per day playing scratch-a-mole with these phantom sensations.

At first, he attempted to shoo away the erotic daydreams. Fancies of that sort, he rebuked himself, should not be entertained in the bed he shared with his wife. Before long, however, all mental self-discipline had dissipated. Free to roam, Russell's mind took him on trips to exotic, tropical places, always accompanied by Jamal. At one fabulous destination after another, they strolled through street markets holding hands and slipped down narrow alleyways, giggling like school girls, in search of shadowy corners where they could indulge in hot, rambunctious sex. They body surfed white-tipped waves alongside smiling dolphins, embraced, belly-deep and dripping with warm, azure salt water, then tumbled onto chaise lounges to mingle their tongues under beach umbrellas.

Russell happened to be luxuriating in one such escapist flight of whimsy when Tess entered the room. Being yanked back into reality was jarring enough. Seeing his wife stirring Metamucil into a glass of water made the contrast between his romantic dream world and reality that much starker.

"Gotta get your motor runnin'!" she proclaimed.

"Oh, thanks, Babe." In spite of having been so abruptly plucked out of yet another exquisite mental getaway with his chocolate love bunny, Russell welcomed the interruption. Among multiple, ongoing discomforts, constipation (a common opioid side effect) was one for which a remedy was readily available. He guzzled down the orange mixture without a second of hesitation.

"Such a good little patient," Tess remarked, before giving her ailing hubby a peck on the forehead. "This just came in the mail." She spun a large, rectangular envelope onto the bed. Russell's face, previously greyish pale, flushed pink, as he looked at the baby-blue paper stock and the rainbow stripes tracing the edges of the envelope flap. "Get well card?" Tess guessed. Russell continued to gape at the colorful envelope. "You gonna open it? Or, are you too busy?"

Having lost any ability to see humor in his circumstance, Russell ignored her tease. Tentatively, he reached for the envelope. The name on the return address, J.A. Diallo, gave him pause. Tess nodded her encouragement. Slowly, cautiously, Russell slipped a fingernail under the flap. It was indeed a feel-better-soon card. Worried that the message might be personal — from one individual, that individual being Jamal — he was relieved to see signatures from the entire Ynonah's Tavern team. Then, as he handed the card to Tess for her perusal, he felt a pang of disappointment, wishing it had actually been a love note from the luscious man who'd been hijacking the lion's share of his convalescent ruminations.

"How sweet!" Tess remarked, with a broad smile. "Those gay boys always do the right thing, don't they." Russell didn't respond. Pressure welling around his eye sockets was spreading back and around his ears, down the back of his neck, over his shoulders and under his armpits, onto and across his upper torso. It was as though someone had lowered an invisible lead blanket onto his chest. This wasn't a coronary episode; although, without a doubt, his heart was aching. This was yet another plunge into depression.

Russell had long been aware that he was a prime candidate for psychotherapy. Still, he'd persistently put off seeking treatment. This reticence was not related to any potential expense; his company health insurance would have covered it. He knew that, in order to receive any substantial benefit from counseling, all of his cards would have to be laid face-up on the table. That meant being forthright about his same-sex attraction and compulsive extra-marital ventures and, ultimately, facing a frank professional assessment.

But he was in dire pain; and not just physically. The broken ribs and punctured lung were only piling additional agony atop the psychic struggle of trudging through day after day in the dual personas known as Russell Deacon. His physical discomfort might even have provided some welcome distraction from this anguish, being as it was, a constant reminder that he was still alive. Still, seeing no escape from a maze of his own construction — at least none that wouldn't cause incalculable ruin — only one solution was making sense. And, on this day, as his wife handed back the get-well card from a group of compassionate, queer softball players, he was contemplating an early exit from what seemed an impossibly tangled thicket of predicaments and private misery.

Russell had come to the conclusion that he was an abject failure in his most important life roles: husband, father, and decent human being. He'd been a selfish, self-serving liar, an egoistic pleasure-seeker, a careless, debauched hedonist. What would his parents, or his wife, or his wife's parents or, perish the thought, his sons think of him if they ever found out? He had lurked along park pathways, loitered outside public restrooms, and entered triple-X bookstores, all to answer a base, animal impulse. The only difference he could see between himself and a chimpanzee at the zoo was that he had yet to fling his own feces at someone. No vision of the future appeared remotely acceptable. Although just 45, with his life's diary barely half-written, turning the page to begin a new chapter seemed too heavy a lift.

Russell had a substantial life insurance policy, with a death benefit large enough to support his family comfortably for a decade. A drug-blurred mind and a melancholic heart told him that Tess and the boys would be far better off with him out of the picture. Surely, they would grieve his passing. But, eventually, they would thank him for making the ultimate sacrifice. Best of all, they would never have to suffer the ordeal of being introduced to his hidden self. If he ended it all without revealing his shadow identity, he would die untarnished, a knight in shining armor. Russell had grown weary of protecting himself. It was time he thought about protecting them... from a very inconvenient, unpleasant truth.

As Russell brainstormed exit strategies, excitement bubbled up at the myriad possibilities. Not only would suicide be a new adventure, it would solve everybody's problems in one single action. Why hadn't he realized this before? Of course, he'd be taking the easy way or, as some say, the coward's way out. But, in this circumstance, the easiest, most expedient thing had every appearance of being a sure win-win. Thus, the coward would be remembered as a hero. So, why not?

"Babe," Tess began.

"Yes," responded Russell.

"I don't know how to say this. So, I'm just going to say it."

"Okay." Suddenly, Russell's heart was racing. He had no clue as to what he was about to hear.

"I'm... I'm really worried about you."

"Okay. What do you mean?"

In a list of subjects Tess would ever want to address, this one was last, and scribbled as an afterthought, in pencil, in the tiniest, cursive script. To her credit, she bit the bullet, took a deep breath, cleared her throat, and looked into her husband's eyes. "I... well... I think you should see somebody."

"See somebody? Like...?"

"You know, like a counselor, a therapist." Having put the subject out into the glaring light of day, her tone became more assertive. "I think you should get counseling. Seriously."

"Alright." Russell found this suggestion somewhat ironic. Tess was not a particularly empathetic person. And, her own personal experience with therapy had not been particularly pleasant, let alone productive. "Because?"

"Babe," she stated. "You're obviously depressed."

"And, what's new about that?" The cynical nature of this quip only served to reinforce her diagnosis.

"Don't be glib. This isn't something to joke about."

"I'm sorry."

"And, don't say you're sorry either. Just... just... just listen to me! I love you. I'm worried about you. I hate seeing you like this."

"I'm on pain pills," he argued. "I'm stuck in this bed. I can't get comfortable. My head is all... you know, messed up. Why wouldn't I be feeling a little bit down?"

"But you're not just a little bit down..."

"What are we having for dinner?" Thirteen-year-olds typically lack the awareness and restraint to inquire if they might be interrupting. Tess stopped mid-sentence and shifted her attention to Hank standing in the doorway. Having commandeered the floor, the boy continued, "Are we gonna have dinner, or what?"

"I'll be down in a minute, Hank," Tess replied.

"Okay, Mom," Hank griped. "But I'm starving. And you always go berserk when I snack before dinner. So..."

"Your mother will be down in a minute, Hank." Oddly, this momentary flash of anger toward his self-centered, firstborn son served to bolster Russell's spirits. He was back in his comfort zone, in the familiar role of paternal disciplinarian.

"Okey-dokey," muttered Hank, in a snide note of resignation, before making his retreat.

Tess returned her attention to the patient in bed. "Thanks," she said, patting the back of his hand.

"For what?"

"For backing me up." Tess and Russell didn't always agree on parenting tactics. So, when they fell into sync, she genuinely appreciated his support. "I guess I'd better..." Tess said, cocking her head toward the door.

"Yeah, right. Can't let the little prince starve."

"You'll think about it?"

Russell didn't have to ask what she was asking him to consider. "Yes," he said. "In fact, I'm inclined to give it a shot."

"I'm so happy to hear you say that." Tess's tear-filled eyes confirmed her statement. She, however, hadn't the first inkling as to what her husband agreeing to therapy could lead to.

Russell's internal to-be-or-not-to-be debate had taken on a new dimension. The issue that, two minutes earlier, had seemed so cut-and-dried was once again fraught with nuance and moral ambivalence. It was becoming apparent to Russell that his permanent absence would not be a clear win-win after all. One aspect he'd previously neglected to put on the "con" side of the ledger was leaving Tess to single-parent the boys; most notably, to deal with Hank's surliness. Doing that would be extremely unfair — unforgivable, in fact. At this inflection point in the boy's development, Tess needed his partnership. And, without a strong father figure, Hank might permanently lose his bearings and spend the rest of his life adrift. Russell couldn't possibly consider vacating his parental role in the household until he was relatively certain that the truculent teen was out of the woods and headed in a more stable direction.

So, with the suicide route forestalled, Russell found himself at a critical crossroads. One sign pointed toward a continuation of the status quo. This pathway, up until a year ago, had served its purpose. Now, however, every step Russell took further into the queer wilderness seemed to make the ground beneath his feet more unstable. Continuing down that course meant that more precarious stretches lay ahead, increasing the odds of being found out, or some other unimaginable catastrophe. The other sign, the one labeled "Therapy," veered off onto heretofore unexplored terrain. Both choices were formidable. Only one, however, held the potential of pleasing Tess... in the short run, at least. That factor, as it turned out, tipped the scales.

TWENTY-SIX

Exiting the medical building, so light on his feet, Russell might have been bounding across the surface of the Moon, pulled by gravity far more forgiving than that of Planet Earth. If he thought he could have pulled it off without suffering a dagger stab of pain in his still-healing rib cage, he would have clicked his heels.

He'd been fretting the appointment for weeks. Sitting on the sofa in the waiting lounge, filling out the requisite forms — page after page of invasive, personal queries — had only served to worsen his anxiety. "Russell?" He looked up from the clip board in his hands to behold the kindest face he'd seen since Mrs. Murty on the first day of third grade. Tallish, with long, straight, shoulder-length, grey hair, Dr. White was dressed tastefully in black stretch slacks and a sweater with a subdued, geometric pattern, reminiscent of a Mark Rothko painting.

"I'm still..." Russell stammered. "I haven't finished..."

"No worries," she said, in a voice that sounded like hot cocoa tastes on a cold, December day. "You can do that later. We've got things to talk about." Russell's nervous knees wobbled, as he rose to follow the psychologist down a short hallway adorned with impeccably framed art and vintage photographs. She ushered him into a tidy room, no larger than twelve-by-twelve. A faux-leather loveseat was positioned against the outside window, flanked by end tables, each supporting a lamp and a requisite box of facial tissues.

"Good. Two boxes of Kleenex," Russell joked, "I might need 'em both."

"Well, that's what they're there for," responded Dr. White. "Please..." She motioned toward the loveseat.

"You want me to sit?" Russell inquired. "Or, lie down? This is all new to me."

"Whatever makes you most comfortable."

Russell perched himself on the edge of the middle sofa cushion, as if he might not be staying long. Dr. White skootched back in her wing-backed chair, upholstered in calming tones of umber and avocado. Smiling pleasantly, she shed her flats, tucked her legs and feet under her and observed. With slow seconds of silence dragging by, Russell felt like a rare, endangered zoo animal under observation. "So, what's next?" he asked.

"You tell me," she said. "What brings you here? What's on your mind?"

"Well..." he began, sliding back into what he assumed would be a more comfortable posture but, instead, wincing and clutching his still-tender chest.

"Something wrong?" She seemed genuinely concerned.

Pleased to have the story of his fractured ribs as an icebreaker, Russell quipped, "Well, long story short, I failed to get out of the way of a charging bull."

"Wow, sounds painful," she said. "Want to tell me about it?" Russell began sharing his passion for coaching baseball and how co-managing the office softball team had provided him a healthy outlet, until a violent collision on the base path put him out of commission; temporarily, he hoped. "That must be difficult," she remarked.

"Yeah," Russell responded, "It's been rough... tedious, really. But... I'm on the mend, as they say." Feeling foolish that the good doctor might think that his inability to actively participate in his athletic hobby was his primary reason for seeking therapy, Russell segued to a more substantive subject. "My wife and I... Tess and I — we've been married for fourteen years now — have two sons..." Sharing the various parental challenges he and Tess had been having with Hank siphoned off a major portion of the session time. Beyond that, Russell shared that he'd been feeling enervated in the work place, while intimating that Tess, although a beautiful person and a dedicated life partner, tended to see him as a two-dimensional caricature and basically refused to appreciate him as a whole human being.

He left the appointment very much looking forward to next week's opportunity to continue unloading his grievances. Having someone listen, comprehensively and objectively, can't help but make a person feel better about everything. He'd taken an immediate liking to Dr. White. And, in one single session, she was already beginning to win his trust.

"Did you talk about me?" This was the second thing Tess asked. Her first query was the obligatory, "How did your therapy session go?" which elicited a glowing report from Russell.

"Only to say what a fantastic wife you are," he told her, giving her a loving peck on the lips.

"Exactly what I wanted to hear." She wasn't kidding. It was what she had come to expect from her perfect partner in their perfect marriage. "You're the best husband ever."

"Let's not go overboard, Babe," he kidded. "There's probably one, maybe even a couple-a guys out there who could give me a run for my money."

"Well, I'm happy with the one I got," she replied. "I'm not looking for anyone else."

Russell felt obliged to respond in kind, to tell Tess that she was the best wife in the entire universe, that she'd always be his one and only love. Instead, he punted. "I really like her... Dr. White."

"That's great," Tess responded. "But, you like me better, right?"

"We'll see," he teased. "I'm gonna reserve final judgment on that."

"You are so bad!" Tess chirped, swatting his behind with a dish towel.

"Ouch!" he protested. "Be careful. I'm still recovering from a head-on collision."

"Seriously, though," she said. "I'm really glad you're doing this. I think it's super, super great."

"Me, too, Babe," he responded. "I really mean it. Hey... look..." He nodded toward the sliding glass doors and placed his arm around his wife's shoulder. Automatically, she slipped hers around his waist. The happy couple stood in their kitchen, watching as, out in the backyard, Rory wound up and fired a brisk fastball across the lawn and into Hank's mitt.

"Steeeeeerike!" Hank called out in umpire speak, before tossing the ball back to his younger sibling.

"Ain't that somethin'?" Russell queried, rhetorically.

"Apparently, miracles never cease," his bride replied. A moment passed. Then, she had an idea. "Maybe we should do it tonight." Once again, Russell knew the proper response. And yet, his tongue failed to give shape to the words. He forced his lips into a creased smile, letting that provide the answer.

It was 11:05 PM when Tess, her naked body still warm and moist from the shower, slipped under the covers. "Are you awake?" she whispered, reaching a hand around her husband's inert body to check the status of his private parts. Russell was indeed awake. His genitals, however, remained cold. He pretended not to hear her.

Russell's manic, first-therapy-appointment high proved to be short-lived. As the weeks of sessions rolled on, he found it increasingly more difficult to hoist himself out of bed in the morning. Without opening his eyes, he'd grope for the snooze button on the radio alarm clock to mute *Morning Edition*, only to repeat this action every time Bob Edwards' voice shook him from his slumber. Only when his bladder insisted on being emptied did he feel sufficient motivation to change his posture from horizontal to vertical. Then, after plodding to the toilet half-awake, he'd return, tumble heavily onto the mattress, and crawl back under the covers. "Just one more dream," he'd mutter to no one. Sleep had become Russell's one and only pleasure. Visiting the unconscious provided escape from an increasingly burdened heart, while offering distraction from a void still unfulfilled.

Mary Ann rapped softly on Russell's office door. After waiting for 10 seconds with no response, she turned to walk away, but changed her mind, mid-stride. She knocked louder the second time. Still hearing nothing from inside, she relayed a warning: "Pull up your pants, Buddy. I'm comin' in." She peeked inside to find Russell seated at his desk, back hunched, his jowls and eyes drooping under gravity's pull.

"Hey..." Russell's greeting was anemic. "What's going on?"

"How about lunch?"

"Yeah. No," he muttered. "Thanks. I really don't have much of an appetite. Besides..." He lifted a policy document from his desk, providing evidence that he had work to do.

What Mary Ann wanted to say was that she was worried about him, that he could always count on her for a compassionate ear. Instead, she asked, "When's your next therapy appointment?"

"Tomorrow."

"How's it been going?" This query was somewhat intrusive and she knew it. "If you don't mind me asking, that is." Mary Ann missed the Russell she'd come to know prior to his injury. He hadn't just had the wind knocked out of him. He seemed to have lost the breath of life.

Russell knew it would be impossible to sum up his therapy experience in a few sentences. But, in his present malaise, even a spontaneous, sociable lunch seemed onerous. Still, he thought, having a friend to talk to might be worth the effort. He swallowed hard and made a conscious attempt at brightening up a notch. "Okay," he said. "Screw it. Let's grab lunch."

"Maybe you'll feel hungry by the time we get there," Mary Ann suggested. On one hand, she was looking forward to spending some long-postponed, one-on-one time with her office confidant. On the other, she harbored a natural sense of apprehension. She knew from experience that no one can take on another person's burden. And, of late, Russell appeared to be lugging around an entire dumpster crammed to the rim with emotional detritus. Maybe, she could convince him that at least a portion of his load could be set aside for the time being. That would relieve her from having to assume the role of emotional Sherpa.

"I guess I didn't realize how hungry I really was," Russell said, as he wolfed down his last bite of rice and vegetables.

The conversation thus far had yet to stray beyond an innocuous, humdrum landscape. Mary Ann had to break the ice. "So, you've got a therapy appointment tomorrow."

"With Dr. White, yeah," Russell responded. "I really like her..."

"I feel a 'but' coming." Mary Ann's intuition was spot on.

"Yeah," he confessed, forcing another pursed-lipped smile. "A big ol' but." Russell's eyes were darting around the room, looking everywhere but directly at Mary Ann. This was out of character for Russell. Typically, he was the one to initiate eye-contact and sustain it, a trait Mary Ann sometimes found unsettling. "How about we get some coffee?" he suggested.

From the day of its grand opening, Bongo Java had clambered with activity. Still, as popular as the spot was, no other place in town offered a better atmosphere for intimate, face-to-face conversation. Caffeine — in this case, a double cappuccino — had a predictable effect on Russell, loosening his lips while suppressing his inhibitions. Tomorrow's session, he informed Mary Ann, would be his fifth with Dr. White. The therapy process had been cathartic from the get-go, permitting him to investigate the sources of certain anxieties, insecurities, and unresolved issues. The sudden, premature death of an adored brother, for one example, was a scarring episode around which, for the previous six years, Russell had managed to tiptoe, leaving residual grief unaddressed.

During the previous week's session, Russell finally dared to broach the very subject he'd steered clear of therapy for so many years to avoid. This meant not only coming clean about his bisexuality, but confessing to the intractable impulses that lured him into habitual, risky behavior. After listening to this part of Russell's story, Dr. White commented, "I had a feeling there was something else going on."

With these cats out of the bag — aptly named Sexuality and Promiscuity — Russell pre-emptively leapt to his own defense, expressing the self-delusional claim that, because he hadn't cheated with other women, his nuptial vows remained unblemished and that his extra-marital adventures were actually a boon to his marriage. "I don't see much difference between what I do and a guy who devotes his free time to dirt biking, or golf, or playing dominoes at the park," he rationalized. "In fact, my little hobby — and that's pretty much what it is — is even better, because it doesn't cost anywhere near what some guys pay for clubs and shoes and greens fees." Withholding her response, Dr. White kept listening with the expectation that Russell would hear what was coming out of his own mouth and realize the absurdity of this pretzel logic. "I mean, Ted,"

Russell blathered on, "he lives like three doors down. This guy spent almost ten grand on a home theater system. All he does, every single night, is sit back in a cushy theater seat in this soundproofed cave, in the dark, and watch DVDs. *Star Wars*, *Saving Private Ryan*, *Glory*, all this macho-manly stuff, on a seventy-inch screen. He's got the subwoofers and the Dolby sound system, and..."

"Russell," Dr. White butted in.

"No, really!" Russell was determined to circumvent the subject he had, just a few minutes earlier, finally put out into the air of his counselor's office. "This other guy, Roger Nelson, belongs to Belle Meade Country Club. Do you know how much that costs?"

"It's expensive, I know," Dr. White affirmed.

"You know?" Russell inquired. "How do you..? You don't..?"

"Whether I... and, no, I don't... or Roger Wilson..."

"Nelson."

"Sorry, Roger Nelson," she said, correcting her error. "Anyway, who belongs to the Belle Meade Country Club and how much they pay for their membership is not what we're here for." It was the first time Russell had detected this tone coming from Dr. White — assertive, almost stern. "Let's concentrate on you. Let's talk about what *you* can control." The psychologist's insistence on focusing on the issue at hand was disturbing. Sensing that he was feeling chastised, the good doctor tossed out a bone of encouragement. "You've just shared something important, essential even, about yourself. You identified as bisexual. You said it out loud. That's huge!"

"Well," he said, "it's not the first time I've said it, so..." He chose not to elaborate.

"It's the first time you said it to me."

"Correct."

"How does it feel?"

In spite of the monumental nature of this breakthrough, had it not been for Dr. White's cue, it wouldn't have occurred to Russell to sit quietly for a moment and reflect. As he took mindful inventory of his emotions, a smile blossomed across his face. "Good," he confessed, pleasantly surprised that the words he'd avoided articulating for so long hadn't yet precipitated a cataclysmic seismic event. For the first time in four visits, his palms noticed the texture of the couch cushions. He drew a clean inhalation. And, upon exhaling, he reiterated, "It feels really, really good."

"Congratulations! Good on ya, Russell."

"Thanks. Thanks a lot." With Dr. White reaffirming that he was on the right track, Russell allowed himself a modicum of pride in his progress. However, he was totally unprepared for the truth grenade the good doctor was about to hurl from her chair to the sofa.

"Now," she said, "before we finish for today, I have two things to say."

"Okay." Russell's gut warned him that he wasn't going to like thing one... or thing two, for that matter.

"First, the impulses and behavior you're describing might — and, I'm not saying this definitively — be symptomatic of addiction."

"Sex addiction." Russell was requesting clarification.

"Yes."

For some time, Russell had suspected that his inability to control his elicit actions might suggest addiction. He found real appeal in the idea of having some legitimate syndrome to blame for his behavior, rather than faulting his own weak will and flawed judgment. Dr. White jotted a book title and its author's name on a slip of paper. Extending it to Russell, she told him, "I want you to get a copy of this book. It's primarily a collection of case studies. See if maybe you recognize yourself in any of them. Will you do that?"

Without glancing at the title, Russell folded the slip of paper in two and pocketed it. "Sure," he promised, "absolutely." *Thing one*, he mused silently to himself, *wasn't so bad after all.*

"Good," stated Dr. White. "Now, this may be somewhat harder to accept. But, I need to set you straight on something."

"What's this," Russell blurted, half in jest, "conversion therapy?"

"No," Dr. White responded, "why would you think that?"

"You said you needed to set me straight."

"Oh," she chuckled. "Sorry about that. I should probably pay closer attention to my word choices."

"Ya think?" Russell was enjoying putting a point the board.

"Anyway," continued Dr. White, "here's the truth." She paused for a second to presage the seriousness of what she was about to say and make sure Russell was devoting his full attention. "You *are* being unfaithful to your wife." Any sense of liberation or well-being Russell had felt from coming out to his therapist abandoned him. "That's the reality you're going to have to face," she emphasized. But that was only a warning shot. She was about to drop the bomb. "And you have to come out to her."

"Fuck me," Russell muttered. He had received thing one, as weighty as such a prognosis might have been, constructively. Thing two, however, was considerably less palatable.

"And, the sooner you own up to yourself and to Tess," the therapist asserted, "the sooner we can start getting down to the real core of your depression."

While draining the final drops of his cappuccino, Russell's eyes took a quick survey of the adjacent tables at Bongo Java. "Then," he recounted to Mary Ann, "The good doctor laid out the agenda for our next session..."

"Tomorrow," Mary Ann assumed aloud.

Russell nodded. "Tomorrow, she plans to start helping me compose my coming-out speech."

"She's right you know," said Mary Ann. Russell knew this was merely a kinder way of saying, "I told you so."

"I guess..." he whispered, haltingly. The specter of setting off what would, in all certainty, be a world-destroying nuclear explosion was overwhelming. "I guess so. God *dammit*!"

TWENTY-SEVEN

Strong coffee had an additional effect on Russell. A mid-afternoon cup tended to rouse his libido. As he scanned through a 14-page policy-renewal agreement for a longtime client, a stirring in his lower belly effectively sent words on the page scattering like cockroaches on a linoleum floor. After attempting to read the updated exemption clause three times, his over-active brain still failed to decode the legalese. He checked his watch: 4:48. The Pirates' game was scheduled for six. *No harm in getting to the ball field early*, he decided. *And, right now, I could use some fresh air.* In reality, his java-stimulated imagination was picturing a stroll down memory lane which, in this case, meant the path through the woods by the ball field. And, the more vivid that vision became, the more the cadence of his heartbeat quickened. He swept the contract aside and pushed his chair back from his desk.

As Russell pulled his Celica into the gravel parking lot, the only people on the diamond were a pair of boys from the opposing squad, playing catch. He checked his watch again: 5:14, 46 minutes until game time. Jogging around the bleachers prompted his still-sore ribs to advise, "Walk. Don't run." By the time he reached the path, players and coaches from both teams were arriving and readying themselves for the evening's contest.

"Barry Larkin takes the field!" Russell immediately recognized Rory's boyish impersonation of his major-league idol. Midway into the 1995 season, the 10-year-old was making major contributions to his team's competitiveness, becoming more adept with the bat, wilier on the base paths and, much to Russell's pride, emulating his father at the shortstop position. Logically, Russell should have let his son know he was there and offer to help the Pirates go through their warm-up routines. Reason and fatherly responsibility, however, were being shouted down. He stepped onto the path and began power walking. As he rounded the bend and out of sight of the baseball diamond, a man came into view, ambling in the opposite direction. As they drew nearer to one another, a subtle exchange of smiles suggested they had both come there for the same reason.

The man stopped next to a trailhead veering off into the pines. Russell slowed his pace. The man shuffled about 20 feet into the shade before turning around to see if Russell was following. Russell gave him a two-second, head-to-toe evaluation. Wiry, ginger-haired, and freckled wasn't Russell's favorite flavor. But he wasn't there to fall in love. Every other thought said, *Don't do it*. The game would be starting soon. But, his animal brain wasn't interested in what time it was. The ginger-haired man fingered his crotch. Russell initialed the silent contract with a head nod and took his first stride into the woods.

Approximately 50 yards down the trail, the ginger-haired man slipped behind a large boulder. Russell stopped to survey the environs and listen for voices. Reassured that he was not being observed, he joined the ginger-haired man, who, by this time, was unzipped, and freeing something quite magnificent into the humid July air. Involuntarily, Russell's salivary glands responded, secreting slippery fluid into his mouth. Resistance was futile. He dropped to his knees.

All human beings need and seek connection, heart-to-heart, mind to mind, body to body. Behind a boulder, beneath a canopy of green, Russell was, at that moment, directly connected in the most literal sense to another human being. The fit was finely engineered: Insert tab "A" into slot "B." Could such impeccably designed tooling be anything but intentional? One orifice, expandable and self-lubricating, provides a round hole for a round peg. The entire concept of intimacy was taking on new dimensions. There is good reason, Russell realized, that the phallus has been revered since the dawn of history. While he'd always found immense pleasure being on the receiving end, this was fulfillment on another level altogether.

It was the bottom of the second inning by the time Russell slipped into the bleachers. That Tess was absent from the crowd provided him a measure of reprieve. He relished having time to savor the delectable aftertaste of his encounter under the trees. Right on cue, Rory proceeded to bunt for a single, steal second, and score on a dropped fly ball. The boy's assertive play gave the Pirates a one-run advantage, a lead they never relinquished on their way to winning the game handily.

As a spectator, Russell cheered boisterously for every strike the Pirates' pitchers tossed, every out executed by the defense, and every swing at the plate. He was filled with a rare feeling, one he had seldom known, and one to which he had never assigned much value. *Happiness*, he'd always posited, *is superficial and transitory*. Russell assigned far more importance to a more lasting experience: fulfillment. Thus, he'd chosen to assess the quality of a day in his life based on whether he'd spent his time productively, if he'd accomplished something tangible or, at the very least, made measurable progress on a worthwhile endeavor. Still, there he was, a passive bystander watching a Little League game, feeling genuinely happy. Certainly, witnessing the Pirates' impressive performance was a source of pride — as their previous manager, he'd played a substantial role in setting these youngsters on the path to self-belief and ultimate victory. But this mood was actually born of something else altogether, something intangible and mystifying. Fellating a guy behind a boulder in the woods was nothing to crow about. Bringing another man to orgasm wasn't some great accomplishment. He might even have felt shame after having participated in such questionable activity. Russell, however, felt neither pride nor shame. He simply felt happy.

He knew this meant he would have to sneak off to the clinic for STI testing. It would require dodging sex with Tess until he had conclusive (hopefully negative) results. But, he didn't care. Those delicious 15 minutes had injected him with contentment on a level he'd seldom experienced. Even knowing that this feeling would be short-lived, he didn't fight it. He marinated in it.

"Where were you?" Rory asked. "I saw your car."

"I got here early," Russell responded. "I decided to take a walk."

"What happened? Did you fall or something?" Rory was curious about the soiled patches on the knees of his dad's pants.

"No, no," Russell responded quickly. He'd had some time to anticipate this question. "Some creature crawled across the path into the bushes. And, I wanted to see what it was."

"What was it?"

"A snake." Although Russell hated lying to his son, at least this fib had an iota of truth to it. "Yeah. Turned out to be a snake... a big one. Where's your mom?"

"She had that thing."

"Oh, right..." Russell nodded, as if it was all coming back. "That thing."

"Some meeting... about recycling, or whatever."

Father and son shuffled through the parking lot. "Great game!" Russell said. "You played really well!"

"Except," the boy grumbled, "the ball got stuck in my mitt, and we missed getting that double play."

"Happens, you know... even Barry Larkin's glove gets sticky sometimes. Besides, it didn't cost you any runs. And that's the important thing."

"I wish you could hit some grounders to me. I really need to practice my move to second."

"Won't be long," Russell said, pointing the key remote at his Celica. "Another week or so, my ribs should be right as rain."

Rory tossed his bat and glove into the back seat. As he slid into the passenger seat, he noticed his father dawdling by the open, driver-side door. "What's goin' on, Daddy-O?" On the adjacent field, the Ynonah's Tavern team was taking infield practice, preparing for a 7:30 p.m. contest. Jamal, standing at home plate, punched a grounder to Bryan at third. Sending a wave in Russell's direction had left Bryan totally unprotected against the bouncing orb that struck a bullseye in the center of his groin. Jamal seemed less concerned about his stricken teammate and far more interested in what (or whom) had distracted Bryan. Discovering that the attention grabber was Russell, he stood transfixed, gazing across the hundred-yard expanse.

"Isn't that the guy?" Rory asked, squinting through the windshield glass.

"What guy?"

"You know, the guy who knocked you on your butt."

"Yep," Russell said, his eyes still fixed on the large, chocolate hunk with the aluminum bat poised on his shoulder. "He knocked me over alright." On impulse, Jamal blew Russell a kiss.

"Why did he do that?" Rory asked. The Celica kicked up dust, as Russell steered toward the road.

"Why did who do what?"

"Why did that guy blow you a kiss?"

"Oh, that?" Russell explained. "It was just a joke. Not a real *kiss*-kiss. More like a mock kiss."

"You guys are weird." Russell wondered how weird Rory would think he and Jamal were if the truth were revealed. Or, would his son use a different word to describe his father and the man for whom his dad harbored a hopeless crush. Russell detected a trace of acidity on his palate. He asked his son to grab a bottle of water from the floor behind the passenger seat. After sloshing the warm liquid around in his mouth, he stopped the car, opened the door and spit out the mouthful onto the pavement. The flavor of sperm was lessened somewhat. But the memory of where that taste came from could not be rinsed away so easily. By taking a prayerful posture in those woods, Russell had crossed the Rubicon into new, wondrous, and potentially treacherous territory. He was astonished by how much he had loved being on the giving end of oral sex with another man. And, he couldn't help but wonder how it might feel to take communion at the altar of someone he knew and genuinely cared about. Surely, he was convinced, receiving Jamal's offering would open up even more inexplicable dimensions of joy.

An expanded universe had opened up for Russell's same-sex cravings. A little more than a year ago, he'd been nothing more than a voyeuristic masturbator. So much had changed in the interim. Since then, he'd wrestled with a bear in a peep booth, and spooned all night, naked, in the same bed with a girthy salesman from Chicago. Today marked a cliff dive far deeper into the mysterious waters of queer sex. And tomorrow, he would be sharing this major development with his therapist.

TWENTY-EIGHT

"**Y**ou seem particularly at ease today, Russell." Dr. White was a keen observer of body language. Seldom was her radar more than a millimeter or two off base.

"Really?" Russell was still feeling a residual buzz from yesterday's coupling under the pines. *Is it possible*, he mused to himself, *that the good doctor is seeing a changed man*?

"Any particular reason?"

"Not really." Of course, there was a reason, a particularly significant one, and he was dying to trumpet it from the rooftops.

"Okay." Intuiting Russell's evasiveness, the tone of this "okay" conveyed her disbelief. "Have you done any thinking about what we talked about last week?"

"You mean..." Russell swallowed hard, "... have I thought about..." He dug deep, summoning up the gumption to say it aloud, "... coming out to Tess?"

"Well, yes," Dr. White replied. "But, not about *whether*. We've already decided that needs to happen. Right?" Russell's nod was nearly undetectable, as the color began leaving his face. "So, have you thought about a timeline, when you might do it, or what words you might use?"

The feeling of contentment and self-acceptance Russell had carried into the room was vaporizing quicker than a dew drop on a Joshua Tree at sunrise. A sudden tightening in his chest made it difficult to draw air into his lungs. Russell had entered the space knowing this would be today's theme. While, over the course of the week, he'd taken a few, tentative stabs at imagining a constructive script, the specter of delivering such unwelcome and disturbing news to his wife painted a pitch-black funnel cloud across his horizon.

Upon spying an approaching tornado, one's first instinct is to hightail it in the opposite direction at maximum speed. Sticking around to face the approaching winds only meant pending disaster. "I..." Russell stuttered, "I..." His face was greyer than a buffalo nickel and his leaded heart was sinking into his belly. "Jesus!"

"Let's just take a pause for a minute." Seeing Russell's discomfort, Dr. White instructed him to stand. Following her lead on a series of relaxation exercises — deep breaths, shoulder rolls, neck swivels, extreme yawns, shaking out his arms — Russell imagined himself as a kindergartener receiving a doting teacher's special attention for separation anxiety. The silliness of this mental image resulted in involuntary laughter. Dr. White seemed to catch the giggles as well. "What?" she asked, between titters. "What's going on?"

Russell plopped back down on the couch cushion. "I did something yesterday," he blurted.

"Uh huh." Two innocuous syllables asked for more information. She pushed back into her chair and crossed her legs, waiting for Russell to drop the next shoe.

After five interminable seconds, he had to fill the silence. "I... I don't... I couldn't resist."

Several more tense seconds passed. "And, what was it you couldn't resist?"

"Well ..." Once again, a short spate of laughter released some pent-up anxiety. "We were... in the woods."

"Who, Russell?" Dr. White asked. The time had come to press for more detail. "You were with someone? In the woods?"

"I don't know his name. He had sort of reddish hair."

"Okay. And?"

"I kind of... went further than I'd ever gone before."

"Kind of? Or..?"

"I definitely went further." Russell's utterance was barely more than a whisper.

"So..." While Dr. White was urging him to continue, she wasn't asking for precise erotic details.

"I blew him."

A veteran psychologist is rarely shocked. But Dr. White found herself disarmed by the bluntly unambiguous nature of this revelation. At a loss for a more custom-crafted response, she reached into her bag of tricks and came up with her profession's most ripened chestnut: "How did that make you feel?"

Hearing his therapist, for whom he held ultimate respect, resort to this stock query re-tickled Russell's funny bone. Breaking into peals of uncontrollable laughter, he snatched up a throw pillow and buried his face into the satiny fabric. Like a free diver coming to the surface after a record-breaking descent, Russell gasped for a lungful of air before screaming into the pillow with the shrillness and ferocity of a jackrabbit being chased by a pack of coyotes. Although Dr. White managed to maintain an outward calmness, her eyes revealed something else. This could be a pivotal moment in Russell's progress, a major inflection point. Sessions like this required switching off autopilot and summoning up all of her training, skills, and experience. She'd been trolling the Caribbean, periodically feeling a tug on her line, and now she'd hooked a blue marlin. It would take strength, stamina, and sound strategy to reel in this prize catch.

"I'm sorry," Russell muttered, dabbing his tear-filled eyes with a tissue. "It's just..." He paused to blow his nose loudly, only to be once again overtaken by nervous laughter. Sharing something this revealing and explicit had left him feeling extremely vulnerable. Still, lifting the curtain on this reality also gave him wings. He suddenly felt buoyant, even giddy. "How did that make me feel?" The question bore repeating. "How did that make me feel?" He pondered for a few seconds, then grinned and shook his head in disbelief. "Happy," he confessed. "It made me feel happy."

"Happy," the therapist repeated.

"I knew what the risks were." Russell was thinking aloud. "I knew the potential consequences. But, afterwards, I felt so... so incredibly... happy."

"By consequences, what do you mean?"

"Oh, you know..." Russell cocked his head to one side. "I'd have to get tested again. For STI's. I'd have to avoid having sex with Tess until I got the results."

"So, to be clear, it didn't make you more inclined to..."

"To come out to her?" As he completed her sentence, Russell was still oblivious as to the convoluted nature of his thinking. He'd left the previous session with a daunting homework assignment: to begin contemplating and planning his truth reveal. Logically, his acting out in the woods should have reinforced the urgency of setting the coming-out process in motion. Rather, his default thought process went directly to compiling everything he'd need to do to cover up his wayward behavior. For 22 hours, he'd luxuriated in residual delight. He knew this was a breakthrough. But he hadn't fully considered how much of a game changer it was. In self-defense, he resorted to bitter sarcasm. "So, I guess I don't have the right to be happy every now and then."

"You don't really mean that, Russell."

Here was a rare instance of Dr. White's finely tuned insight going slightly catawampus. In actuality, Russell's expression of egoistic self-pity was absolutely sincere. He was feeling misunderstood and alone. Still, he pretended otherwise. "Nothin' gets past you, Doc. Guilty as charged. Of course, I was joking."

"This is nothing to joke about," she said, quietly, but sternly. Feeling like a chastised child, Russell had to fight the urge to bolt up from the couch and make a quick escape, with the intention of never returning to this chamber of reckoning. Previously, therapy seemed a safe place to unveil his secrets and vent his pent-up frustrations.

Now, the walls of the confessional were closing in. By volunteering too much, Russell had shot himself in the foot. This was the outcome he'd always feared, the very reason he'd so conscientiously avoided therapy, as any cautious, rational person would a nest of rattlesnakes. Honesty is a double-edged sword. Telling the truth can lift a crushing weight from a person's soul. But that's never the end of it. Once truth makes its entrance, accountability and appropriate action are there waiting in the wings, listening eagerly for their cues to join the ongoing drama.

"I was happy," Russell reiterated. "I hadn't felt like that in... I don't know... like forever. I didn't feel guilty... or... or ashamed, or scared. I was just... happy. Thinking about it still gets me all..." A thrill shiver through his shoulders completed his testimony.

"What if you could feel that way more often?" the doctor inquired. "Have you thought about that?" The leading nature of this question was intentional.

But, Russell's imagination had already meandered down that path, only to be blinded by the view at trail's end. "Yeah, right," he said. "It would be great, wouldn't it? If we could all have our cake and eat it, too." He didn't know if this remark was sardonic, or wistful. Maybe it was both in a befuddling, contradictory mishmash. Regardless, he was certain that he could (and would) never have it all, that he couldn't possibly be deserving of family and marriage while, at the same time, openly satisfying his same-sex needs and desires.

"There's only one way you'll ever find out."

Easy for you to say. Not only was the good doctor parroting the obvious, she wasn't the one surrounded on all sides by multiple bogeymen. She wasn't taking a mind-numbing multiple-choice quiz feeling the absolute certainty that any answer, A, B, *or* C would result in a bold red check mark. Till now, Russell had been savoring his bliss, squeezing every last, remaining drop of sweetness from the previous day's encounter in the woods. But the happiness sponge had been wrung dry. As the doctor had correctly stated, there was only one way he could ever find out if true, sustained happiness was possible. And that meant owning up to Tess. "I guess you're right," he muttered, with sorrowful resignation.

"Okay, good," the doctor said, softly. "I'm glad you agree. Next week, let's start brainstorming on how and when."

Russell felt a tear trickling down his cheek. He'd arrived at his therapy appointment still vibrating with residual joy. Over the course of 50 minutes, he had run the gamut of emotions, from ecstatic giddiness to sidesplitting hysterics. From there, he'd passed through peak anxiety, bitter exasperation, and on to sheer panic. He'd paid a visit to victimhood, made a pit stop at resentment, only to land in ultimate surrender. He would depart Dr. White's office on feet weighed down by sorrow, and legs waterlogged with regret.

The dinner party had completely slipped Russell's mind. As he pulled into the driveway, two extra vehicles parked in front of the house reminded him that he had been assigned one simple task: picking up canned clams for the linguine Alfredo sauce. Choosing expediency over price, he raced to the corner market. There, he was pleased to find two small cans in stock. Both were dusty, evidently from a lengthy linger on the shelf. Brushing them off revealed that they were nearly a year past their recommended use-by date. He immediately set them back on the shelf and began striding purposeful toward the exit, feeling peeved over having to drive the additional four miles to Kroger's.

Either Tess hadn't noticed that Russell was 25 minutes late, or her impatience had been dulled with libation. It was always evident to Russell when Tess had reached her ideal blood-alcohol level. Having imbibed approximately a glass and half of wine, she would invariably be floating a few inches off the carpet, with a rosy blush in her cheeks, exuding an effortless charm. In truth, she thought she was being charming. Russell, however, saw right through this act. Not only did he consider the slightly tipsy version of his wife disingenuous. He had come to find her booze-affected persona borderline obnoxious.

"Oh, look!" Tess squawked from the sunken living room, sloshing her half-full schooner of vino in Russell's direction. "I gave my honey his honey-do, and my honey did it! How lucky am I?" She was acknowledging the two containers of canned clams Russell was setting down on the kitchen counter top.

"I can't tell you how many times I've had to send Josh back for something he forgot to pick up." Russell hadn't met the woman sharing this mundane anecdote. Lean, dark hair pulled back into a high ponytail, with a sharp, axe-blade nose, and slender wrists, Marlene appeared the perfect image of the woman a man's 40-ish wife would befriend in yoga class. As he positioned the first can of clams in the electric can opener, Russell sent a smirk and a finger wave from the kitchen, past the dining table, and into the sunken, carpeted area where Tess was socializing with the two couples she'd invited for drinks, pasta, and snappy repartee.

Mary Ann poked her head out from behind a corner to send a thin-lipped grin in Russell's direction. For the last nine months, Russell and Mary Ann had been sharing their most intimate secrets with one another. Seeing her standing in his living room felt wrong. Selfishly, Russell had hoped the gal-pal bond between Tess and Mary Ann — burgeoned so spontaneously during last December's office Christmas party — would peter out. Instead, side-by-side sun salutations every Wednesday morning had only served to solidify their ongoing friendship. And tonight, Mary Ann, along with her boyfriend du jour, were in his house, sipping wine, bantering, and opining about everything from laundry soap to politics.

This same afternoon, Russell had experienced a meltdown in his psychologist's office. How could he possibly relax and interact naturally in the presence of these two women? One, who knew about his queerness and his surreptitious same-sex pursuits, had been unreserved in her opinion that he must finally be honest with the other. Add two presumably straight men and a straight woman he'd never met to the mix, and the hours to come hovered overhead like an ominous cloud, threatening an impending deluge.

An unusually tall, gangly fellow ambled toward the kitchen holding an empty wine glass. Russell, executing a quick hand wash at the kitchen sink, turned off the spigot to hear the glug-glug sound of wine being poured from bottle to glass. He snatched up a dish towel to dry his damp hands, took a deep breath, pasted a smile on his face, swiveled around and extended his right hand. Before he was able to articulate half of "Hi, I'm Russell," his forehead met the jagged corner of an open cupboard door. The pain was immediate and intense. "God, fucking dammit, Tess!" he howled.

More times than he could count, Russell had felt a twinge of anger after nearly colliding with a kitchen or bathroom cabinet door carelessly left ajar. Over time, he'd taught himself to take a deep breath and shake off his exasperation. After all, what good would it do to blow an all-too-frequent, but relatively insignificant act of thoughtlessness out of proportion and, by doing so, turn it into a major bone of contention? Tonight, however, Tess's penchant for failing to close kitchen cabinets had resulted in a worst-case scenario. The emotional rawness Russell carried into the house had left him unprepared for superficial socializing. Then, upon his entrance, Tess's semi-inebriated zeal had grated against his eardrums like a jackhammer on blacktop. Add those irritations to her barging into his friendship with Mary Ann. Now, due to her chronic neglect, Russell's head was throbbing and blood was streaming into his eye and down his cheek. He wilted onto the kitchen floor, pressing the dish towel to his wound.

"That's not a good idea." The tall man snatched the towel away and lobbed it into the sink. "There's gotta be a ton of bacteria on that thing! Real good way to get a serious infection." He grabbed a roll of paper towels from the counter, tore off several sheets and handed them to Russell.

"Thanks," Russell responded, applying the more sanitary compress to his gushing wound. "As I was saying, I'm Russell."

"I figured as much," the man said, folding his lanky, praying-mantis limbs, and crouching down to take stock of Russell's condition. "Tommy," he replied. "You're probably going to need stitches."

"Not Josh?" Russell asked.

"Nope. Josh is Marlene's husband. I'm here with Mary Ann."

"Hmmm..." Russell was picturing how ungainly this angular, bony stork of a man would look while having sex with Mary Ann. "I don't know Marlene."

"Let me take a look," Tommy said, extending his hand to lift the blood-soaked paper towels.

"Fuck, that hurts!" complained Russell.

"I'll bet." Tommy grimaced. "Wow. You've got a heck of a gash there."

"You and Mary Ann been dating long?"

"Not really. A couple-a months."

"*Jesus!* What the...?" Tess, having finally lollygagged over to see what was happening, was understandably alarmed at the sight of her husband sitting on the kitchen floor with one side of his face smeared with blood, and the crimson-stained paper towels in Tommy's hand. "Are you okay, Babe?"

"What's it look like?" spat Russell.

"What happened?" she asked. Russell pointed to the still-open cupboard door. "You gotta walk around those things," she teased.

"Yeah, next time you leave a cabinet open," he responded, "I'll try to remember that."

"Oh," she shot back, "so, this is *my* fault!"

By now, Tommy was helping Russell to his feet. "He needs to go to the emergency room," Tommy stated.

"Drama, drama, drama." Tess wasn't convinced. "Let's have a look..." A quick glance at the laceration confirmed Tommy's prognosis. "Holy shit, Babe! You really did a number on yourself."

"Yep," Russell muttered. "Dumb-ass me!"

The irony of her husband's self-deprecation evaded Tess. "Well," she admitted, "It would probably be ill-advised for me to drive you."

"First sensical thing she's said since I got home." Russell directed this snide remark toward Tommy, implying a wink.

"Okay," Tommy responded, with another grimace. "I really don't wanna get invol... you know..."

"No," Russell interrupted. "Sorry, Man. You're right. I shouldn't have... I just thought, you're a guy, and..."

"I guess," Tommy interrupted, steering the conversation away from the disconcerting bickering of his hosts. "I guess I could give you a lift."

"We'll take him." It was Mary Ann. "I can drive. I've barely had a sip."

"I thought you were a Chardonnay girl." Tess was suddenly having rare doubts about her hostessing prowess.

"Not really," Mary Ann responded. "I'm more into the reds. Pinot Noir. Merlot."

"I feel horrible," Tess whined. "I usually have a nice red on hand."

"I'm okay with a Chardonnay or a Sauvignon Blanc," Mary Ann explained, "but..."

"Jesus Christ!" protested Russell. "Are you two really gonna stand here bantering about wine all night while a man bleeds to death?"

"So, how bad does the other guy look?" The jocular ER doctor was snipping thread, having just finished the fourth stitch.

"Oh, she looks great." Russell was only half joking. The doctor's brow furrowed. If this was a case of domestic violence, he might be legally obligated to report his suspicions to authorities. "It was a cupboard door," Russell explained. "My wife doesn't seem to understand how they work."

Okay, the doctor was thinking. *Here's yet another wrinkle in the "I walked into a door" gambit.* Still, as the victim in this case was the husband, he decided to keep the banter light. "From my experience," he joked, "it's best to use one's hand to close a cabinet, and not one's forehead."

"I'll keep that in mind next time," parried Russell.

The doctor snapped off his vinyl gloves and tossed them into the wastebasket. Before making his exit, he blurted a quick list of post-op instructions before instructing Russell to make an appointment with his primary care provider in 10 days to remove the sutures. "You probably shouldn't drive for a day or so," the physician advised. "Someone taking you home?"

"Yeah," said Russell. "At least, I hope my friends are still here."

Russell was still feeling woozy as he negotiated his way through the waiting area, sidling past moaning patients, coughing children, and tiptoeing around scattered toys, fast-food sacks, backpacks, and handbags. "Ready to head out?" Mary Ann was standing by herself, next to the exit door.

"Sure thing," Russell answered. Stepping into the humid evening air, he inquired, "Where's the Jolly Green Giant?"

"Tommy?" she replied. "He's waiting at my place."

"Seems like an okay guy."

"I guess so. Yeah. But don't get any ideas. He's definitely straight."

"What do you think? That I'm always cruising? That, every time I see a good-looking guy, I have no other thought but to..."

"Honestly, Russ, I don't know *what* to think." Her vocal inflection expressed a blend of emotions: one part exasperation, two parts surrender, wrapped in a shell of dead seriousness. There was a pause in the conversation long enough for them to cross the pedestrian bridge.

"Yeah." Russell's voice cracked. "I don't know either."

"Sorry?" said Mary Ann.

"I don't know what to think, either." This admission wavered with emotion. "I don't have a fucking clue. I'm a fucking disaster, a mess. I honestly don't know what..." Russell's throat was constricting to the point that he was straining to get the words out. "I honestly don't know what to do."

"That's good," she said, with a tender, empathetic smile.

Russell wasn't prepared for this response. "Good? What the hell are you saying?"

"Well," she posited, "maybe you've hit rock bottom."

"Oh," he wondered aloud. "And that's a good thing?"

"Sometimes, that's what it takes. Only one way to go from here."

"I'm about to explode my whole world," he announced.

"Whoopee!" Mary Ann giggled. "It's about damn time."

TWENTY-NINE

"Lately, everything she does just pisses me off." Russell's hand automatically traveled to his lacerated forehead, fingering the stitches that were due to come out in three days' time.

"What's changed?" Dr. White inquired.

"Nothing, really." Russell pondered the question. "That's the weird thing. She's not really acting any differently. But, even when she does the same ol' stuff, it irritates me."

"What kind of stuff?"

"Oh, you know... like leaving a mat bunched up in the bathroom for me to trip on. When she reminds me to do a chore — putting the trash cans out, or changing a lightbulb — she might as well have given me an order to... I don't know... to do nine-hundred push-ups in the middle of the street."

"Did it ever occur to you that she's not what's irritating you?"

"What do you mean?"

"Okay," the therapist said, preparing to choose her language with special care. "I'm wondering, struggling, as you are, with your sexual orientation and your cravings, if you believe you deserve Tess."

"Interesting." This insinuation had set off a chain reaction, one thought leading to the next. "You know what I think about sometimes?"

"Tell me."

"It's not that I don't deserve *her*. It's more that sometimes I can't help but think, and I really mean this, that she deserves a better man than me."

"Better in what way?"

"Well, straight, for sure."

"Okay. What else?"

"Honest."

"And?"

"Faithful, true, monogamous. All that."

"Sounds like you're beginning to come to terms with your infidelity."

"Wow." Russell grimaced at this spot-on observation. "It does, doesn't it."

"Is there anything about yourself that you *could* change to become more like the better man you're describing?" Russell's expression indicated that he was flummoxed by this query. Dr. White sought to provide clarification. "You say this better man — your words not mine — would be straight. But you can't just decide to become straight, can you?"

"I would if I could."

"Do you really mean that?"

"Well..." He took a second to reconsider. "Okay. I know I can't deny who I am." Dr. White sat silently, allowing Russell to hear the echo of this statement. "Been there, tried that, doesn't work."

"But, because you're not straight," the doctor suggested, "you think you're undeserving."

"Sort of," he muttered, reluctantly, "I guess."

"That seems like something we should examine more thoroughly."

"I can't change what I've done... or what I keep... wanting."

"Exactly. You are who you are: not straight. And, you've been unfaithful. What's done is done." It seemed clear that she was priming him for some sort of reckoning. "So," she continued, "what *can* you change?"

The answer was as obvious as it was inescapable. "I guess I could be more honest."

"Excellent! Yes!" While this level of breakthrough can make a therapist's entire week, Dr. White wasn't about to rest here. "But, *more* honest? Or, just honest."

"I guess that depends on what you mean by honest."

She wasn't about to let the patient get away with semantic game playing. "You brought it up. What does it mean to you?"

"Well..." Russell was about to be too clever for his own good and he knew it. "I don't think any person is a hundred-percent honest. I mean, we all have secrets, right? Stuff we don't want other people to know. If someone just blathered everything to everyone, they'd be... intolerable."

"But, is that what honesty means, really?"

"Hmmm?" Pretending he needed further elucidation seemed a good way to further postpone confronting the question.

"Isn't being honest with one's self different, or at least somewhat different than being honest with others?"

"Still not following." Russell's mind was racing, scanning for an opportunity to veer off to a less-vexing topic.

"Being honest with Tess, or your boss, or a close friend isn't about blurting out everything you're thinking. Right?" Russell's furrowed brow provided Dr. White the cue to make her point. "It's when somebody confronts you with a direct question... isn't that when your honesty is really tested?"

"Yeah, alright," Russell concurred. "But what about when your conscience starts nagging, when you're finding it difficult... even impossible... to handle the deceit?"

"Ah..." Dr. White took a sip from her tea cup. "So, you've practiced deception, you feel guilty, and the angel on your shoulder starts whispering that it's time to own up to it."

"Dang," remarked Russell. "You're really good at this."

"Thank you, Russell. I appreciate that."

"Well, you deserve all the kudos."

"But this isn't about me." With his attempt at flattery failing to knock the session's trajectory off course, Russell felt his anxiety level skyrocketing. It was as though he'd been bitten by a Black Mamba and the serpent's venom was contaminating his bloodstream. Knowing where this dialogue was going, and sorely aware there was nothing he could do to avert the inevitable, he sat in numbed silence. This, Dr. White decided, was the moment for some tough love. "You're going to get a lot more from this process if you..."

"I know," Russell blurted. "I know! *I know! I KNOW!*" Each one of four consecutive "I knows" were expressed louder and more intensely than the one before.

"You sound angry, Russell."

Russell wasn't merely angry. He was furious; furious about having to sit there as this know-it-all therapist used her professional advantage and expertise to disarm his every attempt at evasion; furious at that framed diploma, for giving her license to puncture his armor without providing him so much as a dram of anesthetic; furious at his wife, for loving the man she thought she'd married, the man he knew he could never be. Ultimately, he was furious about finding himself painted into a corner, only to look down to see the offending paintbrush gripped in his own hand.

"I'm not angry." Russell's eyes darted around the room, hoping to discover a trap door. Instead, they landed on the clock. Half of the session still remained. He doubled over, clutching his midsection.

"Russell, what's going on?"

"I hate myself," he muttered, shaking his weary head and staring down at the paisley patterned Egyptian rug. "I'm an awful, horrible, pathetic person. An awful, horrible, pathetic excuse for a human being. A sad, lonely, closeted faggot!"

"What do you expect me to say?"

"Do your damn job. Tell me I'm not awful, that I'm just less than perfect. You know, flawed, like everybody else."

"Okay," Dr. White responded. "Russell, look at me." Like a naughty child caught in the act, Russell lifted his heavy-lidded gaze. "Please, please, listen to me. You're not awful, or horrible, or pathetic. And, you're not perfect, either."

"No shit, Sherlock." Russell's voice had been reduced to a raspy whisper. "What was your first clue?"

"You've got real issues to deal with. Still, don't forget... and, this is important. People love you... your sons, your wife, your parents."

"But they don't really know me." Extreme facial contortion broadcasted Russell pain. "They think they do. But they don't."

"They know your heart."

"My heart is sick. It's tainted."

"Look, Russell..."

"Fuck! I hate it when people start a sentence with 'Look.' It sounds so goddam condescending."

Dr. White sat back in her chair and drew a deep inhalation. "Noted," she said, contritely, on her exhale. "You're absolutely right. Thank you for pointing that out. I'm going to work on that."

"Good." The knot in Russell's belly loosened. He couldn't hold back a smile. "You *should*... work on that, because..."

"Because that's the last thing a patient wants to hear from their therapist."

"Exactly."

"Excellent. Now that we're both being honest..."

"Oh, Jesus!" exclaimed Russell. "Can't we talk about something else?"

"Tell you what..." The tone of the kind woman's voice signaled that she was about to propose a change in strategy. "I'm going to leave you alone... for, let's say, ten minutes." She reached over to a nearby shelf to pick up some blank note paper and a pen. "Your assignment is to start coming up with some language you might use to come out to Tess." As he accepted the paper and pen, Russell's shoulders slumped. Like a kid knowing there's no escape from a painful booster shot, he sighed, gritted his teeth, squinted his eyes, and creased his lips into a pout of reluctant resignation. The time had arrived to roll up his sleeve and take his medicine.

By the time Dr. White reentered the room, Russell had scribbled a half dozen half sentences, only to cross them out. Everything he'd come up with had seemed half-baked, passive-aggressive, self-serving, and/or simply inadequate.

"Do you mind if I take a look?" she asked.

"You won't be happy." Russell predicted, handing her the sheet.

After scanning through the incomprehensible scrawls, she smiled. "It's a good start." Dr. White was betting that this exercise had served its purpose. She knew that simply jotting a few words on paper can function as a pump primer. Picking up the pen demands thinking about what to write. Actually writing something down — *anything at all* — is like tossing a pebble into a pond. The initial plop may seem insignificant as the stone plummets quickly downward, disappearing into the silt. But, back on the surface, ripples have been sent in every direction. Rejecting one way to say something signals to the brain that the search for a better way to say it has begun.

Russell barely slept that night. After weeks of distraction, procrastination, and deliberate avoidance, his mind, now tasked with deciphering an unsolvable riddle, had taken the prompt to get busy.

A few minutes after seven a.m., Hank shuffled into the kitchen, bleary-eyed and yawning. Having picked Reptar Crunch as his breakfast du jour, he emerged from the pantry and, like a somnolent robot, snatched a bowl from the cupboard, a spoon from a drawer, and milk from the fridge. As he tilted the milk carton over the filled bowl, his sleepy eyes bugged out. "What the..?" he squealed. The alarm trigger was the peculiar specter of his father standing on the back patio, barefoot, and clad in nothing but a saggy pair of boxer shorts, staring out into the void, and mumbling to himself.

"What's he doing out there?" asked Rory.

The unannounced entrance of his little brother startled Hank for the second time in less than 15 seconds. His involuntary response was a rapid, reflexive swivel. Centrifugal force sent a stream of milk across the kitchen counter, down a stack of drawers, and onto the floor. "Fuck, Dude!" Hank chided Rory. "Don't sneak up on me like that!"

"Seen the Reptar Crunch?" Rory inquired. A younger sibling learns that ignoring a big brother's reprimand tends to cause him even greater frustration. That, after all, is the primary role of the little brother, to exasperate the firstborn at every opportunity.

"Open your eyes, Dumb Ass!" snapped Hank, nodding toward the box on the counter top.

"Okay, that's it!" Russell was stepping inside through the sliding glass door. "How many times have I told you, Hank? Warned you." Hank, his mouth stuffed with sugary cereal, was incapable of a response. "First of all," Russell lectured, "I will no longer let you get away with talking to your brother like that..."

"But, Dad!" Hank's protest was muffled by the partially masticated glob. "He..."

"I don't care what Rory did. I don't care what he said!" Hank once again attempted to give voice to his own defense. "Nope. You don't get to talk. Zip it." Russell took notice of the milk waterfall cascading down over the kitchen drawers. "And, look at this mess! This is the last straw. Go to your room. Now. No video games."

"For how long?"

"For a week."

"A week? Why?"

"I guess you'll have plenty of time to think about why."

"Fuck you, Dad!" screeched Hank. "I hate you! You're an *asshole!*" The irate boy lifted his bowl over his head with both hands and hurled it into the sink, sending shattered fragments of porcelain, brownish milk, and soggy Reptar Crunch splattering onto the walls and windows. To top off his violent tantrum, he deliberately knocked the milk carton off of the countertop. In the wake of this tantrum, a tense silence descended upon the Deacon kitchen.

"Do what your father says, Hank." Tess's voice was calm, but firm. She looked over at her husband, standing in his underwear, fists clenched and face flushed. Her baffled expression and confused head shake asked, *What the hell is going on here?* Glaring at Rory through squinted, spite-filled eyes, Hank began tearing off sheets of paper towels. "Leave it, Hank," commanded Tess. "I'll take care of it."

"But..." the boy stammered.

"Listen to your mother." Russell's order was clipped and direct. "Go to your room."

As a parting statement, Hank impulsively kicked the half-empty milk carton — "Oops," he said, with adolescent scorn, "clumsy me," — before stomping heavily out of the kitchen and up the stairs.

While waiting to hear the slam of Hank's bedroom door, Tess took a second gander at her nearly naked husband. "Up at the crack of dawn, I see. No time to put on some clothes?" Russell stood, slack-jawed. Words escaped him. At this moment, any attempt to explain his state of mind to his wife would have been futile.

"You guys are freakin' nuts," mumbled Rory, as he toted his cereal bowl to the kitchen table.

Tess approached, coming nose-to-nose with Russell. Then, she rose up on her tip toes and whispered in his ear. "You look pretty sexy in those boxers, Babe. And, the way you took charge right then with your son? Very manly, indeed. It kinda got me hot."

This was not what Russell expected to hear. Still, having his fragile masculinity stroked sent blood rushing to his groin. Blushing, he placed his hands over the tenting of his underpants. "I'd better go get dressed," he said, as he scooted out of the room.

"Really freakin' nuts," reiterated Rory, munching a mouthful of Reptar Crunch.

"You said it, Kiddo," Tess agreed, before switching her attention to more mundane matters. "I wonder why your dad didn't get the coffee started."

"I need some advice." Russell was standing in the doorway of Mary Ann's office. "You got a couple-a minutes?"

Mary Ann looked up from her calculations. "So, you just barge into a co-worker's office and expect her to drop everything? Is that how it goes now?" Exhausted and anxious, Russell was fresh out of snappy comebacks. "Come on in," she said, offering a hint of a smile. "I could use a break." Russell shuffled over to a guest chair. "You gonna shut the door?" Mary Ann inquired. "Or, is this something you wanna share with the entire floor?"

"Right," he replied. As he reached to pull the door closed, he saw Ed who, as usual, was peering out from his office doorway, his inquiring eyes radiating perverse curiosity. "On second thought..." Russell said, pasting on a less-than-convincing smile. "Never mind. We can talk another time."

"You sure?" Mary Ann asked.

"Yeah, it's not urgent," he fibbed.

"Okay," she responded, her eyes automatically returning to her spreadsheets. "Lunch tomorrow?"

"I wish," he said. "Gotta get my stitches out."

"Thursday then?"

"Good. It's a date."

"You know what your problem is?" Minutes ago, Ed had been spying on Russell as he entered, then left Mary Ann's office. Now, he'd trailed Russell into the breakroom.

"Tell me, Ed," snapped Russell, looking up from stirring Half and Half into his coffee. "What's my problem? I'm fucking dying to get your sage opinion."

"Jesus, man!" the bald man protested. "You don't have to be a prick about it."

"Look, Ed..." In normal conversation, Russell conscientiously avoided beginning a sentence with the word "look." To him, it always sounded pompous and pedantic. In this circumstance, however, pomposity was exactly what he was striving for. "It may surprise you," Russell continued, "being someone who has less than zero self-awareness or sensitivity to the people around you. But... I could give a flying fuck about your opinions, especially when it comes to my life. So, why don't you deal with your own shit, save your foul-assed breath, and get the fuck outta my face?"

"I... I was just gonna say..." Ed stammered. Russell's lasered, squint-eyed stare halted him mid-sentence. "Never mind," Ed muttered, turning to leave the breakroom. "Catch ya later."

"Not if I can avoid it," mumbled Russell. For a full minute, Russell savored his coffee, feeling proud of himself for putting imbecilic Ed in his place. This elation, however, didn't last. The guy hadn't deserved such a barbed harangue. *Ed might be a dimwit*, Russell chastised himself, *but he's not manipulative or malicious... like his pig-headed pal, Mike.* He just happened to step into the crosshairs of Russell's ire at the worst possible moment. The last thing Russell needed was to add yet another turd to his ongoing shit storm. Normally, the office provided a reliable escape from his personal issues, a place where he could slip into routine, where his professionalism and position offered some illusion of control. Previously, when a colleague disregarded boundaries — and Ed was by no means the only offender in this regard — Russell would reserve comment. *Don't make waves*: rule number one in avoiding interoffice conflict.

Feeling a sense of regret, Russell stepped into the corridor, coffee cup in hand, only to see Mike Terzian charging towards him like an enraged bull, projecting a squint-eyed scowl, exhaling steam from his nostrils. Russell felt a hot breeze as Mike barreled past, while emitting a succinct and less-than-complimentary utterance: "Asshole." On the way back to his office, out of the corner of his eye, Russell noticed a female intern standing in front of Ed's desk. Ed said something to her and nodded in Russell's direction. The intern turned her head to send Russell, who she had never met personally, a glower of disapproval. The bad vibes were already spreading across the third floor like *The Blob*.

"Hey..." Jamal's mellow voice was welcome, soothing.

"Hey..." Russell had been sitting by himself on the top row of the park bleachers for an hour, gazing across the vacant baseball diamond at the grove of trees beyond the outfield fence. He'd begun the day standing barefoot in the backyard, clad only in his boxer shorts, watching the dawn sky transform from dull grey to translucent blue. Feeling confused, distracted, and isolated, he'd been unable to focus at work, which led to his unloading on Ed Stengel in the office breakroom. Once again, he found himself alone, haunted by self-disparaging thoughts, and mourning the lie he'd made of his life. He longed to feel accepted, understood, and known. "Thanks for coming," he said. "I didn't know if you were in town."

As Jamal took a seat on the next bench down, the aluminum, erector-set bleachers shifted and squeaked under his weight. "I'm glad you called," he said. "I've been thinking about you."

"That's really nice to hear." Russell's words sounded stiff and formal. "Good thoughts, I hope."

"Only good thoughts." Jamal swiveled around to straddle the bench. He looked up at Russell. "How *are* you? What's going on?"

Russell exhaled, inhaled deeply, and allowed his tight shoulders to drop. Such a relief to be with another man, a queer man, a friend, with whom he could be totally forthright and unguarded. "To be honest," he said, "I feel like... like I don't belong anywhere. My wife doesn't know me. My son hates me. I'm alienating my co-workers. I can't concentrate. You know. Normal stuff."

"Sounds like being Russell sucks."

"Pretty much, yeah."

"I can relate."

"Really? Seems like you've, you know, sorta got all your little duckies in a row."

"Yeah, right." Jamal pursed his ample lips and shook his head. "I hardly ever feel like I really belong... anywhere."

"What do you mean?"

"Look at me, Russell. You notice anything?"

Russell's eyes feasted on Jamal's imperfectly perfect visage. "All I see is the most adorable face I've ever seen."

"Okay, you can cool it with the flirting."

"I'm just being honest."

"Well, then, thanks for the compliment. Really. But you're being kind of evasive."

"That's what I do," Russell joshed, evasively.

"Look again," Jamal suggested. Russell took another gander. Still, he had yet to catch Jamal's train of thought. "Here's a hint. What color do you see?"

"Oh, damn! Sorry. I getcha."

"You know how many Black, male flight attendants there are?"

"I never thought about that."

"Why would you? You know how Black communities, how Black families see gay men like me? You know what it's like to hear your granny tell you you're going to Hell?"

"Shit. That's... that's awful. I guess being Jamal sucks, too."

"I don't look at it like that. Not if I can avoid it, anyway. Life... it's not easy for anybody. How we see it is a choice."

"Okay, Shirley MacLaine," scoffed Russell.

"Who's that?" The baffled expression on Russell's face amused Jamal. "Just kidding, Man." Jamal chortled. "Of course, I know who Shirley MacLaine is. *Out on a Limb* is a great book!"

"I'm seeing a therapist," announced Russell.

"Good for you." Jamal seemed genuinely pleased. "And how's that going?"

"Good. Good." Russell's response was unconvincing.

"Something tells me I'm about to hear a 'but.'"

"Man, oh man! You're not just cute. You're perceptive." Jamal's expression said it was time to quit the sweet-talk and cut to the chase. Russell cleared his throat. "Dr. White says... no, she *insists*... that I have to come out to my wife."

"Surprise, surprise."

"Yeah, I know. I pretty much knew this was inevitable when I signed up."

As Jamal drew a deep breath, his cheeks tightened. "Russell, can I ask you a personal question?"

"Fire away," Russell assured him. "For you, I'm an open book."

"Don't you think you'd feel a whole lot better about yourself if you... you know, if you... could..."

"What? Be honest?"

"Not just honest. Don't get me wrong, that's important. But, it's more than that. You've been hiding a secret. A big secret. What if you could get that load off your back?"

"Sure. Maybe. But..."

"Ah, ha! There it is!"

"What?"

"I knew that 'but' was coming."

"Jamal, I'm married. I love my wife. We have kids... and, and... a house."

"Oh, I get it. Because you have a wife you love and kids and a house, you can't be your true self." Jamal proceeded to sharpen his point. "Just like a million other closeted guys out there, all in the exact same boat." Just then, Russell noticed a figure in the distance, strolling the path next to the grove of trees. Knowing what that man was looking for confirmed what Jamal was saying. From those voyeuristic years through last week's unexpectedly joyous tumble to his knees, Russell had seen countless wedding rings on the fingers of countless guys. Prowling the peep booths, the park paths, and the restrooms, myriad men, like him, presumably married to women, were driven by an insatiable need for male-on-male physical contact and risking everything to satisfy an unrelenting, unquenchable, unutterable thirst.

"Fuck!" A dull ache welled up in Russell's heart. "When I think about the pain... the damage my coming out would cause, I just..." His voice caught in his throat.

"Go ahead, Man. Let it out."

"I just... wanna die." Russell had not yet confided his suicidal thoughts to his therapist. And, here he was spilling his guts to Jamal.

Placing his pudgy hands on Russell's knees, Jamal attempted to make eye contact. "Stop. Look at me." Sheepishly, Russell's tear-filled eyes met Jamal's. "You are a great guy, a wonderful human being. Your life has value."

"I'm a liar and a fucking philanderer, and..." Again, the words got bottlenecked in Russell's larynx.

"But, you can change those things. You can do better... starting today, and tomorrow, and the day after. The only thing you can't change is that you're gay."

Russell's own sad laugh took him by surprise. "And what *you* can't change is that you're Black *and* gay."

"Nobody's perfect," Jamal quipped.

"I don't know," argued Russell. "You come pretty close."

"Shut up. You're making me blush."

"Hold on! Wait a minute!" By now, the sadness had left Russell's laugh. "Do Black people blush?"

"All human's blush," Jamal retorted, playfully. "You think Black folk are sub-human?"

"Certainly not," Russell stated. "And, by the way, I'm not gay. I'm bi."

"Whatever." Jamal's eyes rolled up into their lids.

Russell was not only surprised by this evident incredulity. He was surprised by how much it hurt. "You don't believe me?"

"We'll see," said Jamal.

Russell would have pursued this subject further. But the tender, compassionate smile blossoming across Jamal's mug sparked a delicious thought. The physical sensation that accompanied this brainwave was all-too familiar. This time, however, the buzz arrived with deeper meaning. Now, he was the one blushing. "This may sound crazy," he said. "But, how 'bout we take a walk in the woods?"

Although it took a few seconds for Jamal to fully comprehend this come-on, his response was decisive. "I've got a red-eye tonight." In one swift motion, he pivoted back around and hoisted his substantial frame to a standing position. "Gotta get home to pack." A wave of self-consciousness and insecurity swept over Russell. Surely, propositioning Jamal in such an overt fashion had been a mistake. Jamal turned around and took Russell's face in his soft hands. "I like you," he whispered, "a lot." Hearing this made Russell's heart flutter.

"But you've gotta deal with your own situation first." Then, Jamal delivered the ultimate surprise, by planting a wet, sustained, goodbye kiss on Russell's lips.

As the two men climbed down from the bleachers, another idea occurred to Russell. "Maybe you could help me with my coming-out speech."

"Absolutely not."

"Can I run it by you and get some feedback? It would give me a chance to see you again."

"You don't need an excuse to do that." Turning toward his motorcycle, Jamal tossed a parting wave over his shoulder. Just then, the clank of an aluminum bat bouncing off the gravel grabbed Russell's attention. He hadn't noticed the father and son, unpacking athletic equipment from the bed of a king-cab pickup.

"Hey, Mr. Deacon!" Russell recognized the boy hailing him from across the parking lot as one of Rory's teammates.

"Oh, Jacob. Hi." Fret rippled through Russell's torso. Had the boy observed him in the bleachers with Jamal? Of even greater concern was the possibility that Jacob's father might have witnessed him kissing another man — a Black man, at that. "How's it going, Bill?" Bill Walker pretended not to hear. With no response forthcoming, Russell could only suspect the worst.

THIRTY

Seven counseling sessions had stripped Russell of his most reliable survival skill: compartmentalization. After weeks of supervised self-scrutiny, he could no longer keep his quasi-straight, public persona separate from his secret, bisexual self. Although these dueling identities had yet to make peace with one another, the lying philanderer in the mirror could never be unseen. Truth, once acknowledged, he'd come to realize, refuses to go back into hiding. But knowing the truth is not the same as facing it; and facing it is yet another giant step away from speaking it out loud.

Words that begged for articulation kept clanging around in Russell's troubled brain cave. Phrases of confession and apology reverberated like shouts into a bottomless cavern. *Babe, there's something I have to tell you.* Jesus, no! Was there ever a more ominous sounding opening line? *There's something important we need to talk about.* Not all that much better. *There's something I need to get off my chest.* Maybe. *Babe, we're friends, right?* "Of course. Why would you even need to ask?" *Well, if a friend had something they needed to tell you, friend-to-friend, heart-to-heart, something you might find painful, would you be willing to listen without judgment?* What a crock of shit!

He was still struggling to come up with an introductory line to kick off his coming-out speech. *Which Jenga block*, he wondered, *does one pull out first without immediately sending the tower toppling to the ground?*

"Whatcha thinkin' about?" Tess whispered from her side of the bed.

Russell hated it when she asked this question. More times than not, his thoughts were not anything he cared (or dared) to share. Once again, he found himself scrambling for a quick and credible response. "Did we get the boys' sleeping bags out of the storage shed?"

"Mmmm, hmmm," she responded. "All of their camping gear is piled up in the foyer." Today, Tess would be driving Hank and Rory to Knoxville. It was the final week of summer vacation and the boys had been invited to go camping with their cousins. This jaunt would serve a dual purpose for Tess, providing her the opportunity to spend a day and a night with her parents, help her mother with some domestic tasks, and give her ailing father some daughterly love. Although a new experimental medication had slowed the steady degeneration of Henry's Parkinson's, Tess worried that it was only a matter of time before he'd relapse again, perhaps for the final time.

With herculean effort, Russell raised his head from his pillow, lifted his legs, and placed his feet on the floor. To his own surprise, his grey matter was being tickled by the first clearly constructive thought he'd had in weeks. One reason it had been nearly impossible to even imagine coming out to his wife was that there never seemed to be an opportune time to broach the subject. Russell and Tess almost never had a private moment outside their shared bedroom, where they were invariably either exhausted at day's end or clambering in the morning twilight to get a new day underway. And, should he dump such an unwelcome revelation on her at home, in the midst of their familial routine, it could cause very real turmoil and trauma within the family unit. Russell surmised that Tess might find it less jarring if he were to deliver the news at a neutral location. And, post-confession, having consecutive days free from maternal obligations would give her some time to absorb a new reality and consider next steps. Maybe, just maybe, they would be able to talk it out and come to a mutually favorable solution. "Maybe I'll go *with* you," he suggested.

"Really?" Tess was equal parts stunned and thrilled by Russell's unexpected offer.

"Yeah." Observing Tess's delight at this out-of-the-blue proposal enabled Russell to manufacture a smile. He still loved making her happy. "Really." Suddenly, the heft of the commitment he'd just made landed on him like a piano falling from a second story window. First came the ominous realization that he'd best get busy composing the speech on which he'd, over a three-week period, made precisely zero progress. Then, he would have to muster up the fortitude to look his wife in the eye and speak those impossible words out loud. Finally, he would have to endure the unpredictable aftermath. And, should he continue to allow cowardice to muzzle his confession, he might be tempted to resort to even more desperate measures.

"Oh, my God!" Tess exclaimed. "That would be so much fun! On the way back, we could stop at the Catfish Cabin for lunch." Tess was already setting the itinerary for their return drive. She, however, remained oblivious to the plans her husband was contemplating.

"I was thinking," Russell posited, "maybe we could even take a little hike at Cumberland Mountain."

"You're the best, Babe!" Tess planted a kiss on the top of his head. "I don't care what anybody says." From the shadow of his malaise, Russell couldn't help but wonder whether she was joking.

It hadn't taken long for Hank to express contrition for his explosive, profane cereal-bowl toss. Being confined to his room, Nintendo-less, had given the lad time to mull over his words and actions. The day after the outburst, without provocation, he apologized. So, although the words spat so vehemently by his firstborn son still reverberated in Russell's head — "I hate you! You're an asshole!" — and Hank had retreated into his default egocentric posture, the three-hour drive to Knoxville was considerably less tense than it might have been. Of greater concern to Russell were the squinted glances he kept noticing from Rory. He decided to do some subtle interrogation, hoping to find out what, if anything, was on his younger son's mind: "Hey, Roar, have you talked to any of your teammates lately?"

"Like who?" the boy asked.

"Oh, Jacob, Sean, Dylan... Are they all planning to play for the Pirates next summer?"

"I think so. But Jacob's dad wants him to join a travel team."

"Oh, so you talked to Jacob?" This was the exact information Russell sought to extract.

"No. That's what Dylan told me."

Paranoia struck. It was possible that Jacob and his father had witnessed the kiss in the bleachers. And Russell knew Jacob as an impetuous kid with a propensity for blathering whatever happened to be on the tip of his brain. Understandably, Russell had feared that Jacob would relay what he'd seen to Rory. Until now, it hadn't occurred to Russell that the entire Pirates squad, perhaps their parents as well, might be nattering among themselves about this sighting. Fresh in his memory was the tongue-wagging about another queer Pirate dad, Bryan. Russell was feeling even greater pressure to reveal the truth to Tess before she caught wind of the scuttlebutt through the grapevine.

"Oh, Russell..." Miriam's feigned enthusiasm was transparent. "Look at you. It's been forever." Russell's mother-in-law could have taught a doctorate class in passive aggression. He took a step toward her for the obligatory hug. Instead, she quickly put that notion to rest, fending off his advance by placing a firm hand on his forearm.

"We can only stay tonight," Tess informed her mother. "Russ and I have plans for tomorrow."

"Oh," Miriam responded, "Well, I wish I'd known he was coming. I would have made up the queen bed. It's not as though I don't have enough to do around here."

"That's okay, don't worry about it," Russell assured her. "Tess and I can sleep anywhere." In fact, of late, where Russell bedded down wasn't all that important. Rest had been eluding him, regardless. And, considering what he was planning for the following day, he couldn't help but anticipate another restive night ahead.

Russell got along passably with his father-in-law, their shared passion for televised sports being the primary bonding element. Russell found Henry in the den, sitting in his favorite Lazy Boy recliner, watching Sports Center. Russell was stunned by how much Tess's father had aged over the months since he'd last seen him. The first weekend of the college football season was only days away, with the hometown University of Tennessee team, under Coach Phillip Fulmer, preparing for their opening-day gridiron clash versus UCLA. The buzz of the moment concerned young Peyton Manning's surprise decision to pick Tennessee over Mississippi State, where Peyton's father had starred at quarterback before enjoying a hall-of-fame pro career. Henry eschewed normal etiquette, not even offering a *hi, how are you*. "I wonder how Archie Manning feels about his boy signing with the Vols." The elderly man's voice warbled tremulously, and his neck jerked as he spoke.

"Fulmer must have done some pretty sweet talkin' to pull off that coup," remarked Russell, taking a seat on the couch. He waited for a response that failed to materialize. "How are you feeling, Henry? You doing okay?"

"Colquitt will be starting on Saturday." Henry continued to stare straight ahead at the new state-of-the-art plasma screen.

Russell didn't fault Henry for purposefully avoiding the subject of his health status. Clearly, the disease had seized greater control of his motor skills. Returning to the more comfortable subject of college football, Russell offered his two cents. "They say Todd Helton is pretty good, too."

"Peyton is the future, though." Henry had never been reticent to express an opinion. His initial assessment of his future son-in-law, 15 years earlier, had been unabashed. Certainly, it's not unusual for a father of a beautiful daughter to deem his progeny worthy of the most dashing, upwardly mobile partner. And, by Henry's estimation, Russell had never been an ideal suitor. To win his favor, Russell relied on the same, fundamental tactics he'd used over the years since to build a loyal insurance clientele: native charm, listening more than talking, expressing interest in the other person's needs, and taking every opportunity to be their problem solver. The strategy worked. Henry had no idea of the degree to which he'd been manipulated by his salesman son-in-law. Bit-by-bit, the two men had developed a pleasant rapport, along with a measure of genuine, albeit guarded, affection for one another.

"You need anything, Henry?" Russell asked. "Can I get you something from the kitchen?" Although he'd only just sat down, listening to the clicking sound coming from Henry's throat with every attempt to swallow was already verging on insufferable.

"I've got this." Henry was thrusting a palsied finger in the direction of a bronze bell sitting on the TV tray beside his chair. "If I need something..." He swallowed again, his throat emitting an evident click. "... I ring."

"I think the ladies are busy with some chore," Russell informed him. "So, if you need anything, anything at all, I'll be happy to get it for you."

"Women's work," Henry scoffed.

"Okay," responded Russell. "I don't look at it that way. But..."

"A man should be a man."

Sitting passively while this feeble old chauvinist espoused such archaic drivel seemed ill-advised. In his present raw emotional state, the last thing Russell needed was to get himself embroiled in yet another heated, personal conflict, especially one involving his wife's gravely ill father. "Tell you what," Russell said, "I'm gonna go check on what those women are up to." He lifted himself up from the couch and traipsed toward the hallway. "I'll be right back."

Leaning on the railing of the cedar deck, overlooking a stand of tall pines, Russell paged through his mental thesaurus for some useful coming-out language. Still, adequate words failed to rise to the occasion. The balmy, moisture-laden August atmosphere was making him drowsy. He shuffled over to a chaise lounge. Brushing off the pine needles, leaf fragments, and mud spatters seemed like too much work. He dropped down wearily and reclined. Within minutes, slumber had overtaken him. Soon thereafter, his eyes were darting back and forth beneath their lids.

Russell's dream: He pushes open the heavy, creaky door of a small boutique. Oddly, the sound of the bell dangling from its handle is faint, as if it's coming from a distance. After closing the door behind him, the jingling resumes, in sporadic bursts. As his eyes adjust to the darkness of the dimly lit shop, a bizarre inventory appears. Brass and pewter figurines populate the shelves, depicting grotesque hybrid creatures. A goat with the beak of a hawk sits next to a serpent with a horned bull's head. The forked end of a dragon's tongue bares shark's teeth. Vertical veins protrude from a giraffe-shaped creature's neck, topped off with a mushroom-shaped crown. Recognizing this overtly phallic image, Russell's dream persona becomes sexually aroused.

A man's angry voice shrieks from somewhere outside the shop walls: "God *damn* it! What the hell is going on?" Feeling obligated to offer assistance, Russell turns toward the exit. But the door quickly grows smaller, as if the room is stretching, the escape route retreating beyond his reach. Meanwhile, the distant bell jangles repeatedly, now with more insistence.

Angst mounting, he scours the space, hoping to find a secret escape hatch. Behind the counter, he stumbles upon man lying flat on his back, prone on the hardwood floor. The man's trembling hands reach up toward Russell. Although he doesn't look like Henry, Russell recognizes him as his father-in-law. As he crouches down to examine the man's condition, the man's bony fingers grasp at Russell's shirt. A devilish grin reveals the man's toothless gums. It's not Henry, after all. It's the old fellow who, during the Spring of the previous year, serviced Russell with Blowjob #2 through a glory hole at Madame X's Adult Emporium. Terrified and revolted, Russell attempts to pry the man's viselike grip from his shirt. Instead, the man pulls Russell's lips to his and inserts his tongue into Russell's mouth.

"Russ!" The sound of his wife's voice sends Russell's heart into palpitations. Straddling the border between sub-consciousness and lucidity, he feels certain that she's caught him in the act of kissing this toothless codger. With a start, Russell's eyes sprung open to a twilight sky that could have been anywhere on Earth. His chin was coated with slobber and his shirt was damp with drool. "I thought you were keeping Dad company!" Tess stood over him, obviously disgruntled to find him napping on the deck.

"I was," Russell stammered. "I..."

"Well, he's been shaking his bell for who knows how long. Didn't you hear it?"

Yes, he'd heard the ringing; but only in his dream state. "I'm sorry, Babe. Is your dad okay?"

"He wet his pants," she informed him. "Mom's cleaning him up."

"Shit." Russell's murmured expletive was more about convincing Tess that he cared, and not so much coming from a genuinely caring place.

"Well, I sure hope you had a nice little snooze." Russell detected a note of bitchiness in his wife's voice. "Whenever you feel inspired to join us, we'll be inside," she informed him, before slipping back into the house.

Knowing he should at least offer to help with dinner preparations, Russell summoned up enough energy to extract himself from the gravity of the lounge cushions. Swinging a leg over, he placed a foot on the decking and stalled there, literally forgetting what to do next. For weeks, all but incapacitated by melancholy, Russell had been dancing dizzily around the May pole of truth, trying to catch hold of a ribbon that consistently eluded his every grasp. Now, a fresh perspective was flashing across his mind screen, one that enabled him to visualize tomorrow's revelation from a different angle.

Russell's first lie about his true identity and sexual orientation, at the age of 18, had left David Mangold believing that he'd traumatized an innocent, arrow-straight young man. In Atlanta, after the celebration of David's life, one of the deceased's closest friends identified Russell as the source of David's prolonged anguish and castigated Russell for putting another queer man through years of unnecessary emotional turmoil. If, Russell reasoned, David had been compelled to air his resentments to someone who didn't know Russell from a department store manikin, why would David have withheld those same hard feelings from his friend Tess, the other primary victim in Russell's long-running spree of duplicity?

During the months between his lunch-table confession and David's passing, Russell had spent an inordinate measure of energy harboring a desperate hope that David hadn't spilled (and would ever spill) those beans to Tess. Paradoxically, in Russell's current state of semi-clarity, this worry was flipping on its head. Perhaps, by reporting those details to Tess, David had actually done Russell a favor by authoring the foreword to a sordid story. If so, maybe, just maybe, David had already served as advance man, laying the groundwork for Russell to relay the remainder of the tale.

"Oh, my God! Yes! I know all about it, Babe!" There was an odd tone of genuine relief in Tess's voice. And, her smile, in tandem with the gentle hand she placed on Russell's forearm, exuded loving reassurance. "Is that what's been eating at you?"

"Sort of, yes. But..."

"Dang!" she exclaimed. "I thought you were going to tell me you wanted a divorce."

"No, but..."

"David told me the whole story..." She seemed to be in rush to offer him comfort. "... about how adorable and irresistible you were, how horribly guilty he felt... you know, for grooming you like that, and seducing you."

Sitting in that corner booth at Solario Cantina, Russell thought David was being cavalier and presumptuous to suggest that the queer side of Russell's nature was the pink elephant in the Deacon household. Many families, after all, cope with evident but uneasy truths by pretending them away. When Dr. White informed Russell that he needed to come out to his wife, the therapist might as well have dispatched that unmentionable pachyderm to sit directly on his chest. Over the interim weeks, he'd been living under Dumbo-sized pressure. Now, Tess's light-hearted response had turned that imaginary beast into a plush toy. He could breathe again. "Wow!" Russell mused. "So, that's *all* he told you?"

"Pretty much." It only took a second for Tess to detect the unspoken implication in this query. Question marks appeared in her eyes. "Why?" she probed, "You were just experimenting, right?" She forced a chuckle. "I mean, pretty much everyone does some exploring at that age." Russell sat silently, gazing out into the forest beyond the creek, trying to collect his scattered thoughts, hoping to assemble a next statement, the one that would surely blow the lid off. "Is there something else?" Tess asked, a crescendo of concern in her voice. "Babe?"

The morning had begun in Tess's parents' kitchen with some banal chitchat over a cup of weak drip coffee. As usual, Tess's mother had delivered her Madame-of-the-manner performance with aplomb, syrupy sweet with a vinegar chaser. Russell passing on breakfast didn't go over well with his mother-in-law. He didn't care much for grits, his gut was stirring with toxic juices, and he and Tess were planning an early lunch in Crossville. Once there, as it was an exceptionally pleasant summer day, the couple decided to order their food to-go, rather than take a table at the Catfish Cabin. As they motored into Cumberland Mountain State Park, Tess's SUV was filled with the potent aroma of deep-fried fish. After parking, they commandeered a picnic table with a view of the old dam.

"Isn't this beautiful," Tess remarked. "You never cease to amaze me. Sometimes you can be so romantic." Russell gritted his teeth. *Oh, I'm about to amaze you*, he was thinking, *you can be sure of that*. Thanks to a highly accelerated metabolism, Tess had always been capable of devouring twice as much as her husband without gaining an ounce. After finishing her serving, she poached a couple of hushpuppies from Russell's portion. With his nervous stomach churning, Russell could do little more than nibble at his meal.

After disposing of their trash, they set off strolling hand-in-hand toward Byrd Creek Trail. "Oooo," Tess squealed, pointing at a group of saggy-drawered kids taking turns swinging on a rope from the bank and plunging into the clear, green reservoir. "I wish I had my swimsuit. That looks like so much fun!" With his mind mulling other matters, Russell's response was no more than a barely discernible grunt. A half-mile down the trail, after several more minutes of non-communication, Tess felt compelled to ask, "Where've you been, Babe?"

"What do you mean?" Russell knew precisely what she meant. This was a stall.

"You've been so... I don't know... so distant, so far away, lately."

"Could we sit down for a minute?" Russell requested.

"Sure," she responded. "Or, we could always talk while we walk."

"I need..." Russell's heart was pounding with such intensity, he could barely hear his own voice. "I need... There's something..."

"Shit," muttered Tess, her voice modulating downward in pitch. "Sounds serious."

"Yeah. It is. It's... How about here?" Not waiting for her agreement, Russell sat down heavily on the creek-side bench. Tess took a far more tentative posture, beside him, on the edge of the wooden plank. Russell drew a deep breath and exhaled before extending his arms and shaking out his wrists. Seeing her husband's face flush and his hands tremble served to augment Tess's growing trepidation. Something dreadful, she agonized, must be forthcoming. "Listen," Russell began, "did David ever tell you anything about what happened back when I interned for him in Atlanta?"

This is when she informed him that, yes, she had heard all about Russell's long-ago brush with man sex. While Russell was pleased that she hadn't found David's report alarming or concerning, his relief was short-lived. Asking if that was the sum total of what David had shared served up the suggestion that there was more to the story — which, of course, there was. Tess immediately picked up on that insinuation and began pressing him on it. Russell's gaze fell on the crystal clear creek, water surrendering to gravity, cascading over and past rocky impediments. Continuing to withhold the truth, he realized, was as impossible as holding back the river. "Yes," whispered

Russell, turning his tear-filled eyes to meet hers, "there is something else."

"Okay," Tess responded, gripping the bench and girding herself for the blow. "Fire away."

THIRTY-ONE

Russell fumbled with the front-door key in the dark in a blind attempt to insert it into the lock. The metallic rattle of the turning deadbolt seemed harsh and brittle, reverberating off the foyer tile. The door closed with a heavy clunk, followed by oppressive silence. He couldn't remember ever feeling so alone. Vision blurred through tear-filled, bloodshot eyes, he dragged himself to the kitchen and quickly guzzled two tall glasses of tap water. Having shed a gallon of tears over the previous five hours, hydration seemed wise.

After filling his glass for the third time, he dragged himself to the stairs, and began climbing ponderously, on weary, wobbly legs. With each step, water sloshed over the rim of the glass onto the carpet and his hiking shoes. He didn't care. It wasn't important. He set the dripping glass next to the clock radio and tumbled onto the mattress like a carelessly tossed rag doll. His stomach muscles ached from sobbing. Still, the tears kept flowing unabated. He despised himself for hurting Tess so severely, for blowing her entire world to bits. The emotional agony was unbearable, the shame devastating, the guilt crushing. He roiled and flailed, wept and blubbered, whimpered and wailed. "I am a worthless piece of shit! A worthless, fucking, slimy, stinking piece of shit!" Feeling a sudden need to see himself in all his ugliness, he caught his reflection in the mirror over Tess's antique dressing table. The face he saw was twisted and grotesque, with blotchy, discolored skin, red-streaked eyes, and grimacing lips. *That man is a monster*, he thought to himself. *And that monster is me.*

Russell replayed his coming-out debacle for the seventeenth time. He and Tess, sitting on a bench beside Byrd Creek in Cumberland Mountain State Park; his tongue dryer and rougher than a floppy scrap of felt. A convulsive inhalation, forcing a raspy cough to dislodge the lump in his larynx. Tess sitting speechless, eyes wide and wary, as if she were the last team member left on her side of the dodgeball court, awaiting the imminent high-velocity barrage from across the center line.

"I'm..." Russell stammered, "I'm... Fuck! How do I say this?"

"Just say it," Tess urged, with nervous impatience. "You're killing me!"

"I'm... bisexual." Speaking this essential truth about himself, out loud, to his life partner, the mother of his children, felt surreal.

"What?" Tess sounded amused and incredulous in the same breath. "No, you're not!"

"I am, Tess," he insisted, with no sense of shame. The smile burgeoning across his face wasn't forced. Rather it sprang from a previously untapped well of joyful liberation. The truth was setting him free. "I am. I'm bisexual."

"Just because you had one experience twenty years ago doesn't make you bisexual," Tess argued. "Is that what you think? That's... that's just silly."

Russell's instinct, from thousands of sales pitches, was to allow the other party adequate time to absorb the new perspective he had just shown them. A potential client needs to entertain the real inevitability of their demise before they can seriously consider forking over a monthly life-insurance premium. While not exactly a life-and-death matter, the information he'd just dumped on his wife came with every potential of precipitating the demise of a 14-year marriage. Russell sat quietly, owning his declaration, buzzing with perverse exhilaration from having spoken those five honest syllables... twice: "I'm bisexual."

"Okay," Tess said, her eyes squinting and her forehead furrowing, as she attempted to comprehend this new landscape. "I'm supposed to... to assume... that you're serious right now." Russell nodded, his smile growing pursed. "I mean..." she continued, "bisexual. What does that even mean? I know you're not gay."

"No," he confirmed, "I'm not gay."

"So, you're telling me that you're sexually attracted to men."

"Yes," he admitted, "I am."

"Well, Jesus, Babe! How do you know?"

"You just know, Tess." Russell placed his hand on her knee. "You just know."

"Well, then..." Tess took a momentary pause to draw a deep breath and collect her thoughts. "I'm glad you told me. I guess so, anyway." She shook her head and forced a sympathetic smile. "Wow, that must have taken some real courage."

While Russell was feeling good about himself for having shed light on an essential portion of his truth, more courage was called for. Yes, he'd ripped the door to a taboo subject from its hinges and, thus far, the house hadn't crumbled under the weight of gravity. Now, the moment had arrived to air a far more devastating truth. "There's more," he announced.

"Oh, God!" Pure terror flashed in Tess's eyes. "You haven't found someone, have you? A guy? You're not..."

"Not one guy."

"What the fuck do you mean by that?"

"There've been... I've been with... several men."

"Who?"

"I..." Russell's eyes shifted from tree branches to the sawdust trail, avoiding direct eye contact. "I don't even know their names. I *never* knew their names. Most of them anyway."

"That's..." For the first time in their 15-year relationship, Tess felt loathing for this man. "That's disgusting! You... How could you do that to me? *Oh, my God*!" She put her hands to her face, hunched over, bursting into a spate of bitter laughter. "I married Todd Moore!"

When Russell met Tess a decade and half earlier, she was on the rebound from a broken engagement. The ex-fiancé's name, Todd Moore, represented the entirety of Russell's knowledge about her romantic history. To avoid any needless pangs of jealousy, Russell had never probed into her past. Now, hearing this insinuation about her previous beaux, he was wishing he'd expressed more curiosity. Tess sprang to her feet, turned in a quick, half circle, looked up into the forest canopy, and raised her arms to the treetops. Laughing and crying simultaneously, she shouted, "I can't believe it! I married Todd fucking Moore!"

Being so fully absorbed in their own drama, Russell and Tess had blocked out all awareness of the proximity of other humans. "So sweet to see young people in love." Although the person's words were directed at a companion, they were clearly audible. Russell swiveled on the bench to see a pair of elderly hikers approaching on the path. At first glance, he assumed they were male and female, probably husband and wife. The closer they came, the less certain he was about the precise gender of either of them. As the pair shuffled past, the second of what turned out to be two women smiled at Tess and said, "Congratulations on your marriage."

Tess's laughter was piercing and acidic, erupting from a dark chamber of cynical self-deprecation. "Why?" she wailed to the universe. "Why do I keep doing this to myself?"

By now, the two hikers were 10 yards down the path, still well within earshot. One of them stopped and turned around. "Look, I know it's none of my business. But, it's only natural to feel fearful at first. Love is a rollercoaster." Noticing the stink eye coming from Tess, the woman backed up a step. "Sorry," she mumbled, "I was just trying to help."

"You don't know shit!" Tess shrieked. "Why don't you keep your ugly, fucking, butch-dyke nose out of other people's business?" The woman's eyes bugged in shock and insult. She grabbed her partner's hand, and they quickly bustled down the path. Russell sat, stunned. His bleeding-heart liberal wife had just hurled a homophobic epithet at a complete stranger, someone who definitely should not have butted in but had simply been offering a few words of wisdom and encouragement. "Take me back to Knoxville, Russell," Tess demanded.

"Can't we talk about this, Babe?"

"Oh, yeah," she said. "You can bet your sorry ass we'll be talking about this. But, right now, you are gonna drive me back home to my Mom and Dad."

"Well... I'm sorry," he retorted, "but I don't exactly feel comfortable, you know... going back to your parents' place."

"What?" she scoffed. "You think you'd be welcome there anyway? I don't want you in my bed. You've been... playing Russian roulette... with *my life*!"

"I know." Russell's voice was laden with sorrow and regret. "That was wrong. And, I am *so* sorry."

"Save it." Tess's daggered glower was chilling. "We're gonna drive back to Knoxville. Right fucking now. You're gonna drop me off. End of discussion."

Russell and Tess approached the parked vehicle in muted silence. Across the lot, the elderly lesbian hikers were stashing their trekking poles and backpacks into the trunk of a Volvo 240. "Good luck," one of the women called out, sending a wave. "It'll all work out." Russell obliged with a head nod and a meek wave in return. Tess glared at her husband with evident scorn, before climbing into the passenger seat and slamming the car door.

Tess spent most of the hourlong drive crying softly. At one point, she reached over to place her hand on Russell's hand. "I love you," she muttered.

"I love you, too, Babe," Russell managed, a first tear meandering down his cheek. "Never doubt it."

Russell was cried out. It was approaching 11 p.m. Realizing that he had yet to notify Tess of his safe arrival, he grabbed the bedside phone, pushed "one," then area code 965. He was trying to recall the prefix to Henry and Miriam's home phone when he was startled by the ringing doorbell. *Who could possibly be dropping by unannounced at this hour on a Monday evening?* He placed the receiver back in its cradle and listened with intent ears. Against the quiet, the second ring was more spine-tingling than the first. Seconds later, rapid pounding on the door shook the house, along with the muffled sound of a male voice. "Come on, Man!" the night visitor hollered, "I know you're in there." Again, a fist pummeling the door vibrated the walls, followed by repeated rings of the doorbell.

Under the cover of darkness, Russell crept downstairs and into the foyer, an aluminum baseball bat clutched in his hand. A sneak peek through the beveled glass revealed the identity of the surprise caller. Russell unlocked the door, cracked it open, and looked out at the handsome man standing on the front porch. "Bryan," he said, "what's happening?"

"Oh, Coach! Thank God!" Bryan answered. "I was worried... you know, that you might have..."

"What are you talking about?"

"Tess called Diane, and..."

"What do you mean?" Russell queried. "Tess doesn't even like Diane."

"It was kind of a betrayed wife commiseration call, I guess." Russell was dumbfounded. That Tess would seek out Bryan's ex for sisterhood and succor defied logic. Tess had always been a free spirit. She espoused progressive values and possessed an artistic temperament. Diane was a prototypical daughter of the Old South, a haughty belle who would smirk and utter, "Bless your heart," before stabbing you in the back. Russell tried to picture Tess sitting next to Diane in a church pew, both women dolled up in their Sunday frocks, nodding solemnly and passing judgment on the other parishioners, while some portly, sweaty browed preacher rained fire and brimstone upon his congregation. "Would it be okay if I came in?" Bryan asked.

"Oh, sure," responded Russell. "Yeah. Stupid to be, you know..." He opened the door wider and stepped aside. Bryan strode over the threshold and, without waiting for the door to close, grabbed Russell by the shoulders and pulled him into a bear hug.

"Everything okay, Deacon?" This voice of concern was coming from the far end of the driveway. Peering out through squinted eyes, Russell immediately identified the stocky figure: Frank from next door, partially camouflaged by the hedge, looking down the scope of a semi-automatic hand gun. "I heard some noise," Frank called out. "I thought maybe it was a home invasion."

"Nope," Russell reassured him. "All's well here. You can stand down, Frank." The man obliged by lowering his pistol. "But thanks. I appreciate it. You're a good neighbor." Russell started to swing the door closed.

"Okay." There was a dubious tone in Frank's voice. He squinted his eyes in an attempt to discern the identity of the person Russell had just been embracing. "You never know, you know."

"Yep, you're so right," said Russell. "Better safe than sorry."

Bryan held his laughter until the door was shut. "Fuckin' hell!" he said between guffaws. "If you hadn't answered the door, that vigilante might have shot me."

"No doubt," Russell quipped. "Frank is one trigger-happy dude!" For the first time in days, Russell gave somber self-pity a reprieve. He'd forgotten how cleansing mirth could be.

"And, if good-neighbor Frank hadn't filled me full-a lead," Bryan kidded, pointing to the bat in Russell's hand, "I guess you were planning to crack my skull."

"You got that right!" Russell shot back. "Show up at someone's house in the middle of the night? What do you expect?"

Bryan took a closer look at Russell. "You look like death warmed over, by the way."

"It's great to see you, too," Russell parried, motioning with the bat for Bryan to tag along to the kitchen.

"But, seriously, Coach," Bryan said. "I've missed you."

"Missed me? Why?" In his mind's eye, Russell shuffled through a slide show of Bryan memories: his volunteer assistant's dazzling blue eyes during Pirates' infield practice, stumbling upon him receiving oral sex on the creek bank, that risky-yet-arousing thigh grope under the dinner table, that tearful plea for mercy at Rory's Chuck E. Cheese birthday party, Bryan flagging Russell down outside Ynonah's Saloon and inviting him inside to experience a first sampling of the gay-bar social scene.

"I don't know," said Bryan. "I guess I've always felt like me and you, we have a lot in common." Russell understood. Both men had faithfully followed the same hetero-normative, happily-ever-after script to the letter by marrying women, fathering children, and betting the house on white-picket-fence domesticity. Too, they both shared a passion for sports. However, those commonalities would scarcely be worth mentioning if either of these two married-with-children guys hadn't spent years secretively hound-dogging down parallel trails, noses to the ground, determined to catch the scent of a warm, willing body and a next clandestine, tangle-free, same-sex encounter. But, although certain undeniable impulses lured each of them to a common pursuit, Russell and Bryan had, for the most part, operated on separate frequencies. Only recently had Russell begun engaging in risky business. Bryan, on the other hand, had thrown caution to the wind from the get go, making his a double-or-nothing game of chance.

"Yes," Russell responded, "and no."

"Right," cracked Bryan. "I've got blue eyes and you've... What color are yours?"

"Right now," Russell chuckled, "probably red, white, and hazel." Russell opened the refrigerator door. "Wanna beer?"

"I was thinking we could go down to Ynonah's for a couple..." suggested Bryan. With Russell continuing to gawk blankly into the fridge, Bryan sweetened his offer. "I'll buy."

Just 10 minutes earlier, Russell had felt more alone than he could ever remember feeling in his life, flailing on the bed, weeping, wallowing in despair. Now, he was in the presence of a friend who cared, who not only understood his situation, but was freshly familiar with this exact kind of emotional turmoil. Too, Russell was now presumably free to act in a way consistent with his self-identity and desires. What could be more fitting than to top off his coming-out day by strolling proudly onto the deck at Ynonah's with one of the handsomest, hunkiest guys in Nashville?

But, inexplicably, the idea of cruising a gay bar lacked any allure. Now that he'd finally laid his bi cards on the table and confessed to his covert infidelities, Russell felt zero compunction to go right out and wave his rainbow flag. To celebrate blindsiding his wife with such unwelcome, hurtful news seemed wrong. Certainly, he looked forward to being welcomed as an authentic member of the queer community, by men with whom he could be his open, honest, true self. However, being out also meant that, from henceforth, before indulging in man sex, he'd be obliged to ask questions, learn names, and take precautions. "I'm not..." Russell closed the fridge and turned around, gripping a long neck in either hand. "It's too soon. I don't think I'm... quite ready."

"Okay..." Grinning slyly, Bryan was detecting a coded message in Russell's reluctance to attend the club. "You're right. It's late. Monday night. The bar is probably dead anyway."

Russell handed Bryan a beer. After twisting off the caps, they toasted by clicking bottle necks. "Here's to friendship," said Russell.

"To friendship," Bryan said, smiling that smile. "And to coming out. I'm proud of you."

The frosty brew tasted heavenly. After draining half the bottle in a single pull, Russell said, "Thanks for coming over, Man... you know, to check on me. Seriously."

"Don't mention it," responded Bryan, taking a step forward, backing Russell against the refrigerator door. Russell lowered his eyes to the floor tile to evade Bryan's hypnotic gaze. His heart accelerated. Bryan reached out and gently lifted Russell's chin, preparing to plant a kiss on Russell's beer-dampened lips. At that moment, Russell noticed something on Bryan's neck, dark in pigmentation and ovular, like the shadow of a tiny bird's egg.

"What's that?" Russell inquired, with evident concern.

"What's what?" Bryan traced Russell's sight line to the spot on his neck. "Oh, that. You must know what that is."

"No," Russell insisted, "I don't." He was hoping he didn't know what it was, that it was something else altogether, that he was leaping to an incorrect conclusion.

"I thought everybody knew." Bryan was attempting to hide his shame under a dispassionate swagger. "Yeah," he confessed. "I tested positive. About two months ago."

"For H.I.V."

"Yep, but worse. I've got it."

Waves of conflicted emotion swept over Russell: revulsion mixed with pity, disgust blended with compassion, with a heaping scoop of fear plopped on top. His last risky woodland encounter had risked the same fate. Three weeks plus had passed since possible exposure, and he'd been checking himself anxiously every day for symptoms. "So, you were really going to kiss me?" This seemed inexplicable to Russell. "What the fuck?"

"Old habits die hard, I guess." *Bryan couldn't possibly think this was an adequate explanation*! "I'm still horny as hell. You're a sexy guy. I've told you that before."

While Russell knew it was insane, he still couldn't help but feel flattered. After all, what human doesn't get an ego boost upon hearing that another attractive human finds them desirable? Still, the thought that another man infected by a killer virus, one, research had revealed, was transmitted through an exchange of bodily fluids, would attempt to kiss him was beyond comprehension. "Jesus!" It was the only thing Russell could think of to say.

"We could use condoms," said Bryan. "I brought some."

"No we can't," Russell argued. "We *can't!* I'm not gonna... Are you out of your fucking mind?"

"I getcha," responded Bryan, taking a stride backward.

"Do you, Bryan? Do you, really?"

"Look, I guess I stepped over the line, here."

"Ya think?"

"It's not the first time." Bryan coughed, then coughed again. Russell stood, brow furrowed, jaw clenched, wondering how much weight Bryan had lost. "And, it probably..." — another cough — "... won't be the last time, either."

"Like I said..." By habit, master salesman Russell made diplomacy his first priority. "I really appreciate you coming over... you know, to check up on me. That was a very nice thing to do. But..."

"Yeah," Bryan interrupted, with clipped impatience, "you've had a traumatic day. You're probably beat."

"You' got that right."

"So..." Bryan set his barely sampled beer down on the counter top. "I guess I'll just push along." He started toward the exit, then stopped. "No hard feelings, I hope."

Russell stood speechless, wrung out, overwhelmed by this and every other life-changing event that had taken place over the course of this pivotal, monumental day. Still, the thought of rattling around this empty house by himself injected a megadose of dread into his bloodstream. "No, stay." Russell was surprised to hear his own voice articulating these words. "Please."

"Are you sure?" questioned Bryan. "Because..."

"Just hold me," Russell pleaded. "I just need some human contact. And... I don't wanna be alone." The two men threw their arms around one another and locked in a muscular embrace. Tears again cascaded down Russell's cheeks. He wasn't cried out after all. "I'm so scared!" he confessed.

"I am, too, Honey," whispered Bryan. "I am, too."

THIRTY-TWO

"If you really wanna know... I wanted to die." Russell set his fork down on his empty plate before blotting his mouth with a cloth napkin.

"Wow, Dad." Rory, now 20, and sporting a wisp of a mustache, shook his head in disbelief. "Really?" Reaching under the dinner table, Russell's second-born son squeezed the hand of the pretty, brown-skinned girl in the adjacent chair.

"I had a half-million dollars in life insurance," Russell replied, "plenty enough to take care of you and your mom, at least until you guys graduated from high school. I came to the conclusion that you and your mom would be much better off with me out of the picture."

"Why would you ever think that?" inquired Rory.

"I hated... no, worse, I *despised* myself. Not because of who I am. That's important, and I want you guys to understand that. I'm not ashamed of being queer. I hated... *despised* myself for hurting your mom so badly, for lying... to her... and to myself. She didn't deserve that."

"Well," Tess interjected, "in your defense, I kind of, you know... had my blinders on."

"In case y'all hadn't noticed," Russell quipped, "your mother likes to see people the way she likes to see them."

"Yeah," agreed 22-year-old Hank, no longer a soft, chubby lad, but a husky, buff, full-grown man. "That's my mom. Once she's pegged you in a certain role, you're gonna be typecast for life."

"But, really, Tess," Russell said, "You deserved better."

"Okay, sure," Tess responded. "But just because you didn't turn out to be the husband I wanted you to be didn't mean you should cease to exist."

317

"Well, I'm delighted to hear you say that. Because I'd hate to think that I disappointed you one more time... you know, by failing to..." Russell finished his sentence by miming slitting his own throat.

"Not to say that I didn't *wish* you were dead... for a time, at least." Despite her good-natured tone, it was unclear if this statement was even partly serious. An uncomfortable hush came over the table.

"As you informed me very succinctly..." Russell pointed out, "in writing. That letter was brutal, truly brutal."

It was Thanksgiving dinner, 2005. Around the table sat Russell, now 55, his ex-wife Tess, 52, their adult sons, Hank and Rory, Hank's wife Cyndi (her 15-week pregnancy beginning to show) and Rory's girlfriend, Mia.

"Who's ready for pie?" Jamal swept into the dining room balancing rhubarb in his right hand, and pumpkin in his left.

"Oh, my god, Jimmy!" exuded Tess. "They look so delicious!"

Mia took the initiative to remove the cornucopia centerpiece from the table to clear space. "Thank you, Sweetie," Jamal said, as he lowered the pies onto a pair of matching trivets. "Wait, wait, wait, everybody," he instructed, gliding back toward the kitchen a la Brian Boitano and crooning in a singsong voice. "We have ice cream and Reddy Wip."

"Jamal is becoming a baker extraordinaire," boasted Russell.

"I can tell," ribbed Hank. "Looks like you're packin' on some love handles there, Daddio."

"Rustypuss needed some more meat on those scrawny bones," remarked Jamal, as he placed the toppings on the table. "Eat it up while it's still hot!"

"So, what's your secret, Jimmy?" Tess asked.

"Lard, Honey!" Jamal declared. "As my granny always said, 'Everything's better with Crisco!'"

Everybody laughed as Tess began portioning the pumpkin pie into generous slices. "Well," she said. "I guess it's okay to indulge one's self every now and then."

A well-worn aphorism was, once again, being proven truthful: Time heals all wounds. This old saw was particularly germane to the life journey of Russell Deacon. A decade's passage had softened the blow caused by his belated, surprise revelation. Immediately post-disclosure, he hadn't been certain self-preservation was worth the effort. Having been relegated to sleeping on the couch, he spent his nights guzzling vodka, replicating Nicolas Cage's Oscar-winning performance in *Leaving Las Vegas*. While alcohol indulgence temporarily numbed the pain, his suicide attempt via the bottle ultimately fell short for two primary reasons. First, he would invariably lose consciousness before a fatal level of toxicity could be attained. Secondly, as his ongoing efforts to self-destruct continued to flop, he simply got sick and tired of feeling sick and tired.

During the two-month period between Russell's coming out and Tess's decision to make the permanent move back to Knoxville, spousal communication was facilitated primarily through an exchange of handwritten letters. Russell's heart would leap into his throat and sweat would bubble up on his brow every time he discovered the creased pages of lined, yellow paper awaiting him on the kitchen counter, next to the toaster. With trembling hands, he would unfold his wounded wife's daily missive. Tess's barrage of vitriol and victimhood sometimes stretched out into three legal-sized pages.

Russell accepted this ritual as penance, knowing that it would be unwise and inappropriate to react defensively. Tess had every right to express her bitterness, to hurl every pejorative she could conjure in his direction. And, to her credit, she demonstrated surprising adeptness at coming up with sharply barbed, precisely aimed prose. Russell perused each written tirade comprehensively, at least twice.

The initial reading was for the purpose of absorbing and accepting her wrath, as if, for those 62 consecutive days, he was making an intentional choice to stand before the firing squad without a blindfold. Subsequent readings served to inform his response. He found it important to make his return messages as succinct and dispassionate as possible, while addressing all of her concerns. To this purpose, he avoided assuming an argumentative or self-justifying posture, while expressing sincere apology and taking full responsibility for the pain he'd caused.

Ultimately, Tess grew weary of his scrawled acts of contrition. For her, no number of apologies would have been sufficient. But, she was George Forman fighting Mohammed Ali. Having pinned her opponent against the ropes, she was only exhausting herself by delivering blow after blow, losing steam, and never getting the result she desired. Meanwhile, Russell had run out of ways to say how sorry he felt for subjecting her to such disillusionment and heartbreak. Left with but one final gambit, he wrote, "Sometimes, I can't help but think it would have been better for you and the boys if I'd just killed myself."

"Maybe it would have been easier if you *had* died," Tess scribbled in her next screed. "At least then I would have had the memory of our wonderful years together. Now I know our marriage wasn't real, and I don't know how to take my next breath." Seeing these words penned on paper by someone he loved, someone with whom he'd shared a life and a bed for 15 years, was devastating for Russell. Tess had finally delivered the knock-out punch. Any attempt to lift himself off the canvas would have been for naught. He was down for the count.

Fortunately, Russell had a pair of close friends in Bryan and Jamal, who understood him, loved him, and accepted him without condition. Mary Ann, too, was there to lend a sympathetic ear and a shoulder to cry on, while acting as a translator of sorts, offering a female perspective, and urging him not to give up on himself, to keep working on the restoration of a badly burnt bridge. And subsequent sessions with Dr. White proved essential as Russell stumbled along the steep, winding path back from self-hatred and intentional self-destruction.

Being welcomed into Nashville's burgeoning Church Street LGBTQ community also buoyed him emotionally. However, he was taken aback to discover that declaring a bisexual identity was not universally accepted in gay circles. Telling another guy the truth — that he was as attracted to women as he was to men — frequently received a shake of the head and a patronizing smirk in response. He couldn't count how many times he'd been mocked with some version of, "Come on, Russell, you're gay. Why don't you just admit it?" He found it curious that this binary, either-you-is-or-you-ain't attitude was nearly as pervasive within queer culture as it was in the straight world. For this very reason, Jamal spurned Russell's initial romantic overtures. Until Russell was ready to admit to being gay, Jamal was determined to keep his distance, both physically and emotionally. Russell was irresistibly drawn to Jamal. Their chemistry had been undeniable from the instant he first beheld those chocolate-cupcake cheeks. Jamal was everything Russell had ever dared dream of in a male partner. But, after having lived a lie for so many decades, he wasn't about to fall back into pretending he was something he wasn't. His mental health relied on adhering to a solemn vow of honesty. The only strategy left was to keep expressing his love in the hopes that, eventually, Jamal's self-erected barrier would crumble. After a year of keeping Russell at arm's length, Jamal finally surrendered to his mutual feelings for him. They'd been partners ever since.

Bryan succumbed to AIDS-related complications in 1996. Russell and Jamal were at his side till the very end, along with several other men from the Ynonah's crowd. Sadly, yet unsurprisingly, Bryan's ex, Diane, not only eschewed any contact, but forbade their son Carter from visiting his father, even in Bryan's final days. Carter not only grew to resent his dad, but became brainwashed by his mother's biblical-based intolerance of non-straight folk. Russell was grateful that Carter hadn't succeeded in infecting the Deacon boys with the contagion of anti-queer bias. Although Hank and Carter had been tight for years, Carter eventually drifted away from Hank, siloing himself with others who shared his bias. Losing Carter's friendship gave Hank yet another reason to harbor anger against his father.

While it took nearly six years for Tess to fully excise the residual toxins from her embittered heart, she took extra care not to poison the boys' feelings for Russell. Weathering their parents' separation and divorce had been traumatic enough. Tess insisted that Russell sit the boys down to explain the real reason for the split. Predictably, Hank was especially disturbed and conflicted by the revelation of his father's bisexuality and chronic indiscretions. Rory was less overtly judgmental, making a greater effort to find empathy. Still, the upheaval hadn't been easy for either of the Deacon lads.

It was of utmost importance to Russell to win back the trust of his progeny. Restoring this broken bond received a backhanded boost when Tess started dating. Russell couldn't help but feel some satisfaction when his sons — by then, two gawky, pimply, hormonal teens — separately shared their skepticism about their mom being with any guy who wasn't their dad. At the same time, Russell worried that his own bad faith might have imbued them with misgivings about men in general. It also seemed grossly unfair to Tess that the boys' natural resistance made it that much more difficult for her to move on with her life. When things began getting more serious with one gentleman, including overnight stays and awkward breakfast-table conversations, Hank and Rory petitioned to move back to Nashville to live with their father. Once again, Tess made the greatest sacrifice. To avoid additional upheaval in the household, she made the difficult decision to prioritize her maternal responsibilities over her own need for companionship. This didn't sit well with the suitor and the budding romance withered.

Adding to the simmering fury about Russell's infidelities and the lie he lived for so long, Tess expressed yet another resentment: "I can't believe I let you waste the best part of my life!" she exclaimed in one of her written rants. "Now that I've got cellulite and my boobs are sagging, that's when you drop the bomb on me." She seldom missed an opportunity to remind him that he had stolen those years of youthful vigor and effortless beauty and how much more challenging attracting a mate invariably becomes for a woman of a certain age.

For Tess, putting her love life on the back burner had positive benefits as well, allowing her to focus more on her career. With the boys both graduated from high school, her own father gone to his final reward, and her cantankerous mother ensconced in a premier assisted living facility, Tess moved to Atlanta to assume David's prior position, as Executive Director of the Georgia Bridal Show. There, she met her new husband, Arthur, who worshipped her, cellulite, sagging breasts and all. This new pairing came with an extended family, a stepdaughter, now 27, and two step grandkids, with whom Arthur was celebrating Thanksgiving back in the Peach State. It wasn't easy for Tess to overcome the irksome notion that somehow, as a woman, she had never been enough for Russell. She still loved him. However, it was impossible not to develop genuine affection for Jamal as well. This gentle, black bear was, after all, enormously likeable, kind, patient and, so obviously, good for Russell in countless obvious and intangible ways. Russell was a different person with Jamal, relaxed, less brooding, more open and unguarded. And that made Tess miss him all the more.

Russell's feelings surrounding Tess and their shared history were quite different. He liked her. But, he wasn't certain he'd ever really truly loved her, at least not in the same way he loved Jamal. After emerging from his post-separation hell on earth, he never felt the inclination to ruminate on what might have been. Surviving his run of the gauntlet had made him a stronger, more decent human being. He'd come out the other side more self-aware, less judgmental, and unafraid to be vulnerable, thus vastly more prepared to give and receive love. He was finally living honestly. And when he allowed himself any measure of pride, it was for that.

The house resounded with the chiming doorbell. "Hello!" the woman's voice called out from the foyer.

"Come in, come in!" shouted Russell.

Mary Ann appeared, pulling her handsome, younger date along with one hand, and gripping a large bottle of liqueur in the other. "I brought Tuaca!"

"Your timing is perfect, Girlfriend," bubbled Tess, rising from her chair. "Jamal just put two scrumptious, homemade pies on the table." Tess opened her arms to give her nascent pal a welcoming hug.

"Goodie goodie," sang Jamal, "I'll get the apéritif glasses!"

"They're in the…" Russell began.

"I know, Honey, I know," Jamal chided playfully. "Don't worry your little head about it. You just sit back and enjoy your family and friends."

"I love you." Russell didn't have to think about it. The words, along with the sentiment, simply spilled out.

"As you should," replied Jamal, bustling to fetch the glasses. "I treat you like a king."

Noticing Hank and his brother exchanging smirks, Cyndi pinched her young husband's leg under the table. "Stop it," she chastised.

"Ow!" Hank protested, with a pained grimace.

"Be good," she instructed.

"Anybody need anything else?" Jamal asked, gliding weightlessly around the table, distributing assorted cordial glasses.

"Why don't you just sit down and relax?" Russell suggested. "I'm gonna make coffee in a minute." Rory's eyes widened, as Jamal set a glass down next to his placemat. "Just one, Son," insisted Russell. Rory made a face that expressed how much he hated being treated like a child. "We don't want another D.U.I. Right?"

"You got a D.U.I.?" queried Mia. "When did that happen?"

"Way to go, Dad," Rory groused.

"Hey!" Russell responded. "I wasn't the one who got shit-faced and crashed his car."

"Okay, you guys!" said Tess, slipping back into her accustomed role of family referee. "It's Thanksgiving. Let's not..."

"You're so right, Tess," admitted Russell. "I'm sorry."

"Whoa!" chortled Tess. "I'm assuming everybody heard that. Right?"

"When you're right, you're right, Woman," Russell acknowledged. "And I'm not too proud to say right it out loud."

"Well," Tess said, "that makes my Thanksgiving even better."

Smiling warmly at his ex, Russell rose to his feet. "We all have a lot to be thankful for," he announced, raising his glass. "Let's toast..." Glasses lifted around the table. "... to family, friendship, and love."

Jamal sidled up, encircling Russell's shoulder with his beefy arm and kissing him sweetly on his temple. "To family, friendship, and love," Jamal repeated, accompanied by the high-pitched tinkle of glass clinking glass.

Some version of a smile spread across each face as they all sampled a sip of sweet, caramel-colored liqueur. Even Hank, typically sullen and withdrawn, showed a momentary glimmer of contentment. One voice after another spoke: "Happy Thanksgiving."

Russell and Jamal stood at the head of the table, nose-to-nose, lost in each other's eyes. "Happy Thanksgiving, Jimbo," Russell whispered.

"Happy Thanksgiving, Rustypuss," purred Jamal.

THE END

About the Author:

Rand Bishop enjoyed a 45-year music-business career as a major-label recording artist, touring musician, hit songwriter, platinum record producer, talent development executive, and music publisher. He garnered a Grammy nomination, several BMI Awards and more than 300 songwriting credits with artists as diverse as the Beach Boys, Heart, Toby Keith, Tim McGraw, Indigo Girls, Cheap Trick, and Sheryl Lee Ralph. His compositions have been featured in more than a dozen feature films and several stage musicals.

Bishop has authored six books, penned award-winning and optioned screenplays, a stage play, numerous essays and, for six years, contributed a bi-monthly column to *American Songwriter Magazine*. *Medium* lists Bishop among the Top LGBTQ+ writers on its platform.

Long Way Out is Bishop's second novel. He resides in Newport, Oregon, where he acts as music director for the Oregon Coast Unitarian Universalist Fellowship.

Other Books by Rand Bishop:

My List: 24 Reflections on Life's Priorities

Makin' Stuff Up: Secrets of Song-Craft and Survival in the Music Biz

The Absolute Essentials of Songwriting Success

Grand Pop

TREK: My Peace Pilgrimage in Search of Kinder America